THE ROMANCE OF ELEANOR GRAY

HARDSCRABBLE BOOKS—Fiction of New England

Laurie Alberts, *Lost Daughters*
Laurie Alberts, *The Price of Land in Shelby*
Thomas Bailey Aldrich, *The Story of a Bad Boy*
Robert J. Begiebing, *The Adventures of Allegra Fullerton; Or, A Memoir of Startling and Amusing Episodes from Itinerant Life*
Robert J. Begiebing, *Rebecca Wentworth's Distraction*
Anne Bernays, *Professor Romeo*
Chris Bohjalian, *Water Witches*
Dona Brown, ed., *A Tourist's New England: Travel Fiction, 1820–1920*
Joseph Bruchac, *The Waters Between: A Novel of the Dawn Land*
Joseph A. Citro, *The Gore*
Joseph A. Citro, *Guardian Angels*
Joseph A. Citro, *Lake Monsters*
Joseph A. Citro, *Shadow Child*
Sean Connolly, *A Great Place to Die*
J. E. Fender, *The Frost Saga*
  The Private Revolution of Geoffrey Frost: Being an Account of the Life and Times of Geoffrey Frost, Mariner, of Portsmouth, in New Hampshire, as Faithfully Translated from the Ming Tsun Chronicles, and Diligently Compared with Other Contemporary Histories
  Audacity, *Privateer Out of Portsmouth: Continuing the Account of the Life and Times of Geoffrey Frost, Mariner of Portsmouth, in New Hampshire, as Faithfully Translated from the Ming Tsun Chronicles, and Diligently Compared with Other Contemporary Histories*
Dorothy Canfield Fisher (Mark J. Madigan, ed.), *Seasoned Timber*
Dorothy Canfield Fisher, *Understood Betsy*
Joseph Freda, *Suburban Guerrillas*
Castle Freeman, Jr., *Judgment Hill*
Frank Gaspar, *Leaving Pico*
Robert Harnum, *Exile in the Kingdom*

The
ROMANCE
of
Eleanor Gray

A NOVEL

Raymond Kennedy

University Press of New England

HANOVER AND LONDON

Published by University Press of New England,

37 Lafayette St., Lebanon, NH 03766

© 2003 by Raymond Kennedy

Printed in the United States of America

5 4 3 2 1

Library of Congress Cataloging-in-Publication Data
Kennedy, Raymond A.
The romance of Eleanor Gray : a novel / Raymond Kennedy.
    p.   cm.—(Hardscrabble books)
Includes a reading group guide and interview with the author.
ISBN 1–58465–291–8 (alk. paper)
    1. Young women—Fiction. 2. Massachusetts—Fiction. I. Title.
II. Series.
PS3561.E427R66 2003
813'.54—dc21   2003010746

To David Gordon

Into many a green valley

Drifts the appalling snow.

■

—W. H. Auden

THE ROMANCE OF ELEANOR GRAY

one

M **R. WALKER** was the driver of the horse and wagon that was transporting Eleanor to her new post in the Berkshire hills. While he was in no way brusque or unpleasant, he was not a talkative man. He was one of those thousands of a similar type that continued to give New Englanders a reputation for being wry and short-tongued. Eleanor did, though, learn a few things about him along the way. Myron Walker was the local Star Route man. That meant he carried the mail to rural deliveries by special contract with the U.S. Postal Service. The year was 1910. In those days, letters sent to out-of-the-way addresses bore the stamping of a red star—and these were delivered in the East Becket area by Mr. Walker. Also, twice weekly, he made the twenty-five-mile round-trip wagon ride to the little factory town of Westfield, where he collected all mail coming in from the east.

"What would people do without you?" Eleanor asked, in a playful tone, as they clopped along into the wooded foothills. He was slow to reply. The sun, blinking in the cedar trees overhead, threw pale coins of light on the gravel road before them, and over the head and withers of Mr. Walker's horse.

"They'd get on just fine," he answered, in an unhurried drawl. He said the words as though remarking on the meaninglessness of his own role in the great scheme of things, as in the coming and going of day and night, or the shifting of seasons.

He repeated himself a minute later, while reaching for his tobacco.

"They'd all get on just fine."

Eleanor smiled to herself, but sighed then, and took a deep breath. For the hundredth time that day, since starting out by train from Fall River at dawn, she suffered a stab of anxiety. With the passing miles, there took form in her breast a troubling sense of the isolated world to which she had consigned herself. The day-long journey struck her at times as a kind of regression, as though she were traveling backward in both time and space, retreating mile by mile from the crowded electrically lighted world of her growing-up years in Fall River to some remote agricultural outpost, where—how should she put it?—where time had stopped, where tilling and planting and harvesting—and milking and wood gathering and other such rudimentaries—had probably not changed in centuries. In fact, she experienced a deepening concern that she was not equal to the post that she had secured this summer. She had never taught anyone. In June, she had graduated from the two-year normal school in Framingham, which certified her—a piece of paper!—to exchange her expertise in a classroom full of children for actual pay. It was sometimes a daunting thought.

Eleanor sat with her hands in her lap, jouncing gently to the incessant movement of the wagon.

"Were you ever away from home, Mr. Walker?" she inquired, finally.

"Years ago," he said. "Spent two years down in the Secession War fields."

"Oh, my!" Eleanor regarded him sidelong, taking in his weathered complexion and tomahawk profile. Somehow, she had not thought him quite old enough to have served in the War Between the States.

"I joined up forty-eight years ago this winter. Came back," he added, melodiously, "forty-five years ago this past Easter." He looked at her. "Got home on Easter Day itself."

"It's still clear in your mind," Eleanor averred.

"Yes, it is," said Mr. Walker. "Walked this road, in fact."

"My grandmother, they tell me, lost some family back then."

Mr. Walker nodded, then ended the topic. "Lots did, miss." He flicked the reins, and straightened in his seat, flexing his back.

Eleanor wanted to ask Mr. Walker about the town of East Becket, but was not encouraged to do so. As before, while glancing up at the narrow band of sky that divided the treetops, and seemed to point the way to a receding horizon, she breathed deeply. On the wagon bed behind her lay a worn leather trunk, filled with enough personal things to last her through fall to Christmas. As the road rolled on higher into the hills, a late-day chill developed. Eleanor pulled on her dark gray cardigan sweater, fluffed back her hair, and rubbed her palms together briskly. Not a moment later, a magnificent prospect began revealing itself up ahead. The earth seemed to drop away precipitately, and she could see across a great gulf of sunlit air to a smoky skyline ten miles off. Then, moment by moment, the valley below came gradually to view, as though the lid of a pot were being lifted by an invisible hand, and inside rested the end and aim of her journey.

Eleanor put her fingers to her mouth. The sight took her breath away—the green geometries of the farmlands, a tiny white church spire discerned amid a cluster of trees, and widely scattered rooftops then of barns and houses.

Mr. Walker's horse, at the same time, shook his head, and quickened the pace. The steel-rimmed wagon wheels grew noisier in the pebbles.

"I guess he knows home is getting near," said Eleanor of Mr. Walker's horse.

"If he doesn't know by now," replied the Star Route man, "he ain't ever going to. He's been this road, back and forth, more times than a person could count. Yes," he said, "he knows."

Within thirty minutes, the wagon was moving along the foot of the valley, passing between orchards and fields. The road was following a stream now. Beyond a spectacular barn and silo to her right, several hands were busy in a field of impressive dimensions. Quite far off, two teams of horses stood in the shade of a majestic elm.

"What are they doing?" Eleanor asked, signifying the men at work.

"Just what they look like they're doing."

"And what is that?" she persisted, amused now by Mr. Walker's evasive way of answering a question.

"Haying." Mr. Walker looked at Eleanor, and smiled. "Just haying."

Indeed, Eleanor could smell it on the air. The fragrance of the mowed grass was all but intoxicating. For a moment, she wished she were coming here just to visit, and not instead, as it was, to prove her worth as a human being, as an adult of twenty years going out to meet the world—not to say as a skilled teacher of small children. For it was like Eden itself. The word pastoral took on vivid meanings.

Mr. Walker and Eleanor were moving at a clip now. The horse—whose name she now learned was Ben—was moving smartly.

"Ben, don't you break a shinbone!" Myron Walker spoke up, while creating some tension in the reins.

"He's ready for his stall," Eleanor surmised.

"And his supper," said the other. "You're right as rain about that, miss."

"Where'd you get the name Ben, Mr. Walker?"

"Well," Mr. Walker raised his voice in offering his pat answer, "like Ben Franklin, he doesn't see all that well. Only difference is, he's got no spectacles, this one. Isn't about to invent any, either."

Eleanor laughed outright. She liked Mr. Walker.

They were approaching now her actual destination, a sizeable colonial house situated at the crossroads—at the very axis, as it were—of East Becket. Eleanor reached around instinctively for her knitted carrying bag, to get at her purse, in order to pay Mr. Walker for the long ride in, but as she did so, her attention was drawn to a most arresting sight. On the horizon to the north, at the point where the rising sunlit pasturelands of East Becket came to an end, appeared a black wall of trees, extending to left and right as far as she could see.

"What an unusual sight!" Eleanor exclaimed, speaking half to herself. She straightened in her seat. "Those trees look lined up for battle."

Mr. Walker gave a cursory glance to the north, and returned his attention to the road. "Just trees, miss."

Eleanor laughed over that. "I know they are trees, Mr. Walker, but they present such a brooding, forbidding aspect. Look how they swallow up the sunlight! It's so baleful-looking, so prehistoric. What lies beyond them?"

As ever, the Star Route man was slow to reply. He continued staring at the road ahead. "Just more trees, miss."

"I mean *beyond* the more trees," she said, delightedly. She pointed. "That road leading up to the trees—where does it go?"

"There are a couple of towns up there that used to be."

"Used to be!" Eleanor was getting used to Mr. Walker's dry humor. "That once were towns, you mean. It's all so mysterious."

"Isn't mysterious," he replied. "What were once roads up there are something less than that now. Where there were houses and barns, and a town hall or two, and maybe tobacco growing and corn, there's trees coming back."

Truth was, while Eleanor enjoyed bantering back and forth with Mr. Walker, the dark brooding tree line to the north had imprinted itself upon her mind and senses. It was like a picture of something dark and invidious materializing for the first time within the precincts of her imagination. It gave her gooseflesh.

Not one minute later, the Star Route carrier let fall what Eleanor thought was an all but clairvoyant remark. He said it with soft matter-of-factness. "You're going to do just fine, miss, in your calling."

Eleanor was moved instantly. "My *calling!*" she said. "What a kind thing to say to me."

Here, Mr. Walker steered Ben off the road, and up a short drive to the house. It was a big house, and an old house, but portrayed an inviting look. The owner, Miss Alice Harrison, an unmarried lady in her later thirties, was one of East Becket's more prominent citizens.

Myron Walker drew Ben to a halt at the front door. Eleanor took notice of the little column of lilac-colored windows on each side of the door. They were called sidelights. She knew such windows from some of the very old houses back home in Fall River. The glass was very early. The panes were clear when first made and installed. They turned lilac with age. Eleanor opened her knit bag and took out her purse to pay Mr. Walker, while he— the Star Route driver—got down her trunk.

two

N THE HOUR before supper, Eleanor settled into her room in the upstairs rear of the big colonial house, unpacking and putting away her things. More than once, she returned to the window, to enjoy again the sunlit country landscape. A light breeze set the leaves of some nearby fruit trees aflutter. From a distance came the rather mournful sound of a dairyman calling in his cows, and, from time to time, even more distant seeming, the actual gonging of a cowbell, as the herd doubtless made its way homeward from the pasture. For a city dweller like Eleanor, who had not spent one day of her life in farm country, the atmosphere was one of unmixed enchantment. She could understand now how some of her New England family ancestors, as in the time of Eugene Lloyd Gray, who was her grandfather, and friends and contemporaries of his, like Bronson Alcott, or Margaret Fuller herself, had waxed lyrical upon the everlasting beauties of nature, and of the desirability of going back to it—or back to God, as it were—by re-entering that ancient harmony.

Eleanor had finished moving in. She had placed her dozen or so books in a neat row next to the oil lamp on the oak desk, and put away her clothing, underthings, toiletries and such, either in the closet or in the top drawers of the cherry wood highboy. That done, she took her ironstone pitcher from its basin, intent upon going downstairs to fill it with water—but really just to familiarize herself with the house—when a set of voices from the hall arrested her in place. She was actually gripping the brass doorknob when she turned stockstill. Both the voices were hushed. It was a man and a woman.

"It isn't for you to say, Evangeline," said the first, in a hoarse whisper.

"I only know," countered the other, with apparent urgency, "that I cannot stay here."

"Next week is time enough," the man sought to dissuade her.

"I require your help!" said the woman, more boldly. She said it twice.

To her own chagrin, Eleanor discovered herself pressed up against the door, her ear to the wood, her fingers to her mouth, listening breathlessly. While no one was there to notice it, she blushed to the roots of her hair upon realizing what she was doing, and stepped away. Despite her stealth, a floorboard underfoot made a squeaking complaint. For whatever reason, the voices ceased, followed by the sound of footsteps descending the back staircase. Eleanor retreated to the center of the room, and stood there, pensively, with the pitcher dangling at her side, looking for all the world like a sculpted figure.

For minutes thereafter, Eleanor was understandably reluctant to leave the room, lest her presence behind the door be construed by those two persons—the owners of the surreptitious voices—as nosiness, prying, meddling. The thought of it appalled her, as she thought herself to be above such things. As it happened, however, her remaining thus in the room for five or six long minutes, inadvertently put her in position to catch an actual glimpse—more than a glimpse—of a particularly compelling human being. She heard the soft report of a screen door closing on the summer kitchen below, and went without any conscious impulse to the window, as though drawn to it on an invisible lead. Looking down, she found herself staring at the top of the head of a young female possessed of hair as pale as cornsilk, her skin all but translucent. The girl stood at the summer kitchen door as motionless as the door itself. Clearly, it was she whom Eleanor had overheard. She appeared to be lost in her thoughts. At last, after an interval, she started away from the door, while, in that same motion, suddenly looking up! Eleanor never knew whether their eyes met in that second or not, because she recoiled instantly, even guiltily, retreating from the curtains.

Later, as she departed her room and went down the back stairs to the ground floor, she was astute enough to realize that her extraordinary response to the whisperings in the hall, and to the rather apparitional figure at the door below, could not be disentangled from the fact of her having arrived here only an hour ago—the newness of the house to her and her unsureness about her future post.

"I hope that we are as fortunate as I think we are," said Mr. Chickering at the supper table, after Eleanor had been introduced round to the other boarders. "Is it a fact that you count among your family that romantic thinker and iconoclast—the Reverend Eugene Lloyd Gray himself?"

Eleanor colored with embarrassment. "How on earth, Mr. Chickering," she returned, in a faint voice, "did you ever learn such a thing?"

"My sources," said the other, as he spread his napkin, "insist on perfect secrecy regarding all such intelligences forwarded to me. Is it," he persisted, "true?"

"It is, sir—yes," Eleanor answered. "He was my grandfather."

"What bloodlines!" Mr. Chickering declared, addressing himself to the others at the supper table. "What historic bloodlines."

From the want of expression on the faces of the other boarders, however, it was clear that the Reverend Eugene Lloyd Gray was an altogether unknown entity. The only possible exception was Miss Alice Harrison herself, the owner of this house. She was sitting at the head of the table, and had placed Eleanor conveniently at her left side. While Alice was a lady not yet out of her thirties, she gave an unmistakable air of being somewhat older. Eleanor liked her at once.

"Was he a Quaker?" Alice asked her latest boarder, while showing a polite and thoughtful air—as though the man's religious following were something that she had once perhaps known about and subsequently forgot.

"I believe," said Eleanor, "he was one of those writers and preachers whose writings and preachings often exceeded the scope not only of the doctrines of all others, but even of his own."

At the opposite end of the table, the garrulous Mr. Chickering gave out a horse laugh. "That is so beautifully put! So true. *Too true!*" He cried. "Too true!"

At once, though, Eleanor blushed furiously, as she realized that her reply was much too smart-alecky. Looking down at her plate, she blushed anew.

As supper progressed, Eleanor became familiar with Miss Harrison's other boarders. They all struck her as being modest, up-standing New Englanders. The only outsider in the company at table was Alonzo Klaw, an artist who hailed from New York City, and who was spending time in the dry air of the Berkshires as an antidote to a respiratory condition.

"Alonzo is East Becket's visiting artist!" Alice Harrison de-clared, with evident pride, and looked over at him. "I hope he'll show you some of his work."

"Oh, I will," he attested. "You may be sure. I never miss a chance." He smiled at Eleanor. "I am very vain."

"He says that jokingly," Mr. Chickering put in, without missing a beat, "but in fact it is no joke. He is very vain." He opened his hands, to signify the obviousness of his retort.

The two men laughed over the exchange.

"Look!" said Alonzo, all at once. He pointed out the dining-room window to the road nearby.

"Oh," said Miss Harrison, "they are an unusual pair."

Eleanor turned round in her chair just in time to see a long-legged bearded man followed by a young boy vanish from sight be-hind one of the elms.

"Two of our town's eccentrics."

William Bayles, who was Eleanor's associate and superior at the local school—he taught the upper grades, six through nine—had just entered the room.

"I am sorry I'm late for supper, Alice."

"It's all kept warm for you, William."

Turning, Miss Harrison introduced Eleanor to her superior at the schoolhouse. Eleanor extended her hand to the young man.

"Miss Gray arrived in town only two hours ago," Alice explained.

"We were just talking about old Conboy," Mr. Chickering interrupted, waving a finger at the outdoors. "Just went by with the boy."

"The boy," Alice confided to her latest boarder, "is a ward of the town. He's a sort of orphan or runaway from upcountry. He was boarding here with us till last winter, while attending school, but insists now on living with Mr. Conboy—who is a sort of hermit."

"Mr. Conboy," Charles Chickering elucidated, "is the former *Captain* Conboy, veteran of the Third Massachusetts, a regiment that saw some of the fiercest battles in the Civil War. He is somewhat strange."

"They are both strange."

Eleanor's associate returned from the kitchen, and took his place opposite her. "The boy's name is Justin Judd," he said. "He was a student of mine for three years. He marked time."

"Marked time?" Eleanor showed her wonderment.

"That means marching in place," said Alonzo Klaw.

"For three years," William Bayles added, while drawing up his chair, "the others went by him. He doesn't learn. He doesn't progress."

Alonzo pointed at a vacant chair. "Sat right there—quiet as the trees."

"I am sorry to hear that about him." Eleanor winced. "He's so young. To be alone."

"He's maybe fourteen," said the schoolmaster. "He's growing up now."

"And the town confers a small monthly stipend on Mr. Conboy—whose own plight is thereby eased, also," said Miss Harrison.

But Eleanor's attention lingered somewhat upon the young schoolmaster's remark of a moment ago about Justin Judd's age; not so much upon what he had just said, however, as upon the quality—the timbre—of his voice. She wondered, that is, if it was not he, her fellow teacher, whom she had heard outside her door. At once, the sight of a luminously pale young woman looking up at her window flashed back to her mind. It gave Eleanor a chill. She glanced across at William Bayles, and studied him in profile, as he had turned to speak to Alonzo Klaw.

AFTER SUPPER, Alice took Eleanor into the parlor to acquaint her with some facts about the town and about her post at the school. Miss Harrison was one of the elected board of selectmen responsible for the taxation and general administration of the entire East Becket Township.

Eleanor seated herself on the long mahogany bench at the piano.

"We are very pleased to have such a bright young lady come to join us from one of our big cities. The dean at Framingham wrote to say that you were the leading light in all your class! You'll be a breath of fresh air to all of us out here."

"That is so kind of you to say." Eleanor colored with pleasure. She smoothed her skirt and looked away.

"I hope that Charles Chickering does not tease you unnecessarily."

"On the contrary," Eleanor came right back. "I find him very engaging, very flattering. He's a great deal of fun."

"Charles," Miss Harrison explained, with obvious fondness, "is one of those men who takes his lively view of things from Teddy Roosevelt himself. He doesn't believe in pessimism."

"Where does Mr. Bayles come from?" Eleanor asked, attempting to be casual.

"William is from out this way. He was raised in Tolland, and spent two years at a technical school in Pittsfield. He is something of a technical genius. If you so much as *think* about radio telephony—whatever that means—he'll talk your ear off. But he is very bright. We were lucky to catch him." Alice Harrison let fall here one of her characteristic expressions. "In a pond full of pumpkin seeds and bullheads, William," she said, "is a rainbow trout! He is really quite a genius. He has published articles!" Alice widened her eyes expressively, as though to convey something of the mystery of the young Mr. Bayles's writing skills and of his attainments in the world of the new technologies.

"I hope that he will be satisfied with my teaching," Eleanor admitted, with a twinge of anxiety.

"You will find," Alice assured her, "that the children are wonderful. They practically do the job for you!" she exclaimed. "They really do. That's what Margaret Laughlin always maintained. She taught our school for years and years. She was my own teacher—through *all* the grades, one through nine." Alice looked about herself. "I was born in this house—thirty-eight years ago, in eighteen seventy-two."

"It's a wonderful house, I think," Eleanor observed, "and wonderfully situated."

Alice Harrison laughed. She offered a candy dish of mints. "My father used to say that we stood at a crossing of roads going nowhere."

"Miss Harrison," Eleanor spoke up, as she politely selected a mint. "I saw someone earlier outside my upstairs window. A young lady. A young lady with . . . white-blond hair and the palest complexion I think I have ever seen."

"Please call me Alice," the other interjected.

"Are you sure?" Eleanor inquired in earnest.

"I'm very sure."

Eleanor nodded, but said nothing after that, lest she blunt the thrust of her own question.

Alice nodded gravely. "That would be Evangeline Sewell," she said. "You saw her here?"

"Directly beneath my window," Eleanor attested. "Standing by the back kitchen door."

Alice reflected on that coincidence. "She sometimes poses for Alonzo. . . . Right in this room, in fact." Alice indicated her surroundings.

"What a wonderful subject she must be for an artist," Eleanor breathed out quietly.

"Like the boy"—Miss Harrison gestured toward the road, signifying the man and youth who had earlier strode past—"Evangeline is from upcountry. A place called Wisdom Way."

"She and the boy are related?" Eleanor exclaimed.

"Not at all." The other shook her head. "They are as different as day from night, except as both tend to be quiet, maybe even secretive. Those towns!" Alice laughed as before.

"When you say 'upcountry'. . . ," Eleanor began, encouraging Alice to explain.

Alice nodded. "Life is hard in the towns north of here. Mostly high woodlands. Not very suitable for farming, I'm afraid. They scratch out a living, at best. An acre or two under cultivation. Some chickens. A cow. You understand."

Eleanor was by now quite affectionate of Alice, whom she saw as an old-fashioned spinster lady, but deceptively insightful and understanding of others. She guessed that Alice made her living principally from her boarders. Eleanor wondered in passing if Alice, as a young lady, had ever known romance. She guessed perhaps not.

The parlor was filling up with shadows. A single horizontal beam of sunlight ignited the front windows, while the evening air remained redolent with the powerful scent of mowed hay.

While not prompted to do so, Alice Harrison enlarged upon the subject of the girl in question. "Evangeline," she went on, "was raised up there by her grandmother. Her mother, who was unknown to most of us, took her own life a few years ago. She never speaks of that, of course. She boards with the Trumbulls—about a half mile from here—and goes up home for summers and Christmas. She and that boy you saw, Justin Judd, are the only ones who have come down to our school in recent times. There used to be more. But that country up there is getting depopulated."

Eleanor nodded. "While riding in this afternoon, I remarked to Mr. Walker on that dark tree line north of here. It has such a brooding look about it! Very foreboding." Eleanor laughed. "It gave me quite a chill. Mr. Walker called it a place that 'used to be.'"

Alice laughed over that. "My father used to say that its past was our future."

Before continuing, Eleanor weighed her next remark. She did not want to seem over-interested. "The Sewell girl," she said, at last, "is she . . . strange?"

Alice Harrison waved her hand dismissively. "Oh, not really," she said. "Not in the way that Justin might be."

"Is she . . . mysterious?"

Miss Harrison did not reply at once, nor show any sign of surprise over Eleanor's questions. She reflected momentarily. "Yes. . . ," she replied, at length, but with obvious hesitation, as though giving voice for the first time to a persisting suspicion. "I think so."

"She looks unearthly," Eleanor blurted.

"She has a most magnificent way of looking at you sometimes. She has those ice-colored eyes! I declare!"

"She looks delicate," said Eleanor.

Alice laughed heartily over that. "She is anything but delicate! As I said, they are not like that. They are very hardy people up there."

The evening sun flickered several times on the windows, and then withdrew, as though drawing a curtain on their talk. "I hope you like your room upstairs," said Alice.

"Ever so much!" Eleanor piped, enthusiastically. "It's far more gracious and comfortable than anything I expected."

"Tell me again," said the other. "Who was your grandfather? Should I know of him better than I do?"

"He called himself the last of the Transcendentalists. He was captivated by the writings of Mr. Carlyle and Mr. Emerson. He was a preacher in Taunton, and published collections of his sermons. I never knew him. And my father—who was given the name Amos, in honor of Mr. Alcott—was never much loved by his father."

"I'm sorry to hear that, Eleanor."

"I put that unfairly," Eleanor corrected herself, as she and Miss Harrison stood up. "My father was at odds with my grandfather. They were at loggerheads. To this day, the name Eugene Lloyd Gray brings a smirk to my father's lips. . . . Naturally," Eleanor added, "I side with my father."

"Naturally," said Alice, nodding gently, closing and opening her eyes in understanding of the young schoolteacher's natural bias. "And your father, then . . . is a minister?"

"My father is nothing like a minister. He is an engineer at the Held McDermott cotton mills in Fall River. I'm afraid he could never preach. You can't get six words out of my father. He's as silent as his pipe."

"I would imagine you're his great favorite?" Alice interposed, questioningly, as they departed the parlor.

"As I have no brothers or sisters, there is only me to *be* his favorite. . . . But he does love books and letter-writing, and places great stock in schooling. My parents scrimped and saved that I might go to normal school."

"I think," said Alice, "that your mother and father have done wonderful things in raising you."

"I have been very fortunate, I feel."

Eleanor was reminded momentarily of her neighborhood back home, of the droves of children in the backyards and streets, some of them French-speaking from Canada, and others like herself of old stock—and of the great liveliness there amid the relative want. East Becket, by comparison, seemed altogether blissful—like a Currier & Ives scene shown by magic lantern upon a wall.

After darkness had fallen, before going to bed, Eleanor wrote her first letter home. She lighted the big glass-shaded oil lamp, turned down the wick, and addressed paper with pen. In her secret heart, Eleanor fancied that she would keep a memorable year-long record of her new life. She had never been away from home before, except of course for her overnight stays at Framingham Normal School, and looked upon the weeks and months to come as "An Adventure Among the Familiar."

She uncapped the ink bottle, dipped in the metal nib of her pen, and began to write.

"Dear Father. Let me begin by describing to you a certain hawk-faced individual of extraordinary taciturnity—a local wagoneer—who is known to his fellow citizens in the town of East Becket by a very enchanting sobriquet. He is called the 'Star Route man.'"

So began Eleanor Gray's nightly recording of her "adventures" among the commonplace.

three

Y LATE MORNING of her first day in the schoolhouse, Eleanor knew that Miss Harrison's reassurances regarding the children, and about her own capacities to teach and maintain order among them, had already been borne out. With each passing hour, she felt a burden lifted from her mind. She was following the precepts and suggested teaching formats of her normal school training, and was thrilled to see how efficacious they proved themselves out in reality. Nevertheless, by three o'clock, when she heard the sudden sound of a bell being rung jubilantly next door—doubtless by one of Mr. Bayles's male students—Eleanor was bone tired. When the children had departed the school—running off in all directions—she swept up the classroom, returned the readers and workbooks to the long table by the windows, and sponged the blackboard. Every now and again she gave an involuntary sigh and collected her breath. It was a trying day, but not without its minor victories.

Later, after going across the road to the Harrison house and getting out a cardigan sweater, Eleanor went for a walk. She followed the road west toward the church spire she had spotted yesterday while coming down the mountain road with Mr. Walker. She could see it now, the pristine white needle showing above a line of trees. There was a covered bridge up ahead, and within minutes the sound of a rushing stream reached her ears. As she stepped along, breathing in the fragrant air of the pastures flanking the road, Eleanor couldn't help feeling a bit self-congratulatory— happy with herself—that she had taken the extraordinary decision weeks ago to transplant herself from her house, more than a hundred miles away, to this quiet sunlit place. The mountainy atmosphere was invigorating beyond description.

While walking along the shoulder of the road, Eleanor noticed she was attracting sprigs of hay to the hems of her ankle-length skirt. Obviously, a hay wagon had come this way. To her right, as she approached the covered bridge and trees, she found herself being examined in passing by a dozen or so Holsteins. The cows, standing in the shade at the edge of the pasture, watched over the wire fence as she paced past toward the bridge. The sound of the little river—which was particularly rapid at this point in its career—reverberated noisily under the high roof of the bridge. Eleanor smiled to think that the stream, splashing its way seaward, was sending up a perpetual shout—a salutation!   to the stodgy bridge under which it came frolicking.

Emerging from the sheltered bridge, she could see up the gravel road on her left to a small town common, several houses, the church, and a white churchlike edifice that she rightly guessed to be the East Becket town hall. The town green consisted of an oval of grass formed by the bifurcating road, a stand of American elms, and a bronze figure standing atop a granite pedestal. Where the sandy road divided to embrace the small town common, Eleanor came to a halt, as there rose from behind her, from the direction of the bridge, the echoing of a horse's hooves drumming on the floorboards. Eleanor turned around instinctively, just as the horse and rider appeared, coming out into the patch of sunlight at the near end of the bridge. It was Evangeline Sewell. Her horse, a magnificent mare, black as anthracite, came on at a slow amble. Behind her, about six feet back, strode the two individuals that Eleanor had seen outside Alice's dining room windows last night.

Mr. Conboy, the first of the two, was a tallish, angular man, with a grayish beard, and a loping purposeful stride. He was carrying over his arm a shotgun. The golden-haired boy followed behind, stepping along briskly.

Only in the days to come would Eleanor learn that the horse belonged to the Trumbulls, where Miss Sewell boarded, and that she had learned to ride at a young age. The sight of Evangeline Sewell riding about the roads and woodlands of the neighboring countryside was commonplace. Eleanor noticed that the girl was wearing some type of denim trousers, an outfit that was altogether at variance with the customs of the day. A child might attire herself thus, but not an adult female. Miss Sewell straddled her horse like a male.

As the three of them came up the grassy incline behind her, Eleanor looked away, almost guiltily, and continued walking. She recalled the moment of her eavesdropping on the two voices in the hallway outside her door. On reaching the bronze Civil War soldier, she paused, and affected to be examining the names of battles that the sculptor had chiseled into the granite pedestal on all four sides. Eleanor read the names—Richmond, Antietam, Wilderness—but her senses were absorbed by the soft rhythmical thud of the hooves in the grass behind her. She caught on the air the jangle of a stirrup, then the sound of the horse's breathing. By this time, though, Evangeline had begun bevelling her mount to the right, in the direction of the side portico of the town hall. The three of them passed within just a few feet of Eleanor, moving along single file in the shade of an elm. Eleanor glanced over quickly, and glanced away, just as Evangeline came out of the shade. The flanks of the great mare shimmered, as horse and rider emerged into a long bar of sunlight. Evangeline's pale coloring lit up. In all, it was an awkward moment for Eleanor, as neither Evangeline nor the others so much as looked at her.

The sight of Miss Sewell at close range was quite different from Eleanor's earlier impression. She was not the schoolgirl figure she had looked to be when spotted, yesterday, from Eleanor's upstairs window. This figure bore herself with a solidity that belied her age, as did the utter want of expression on her face, or even the casualness in the way she clasped the reins in her pale fists. There was no denying the splendid look of her. The glowing planes of her hair, her ruler-straight posture in the saddle, the translucence of the flesh of her face and neck—there was just no describing it. One detail in particular arrested Eleanor's attention. It was the look of Miss Sewell's shoe in the steel stirrup. It was a paint-spattered man's work brogan of ankle height, with the laces out and the sides flaring open—as in a kind of intentional carelessness, or disregard for custom.

They went past in the sunlight in slow processional. Now and again, the mare raised and shook her head, as though conscious of her great size and dignity, or of the unusualness of her rider.

Eleanor resumed her afternoon walk, but found herself inexplicably shaken by the encounter. She had set out to explore the town, and decided to take the road that led south from the common. This road followed the little river that flowed beneath the bridge, but here, downstream, it took a noticeably more leisurely course. One of Eleanor's pupils, Bobby Dickson, had told her about the ruins of an old jute mill. She spotted it up ahead, an imposing red-brick edifice standing in silhouette against the trees and sky beyond. William Bayles, her superior and colleague at the school, explained that it was a small but very active "manufactory" fifty years back, one of many such places doing contract work for the Union government in those days, making uniforms. After the war, the owner, a man named Billings, tried producing Panama hats. "That failed dismally," said William.

The sight of the gaping windowless structure was somehow poignant, standing alone and abandoned in the midst of a swarm of saplings and second growth trees. Birds flew in and out. To one side, next to a dam, stood the long-inert waterwheel, a rotted portion of which jutted into the spilling waters. Here, the river, backed up, was deep, compared to the relative shallowness of the stream. On sighting the mill, she had departed the main road and was following now a cart path that led in the direction of the jute mill itself. This tributary road was very narrow, all but overgrown with grass and low shrubberies. Eleanor paused in her walking. The sight of the mill had an unexpected effect on her. It set off thoughts in her of the fate of all things mutable. There was, she felt, a certain beauty in desolation, in ruins, something that spoke of men's hopes, and courage, against a backdrop of an indifferent universe.

Eleanor sat in the sun on a boulder by the dam. She took a book of poems from her skirt pocket, but was really too immersed in her thoughts, and in the beauty of the day to concentrate her mind upon reading. The constant din of the waters spilling over the dam deadened her senses.

The figure of Evangeline Sewell came and went in her mind. She smiled to recall how Myron Walker and Alice Harrison had spoken about Evangeline's "upcountry" origins—a bleak derelict region of hilltop towns that were on their way to vanishing. It gave a romantic dimension to things. Eleanor formed a mental picture of the pale, luminous figure making her way on horseback—coming down from the north—descending from a place called Wisdom Way—along a road that was itself subsiding into nature.

She had been sitting no more than five minutes when she heard on the wind the thud of a shotgun. It came from far off. For some reason, Eleanor associated the sound of it with the sudden realization that Miss Sewell had not come to school today. Eleanor knew her to be matriculated. In the minutes to come, she heard three more reports of the shotgun, coming at short intervals. They came from beyond the wooded knoll across the way. She could only guess that the bearded Civil War veteran was teaching Evangeline how to employ a shotgun! Later, while retracing her steps along the grassy wheel tracks of the mill road, and looking away toward the direction of the wooded hill, Eleanor caught a glimpse through the trees of a house that somehow harmonized with the ruins behind her. It looked empty. It appeared in perfect condition, but its red-brick façade connected it visually—architecturally—with the mill ruins.

While walking home, Eleanor encountered Mr. Chickering. She fell in beside him.

"So, you have been out exploring," said he.

"It's unbelievably picturesque!" she exclaimed. "The countryside is so timeless, so beautiful. The farms," she said, "are like pictures of farms."

"I," said Mr. Chickering, "like the way the church and the town hall glare at each other across the green."

Eleanor loved the observation. "What a choice way of seeing things," she said, for it was true. She had noticed how the two white buildings stood on either side of the common, looking at each other.

"An apt symbol of our great nation," he added. 'The flag and the cross—each ever vigilant of the ambitions and fury of the other. Ever distrustful. Ever on guard." He balled his fist illustratively.

They stepped along the road in silence. The fragrance of the mowed fields was exhilarating. Eleanor's color was up.

"Mr. Chickering," she spoke up, at length. "I saw the most unusual sight today. It was Miss Sewell. She came across the town common on a magnificent-looking horse, followed," she stressed, "by Mr. Conboy and Justin Judd. Mr. Conboy carried what I believe was a shotgun. It was all rather peculiar to look at."

Mr. Chickering laughed sharply, putting his fist to his lips, his laughter degenerating into a series of rattling coughs. "Everett," he said, "is a bona fide solitary, but a very resourceful hermit. He has a small kitchen garden. He hunts and he traps. He works the blueberry lots in August. He does chores about town. It was he who taught Evangeline the fine points of riding. She's quite an accomplished horsewoman." Charles Chickering drew a long sail of a handkerchief from his back pocket, and blew his nose.

Eleanor noticed he was smiling to himself. She was enjoying their walk, and the aspect on all sides of the rolling pasturelands. "Is there something you're not telling me?" she asked, in a playful tone. Reaching down, Eleanor drew a long blade of grass, and set it to her lips.

"This past June," Mr. Chickering persisted, while carefully folding his handkerchief, "the Sewell girl rode her mare up to Middlefield, about eight miles from here, to a horse fair, a show, a competition of some type. Everett accompanied her. That was a little while before the boy went to live with him. Odd thing was," Mr. Chickering explained, his voice climbing amusedly, "Everett followed her on foot—all the way up there, and all the way back."

Eleanor guessed at Mr. Chickering's meanings. "You mean, like her *liege man?*"

Charles Chickering lit up. "What an apt expression!" He beamed at Eleanor, his cheeks flushed, as he stepped vigorously along. "What a lovely addition you are to our fair village. That's exactly what I meant. Like her personal footman! As though she were riding off to some feudal tournament." Charles here raised a cautionary finger. "Not walking at her side, mind you. Nothing so presumptuous. Marching in her wake. People along the way noticed it." Mr. Chickering restored his handkerchief to his pocket.

"A carpenter I know up in Middlefield remarked on it," he continued. "He described the two of them coming down the long road into town, past the hostelry and the creamery, she looking like a warrior of old—very stately—and Conboy slogging along dutifully in her wake. Then, this carpenter said, couple of hours later, here they come again, back the other way. She's out front of him, riding along slowly under the big sugar maples up there, and Conboy trying like the devil to keep up."

"And she, I suppose, not looking back at him," Eleanor surmised.

"Right, again!" crowed the other. "Not so much as a perfunctory glance. Unless, I suppose, she wanted something of him. I've seen the two of them like that a couple of times myself."

Eleanor and Mr. Chickering were now approaching the foot of Alice's driveway.

"She certainly has a magnificent presence," Eleanor conceded, softly, conscious of her own gathering fascination for the young woman.

"Don't misunderstand. They're rarely together. If she wants something of him, then, I suppose, she rides out to his shanty, or wherever he might be at the time, and—"

"Leads him away," Eleanor interposed.

As though he had divined it, Mr. Chickering answered the question that Eleanor was just about to put. "These days he's teaching her to shoot. They go to the orchard out behind the town hall."

"That's where I saw them," Eleanor put in.

"I was at the Treadwells' house—the general store—a couple of weeks back, and saw the three of them go into the orchard." Charles smiled over the recollection. "She, Evangeline, gets down from her horse, as nice as you please, and hands the boy the reins to tether the horse for her. Everett, he loads up the shotgun. I know the gun. It's a double-barreled twelve-gage Remington. It's a gun with a good kick. And you can see from a distance," Mr. Chickering continued, as he and Eleanor arrived at the front door of the house, "that Everett's explaining things to her. That done," Mr. Chickering concluded, "he presents her ladyship with the firearm. The boy reaches up an apple or two from the grass, gets round behind her, and lets one fly. As high and far as he can throw it."

"She sounds capable beyond anything."

"Well, Everett knows his craft," Mr. Chickering allowed, with a decisive nod. "He knows firearms. He knows a good many things. He's got skills."

Eleanor considered her next question for a long moment. "Is Mr. Conboy *fanatical* in his regard for Evangeline?" she asked, at last.

"If there is a better word for it," Mr. Chickering replied, as he held the door open for her, "it's in another language."

Stepping indoors, Eleanor took notice of the little lilac sidelights that had caught her attention yesterday on her arrival. It seemed like a week ago.

four

ON **THURSDAY** of that week, while sitting to supper, Eleanor mentioned her visit to the ruins of the old jute mill, and made a point of asking about the red-brick dwelling that she had spotted on the wooded hill across the way.

"The house is very much habitable," Alonzo Klaw replied. "Your predecessor, Margaret Laughlin, claimed that it's one of the grander interiors for miles around. Or, certainly, to be found in a farming town like this one."

On this occasion, Alice's boarders were joined at the supper table by the elderly Annie Sampson, who usually took her meals upstairs. The old woman liked eating at her own slow pace, and was hard of hearing, besides. But she didn't like storms—in particular thunderstorms. Tonight, minutes before suppertime, the heavens over East Becket turned dark blue. A wind came up, flapping the tar-paper roofing of the woodshed out back. Two wagons went rattling past in opposite directions, their drivers intent on getting home, or to the shelter of the covered bridge perhaps. By now, the rain had come pouring down, and was making sudden puffing sounds against the dining-room windows.

"You have not been inside?" Eleanor went on, querying Alonzo Klaw, while holding a serving dish of apple sauce for Mrs. Sampson.

"I've been inside," William Bayles cut in, "but only as far as the front entranceway. There is a great deal of wood-carving—paneling, that is—and the plasterwork of the ceilings is very decorative. But it's an old house, and the owners, the Billingses, do nothing to keep it up or improve it." William turned to Miss Harrison. "Alice, have you ever been inside the Billings place?"

"Oh, no," Alice demurred at once. "In those days, in my girlhood, the Billingses were considered to be like—like Stockbridge quality! The mill was still running then. They were quite aloof."

"Hats!" Charles Chickering fired out, with humor.

Alice laughed. "Yes," she said, "hats. Tropical type hats. It was a small operation, even by the standards of those days. But the Billingses were landowners. They did a lot of real estate banking. To this day, they have a bank up in Hinsdale."

Eleanor reached up a plate of hot rolls for Mrs. Sampson. Then, knowing she would not be insulting the lady by doing it, she selected and buttered one of the rolls for her. Mrs. Sampson showed her a foxy smile.

"You've got a pretty one here," Mrs. Sampson imparted to Alice, and wagged a finger backward at Eleanor.

Alice spoke loudly in order that Mrs. Sampson might hear her. "She is also quite brilliant!"

And didn't I know it! Mrs. Sampson shouted her reply in a big voice, inspiring laughter among all.

During all this week, Eleanor was alive to the fact that no one in the house made even a passing mention of Evangeline Sewell, even though her absence at school was more than conspicuous. More insidiously, Eleanor had to confess that the young woman was much in her own thoughts, perhaps to an unnatural extent. She could not recall anyone having impressed herself more profoundly upon her imagination. Time and again, the picture came to mind of the young woman riding in solemnly under the shadowy portico of the town hall—her snowdrop skin, and the long tail of her lusterless hair—her two retainers following her on foot, like dream figures.

ON THIS EVENING, Eleanor did in fact receive a "revelation," but it came from an unexpected quarter. She had just come from her room, headed downstairs to see who might be socializing in the front parlor, when she was arrested by the voice of Alice Harrison from below. Eleanor paused at the stairhead. Miss Harrison, who possessed one of only six telephones in the entire town of East Becket, was speaking in low tones. She was standing not ten feet from the foot of the front stairs, next to the oak counter and oaken rack of pigeonholes that contained the mail for the town's inhabitants. Eleanor overheard only isolated utterances. "Our worst fears," said Miss Harrison, at one point.

Eleanor retreated a step into the shadows of the upstairs hallway. A long silence ensued, before Alice Harrison spoke again. Then, clearly, she heard Evangeline's name.

Appalled at the prospect of being caught eavesdropping, Eleanor returned on silent foot to her room, and closed her door. It had been dark for more than an hour by this time, and the rain had continued without letup. Tonight, for the first time, one could begin to suspect the nature of Miss Sewell's distress. It pained Eleanor to think it, but the girl was very likely in trouble. What else could it have been to have caused her withdrawal from school, and to create such perturbation in Alice? That, Eleanor conjectured, must have been Mrs. Trumbull on the phone to Alice tonight, as Eleanor knew that the Trumbulls possessed one of the small handful of telephones in town, and Evangeline was their boarder.

In her concern, Eleanor could think of only one person in East Becket to whom she might broach the subject. That person was Mr. Walker. Eleanor and the Star Route carrier enjoyed an unspoken rapport.

LATE AFTERNOON the following day, having stayed longer at the schoolhouse, Eleanor spotted Mr. Walker's horse and wagon under the elms at Alice's house. She crossed the road at once. Indoors, she heard the sound of Alice and the Star Route man talking in the kitchen. "I declare!" Alice said, laughing over some remark of Mr. Walker's. Eleanor decided to go upstairs and wait in her room till she heard him leaving, then overtake him outdoors. The wait proved not a long one; but at one point in those few minutes to follow, Eleanor was a bit nonplussed to discover what she was doing. She had glanced round, and saw herself in the mirror. She was standing by her closed door, perfectly motionless, hands clasped at her waist, listening. It struck her as such an unlikely thing to be doing. Not like herself, at all. She might have dwelt longer upon the oddness of her behavior, but Myron Walker chose that very moment to depart. He was going out the back way. At one point, their voices suddenly shifted; they ceased coming up the rear stairs, and flew in at the open window, as Mr. Walker emerged outdoors.

Eleanor went along the upstairs corridor and waited at the stair top. She stood unmoving for a short interval, till she divined that Mr. Walker would have reached his wagon, then went briskly down the steps and out the front door.

"Mr. Walker!" she cried. "Where are you going?"

As Eleanor approached him, he made no effort to conceal his pleasure at the sight of her. He affected, however, to give her question great thought, as though it contained scientific or philosophic import. He was up on his wagon seat, reins in hand.

"Two miles east," he pronounced, at last, nodding deliberately with each phrase, "two miles south, and two miles west."

Eleanor laughed, her fingertips to her lips. "You are always so profound, Mr. Walker. Isn't it true," she added, "that if you then

.

went two miles *north,* that you would be back where you had started?"

"I'm starting right here," he said.

"That's what I'm saying," Eleanor confirmed.

"I don't have a map, Miss Gray."

"It isn't a matter of needing a map, Mr. Walker, to realize that you were drawing a box—a picture of a box."

"I was doing that?" he returned. He pursed his lips significantly.

But the Star Route carrier gave no sign of being in a hurry to leave during this exchange. He liked talking to the town's new schoolteacher. Eleanor stood in the sun, facing him, shielding her eyes with her hand.

"May I ride with you?" she asked.

Mr. Walker's face changed. He was visibly pleased. "I'll ask Ben," he said, indicating his horse.

"Ben would never say no to me."

"Where are you going, miss?"

Eleanor responded with cleverness. "Two miles east—by horse—two miles south—by horse—two miles west—by horse, and two miles north—on foot."

"Come ahead!" he cried. Mr. Walker gave her a hand up, and made room for her beside him.

"I go out exploring every afternoon," she explained, "right after school. Usually, I change into some kind of walking clothes and walking shoes."

"These look like your Sunday clothes. Today just being Friday," he added. As they turned onto the broad gravel road east, Mr. Walker gave voice to what seemed a long-standing perplexity of mind. "Someone once told me—that was years back—that *Arabs,*" he said, "celebrate Sunday on Friday." He looked sidelong at Eleanor. "That possible?"

Eleanor was enjoying herself already. "I think," she replied, "that they celebrate the *Sabbath* on Friday."

"I know, I know," he nodded. "But the Sabbath is Sunday."

"Not," Eleanor stressed, "for Arabs."

"Just my point," he added. Reaching, he touched a finger to his forehead. "The old lady that told me that was . . . incomplete."

"Sometimes, there's just no talking to you, Mr. Walker."

They were headed east now, toward the mountainside down which they had descended that first day.

"Mr. Walker," Eleanor injected, quietly, as the horse fell into his rhythm, "if I brought up a certain subject to you, could it become something that would remain discreet between you and me?"

"Something private?" he said, turning grave.

"Yes."

"Nothing troubling you, I hope."

"No, it is not at all about me, but about the welfare of someone else. Mr. Walker, it's about the young lady who lives with the Trumbulls."

"Lived," he said.

Eleanor looked at him questioningly.

"She ain't there anymore, miss," he added.

By now, the horse was plodding along comfortably, his head bobbing gently to the motion of his gait. The wheels of the wagon set up a ceaseless grinding in the gravel. Spacious meadows lay to left and right. The grasses that grew tall along the wire fences were choked with daisies and Indian paintbrush. Eleanor waited for the Star Route man to say more. At length, without prompting, he elaborated on his remark.

"Evangeline Sewell departed for home the night before last— took the horse with her—left in the dead of night."

Eleanor's heart sank unaccountably. Or maybe it was just because she had determined this morning to make herself helpful. She was not unaware that her post as teacher conferred upon her a degree of moral latitude denied to others.

She smoothed her skirts, straightened in her seat, wiped her lips with her fingertips. Words evaded her.

At last, she spoke. "Am I correct in thinking, Mr. Walker, that there are some parties in East Becket who know why Miss Sewell has withdrawn from school and that the reason for it is unfortunate?"

"You know," he replied, his voice rising, "you talk beautifully."

He nodded impressively over that, and returned his attention to the road ahead.

Eleanor smiled. "You are the only person I know who can change the subject five times in one minute—then six in the next."

He grunted. "Schoolteachers scold."

"Do you see what I mean? You just did it again."

"Yes, Miss Gray," he sighed, "there are folks around who know why she's gone."

"It is, then," she sought to verify, "what I think it is."

"I've no doubt it's that," he attested. As before, Mr. Walker regarded Eleanor from the tail of his eye.

Eleanor was doing some chronological guesswork. If the girl had been upcountry during the summer vacation, and had got pregnant up there, she likely would not yet know it for sure. She must have got that way months earlier—last spring—when she was here in East Becket.

"I guess it is none of my business," she remarked, at length, with sincerity.

"You're right to ask," he objected. "You have a right to know, considering who you are."

"Is there anything you think I should do?"

"Ain't much you can do."

Following those remarks, Eleanor and the driver fell into a prolonged silence. The perfect temperature and the general beauty of the day produced on Eleanor's senses a sweet torpor. With the sun resting on her back, she fell to reflecting upon the worshipful beauties of the agrarian life, back to an ancient age when the barn was the temple, and the meadow the sacred grove. Had she not come out to East Becket, she might never have known the truth of it.

"It's like the beginning of the world," Eleanor exclaimed, taking a deep breath.

"In about three months," said Mr. Walker, having divined Eleanor's meaning, "you'll get some blizzards that are like the end of the world."

"You always have a contrary point of view!" she bantered back. She straightened in her seat. She was conscious that her playfully scolding retorts had become a part of their natural badinage. "I never knew what a Yankee really was, Mr. Walker, till I met you."

While bandying words with the driver, Eleanor's thoughts turned to William Bayles, as she couldn't help wondering if it wasn't he she heard whispering behind the door that afternoon. She would like to have mentioned that incident to Mr. Walker, but thought better of it.

Surprising even herself, Eleanor suddenly gave voice to the considerable impression that the Sewell girl had made upon her. "I have seen the young lady only twice since my arrival here, but she is very noteworthy, very remarkable to look at." Eleanor colored momentarily. "Sometimes, there is something a little ghostly about her. Although Miss Harrison says that she is anything but insubstantial. She says she is very solid."

"I would agree with that," Mr. Walker affirmed. He smiled over his thoughts. "None of the boys at the schoolhouse ever cared to quarrel with her. She outdoes them all. Outfishes them, outruns them, outrides them—"

Eleanor interrupted. "Mr. Conboy has been teaching her to shoot."

"Oh, she knows how to shoot!" Mr. Walker argued right back. "He's teaching her the finer side of it. Shooting on the wing."

"I'm sorry to hear she is gone," Eleanor admitted, softly. "She sounds so able, and daring. Certainly, she is unusual."

Myron Walker laughed. "She took Todd Trumbull's horse! That's unusual."

"It's a beautiful horse."

"Biggest mare I've ever seen. Seventeen hands at the withers. She's about the only saddle horse out this way. Trumbull's wife, Ivy, used to ride from time to time, but gave it up about two years ago. She grew kind of fat. So, Todd let the Sewell girl ride her. Just to keep the mare busy, I suppose."

"Are you sure that Mr. Trumbull didn't actually give the mare to Evangeline?"

"If he did," sang the other, "he's made a good show of hiding it. Mostly, I think he's more troubled about her taking the horse than he is about the horse."

"Mr. Walker," Eleanor inquired, at length, "if I wrote to Evangeline, would my letter reach her upcountry?"

"They get their mail up there. A couple of them come down to the general store now and then, and they either stop by at Alice's house, or get it from the Treadwells."

Up ahead, a cock pheasant emerged abruptly from a field of cornstalks, and strutted casually across the road, unperturbed by the oncoming wagon. Its feathers gleamed with breathtaking iridescence, shimmering and changing color at every step.

"Isn't he the dandy," Eleanor observed.

"Cock o' the walk," said the Star Route man.

THAT EVENING, Eleanor skipped her usual late-night journal entry, and composed instead a letter to the distressed young lady upcountry. Eleanor was always a stickler when it came to expressing herself on paper, but probably never more so than tonight. She was determined to strike just the right note. She did not want to sound "schoolmarmish." She leaned over her desk, with the glow of the oil lamp illuminating her hands and the sheet of writing paper, and began.

> *The Harrison Homestead*
> *East Becket, Massachusetts*
> *September 18, 1910*

My dear Evangeline Sewell:

> *I was lately saddened to learn of your withdrawal from the East Becket School, and of your return to Wisdom Way. As you know, I am only recently installed here as teacher in the lower grades, but it is a post that I have learned already to cherish. I come from the manufacturing city of Fall River, a hundred miles from here—having just completed my two years of normal school-teacher training this past June. At twenty, I am not so different in age from you!*

Eleanor paused in her writing. She wanted to strike a subtle, conspiratorial note that might inspire confidence in the other. She made an effort at humor.

I was delighted upon hearing that your beautiful black mare could not abide the thought of your going away and leaving her behind, and chose therefore to accompany you home.

My reason in writing to you is to offer my help most sincerely. If you ever wish to have a trustful friend in East Becket — whether to deliver messages to anyone, or to acquire anything you might need, or even just for an understanding ear — I am prepared to be that friend.

Enclosed is an envelope addressed to me at Miss Harrison's house. Please do respond. I am ever so eager to hear back.

> *Yours most faithfully,*
> *Eleanor Gray*

As chance had it, Eleanor found someone heading upcountry the very next day, and entrusted the letter to him. To make it official, she had stamped the letter with Miss Harrison's red Star Route stamp, and was carrying the letter in the pocket of her Kendal-green tweed skirt, when Marjorie Treadwell, owner of the general store, introduced her to a young itinerant minister who said he was heading north. He was driving up to Cold Spring, he said. The coincidence struck Eleanor as auspicious.

"Is that anywhere near Wisdom Way?" Eleanor spoke up.

Eleanor and he were standing opposite Mrs. Treadwell, posted behind her counter.

"If it still has a right to *be* an it," replied the young cleric, with the wry type humor that brought Myron Walker to mind. "I suppose you could say they're near one another. Fact is," he added, "they touch."

"I wonder what will happen when they cease to exist," Eleanor bandied back. She enjoyed regularly now the amusing references to those obscure towns, as well as the quirky Yankee point of view that they seemed to evoke. "Inasmuch as they won't be able to touch any longer."

"Or speak, or hear," he added.

"I'm Eleanor Gray," she offered.

"Howard Allen," said he. The minister was a slender handsome man, who clearly took pleasure in the way he dressed.

"Reverend Allen says a service up there every Sunday," put in Mrs. Treadwell.

Eleanor waited till the two of them got outdoors, minutes later, before mentioning the letter she bore.

First, she remarked on Howard Allen's conveyance. "That's a very pretty carriage," she said. "Is that a cabriolet?" She signified it with her eyes.

It was a light two-wheeled carriage, with a folding leather hood and upward slanting shafts. The horse in the shafts looked young and sprightly.

"I believe it is," he said.

Eleanor changed the subject. "It's very thoughtful and generous of you, Reverend Allen, to hold service up there the way you do."

"I have to be talking someplace on Sunday."

As the young man turned to his carriage, Eleanor screwed up her courage. "Are you familiar," she asked, "with a young lady from Wisdom Way named Evangeline Sewell?"

Howard Allen looked surprised, and in the same moment sought to conceal it. "Yes, I am. Why do you ask, Miss Gray?"

"I'm the new schoolteacher in East Becket. I have a letter I wish delivered to her."

"Is something wrong?"

"My message to her," Eleanor evaded the point, with a shake of her head, "is altogether ingenuous. But I wish it to reach her notwithstanding." With that, she withdrew the envelope from her skirt pocket. She studied it herself. The envelope with its lovely flourish of letters and the Star Route postal marking looked somehow mythical. It bore the blood red ink-stamp star, and beneath that the handwritten legend,

Evangeline Sewell
Wisdom Way

"Would it be possible?" she asked. "Will you likely encounter Miss Sewell at services tomorrow, or anyone of her family?"

Reverend Allen was standing with his back to the carriage, his hands thrust into his trousers pockets. Eleanor liked the young man's looks.

"Miss Sewell, as you call her, has not attended a service of mine in some long while. Or anybody else's, for that matter. I've only been ministering up there for two years. My predecessor, a man of the Presbyterian persuasion—who drove to Cold Spring from Hinsdale—was a very old gentleman named McArdle. He died in his carriage one Sunday afternoon while trotting back to Hinsdale. His horse went blithely along!" said Mr. Allen. "Right up the McArdle drive, and into the open door of the stable. Stood there an hour, waiting to be unharnessed, and fed and watered."

Eleanor endeavored not to laugh. "That is a dreadful story."

"Not at all. The man died in harness—the horse got his feed—and the sun went on shining. As our own Edwin Arlington Robinson put it, Miss Gray, 'There is nothing more to say.'"

He reached then for the letter, which Eleanor thrust at him instinctively.

"The first time I ever saw Evangeline," he said, "she was in the top of a butternut tree, shaking the branches for some children below. Shaking down butternuts."

"That's a lovely recollection."

"I was astonished. She was way up in the topmost branches," he exclaimed, "swaying back and forth in the wind, going from one bough to another. Every now and then the butternuts came raining down!"

Eleanor experienced a sudden clairvoyance. "Did you include it in your sermon that week?" she snapped.

The minister was just about to climb aboard his carriage. He stopped. "What a remarkable lady you are. What a remarkable guess. Yes, I did," he admitted. "I likened the moment to something about . . . Zaccheus."

"I know Zaccheus," said Eleanor.

"Oh, I was sure you would!" The minister laughed.

Eleanor recited: "Zaccheus he . . . did climb a tree . . . the Lord to see."

"That's it!" said the other. "You know me backward and forward."

"On the contrary," said Eleanor. "The endurance in my mind of that little piece of Puritan doggerel is the solitary upshot of nearly ten years of Sunday school."

She watched as he stepped up into his carriage.

"Were you born in the Berkshires, Howard?" she asked.

"Yes," he answered. He flicked his head backward. "Down in Otis. Where I live now."

Eleanor had determined to broach a final question. She followed a step or two behind, as the carriage started to roll. "Do you find, Howard," she said, "that Miss Sewell is one of those persons who is born to be talked about?"

"I think she is one of those figures whom people like either to romanticize or demonize—because she keeps to herself. Christians love a pagan," he said. "If we can't find one, we find one anyhow."

As before, Eleanor felt that the young man was intentionally obfuscating, but could not bring herself to say more.

"I hope I see you again," she smiled, and stopped walking.

"Same time through every week," he called back. "Stroke of noon."

She watched then as he trotted off to his right, going round the oval of the common toward the bridge, the black-wheeled spokes of his cabriolet gleaming, the dappling sun winking and flashing in the elms overhead. He was both handsome to look at and a morally attractive young man, she thought. For all his jocular airs, he seemed to be of serious purpose in putting his talents and education to the best use he could find—and in what was probably a very thankless undertaking.

As she went striding off, she wondered, however—having given him the letter—why he had not asked the reason for Evangeline's being up home this time of year? Surely he knew she was matriculated here. How could he have known of her departure?

five

N THE DAYS to follow, while Eleanor settled comfortably into her teaching routine at the schoolhouse, she was surprised to discover what an enduring impression Evangeline Sewell had made upon her. At odd moments in the day, the other would come unbidden to mind. The most alluring picture of them all was the one that Mr. Chickering had drawn of Everett Conboy, the old war veteran, following grim-faced in the wake of his luminous muse—traipsing mile after mile behind her up the long road to Middlefield. Other times, Eleanor was visited by the sight that day of Evangeline riding under the portico of the town hall—the pale helmet of her hair, the look of ice-eyed indifference. Eleanor knew the notion to be unsupportably romantic, but was pleased to think of that moment on the common as having perhaps mystical significations. More than once she wondered if she, too, were not falling under the other's spell.

On Monday afternoon, when she came in at Miss Harrison's front door, she discovered a letter lying slantwise in her own pigeonhole mail compartment behind the oak counter. As she took it in hand, she was momentarily perplexed by it, as the envelope was addressed in her own handwriting. It was, of course, the Star Route stamped envelope that she had included in the letter she entrusted to the young minister, Howard Allen, for Evangeline Sewell. For a second or so, she felt a stab of concern that Miss Harrison would be privy to her secret communication—till she realized that the address to herself in her own hand naturally masked the identity of the sender. As she mounted the stairs to her room, Eleanor felt flutterings of excitement—if only because of the clandestine nature of the communication in hand. She was moved to think that the strange upcountry girl might, indeed, have responded to her letter with some small amount of genuine relief, or, at least, friendly gratitude.

By the time Eleanor sat to her desk, and began to slit open the envelope, she was sensible to the fact that she had only recently arrived in the town, and had insinuated herself into the heart of a very delicate situation. To her consternation, however, the letter within consisted of nothing more than a penciled note and a sealed envelope. The note was written on a scrap of cheap, yellowed paper.

The message read:

Dear Eleanor,

    Give this letter to Howard Allen next Saturday.

                           Evangeline Sewell

Eleanor was instantly offended. She felt her temples heating up. The other addressed her as though she were a child. Eleanor dropped the note and enclosed letter onto her desktop. This teenage girl, to whom she had extended a hand of helpfulness and affection, had responded in the bluntest, most unmannerly way.

When Eleanor came outdoors, she was walking rapidly. The foliage was turning now, and the air had upon it a smoky autumn haze. She set off for the covered bridge, toward the town green. She was castigating herself for having put herself into a situation from which she could not now extricate herself without suffering some degree of embarrassment. She could not tell anyone in the Harrison house that she had written to the young woman, as that would imply her having somehow received information about the girl's condition. At the same time, she was constrained by her own scruples to transmit Miss Sewell's letter to the young minister. Moreover, Eleanor had *offered* to play the role of go-between regarding such messages. As she strode on past the church and Civil War monument, headed south toward the ruins of the jute mill, her thinking clarified.

She would simply put an end to the matter. She would enclose Evangeline's letter inside a fresh envelope, give it to Marjorie Treadwell at the general store, and ask her to give it to Howard Allen whenever she might see him next. The idea of being finished with the entire business made Eleanor more buoyant, as she turned in at the grassy road leading to the mill. It was her lack of any significant socializing, she was sure, that had embroiled her in this lamentable affair in the first place. Nevertheless, by the time Eleanor came up to the ruins, she had already resolved on a far different course. Moreover, her mind was completely made up in the matter, in the way that sometimes happens when one alternative to act simply displaces its opposite, notwithstanding human reason or scruples. Somehow, her mind was made up for her. She was going to steam open Evangeline's letter to the young clergyman.

In her effort to rationalize this violation of another's rights, Eleanor invoked as a cause for it her own injured spirits. She knew this line of thinking to be specious, but one always has to invoke some self-exculpating motive.

THAT SAME EVENING, as he had promised to do, Alonzo Klaw invited Eleanor to review some of his recent drawings and watercolors. After supper, she followed him up the stairs and along the corridor to his room. She remained in the doorway until he had lighted his lamp, and watched as the glow slowly expanded, invading the nooks and dark corners of the crowded room. Within a moment, Eleanor was gazing straight ahead at the most prominent work of all. It was a pencil portrait of Evangeline affixed to an easel.

Eleanor stepped into the room. The walls were covered with a variety of drawings. A long table was stacked with books and drawings. The room was aswim with pictures and art supplies.

"It's quite a mess," he allowed.

"Not at all," said Eleanor. "It's very busy, very workmanlike, very interesting. Next to it, my room is a mausoleum." But Eleanor made no effort at not showing her reaction to the pencil portrait of

Evangeline Sewell. "Mr. Klaw," she said, "that picture over-whelms me."

"That's quite recent," he said.

"She posed for you here?"

"Downstairs," he replied. "In Alice's parlor."

While marveling at how the artist had caught in pencil the transparency of her face, Eleanor heard herself remarking upon it with words that emerged from nowhere. She was staring at the picture. "She has such an air of purification!" she said.

Mr. Klaw looked at Eleanor over his shoulder. "I can't imagine it better put," he said.

"I think," she said, "that I have never known an artist before. I never even thought to know one. Not till meeting you."

"While we are dealing out praise, Miss Gray, it will please you to know that you are already a great success in your post. The adula-tion," he exclaimed, smartly, "is general. I hear it everywhere."

Eleanor colored with pleasure. "I do feel I am grappling with the job satisfactorily, but it's reassuring to hear you say that."

"Not to dilute it," he said, "but your predecessor, Margaret Laughlin—who vacated the job last year for southern climes—was getting decidedly senile. She reached a point, I hear, where she had forgot her own middle name. But then," Alonzo qualified, "many among us would probably do as well to forget ours."

"What is your middle name?" she asked, amused.

"Guggenheim," he said.

"Really?" Eleanor brightened. "You are one of that famous New York family?"

"I am a part in the machine," he said. "Yes."

Eleanor teased him. "Are you very wealthy, Mr. Klaw?"

"I am not in that part of the machine," he said. "I am in the part where the money is not kept. When the Guggenheim worth is cited, I am any one of the great string of zeroes reaching out to infinity."

Eleanor's hand was closed around the letter in her skirt pocket all this while, as Alonzo Klaw showed her about and commented in passing on many of his studies, in particular a variety of watercolor landscapes. Some of the winter scenes struck Eleanor as being especially beautiful to look upon.

"The winters here must be formidable, if your watercolors are an indication."

"That's why I'm here," he said. "The air in winter is so cold and dry."

"Mr. Klaw," Eleanor inquired, on impulse, "have you ever been upcountry?"

"Upcountry!" he parroted back. "The derelict realm of!"

"It's spoken about by people like Myron Walker, and even Alice, as being such a . . . bleak domain." Eleanor laughed. "I picture old houses covered over with woodbine, sinking into milkweed. Empty barns! The roads, they say, are slowly vanishing."

"There may be more to it than that," Alonzo explained. "A company of men drawn from those towns in the Civil War got itself massacred someplace. Only sixteen out of fifty men came home. Everett Conboy told me that. Do you know Conboy?"

Eleanor chose here to say nothing of what she had learned about the sullen, long-faced Mr. Conboy, and his obsessive attachment to Evangeline. "He has a beard, and walks rapidly," she said, with a smile. "He has that boy with him."

"Justin Judd," said Alonzo. "A very nice boy he is, too—although not altogether clear-headed."

By now, Eleanor and the artist were sitting on straight-backed chairs by the side of the piled-up table.

She was looking meanwhile at several pen-and-ink sketches, and was shown then three other pencil drawings of the Sewell girl. As in the big drawing attached to the easel, the likeness was remarkable. Eleanor fell to studying them. For reasons she could not understand, the cold gaze of the eyes of the young woman left her feeling squirmish inside, oddly fragile.

ON THE FOLLOWING afternoon, while Alice Harrison was attending a choir rehearsal at church, Eleanor set a fire going in the kitchen stove and brought a pot of water to a boil. She couldn't quell the trembling of her fingers as she held the envelope above the steam with a pair of tweezers. In seconds, the glue began loosening. At one point, Eleanor actually sighed aloud. She could scarcely credit what she was doing. She gave a long shiver. She had heard of persons doing this, but had no idea how simple it really was. The envelope was opening right before her eyes.

That done, she poured the water out the back kitchen door and went hurriedly up the staircase at the back of the house. In her room, she leaned against the closed door, her hand flat to her chest. Tonight, she determined, she would make confession to her father of what she had done. She would explain herself in detail. Eleanor had developed by now the conviction that Evangeline had been badly wronged by somebody, and was in a quite forlorn circumstance up in Wisdom Way. Before extricating the letter to Reverend Allen from the opened envelope, Eleanor swore that she would do nothing underhanded or in any way harmful to anybody—following her secret perusal of the letter. She swore further to extend any help she could to Miss Sewell—no matter what the letter might contain.

Eleanor sat at her desk, and shifted her school papers and books to one side. She was listening to her own breathing, as she plucked out the letter, a single sheet of yellow paper similar to the page that Evangeline had addressed to her.

Evangeline Sewell's handwriting consisted of careful, rounded lettering. There were smudges and erasures on the page. It read:

Dear Howard,

> *I don't like the fact that you know more about me than God Himself.*
> *I am going to stay with my aunt Beulah for two months. Then I will*
> *come back! Then we will see who is strong and who is weak.*

> *Evangeline Sewell*

Oddly, the steely feeling behind these sentences did not take Eleanor altogether by surprise. She had sensed it before. She recalled the look of Evangeline's shoe in the stirrup that day—the unlaced work shoe!—and how it had suggested a certain rough spiritedness in the girl. She liked, too, the distinct air of menace that informed that last sentence, as well as the obvious vow to return and settle accounts with someone.

Within a minute, the frayed yellow document lying on the shiny desktop took on for Eleanor a talismanic look—like the page of an ancient manuscript found in a chest dredged up from the seafloor. It was a sickly hue. Eleanor stared lengthily at the yellow rectangle, her hands to her forehead, her eyes going up and down the page. She was scanning another's most private thoughts. She was looking into the forbidden.

She kept the letter in the pocket of her skirt, when, later on, she went downstairs to supper. While reluctant to admit it, she found the fact of her illicitly obtained secret knowledge—not to say the pressure of the envelope against her thigh—vaguely thrilling.

"I don't believe in séances," Mr. Chickering was declaring to all, when Eleanor came to the table, "and I don't believe that Madam Blavatsky herself could take the place of a good Boston churchman in our series of winter lectures. That is what I'm saying. Perhaps I'm wrong." He set the fingertips of both hands illustratively to his chest. "Maybe I'm old-fashioned. Maybe I am not modern enough to believe in ghosts—in spirits rapping on the underside of tables."

"In the dark," William Bayles added.

"Always," said Mr. Chickering, "in the dark! How else? It's funny, isn't it, that beings that cannot be seen in the full light of day insist, anyhow, on traveling everywhere under cover of night."

Miss Harrison laughed over her boarder's clever remarks. "I am not stating my approval of the choice, merely saying, Charles, that the Atheneum board sent a letter of invitation to Annie Besant for our January speaker.

"You would think," Charles Chickering added, "that these seers into the future would have had the foresight to have bought up New York Central common stock last year."

"How are your studies on the watershed going, Mr. Chickering?" Eleanor spoke up, sociably. She had learned only this week that Charles Chickering was a recently retired officer of the U.S. Corps of Army Engineers. While in his retirement, he was concluding an ongoing study of the Housatonic watershed, with a view, it appeared, toward creating a series of small dams.

Mr. Chickering nodded, with a look of exaggerated patience. "Painstakingly."

Eleanor teased him. "It is so hard for a disinterested observer to imagine how the little ponds and brooks that I've seen out here could be of any lasting interest to the United States Army."

Mr. Chickering raised a staying hand. "These same little watersheds create the oceans of the earth, Miss Gray."

Eleanor had a sudden inspiration. "Mr. Chickering," she said, "does your work ever take you up to Cold Spring—to those towns up there?" She avoided saying Wisdom Way.

"Oh, yes. I'm trying to determine the actual volume of water of the two principal streams that contribute to our own little river. They are called the East Branch and the West Branch. The West Branch is formed in Cold Spring. It's the larger of the two. The other, which collects water from a dozen or so little brooks, and from two or three quite prolific springs that erupt in an old granite quarry up there, comes out of Wisdom Way."

Eleanor affected a deadpan expression, and reached to wipe the elderly Annie Sampson's lips with her napkin. She might have imagined it, but Mr. Chickering's mention of the name of Evangeline Sewell's township made for a slightly restive, prickly moment round the table. She glanced then momentarily at William Bayles, her fellow teacher. He appeared both detached and concentrated.

"I have heard so much said about that region!" Eleanor interposed, while taking up her fork.

"We talk about it," said Alice, "in much the same way, I think, that we talk about old battlefields."

"Or the Black Hills," said Alonzo Klaw, adding, "where our least favorite, most vainglorious of generals met a fitting end."

"That," said Mr. Chickering, flushing, "may be a popular view of George Armstrong Custer in New York society, but words like that would get you strung up by the neck at our West Point Military Academy."

"With his long golden curls!" Alonzo added, expansively.

"It *was* about time," William Bayles agreed, "that the Ogalala Sioux got to enjoy a good day in the field for a change."

"It was all so long ago," said Miss Harrison. "I was a girl of but three or four. Some episodes," she said to Eleanor, "stay alive with such clarity in the public mind."

"Especially massacres," said Alonzo.

"Mr. Chickering," said Eleanor, persisting in her interest. "The volume of water originating in the hills must vary considerably from season to season."

"Indeed!" Charles looked relieved to shift the subject away from what had happened decades earlier at far-off Little Bighorn. "The flow of our own East Becket River loses nearly thirty percent of its carriage from April to late summer."

"And it varies from year to year?"

He nodded. "The smaller streams dry up to a trickle by August of the year. This has been a rather ordinary year. I'll be going up-country pretty soon."

"That will not be of a Saturday, I suppose? When I might be free to ride along with you?"

"A Saturday would not be disadvantageous to me!" He bowed to Eleanor with polite amusement. "I feel so favored," he said to the others.

THE FOLLOWING DAY, during a quiet moment in her classroom, while the youngest were napping, Eleanor sat to her school desk and took out Evangeline Sewell's letter to the young minister. She scrutinized it a final time. She marveled still that such a crudely written message, scratched in pencil on a yellow piece of paper, could contain such power and importance. She re-read the conclusion. "Then I will come back! Then we will see who is strong and who is weak."

Eleanor folded the page into its envelope, reached up the little brush from the nearby jar of mucilage, and pasted and resealed the envelope. Tonight, she decided, she would write to Evangeline a second time. She made up her mind all at once, without reflection. She would be candid about her clandestine role. She would assure the other young woman that she had in fact forwarded her letter to Reverend Allen, that she had been pleased to do so, and that she awaited further opportunities to be helpful.

IN HER ROOM that night, before going to bed, she set out pen, paper, and ink.

"The more I wander among the familiar," she wrote her father, "the more rough-textured, and grainy, and compelling it becomes, and the more I sense at the heart of it—or perhaps it is at the back of it—something both ghostly and precious. Something," she added, "beyond my view and sense of things, beyond my door, beyond the reach of my fingertips."

Eleanor broke off the letter, as she knew it to be studiedly intricate and obscure. She folded the paper in two, creased it, and stored it away in her desk.

six

N SATURDAY, Eleanor made sure to put herself in the way of Howard Allen. From the ruins of the jute mill, where she sat in the sun with a favorite volume of Browning's poetry, she could see downriver nearly a half-mile, to a clearing in the trees, where the road coming up from the south drew ever closer to the bank of the river, like a parabola inclining to its asymptote. Sure enough, at noon, she saw his gleaming, two-wheeled carriage come into view. Eleanor smiled upon wondering if the young man's glittering cabriolet and prancing horse were not somehow contrary to the professions of humility that he had doubtless made.

Wasting no time, she clambered down from the brick ledge where she had been sitting for an hour, and strode briskly up the grassy cart path toward the town road and common. She was carrying Evangeline's letter in the pocket of her cardigan, but hidden beneath a scarf and books in her straw bag was a second letter, the one she had written last night. Eleanor would not decide whether or not to give it to Howard till she saw his reaction to Evangeline's communication to him.

She had spent more than an hour the previous night composing various drafts of her note, and settled at last on her very first version.

Dear Evangeline:

I am ever so pleased that you entrusted me with your letter to Reverend Allen. I expect to see him tomorrow afternoon, and will obey your wishes at that time. Let me assure you that I will maintain complete silence in this matter. I will speak of it to no one!

I hope in future that I can help in more practical ways. Tell me about anything you may need, and I will do my level best to get it for you.

I admire your bravery and independence.

Yours, in friendship,
Eleanor

At the moment, Eleanor anticipated being overtaken on the road by the young clergyman. She could hear him approaching.

"Eleanor!" he called, from some distance back.

"Hello, Howard. I was just thinking about you." She waited for him to pull up. "I was thinking that you and your horse and your beautiful piece of machinery cut a rather ostentatious figure for a shepherd of the Lord."

"Of course, you're right. I'm proud—I'm showy. . . ."

Eleanor felt drawn to the young man. She liked his ways. "I think your flock loves you the more for it, Howard. I can't help teasing you."

"Why," he said, "don't you climb up onto the seat with me, and you'll see what fun it can be, being vain and swanky. I'll drive you to the Treadwells' store."

"It's only a hundred feet, Howard." Eleanor nodded at the house in question.

"We'll go the long way round. We'll go the wrong way round the common."

He reached a hand. Eleanor put a foot on the iron cleat, and thrust herself up onto the seat beside him.

"By going to our left," he said, "around the common, we shall defy the rules of modern traffic!"

"I have read, or heard, Howard, that where others go duty-bound to their right, the Devil naturally goes left."

"Then we shall definitely go to the left," he said. "Impossible that way to meet him."

"I have a letter for you, Howard." Eleanor didn't beat about the bush. She said it straight out.

"You wrote me a letter?" he exclaimed, while urging the horse forward.

"No!" she cried. "It's not from me! It's from somebody else. It was sent to me to be given to you."

He examined Eleanor sidelong.

Eleanor explained with exaggerated enunciation. "The letter," she spoke out, "comes from her to whom *I* sent a note—last Saturday—by way of you." She smiled ingenuously.

"Evangeline Sewell?" Howard sounded genuinely puzzled.

"The same, exactly. She," Eleanor stressed, "whom you alleged you scarcely knew."

"I do not know her as well as I might," he said.

"That," Eleanor pointed out, "is wonderfully ambiguous! As well as you are able, or as well as you would like?"

Meanwhile, Howard and Eleanor were going clockwise round the village green, past the town hall on their left, headed in the direction of the covered bridge. Eleanor's thoughts were racing. She sensed subterfuge. She struck a frivolous note. "I hope I am not being asked to play the part of *poste d'amour.*"

"What is that?" he said.

"It is the office of go-between," Eleanor said, teasing him, "in a secret romance."

But the young minister had grown noticeably reflective. "In fact," he said, "she came to the church in Cold Spring, but not to attend my service. I saw her later, outside the church doors, as I was seeing people out. I spoke to her for a couple of minutes. Then we were interrupted, as I was required to perform a baptism. By then, she was gone."

"How far is it from Wisdom Way to Cold Spring?"

"Three or four miles."

"She came the three or four miles on horseback, then."

Eleanor tried to picture Miss Sewell plodding her way on horseback from one bleak upcountry town to the next—or perhaps just sitting atop her mare outside the church doors. She felt reasonably certain what had passed between them during that two-minute interlude outside the church. Surely, Evangeline had spoken to him about her condition. That was why she went to him. But she was surprised then to learn that he already knew. She said as much in her note to him.

For the moment, Eleanor kept silent, intuiting that the other would thus be compelled to say more. The interval widened. She affected to be soaking in the beauty of the October afternoon—gazing off at the splendor of the red and gold foliage in the trees along the riverbank behind the church. Presently, she took Evangeline's letter from her pocket. It felt very familiar in hand by now.

"In Fall River," the minister suggested out of the blue, "you must see a lot of motor cars mixed in with the traffic." While speaking, he took the letter and slipped it with studied casualness in his inside coat pocket.

"They are becoming all the rage," she said. "My father believes that everything will be mechanized. Especially, he says, farming."

Eleanor made up her mind as of now that she would not give Howard her own letter to Evangeline. She would find another method of getting it up to Wisdom Way. Why it should be true she didn't know, but Eleanor wanted to maintain communication with the other more than ever.

The carriage came round now past the Congregational church, completing the circuit of the common, and pulled to a stop in front of the Treadwells'. Howard got down, and prepared to lead the horse to the drinking drum near the general store. For some reason, Eleanor was feeling slightly sickish. She thanked the cleric for their drive, then walked out onto the green, and lay down full length in the sun. Closing her eyes, she hoped he was not offended by the brusqueness of her departure. The warm earth felt good against her stomach and thighs.

She might even have slept for a minute, when she sensed his presence. Startled, she sat up. The young clergyman was standing not five feet away.

"Miss Gray," he said, pleasantly, "how is it that you know so much about Evangeline Sewell?"

"Howard!" Eleanor straightened up, and shielded her eyes from the sun. "Have I done something wrong?" She wondered for a split second if he had divined somehow that she had meddled with the letter, but instantly saw the unlikelihood of that. It was something else. Eleanor followed her instincts.

"Does she have feelings for you, Howard?"

"I think she is not like that," he replied, enigmatically.

"You have, I've no doubt, opened her letter?" Eleanor pressed the point with apparent indifference.

"What it says is not important. That she wrote to me at all is perplexing." He paused. "In her letter," he added then, as if reluctantly, "she asks at one point why you have taken an interest in her."

Eleanor felt a chill dart up her spine. The young minister, standing before her, with his hands in his pockets, was looking her squarely in the eyes. He was lying right into her eyes! (Eleanor remembered her mother's favorite aphorism. "A lie," she said, "is the handle that fits all other sins.")

"But it's obvious, Howard," Eleanor persisted, shrewdly, "that she did not write to you in order to ask you that—especially as she posted it to you by way of me. You ask how I know so much about her. In fact, I know precious little. I have never spoken to her. To me, Miss Sewell is a student who withdrew from school unaccountably, and rode off home on a—a stolen horse!"

seven

O **N A WET** drizzly afternoon, however, while in the kitchen helping Alice with some ironing, Eleanor received a most remarkable jolt. Alice was explaining to her something of the Atheneum winter lecture circuit—of how a notable speaker would go from one town to another, spending a night or two at each stop. Eleanor agreed it was a wonderful custom, and was delighted to learn that in the year of Alice's birth a figure of no less consequence than Mr. Emerson himself had lectured of a December night in East Becket. Wishing to show Eleanor a relic of it, Alice put up her iron, and went to the front parlor to get a copy of the historic notice that her family had kept all those years. It was stored with some documents and the family bible under the lid of the piano bench, she said.

Eleanor had turned on her heel to the partly open window, at the sound of the rainy wind slapping the paper shade, and found herself arrested by the most compelling picture imaginable. The window framed perfectly the moving image of the distant figure. How Eleanor had reached this point—where the living sight of Evangeline Sewell advancing toward the crossroads on horseback would have worked such a startling effect on her senses—was not clear to her. The young woman was wearing a heavy black cape, and came across the intersection of the two gravel roads at a steady mechanical pace. It made Eleanor think of those black silhouette cut-outs that she had made with scissors as a child. Before Alice Harrison returned to the kitchen, Eleanor hurried forward along the central hall and started up the staircase. "I'll be down presently," she said.

Upstairs, she went straightway to the little Palladian window that was situated above the front door, and crouched there to look down, just in time as Evangeline came into view from right to left behind the elms. It was a most extraordinary spectacle. The horse and rider moved across her field of vision with a slow, deadly, percussive rhythm. The rider was bareheaded. Her hair lit up like something unearthly. She was gripping the reins with her left fist cocked before her. The drizzle in the air left the big mare shining like wet coal. Evangeline's white-blond head bobbed to the clock-like rhythm. Clearly, she was returning the horse to the Trumbulls. She was headed that way.

Eleanor hurried back along the upstairs hall to her room, as her own window furnished a succeeding view of Evangeline seen from behind, as she headed along east toward the Trumbulls' place. She watched for three or four full minutes as Evangeline and her mount receded incrementally, until she disappeared over a rise.

Her first coherent thought was that the girl had lost the baby. It was far-fetched to suppose that she was merely returning the mare to its East Becket owner. She would have done that weeks ago. More likely, she was returning altogether, to live with the Trumbulls, perhaps even to pick up her schooling once more. In the minutes to come, Eleanor rejoined Alice in the kitchen, but said nothing of what she had seen.

After helping Alice put away the ironed linens—and after having marveled appropriately over the faded announcement of Ralph Waldo Emerson's 1872 visit to the Atheneum Society of East Becket—Eleanor went upstairs to change her own bed. It was about an hour before dusk. She wound her mantel clock, moved the minute hand forward five minutes—which the clock required her to do every day, as though it needed that attention if it were to keep its side of the bargain—and pulled down her blankets and bedsheets. Her senses were still much taken up with the sight of the young horsewoman going by on the road. A week or two earlier, Eleanor had finally managed to post that second letter of hers to Wisdom Way—the one in which she had assured Evangeline of passing her note along to Howard Allen—and in which she had beseeched the other to make known to her any needs she might have.

Eleanor drew the crisp bedsheets tightly in place, creasing the corners carefully, tugging at them, then shaking the pillow from its slip, and thrusting it into the one freshly laundered. She reflected further upon the obvious correctness of her deduction about Miss Sewell coming back to East Becket, because she would otherwise have removed herself farther away by now, to her aunt Beulah's house, as she had specified in her note to Howard. While tossing and shaking her blanket into place, and experiencing some feelings of relief for the other, she smiled to think how she almost wished that the mystery had gone on a little longer. If she had believed that seriously, however, her amusement would have been short-lived. Because just before dusk, Evangeline was coming back the other way. Only this time, no doubt by coincidence, she had fallen in abreast of Mr. Walker's horse and wagon, coming in the same direction.

The motion of the oncoming figures was like that found in the little "movie machines" that one peeped into and cranked by hand at the penny arcade in Fall River—growing bigger and bigger, moment by moment, in the glowing lens of her window. Eleanor was visibly perturbed. She stepped back and forth nervously, her movements reflecting exactly her indecision. As the two horses came clopping side by side past the wet lilacs, Eleanor seized a sweater from her closet, and went hurriedly out her door and down the front staircase. She was in obvious agitation. She came out of the house, pulling on her sweater, just as Mr. Walker whistled for Ben to turn into Alice's drive. Evangeline continued, meanwhile, going past on the road. Eleanor's situation was most awkward. If they had remained together, the wagon and the rider going by, she could have hurried out to the road to intercept them, as to speak to the Star Route man on some pretext. As it was, he was coming toward her now up the drive, at every hoofbeat widening a space between himself and the rider. Eleanor couldn't run after the other. She did actually start across the driveway toward the road, but stopped after a few steps, at the point where Evangeline was passing directly in front of the house. She was in full silhouette. At this range, it was evident that the cape she wore was nothing more than a rain-blackened blanket. At its fringe, above the stirrup, appeared Evangeline's bare unstockinged ankle, and that same familiar-looking workshoe. Going by, she looked neither to left nor right. That she had seen Eleanor Gray come out the door of the house, though, was all but incontestable. Eleanor glanced around at Mr. Walker, then at Evangeline drawing away, and Mr. Walker spoke to Eleanor in the very second that Evangeline turned her head and looked back at her.

If Eleanor lived to be a thousand, she would never recall what Myron Walker had said, but the picture of Evangeline's suddenly averted head—the brooding backward glance—the pale-as-asphodel face—was imprinted on her mind.

Eleanor dispensed with the usual salutations, as he pulled up beside her, removing his rubber rain hat. "Mr. Walker," she said, "what is happening with Miss Sewell? I saw her go by earlier. I thought she had come back."

"All I know," said Myron Walker, "is that Trumbull told her to keep the horse. I can't say exactly what the man said, because she didn't tell me what the man said. 'He told me to keep her,' she said." Mr. Walker stepped down from the driver's seat, and took his leather mail sack in hand. "So, she kept her," he added, laconically, "and that's that."

For an instant, Eleanor lost her guardedness. "But in her condition," she exclaimed, pointing, "she can't go horseback all the way home again. In the rain! In the dark!"

"Better than walking," he said.

Eleanor protested. "That's very unfeeling of you, Mr. Walker!"

"She was going to walk back, and now she's got the horse."

Eleanor raised her hand to her face. "I feel bad for her! She is so alone. You are all so standoffish and distant, Mr. Walker. You are all such . . . Yankees!"

Her words left Mr. Walker chastened. He glanced round reflexively in the direction of the crossroads, as did Eleanor. Evangeline was by now withdrawing up the northern road beyond the schoolhouse. If Myron Walker were impelled to change his mind—as to go hurrying after her—it was all made speculative. As Evangeline whipped her horse into a gallop!

eight

A S AUTUMN progressed, Eleanor despaired of hearing any further word from upcountry. By December, the nights were cold and the trees bare. At certain places in the woods, or under the trees along the riverbank, the fallen leaves were a foot deep. The smokiness of fall gave way to a brittleness in the atmosphere, and the sun grew white. One day, Charles Chickering called Eleanor outdoors to show her something. He pointed at the heavens. High against the pale, shark-colored sky could be seen successive flights of Canadian geese, coming down from the north, squadrons of them, flying in formation at great altitude.

"It's inspiring, isn't it?" said Eleanor, pleased to have been called outdoors. "Not just that they know what to do, but that they do it with such beauty, such purpose."

"I suspect it's because we humans have to think up what we're going to do next," said Mr. Chickering, "that we're so often confounded by the spot we've put ourselves in."

Eleanor laughed appreciatively. "Well, I'm perfectly happy," she said, "to have thought my way into my present circumstance.

"You seem happy," he said. "But don't you find us to be a dull, uninspiring lot?"

"On the contrary," Eleanor replied, with sincerity. "Nothing has pleased me more since my arrival than the richness of the lives—of the people—I've got to know. My citified ways are like nothing compared to it. And I am not just speaking about Alonzo's artistry, or your own engineering knowledge, or even William Bayles's interest and expertise in something called radio telephony. It's far deeper than that, Mr. Chickering," she said. "I couldn't plant an acre of corn if my fate in the life-to-come depended on it. I can't put up preserves. I can't plow. I can't nail two boards together. Where would I be if I were asked to shoe a horse, or to play Truman Rogers's fiddle at the grange hall next Saturday night? My big-city attainments leave me paper-thin."

"You are being too humble."

"I understand now why my grandfather joined the famous Fruitlands experiment when he was still a youth. They wanted to be philosophers of the soil. They wanted to go back to the origins, to the very basics of the ancient agrarian life."

"Would you like to do that, as well?" Charles inquired.

"No!" remarked Eleanor, firmly.

After a moment, he laughed heartily over Eleanor's unequivocal dissent.

"Not for a second," she said.

"In truth, I don't see you as a commune type, Miss Gray."

"I would not enjoy shelling peas hours on end, or churning up a tub of butter, or sewing big wooden buttons onto homemade sweaters. I am much too spoiled, Mr. Chickering. I am too effete. My father and mother convinced me long ago that my errand in life would be to read and to learn, to write and to teach. I hope they were not wildly overreaching in their aspirations for me."

"You will be a grand lady, a force to be reckoned with, in this new century," Mr. Chickering assured her, as he held open the front door for her. "Are you interested in women's causes?" he asked, as she stepped by him.

"Well," said Eleanor, "we should certainly all be enfranchised. Today, women can vote in the territory of Utah, or in Idaho, but after all these years, the United States Senate will still not discuss the question."

"Your generation will make all the difference," he said. "The young women of today that I've seen, who are active in the labor movement and on the campuses of the women's colleges, will never be stopped. There is no woman in the world like the American woman. Our other inventions—our electrical gadgets and gramophones and automobiles—are nothing next to that. By the end of this century, every woman in the world will want to be an American woman."

Eleanor blushed pleasurably over Mr. Chickering's generous remarks, as she stepped along the hallway. But in this selfsame moment, her eye fell upon something that gripped her attention. It was a letter lying slantwise in her own mail slot on the wall behind the oak counter. She recognized it instantly. It was the self-addressed envelope she had sent to Evangeline Sewell a few weeks earlier. For some reason, Eleanor was reluctant to take the letter in hand while Mr. Chickering was at her side.

"Shall we do a tune on the player piano?" he was asking, gesturing toward the parlor.

"Oh, yes!" Eleanor exclaimed. "Please." She followed Mr. Chickering into Alice's parlor, and waited as he seated himself on the piano bench.

"What shall it be?" he asked, rubbing his hands together expectantly. He picked up one of the player rolls, and read out the label on the box. "'The Sidewalks of New York?'"

"Absolutely," said Eleanor. That's my favorite. But excuse me one moment."

With Charles fixed in place at the piano, Eleanor returned to the hallway and mail desk, and quickly took hold of the letter. She was not disappointed. It was the same envelope that she had sent up north in October. Eleanor pocketed it and hurried back into the parlor.

In the minutes to come, Eleanor and Charles Chickering fell quiet while the piano played on, but Eleanor's thoughts returned again and again to the letter from Evangeline. She felt that a door had opened once again upon that enigmatic upcountry world. She made no effort to open the letter, but saved it to read later on in the privacy of her room. She was also preparing herself against the possibility that the communication might be a distasteful one. Eleanor had once before been offended by the other's unmannerliness.

A quarter hour later, at the supper table, Mr. Chickering raised the subject of Eleanor's grandfather.

"I know something about your family, Miss Gray, that will surprise you!" he said.

"Your recollections never surprise me, Mr. Chickering. You have a prodigious memory."

"This is not a recollection. I looked up your grandfather, Eugene Lloyd Gray, in my *Dictionary of American Biography*. He wrote a book about his boyhood in Portsmouth, New Hampshire."

Eleanor brightened. *"Diary of a Countryman,"* she said.

"Exactly!" said Mr. Chickering. "And of how he worshipped and adored his own father, but rarely saw the man."

"That was Samuel," said Eleanor. "He was forever at sea." Eleanor turned to Alice. "Samuel Gray," she said, "had the indubitable distinction of having four times carried shiploads of ice to Java!"

"Ice?" said Miss Harrison.

"You have spoiled my story," said Charles. "That's what I was about to say."

"I apologize for having anticipated you."

"For your grandfather," Mr. Chickering went on, "that notion—that picture—of his aloof and always absent father—sailing over a measureless tropical sea—day after day, in the equatorial sun—with a shipful of ice! —must have had some special metaphysical meaning. For the schoolboy in Portsmouth, that is."

"That's so insightful of you, Mr. Chickering. It is a rather dismaying picture, isn't it? Sailing the boiling equatorial seas with a harvest of ice!"

As Eleanor was speaking, Alonzo Klaw came into the room from outdoors, slapping his hands together.

"It's snowing?" said Miss Harrison.

Each of the shoulders of Alonzo's mackinaw was decorated with a neat epaulet of snow.

"First of the year," said Alonzo.

"Your supper is in the oven," Alice explained.

"I've been helping the reverend Winslow with some carpentry at his church," Alonzo Klaw called back from the kitchen. "It seems that Mrs. Trumbull split the seat in two in the family pew of the Congregational church." Alonzo returned from the kitchen bearing a plate with a folded towel. He had removed his coat.

Alice Harrison teased him. "Alonzo," she said, "doesn't your faith prohibit you from doing good works in a Christian temple?"

"Not at all." He drew his chair up to the table. "Not any more than any parent would fail to give help to his own wayward child. We Jews have a sense that your centuries of worshipping one of our own sons and teachers entitles you to—"

"Solicitude," Mr. Chickering interjected.

"The *solicitude* . . . of all of Abraham's descendants."

"How did Mrs. Trumbull break the pew?" asked someone.

"She sat on it," said Alonzo.

All at table, including Eleanor, stifled their laughter.

"She was such a delicate girl," said Alice.

"She may still be delicate," Alonzo replied, taking up his silverware, "but not as delicate, apparently, as the wood grain in the pine seat she sat upon. Anyway," he said, "it's right as rain now. A mule could sit in there."

Mr. Chickering offered a joke. "I've seen mules in church," he said, "but they had ears remarkably similar to yours and mine."

"Were they on their hind legs?" said Eleanor.

"They were. And they came in in twos. And they sang 'Rock of Ages' in all but perfect pitch."

"I'm going to read my Jonathan Swift tonight," said Eleanor.

"Good heavens!" Alice burst out, with effervescence. "Our supper talk has never been nearly so clever. I can't keep up. It must be Eleanor," she said.

"In the cake of life," said Alonzo, "you must always have an Eleanor for the yeast, or the cake won't rise."

This time, Eleanor was visibly charmed and flattered. She liked, too, the way Alonzo looked at her. His eyes always lingered a moment longer than expected. His admiration for her was becoming palpable to the senses.

After supper, Alonzo Klaw built up the fire in the front parlor stove and asked would anyone like to play some cards.

"My game is Parcheesi," said Charles. "It doesn't require thinking."

The ancient Mrs. Sampson spoke up. She had been listening all the while, but her hearing was imperfect.

"*Parcheesi,*" she said, in a big voice, "is a game for louts."

"There it is," said Charles Chickering, amid the general laughter that followed. He gestured with an open hand toward Mrs. Sampson. "The Sybil speaks the truth."

Everyone helped clear the table, then Eleanor joined Alice in the kitchen. Alice poured hot water into the sink from a two-gallon pot on the stove, stirred in soap flakes, and started washing. Eleanor stood by, drying.

"You must be feeling some homesickness by now," said Alice.

"Now and again," Eleanor admitted. "But I wouldn't exchange my place for anything. You make us all such a lovely home. You keep everything together."

Eleanor was aware that Alice Harrison's life was a predicament of sorts; that she was one of those women living out in the countryside where the sheer paucity of people had likely deprived her of the chance of ever meeting an appropriate young man. Soon, Alice would pass beyond childbearing years, and could only reflect then in daydreams on what she had missed. And to think that the whole drama of her unfulfilled life should have unfolded in this house — from the days of her infancy, when she crawled on all fours, or tottered gaily about on this same kitchen floor. Why, Eleanor asked herself, don't our talkative, fire-and-brimstone preachers take up the important questions? They are all interested in what we should not do. That was the poignancy in it. That a deserving soul like Alice could feel that her dilemma was vaguely a patchwork of her own failings.

Eleanor went upstairs to her room in a tremulous state. Men, with their forceful ways, and a high-mindedness concocted out of the beliefs and doctrines of those now dead behind them, who contrived such rubble-work in the first place in *their* self-interest, were in some way accountable for Alice standing over her sink, up to her elbows in dishwater.

BEFORE GOING BACK DOWN to join the others in the parlor, Eleanor set a small stack of kindling alight in her fireplace, not to heat the room so much as to create a cheery ambience for herself when she opened Evangeline's letter. Outside her window, the snow was falling. Eleanor sat down at her desk, turned up the oil lamp, and removed the letter from the pocket of her skirt. Before opening it, she counseled herself a final time not to expect a message within that would be in any way personal or cordial. She saw Evangeline now as an untutored soul, who expressed herself bluntly, but who had strengths of character that set her apart from others.

As it happened, she was not prepared for the letter she now extracted from the envelope. As on that previous occasion, the letter was written in pencil on faded yellow paper.

Dear Eleanor:

Go to Everett Conboy and tell him to get me what I need. He can bring it to Wisdom Way and give it to Calvin Tripp the blacksmith.
I also need a coat if you have an old one. My things are worn through. I am cold half the time.

Evangeline Sewell

This communication produced a profound effect on Eleanor. She read the letter twice, set it down before her on the desk, and placed a hand to her temples. She gave an audible sigh. Getting to her feet, Eleanor paced to the hall door and back, sat down on the needlepoint chair that she had set by the fireplace when lighting the kindling, and re-read the letter another time. She had never suspected that the young woman up north might be in true want. Presently, she went to the window, and stood there, watching the flakes falling past on the diagonal, silver and dark, and thanked her good luck that Evangeline had turned to her in her time of need. The piece of paper in her hands, for all its wear and smudges, was like a sacred charge. Nor could there be any denying that

Eleanor had become the medium between Evangeline isolated in her lonely upcountry domain and the world outside of there.

Her thoughts racing, Eleanor went through her belongings in her closet. While doing so, she recalled that Mr. Conboy was supposed to work this evening on the stovepipes in the school. William had said the pipes were clogged with creosote and were not drawing. He engaged Mr. Conboy for the job. Turning, Eleanor went out of her room and along the upstairs hall to the Palladian window, where, indeed—through the snow—she saw clearly the glare of lanterns in the schoolhouse windows. She was impelled to act at once—to go across the road to the school—but knew there was nothing among her things that amounted to a proper winter coat, other than the green loden mackinaw that her mother had bought her last year at Shapiro's in Fall River. She could send that to Evangeline, and would do so in a second, except there was no way to replace it. Eleanor considered going downstairs, and taking Alice Harrison aside, and explaining everything to her—as she knew that Alice had a heart of gold, and likely could come up with any number of heavy suitable coats.

Eleanor dismissed the idea. She decided against telling Alice about her connection with the girl. She recalled the secret nature of Alice's telephone call to Ivy Trumbull. More than that, she prized the secrecy and growing importance of her correspondence with that figure whom many in East Becket looked upon as quite singular. The one figure to whom she could most readily appeal for help would be Myron Walker, of course, but she never knew when or where she would encounter him next. There was only one person in the house to whom Eleanor might turn with some confidence—who struck Eleanor as fittingly close-mouthed and sensitive, who had some fond feelings for *her,* and who would surely be in possession of what she needed.

Eleanor went down the front stairs to the landing, and called to him in the parlor.

"Mr. Klaw," she said, in a ringing voice. "May I speak to you upstairs?"

In seconds, Alonzo came smiling through the doorway. "We are waiting for you," he said. "Chickering tells me that you are going to make brilliant discourse tonight on the subject of the happy tillers of Brook Farm."

"Oh, please, Alonzo," she said, invoking his first name, and started back up the staircase.

"Is something the matter?" he inquired, as she led him to her door.

"Please come inside. I have something of importance to impart to you—to ask of you."

He looked at her more gravely, as she shut the door behind him, went past to her desk, and turned the letter face down in the lamplight.

"If I told you something," she said, stopping before him now, her hands clasped at her waist, "could it remain perfectly private between us?"

"I hope nothing unfortunate has happened."

"It's not me. It's someone else."

Alonzo looked round at the delicate needlepoint chair, took a step or two sidewise, and sat down. Eleanor drew her desk chair along the pine-board floor on its rear legs, and seated herself opposite him.

"I can't continue," she said, "without your solemn word."

"Of course," he said, encouraging her. "I would never speak of it to anyone. Whatever it may be."

"It isn't the secrecy of it that is as important as the fact of your simply not treating what I have to say to you as something discussible with others."

Alonzo Klaw's features brightened. "That is the most recondite sentence I have heard in my life—and I have relatives, Miss Gray, who are Talmudic scholars!"

"I mean to say," Eleanor sought to clarify her words, "that the secrecy of the thing is in less need of protection than is the fact of *my* part in it."

"I think I begin to see."

"I have heard," said Eleanor, "from Evangeline Sewell up in Wisdom Way."

Mr. Klaw muttered something, and pointed a finger queryingly at the yellow page on Eleanor's desk.

"Yes," she said. "She has asked me to tell Mr. Conboy to bring her what she needs."

Before Mr. Klaw might have felt obliged to respond, Eleanor went on. "The reason she has communicated to me—on this occasion, and an earlier occasion—is because I sent her a note back in September, when she failed to start school, and instead withdrew home." Eleanor paused. "The reason I wrote to her was because I had divined that something was very wrong. . . ."

By this time, Alonzo's expression reflected genuine sympathy. Clearly, Evangeline's condition was no mystery to the man who knew her well enough to have executed those pencil portraits of her.

Eleanor continued. "It wasn't really a divination," she said. "It was just a matter of acquainting myself with something that everyone else seemed already to know."

"What does she say she needs?"

"Apparently, Mr. Conboy will know."

Unexpectedly, Eleanor felt a return of the powerful feelings that had assailed her a quarter hour earlier when she first read the letter. Rising, she went quickly to her desk, and retrieved the yellow page. She sat, and read out the last three sentences. She lowered the page. "Mr. Klaw, I feel so bad for her! I didn't know how lucky I have always been until today," she said. "Until this. I can't help picturing her up there—up in that forbidding country without professional help or advice—with the days growing short for her—and being reduced to *this!*" She waved the letter. "Asking for a winter coat!"

Mr. Klaw looked as if he had aged five years in the past five minutes, as he sat forward on the little chair, with his hands resting backward on his knees, his mouth ajar.

Eleanor collected her feelings. "Mr. Conboy is in the schoolhouse this minute, working on the two stoves." She indicated her closet. "I have only my one coat. Surely, Alonzo, you have something."

"Of course, I do," he said. He arose and started from the room. Eleanor followed him at a rapid pace down the hall to his door.

"This should do," he said, pulling up a long black overcoat from a chest on the floor of his closet.

Eleanor was instantly delighted.

"Before coming back to East Becket for my second winter, I made up my mind," said Alonzo, "that I was going to pitch in and do my share of the town's snowplowing. Turned out," he said, and laughed, "I wasn't very good with oxen. This was to have been my teamster's coat. Truman Rogers suggested on my first try that I should paint pictures of the oxen at work, and leave the handling of those genial, even-tempered brutes to experts like Myron and himself.

Eleanor was feeling refreshingly happy. "You acceded to his wisdom?"

"Yes, but not without five or ten seconds of deep reflection on the matter." With that, Mr. Klaw unfurled the coat. He held it up, displaying it in full. It was a garment of obvious expense—what Eleanor believed was called a greatcoat.

She remarked on its beauty. "It's just perfect! It's so dramatic for her. She will be known everywhere up north by her magnificent coat. I'll tell Mr. Conboy to tell her that you sent it."

Mr. Klaw dismissed the significance of it. "There's no need of that."

"Also," said Eleanor, as she took the big coat in hand, "while I am shamelessly improving on your kindness, I hope you will lend—or even give me—one of your drawings of her, as you once offered to do."

"Those are the three best," he said, nodding at an array of his pencil drawings. "Take the one you like."

Eleanor demurred. "I wouldn't do that," she said.

"Choose it, and take it now," he said.

Eleanor could tell by the way he was looking at her at this very moment that he liked her a great deal, and wanted to make her a gift of one of his favorite creations. Of the three, the picture on the easel was surely her favorite, one in which the artist had captured in pencil the dreamy planes of her hair and milky hues of Evangeline's face and hands, but most especially because of the pale enigmatic intensity of her gaze.

"If that's the one," he confirmed, "take it."

Eleanor remained motionless. She felt quite moved by the moment, as she stood in the middle of the room, with the artist's coat folded over her arm, staring at the drawing. Alonzo stepped forward, unfastened it from its wooden pinnings, and rolled it up for her. He tucked it under Eleanor's free arm, and asked then if he might not take the coat across the way to Mr. Conboy at the schoolhouse.

"No," said Eleanor, firmly, but revealing a pathos not seen in her behavior since early girlhood. "I want to follow her wishes, her instructions, exactly."

IN DELIVERING the coat that evening, Eleanor let herself noiselessly out the back kitchen door, and strode rapidly across the snow-whitened grass at the side of the house to the roadway. She could hear occasional banging sounds. A pale bar of lantern light lay along the stoop of the open schoolhouse doorway, and the windows of her own classroom were softly aglare. When she went in at the door, Everett Conboy and the boy, Justin Judd, were working industriously at rejoining the several sections of black metal stovepipe. Mr. Conboy was bent over his work. The boy tapped his shoulder.

"Look, Ev," he said. "It's Miss Gray."

"I am sorry to interrupt," Eleanor announced, making her way among the children's desks. Mr. Conboy, she noticed, had spread several newspapers on the floor beside the big potbellied stove. Atop the papers stood a mound of soot.

Mr. Conboy straightened in place. He said nothing in reply, but stared at her, while flexing his back. His face and beard were flecked with carbon. Eleanor went straight to the point. "Mr. Conboy," she said, "I received a message for you today. It was sent to me in secret, but it's obvious that this person is someone who trusts you, and who needs your help."

"From *herself?*" he said. He looked across at the boy, then at Eleanor again.

"I believe so," said Eleanor. With that, she produced the yellow page, and handed it to him. For a split second, she was tempted to read it aloud to him, as she knew there were persons in the valley who were unable to read. But she guessed that Everett Conboy—to judge by his look of withering shrewdness—would have learned on his own long ago. Also, local lore had it that he was an officer by battlefield commission forty years back, in a unit of the Third Massachusetts.

All this while, Eleanor watched his face for change, to see if Evangeline's words mightn't produce a visible effect on his usual stony expression. Nothing in his look changed, however. He folded up the letter. As he started to slip it into the breast pocket of his denim jacket, Eleanor left no doubt about its ownership. She put out her hand.

"What is it?" asked Justin. Then, in his next breath, the boy's own reference to the young woman up north might have struck a third party as comic. He spoke from the side of his mouth. *"Is it from herself?"* he said.

"It is," said Mr. Conboy, as he relinquished the page to Eleanor, and stood then slapping his soot-blackened hands together.

As a stranger to him, Eleanor had no way of knowing if it was possible to extract any sort of news or information from him. "Will you be going soon?" she asked.

"I know what to do," he sang back, "and who to get."

"Who to get?" Eleanor repeated.

Justin interrupted. "It's from Evangeline?" he asked his friend.

"Yes," Eleanor answered for the other.

"Are we going up there?" said the boy.

"First thing in the morning," said Mr. Conboy. He addressed Eleanor questioningly. "I didn't know you even knew her," he said.

"I don't," she replied. "But I have written her twice, offering any help I can give, and twice she has replied." Eleanor set the coat down on the nearest desktop. "I hope you can bring this to her soon. She must have a coat!"

Mr. Conboy nodded, replying in a deepish voice. His remark struck Eleanor as somehow fateful, as though he neither had nor desired any choice in the matter. "I do what I'm called on to do," he said.

"It's kind and generous of you," said Eleanor. A notion came to her on sudden impulse. "Mr. Conboy," she said, "if I write a note to her, will you deliver it?"

"Of course, I would," he replied. "What else would I do with it?"

For some reason, that response struck the boy, Justin Judd, as especially humorous. He laughed so merrily—gushingly—his tongue clamped between his teeth—that Eleanor and Mr. Conboy joined in.

"What else would anybody do with a letter?" the boy repeated, turning a bright face from one to the other.

Mr. Conboy had earlier assembled the tall stovepipe into sections, with two matching elbow joints, and was ready to connect one end of the entire piece to the top of the stove and the other to the flue high on the wall.

Knowing meanwhile that she had envelopes in her desk, and could write therefore a note of an intimate nature, Eleanor got out pen and paper. Unfortunately, the light of the two lanterns was so wan, and cast much of the classroom in deep shadows, that she was required to take her paper and writing implements to the desk of one of her fifth graders in the middle of the room. Always facile with pen and paper, Eleanor set the words down swiftly.

Dear Evangeline:

It was kind of you to turn to me with your latest wants. I have done as you wished, and given your instructions instantly to Mr. Everett Conboy.

Eleanor hesitated for a second, as she was not sure that an expression of personal feelings was appropriate at this time. In obedience to her heart, she decided to go on with it. She started a new paragraph.

I was deeply moved by your choosing me in particular to get you a proper winter coat, and have succeeded in obtaining one that you will find wonderfully serviceable. It is both warm and magnificent to look at! You will be the envy of Wisdom Way.

Eleanor looked up thoughtfully from her paper, watching with a vacant expression as young Justin stood atop the stove, with his arms wrapped around the tall pipe, while Mr. Conboy, standing on a chair nearby, tapped the upper section of the pipe into the flue on the wall below the ceiling. Eleanor was trying to decide whether to mention Alonzo as benefactor of the coat. In deciding not to do so, she was not unaware that her reasoning was probably spurious. She told herself that the introduction of any unpredictable factor, any name or piece of unexpected intelligence, might be incendiary to such a delicate correspondence.

She dipped her pen, and completed the note without hesitation.

Please know that you are never far from my thoughts. I have complete faith that your bravery will bring you through, and preserve you for future triumphs.

Knowing you and being of aid to you at this important time is my joy. Please tell me what next to do.

Eleanor Gray

Eleanor sealed up the letter, but not before writing out an exact copy of it for herself on a separate sheet of paper. By the time Eleanor got back to her room, her fingers were feeling numb from the cold, and the color was up in her cheeks. She was in high spirits. Who would have guessed a few weeks ago—as on that Sunday afternoon when she first came down the mountain road into East Becket with Mr. Walker—that by the end of fall she would have insinuated herself into the heart of a drama of such provocative character? Eleanor never doubted for a second, though, that it was not the bare facts of the situation that exerted such a gravitational pull. It was not just the unfortunate circumstance of an unknown student who had got herself with child and withdrawn home for the year. Rather, it was the magical effect that this young female worked on some of those around her — not excluding Eleanor herself — that made all the difference.

Sitting on her tapestried chair, Eleanor unrolled the big picture of Evangeline that Alonzo Klaw had given her, and held it up for inspection. The effect was uncanny. It was the picture of an individual both delicate and robust, looking both innocent and yet adamantine of purpose. While staring at it, Eleanor smiled to recall how, in her recent letters home to her father, she spoke no longer about the theme she had set herself — of a "journey among the familiar."

Evangeline Sewell had changed that.

nine

IN THE DAYS to come, the buoyant spirits that Eleanor had experienced that evening at the schoolhouse, when she gave Evangeline's instructions to Mr. Conboy, had deteriorated into a state of nagging anxiety. That was only natural. For Evangeline's instructions to Mr. Conboy implied most strongly that the baby was full term, that childbirth was imminent. It struck Eleanor as ironic that probably she alone among her townsmen was privy to this intelligence, even though she was about the only one of them all who was a stranger to Evangeline Sewell. More than once, Eleanor had considered going to Miss Harrison, and unburdening herself of everything she knew. In any other situation, Eleanor would not have been anywhere near so convinced of Evangeline's plight. It was the girl's call for a winter coat that had begun summoning up pictures of the brutal conditions up there. Still, she could not bring herself to admit, not to Alice, or to anyone, all that she knew. She could not explain to anyone the steps by which she had somehow borne herself to the core of this unfortunate matter.

She knew, too, that such an admission would have no sensible effect. It would not provide Evangeline any appreciable help. It might even have deleterious effects.

ON SUNDAY, Eleanor attended church in the company of Charles Chickering. Eleanor was accustomed since childhood always to wear her Sunday best to church. As it was an uncommonly mild day for December, she wore her long, gray serge skirt with a matching jacket, a white blouse fluted at the throat, and her only expensive headpiece—a brimmed hat of dove gray, with a black hatband and a small black feather. To a stranger, she might very well have looked the part of a well-to-do, out-of-town visitor, inasmuch as the fabric and cut of her costume were noticeably stylish by rural East Becket standards. By now, most of the parishioners knew Eleanor, and looked upon her as their lovely newfound schoolteacher. They took pride in the fact that they had caught themselves a prize from one of the bustling cities of the eastern seaboard.

Following the service, most of the congregants dallied outdoors for a while. They enjoyed the opportunity to socialize. Reverend Winslow stood in their midst, looking diminutive as always, but somehow patriarchal notwithstanding. The children of the parish had not emerged yet from the basement of the church, where they had been engaged in their regular Sunday school lessons. The day was shockingly bright. A light breeze upset the withered leaves piled up under the trees. More than once, Eleanor grasped her hat, lest it blow away. The roadway and field nearby were clogged with horses and carriages. The bell in the belfry began tolling now. One of Reverend Winslow's grown sons attended to that task each Sunday. It was not intended to signify the hour of the day, but just to set the heavens ringing for a minute or so, as an expression of communal joy.

It was during this pleasant interlude, just as the tolling died away, that Eleanor caught sound of the name Evangeline Sewell. Her heart jumped. Everyone around her was talking at once. The voice in question came from someone standing behind her.

Mr. Chickering was just then saying, "The pedigree of this church is that it is a copy of a Bulfinch church in New Hampshire, *which,* in its turn, is a copy of a Christopher Wren church in London."

Eleanor turned slowly on her heel, surreptitiously, and glanced back in the direction of the voice. The speaker was Ivy Trumbull herself.

"*This* church," Mr. Chickering waved his hand, "was copied in three-quarter scale up in Wisdom Way back in the eighteen forties."

Eleanor lifted her face and eyes to the pleasing sight of the white steeple and bell tower, and in doing so, stepped backward, as though to improve her perspective.

"*I heard from Jonathan Hewlitt,*" Mrs. Trumbull was saying, "*that she has been missing these two or three weeks.*"

While straining to hear more, Eleanor did her best to shut out Mr. Chickering's words.

"That Wisdom Way church," he added, "has gone the way of Nineveh."

But Eleanor made out nothing more of the conversation behind her, as Ivy Trumbull had evidently turned to another. All she knew was that someone named Jonathan Hewlitt alleged that Evangeline had been missing for many days. Eleanor knew better than that. For it was only two or three days since Miss Sewell had sent instructions to her for Mr. Conboy, and made her touching request for a coat. Of all the East Becket townsfolk, Eleanor alone knew of Mr. Conboy's mission to the north. Moreover, as she had not seen him in church this morning, she surmised that he and Justin Judd were still up there.

Presently, as the children erupted noisily out the side door of the church—many of the younger ones pressing and clamoring about her—Eleanor spotted Myron Walker not far away, and soon excused herself. Holding her hat brim against the breeze, she made her way through the throng to where he stood. He and the fiddler, Truman Rogers, were sharing a joke or amusing anecdote. "Mr. Walker," she said, "when you have a moment, may I speak with you?"

"You may have him all to yourself right now." Truman Rogers waved a deprecating hand at his friend. "Myron's stories are old stories, and there was never a grain of truth in them to begin with." He turned to Mr. Walker. "Miss Gray," he said, "makes a man want to go back to school."

"You got that correct," said Myron, "except for the scoldings. She scolds me left and right."

"I have a great favor to ask of you," Eleanor started in at once, the moment Truman departed. "First, have you had any news from upcountry?"

"I have not." A grave look came over his face.

"I am speaking now in confidence."

Mr. Walker nodded.

"I just overheard someone say—in private—that Evangeline Sewell is missing. Have you heard that said?"

"No," he replied, "I have not."

"Someone up in Cold Spring, named Jonathan Hewlitt, has reported that Evangeline has been missing for two or three weeks. You must be acquainted with him," said Eleanor. "Who is he?"

"His sister-in-law is a midwife. *He* . . ." said Mr. Walker, "he's like . . . a horse and cow doctor. He's good with sick animals. His wife's dead, so he lives with her sister. She delivers babies up there. Though there aren't many babies getting born up there anymore. Fewer all the time."

Eleanor reflected momentarily before going on. She looked around, as the churchgoers had begun dispersing now. The road and field nearby were crowded with wagons and carriages.

"I know some things, Mr. Walker, that I am not supposed to know. . . , which you must not repeat to anyone."

As before, he nodded.

"Mr. Walker, who is *Beulah?*" she asked, referring to the name in the letter she had steamed open. "There is a woman up north named Beulah. I think she lives in Wisdom Way."

He thought about it. "There's a Beulah Bisonette . . . lives on the lake."

"What lake?"

He shrugged. "I don't think it has a name. Suppose it did once."

Eleanor smiled over his words. "Might she be Evangeline's aunt? You see," she continued, catching the blank look on his face and in his eyes, "I learned some time ago that she was intending to stay with her 'aunt Beulah.' She told someone that she was going 'up' to Beulah's."

"Well," Myron said, and laughed, "the lake is north of where Miss Sewell was born and raised. So, I guess that's *up*. If that's what you're asking me."

Here, in passing, Eleanor wondered if the Star Route man knew anything about Mr. Conboy and Justin having recently gone up-country. Probably not, she guessed.

By now, many carriages were pulling away from the church, most of them headed in a file toward the covered bridge, in the direction of the crossroads out by Alice's house. Children called to her, and Eleanor waved back. She was holding her prayer book to her waist, and, as before, securing her hat whenever the air gusted. Earlier, she would have been startled by what she was about to say. She had made up her mind impulsively.

"Mr. Walker," she said, "I'd like you to take me upcountry this week."

"Really?" he exclaimed, genuinely surprised. "I thought you'd be going home about now. I expected to be driving you to the train station in Westfield any day."

"My mother and father will be up in Mt. Washington on Christmas Day. I'm going home a day or two later. Mr. Walker," she stressed, dropping her voice. "I want to go upcountry Thursday, unless some heartening news arrives before then. School," she pointed out, "shuts down Wednesday afternoon."

"Yes," he said. "I know."

"Am I being too forward?" She leaned to him. "Am I bothering you?"

The soft spot that he held for her was apparent in his face. "I'm pleased as punch," he said, "that you'd look to me before anybody else. That's a fact," he said.

Eleanor felt a rush of affection for him. "I never forget," she said, "that it was the Star Route man who transported me to this valley."

Mr. Walker laughed, and blushed with pleasure.

ten

EFORE HEADING up north that week, Eleanor thought it wise and proper to deliver Miss Harrison of her intentions. Wednesday evening, after helping with the dishes, Eleanor broached the topic.

"We want to see if we can be of some help to Miss Sewell," she let fall, quietly.

"I am surprised," Alice responded, "that you are familiar with that story."

Eleanor hewed carefully to a general line. She would say nothing about Howard Allen or Everett Conboy, or about her own messages to and fro, or even mention the gift of Alonzo's coat.

"I have known about it for some while," she admitted. "I have heard bits and pieces, telltale whisperings. It is none of my business, but I have heard, Alice, that she is in hardship. More recently, I have heard that she is missing." Eleanor blushed slightly, knowing this last statement to be fundamentally untrue; for in all of East Becket, she alone possessed knowledge of Evangeline's whereabouts. "So, Myron Walker and I are driving up there tomorrow." Eleanor brightened. "Also," she exclaimed, "I have such a desire to visit those fabled, run-down towns!"

"There will be less romance in it than you think," Alice cautioned. Holding a little stack of bread-and-butter plates in her hands, she paused by the table where Eleanor was sitting. She spoke thoughtfully. "They are hard people," she said.

Alice's words gave Eleanor a chill. They called to mind the icy, expressionless eyes in the pencil portrait of Evangeline that Mr. Klaw had given her as a gift.

"They are different from us," Alice added.

Eleanor's gaze followed Miss Harrison, as she put away the plates.

"It's difficult to believe, Alice, that they could be describably different from the people of East Becket." Eleanor, who was steeped in the liberal Christian thought and teachings that had come down to her from her grandfather's world, was certain in her heart, if nothing else, of the native innocence of man. She even wondered if Alice was not invoking a useful condemnation of the life and people of those bleak towns as a counterweight to her own deep dismay regarding the Sewell girl, or even, perhaps, to a general sense that East Becket had failed a young ward of the town. If so, Eleanor thought, that was not unusual or blameworthy.

Alice Harrison was evidently thinking along related lines. "A bitter life makes a bitter baby," she said.

"I am sure you're right."

"She violated the generosity and trust, Eleanor, of those who fed and sheltered her."

"It seems to me," Eleanor put in, "that it is the most flagrant and yet least talked about thing that's taking place for miles around."

Eleanor debated momentarily whether to say more. Her curiosity gained the upper hand. "No one," she declared, in quiet tones, "seems to be directing responsibility, however, toward anyone beyond *herself*. Or, at least, so it seems, to an outsider."

In the next breath, as she closed the china cabinet, Alice astonished Eleanor with an unexpected frankness. "There is a young man who passes this way regularly," she said. "They have been close for a long while."

"Is he a churchman?" Eleanor blurted out, reflexively. For it was immediately obvious that Reverend Allen, the young minister from Otis, had been cast—doubtless by everybody!—as responsible for Miss Sewell's predicament. As had happened earlier, Eleanor realized that she was just about the only person in the township who was alive to the truth. Except, she thought, for the schoolteacher upstairs, William Bayles. For Eleanor knew, beyond dispute, that Howard Allen was blameless as a lamb. That was made clear in Evangeline's letter to him.

"Two years ago, this individual," Alice narrated, "held a Sunday service in one of those upcountry towns, a service that he directed at the girl. If you can picture such a thing!" Alice set her hand flat to her cheek. She was genuinely appalled. "The girl was fourteen years old. He called her 'the living hope of these mountains.' He suggested that all present in the church that morning should follow her example in life. That they could take strength from her. It was all but blasphemous. *Imagine* it!" Alice's eyes shone with dismay. Her incredulity was palpable.

Eleanor listened all the while with the keenest attention. What she had vaguely suspected was indeed in some way true. That the young clergyman from Otis was fixated upon Evangeline.

"In Cold Spring," Alice concluded, this time specifying the church, "they have a choir of three. He asked the choir to honor her with a special hymn! He asked them, in other words, to celebrate her presence among them."

Eleanor weighed her words. As she arose from the kitchen table, brushing crumbs into her hand, she couldn't help appreciating the concerns of all. Still, she took Evangeline's side. "Wouldn't that," she said, "earn the young lady an extra measure of sympathy?"

But Alice remained with her own thoughts. "They are a hard people," she said.

BEFORE GOING to bed, Eleanor heard Charles Chickering's voice, amid punctuations of laughter, coming from the front stairway, and decided to apprise him of her plans. Her nervousness gave way all at once to buoyant feelings, and a desire to talk about her up-country jaunt. As pretext, she would ask his advice. Eleanor met him at the stair top, and told him of her intentions.

"I'll let you take my compass," he said.

"*Compass?*" said Eleanor, sensing a joke.

"I never travel without a compass. People get turned around. It can be perilous. Far worse," he whispered behind his hand, "it's embarrassing. . . . I have other little necessaries I shall let you take."

"We are not going to be lost," Eleanor countered, amusedly. "I am going with the Star Route man. I am sure he knows every road up there."

She followed Mr. Chickering into his room—the door to which he left politely ajar. His room differed dramatically from the others. There was a look of Victorian solidity to it. The walls were decorated with handsome walnut-framed prints. There was a big porcelain jardiniere containing a stupendous fern, an overseas trunk at the foot of the bed, and everywhere an impressive collection of books. The drab-colored blankets on his bed appeared to be of army issue.

Bending over, he drew a small leather traveling chest from beneath his bed, and loosened the straps.

"This," he explained, reaching up an item, "is a waterproof match case." He handed her a silver cylinder. "You won't need a canteen," he went on, "as there are streams everywhere up there. But this cooking tin and metal drinking cup may be useful." He set these articles on his bed, and produced then a little velvet pouch. "Your compass, Eleanor."

"Mr. Chickering!" Eleanor was completely charmed. "You would think I was going to Hudson Bay!"

"Take an extra blanket with you, also," he counseled, "and extra wool stockings."

While he rummaged away, she couldn't help remarking the exquisite neatness of all the items stored compactly in the small chest. She suspected that his mind was just as tidy. "You and Mr. Klaw," she said, "are perfect opposites. Your room represents the *calm,* and Alonzo's—across the hall—the *storm.*"

"You are such a lovely young lady!" he declared, impulsively, as he straightened up. His eyes gleamed behind the little gold-rimmed spectacles he wore. "So comely," he praised. "So bright-minded. Some young fellow out Fall River way is going to be ever so lucky. To think that he is unaware tonight of the magnificent good fortune that is slowly wending its way toward him."

Smiling, Eleanor extracted a handsome black-dialed compass from its velvet pouch. "This is far too expensive," she emphasized, "for you to let out of your sight!"

Speaking almost at once, Charles let fall a perplexing sentiment. "All the better," he said, "that it may point you to the land of your heart's desire."

Eleanor blushed, and wondered instantaneously—at the back of her thoughts—if Mr. Chickering had somehow divined the character and depth of her growing fascination. His next words dispelled that suspicion.

"That is a play by Mr. Yeats," he said. "*The Land of Heart's Desire*. I have a very pretty edition of it, put together by Thomas Mosher, a boyhood friend of mine up in Portland. A little artwork in itself."

Here Charles offered Eleanor a glass of port. He took down a bottle, along with a black-lacquered tin tray bearing two tumblers, from the top shelf of a bamboo cabinet.

"It must be a very small portion," said she. "My constitution is not trained for anything more than a taste." She sat down on one of his cane-bottomed chairs.

"A sociable dram!" he agreed, pouring her an ounce or two, before filling his glass. "In the Philippines," he said, "port was my lubricant to sleep. The *bugs out there!*"

"You were stationed there with the military?" Eleanor asked, sipping tentatively from her glass. "Were you a general?"

He laughed. "I'm a retired major. Regular army."

"Then, what is all of this business about 'water tables' and the depleted 'carriage' of certain streams in summertime?" She sipped from her port. She was enjoying herself.

"That is my sideline to being retired. You see, I live here. This is not my station." He waved illustratively at his furnishings. "I came this way on an autumn day back in 'eighty-three, as a very impressionable young man—a cadet, actually—and never forgot it. This valley, which I had never seen before that long-ago day, remained with me, for nearly three decades, the land of *my* heart's desire."

Eleanor raised her glass to that proclamation. "I think that you are everything an army officer should be, and that this verdant valley was fortunate to have captured you."

Charles enlarged on his work. "The Corps of Engineers sends me a certificate now and then for my invaluable findings and reports on the Housatonic watershed."

"I'd bet that this is a wonderful place to get away from bugs," Eleanor observed.

"Oh, they were a damnation to me for four-and-a-half years!" He set his hand to his cheek. "Mindanao can count more bugs in a tree than we can in a forest."

"Is it true, do you suppose," Eleanor went on, brightly, as she set down her glass, "that the English colonized the north Americas, and left the southern hemisphere to the Spanish, because of an English aversion to bugs—and a Spaniard's indifference to the insect world?"

Charles Chickering's fondness for Eleanor broke out anew. "Where on earth," he rhapsodized, "do you locate these ideas? Except for Lizzie Borden, the city of Fall River must produce the most astonishing children!"

"There are many people in Fall River," Eleanor replied, automatically, "who find Lizzie Borden astonishing. My mother's uncle—a man named Baldwin Topp—had cause to go into the Borden house a few weeks prior to the ax murders, in order to put in some gas mantels, and said that the *stench* of the place was something beyond human endurance. He meant that literally. He showed us from his pocket the big, white-spotted, blue workman's handkerchief that he had had to tie over his nose. Next to the Borden house, he said, hell itself would smell like a perfumery."

Limp with laughter, Charles leaned and took a neatly tied length of rope from his travel kit. It was tied in the shape of a bow. "You never know," he said, "when a six-foot strand of good strong Malayan rope may prove useful."

"Well, I'm not in a frame of mind to do away with myself," Eleanor was quick to point out, "nor, I'm sure, is Mr. Walker. *Nor,*" she added further, with mounting humor, "would I desire to pass it along to anyone who might be of such extreme spirits as to put it to use. But you do know best, Charles. If your military training argues for the inclusion of a piece of good Malayan rope for my ten-mile horse and buggy ride tomorrow, I wouldn't question it for the world."

Eleanor took up her port. She wanted very much to allude to Evangeline. She would like to have told Mr. Chickering about their correspondence. Or of how she had sent her Mr. Klaw's magnificent coat. Or that Everett Conboy and his young friend had journeyed north a few days ago, and had not yet returned to East Becket. Instead, she kept her own counsel. So far as Charles Chickering was concerned, Eleanor was accompanying Myron Walker on an exploratory, one-day expedition up north tomorrow. That was enough said.

eleven

OOD TO HIS WORD, Mr. Walker arrived early the next morning outside Miss Harrison's front door. Eleanor was dressed warmly for the occasion, in a woolen skirt and stockings, her heavy loden coat, and a big knitted cap to pull over her ears if required. In addition, she carried a small canvas ruck-sack belonging to Mr. Chickering, containing the field-trip articles he had urged upon her, along with a parcel of food and some extra clothing. She had earlier prepared a half dozen sandwiches, and got some biscuits and a tall thermos of tea from Alice. She also included in the rucksack — as gifts for Evangeline — her favorite scarf and a pair of matching gloves. Last of all, she thought to include among her things a purse full of coins, as she anticipated that hard currency would go a long way up north.

Within minutes, she and Myron Walker were underway.

"Ben," she said of the horse, "is so vigorous!"

"It's the winter air," he replied. "You can tell how cold it is by counting his hoofbeats."

At the crossroads, they turned north. They were at the point in the road at which Evangeline—on that rainy day—had leaned forward in the saddle and whipped her mare into a gallop. Squinting in the warm morning sun, Eleanor studied the landscape rising before them. Far ahead, where the climbing white ribbon of the road vanished over a hilltop, a mile-long wall of dark conifers stretched perpendicularly across the horizon. They looked like helmeted soldiers, thousands of them, drawn up in battle array.

"I hope we are not in for snow today," said Eleanor. "The sky above those trees looks gray and smoky."

"I have it from Truman Rogers," said Mr. Walker, "that the *Farmer's Almanac* guarantees nothing worse than wind and sunshine from now to Christmas—from Lake Erie to Cape Cod Bay!"

"I would find that reassuring," Eleanor remarked, playfully, "if I had never read a book or been permitted an original thought. The *Farmer's Almanac* is a catalog of superstitions and old wives' tales."

Myron turned wry. "That's why Truman likes it."

Eleanor and Mr. Walker rode on in silence, the road rising slowly before them toward the dark wall of cedars, the wheels of the wagon grinding a mechanical rhythm in the gravel. The motion was conducive to reflection. Eleanor noticed how the pastureland on both sides of the road was giving way to stone outcroppings, with saplings growing out of them like plumes springing from a bonnet of rocks. Here the tail end of the carved-out farmlands of East Becket made uneasy discourse with the soughing, brooding forest beyond. The forest—she thought—which was father to the farm. Not a loving, benign father. An Old Testament father. With his bearded legions gathered about him.

As they approached the tree line, the rocky pastures gave way to a growth of shiny-leaved sumac. Beyond that, where the road entered the forest, a veritable door appeared to view among the cedars, a narrow man-made passage cut into the trees long ago. Eleanor remarked upon it, while being jounced about a bit on her seat.

"It looks like a door in a fairy tale," she said.

As she and Myron approached the narrow slotlike opening in the black palisade, it pleased Eleanor to picture Evangeline Sewell coming this way atop her black mare, holding the reins high, her back ruler-straight, her mount stepping along unhurriedly. Nor was she unaware of the romantic sense growing up within her that the portal in the dark, serrated tree line up ahead was the fabled doorway to Evangeline's private domain.

"I am surprised," said Eleanor, as their wagon rolled in among the tall trees, "that such a bumpy, inconsequential road should be the only real thoroughfare to these upcountry towns."

"A road into a place," said Mr. Walker, with a grumble, "tells you a lot about the place,"

A long, cool shadow fell across the wagon.

"Your wisdoms," said Eleanor, playfully, as she felt the chill of the forest, "are like rubies, Mr. Walker."

Here he made a slow, broadcasting gesture with his arm. "You can see by the bushes and small second-growth trees on both sides that this 'thoroughfare' was once not so skimpy."

Eleanor looked about herself as with a new eye. "That's a wonderful observation! I can actually *see* the original breadth of the thing." With a little effort, she could make out, among the ferns and young conifers, the general levelness reaching away from the road on both sides.

"You can tell by the curves up ahead," he added, "that nobody has tried to repair or straighten this road. This road was built with oxen. They never heard of dynamite back then. They never heard of blasting! Not the way we know it." He looked across at Eleanor. "Dynamite was only discovered about fifty years ago. Some Italian found it. So you know what it was first used for?"

"I can't imagine."

"This is true, " he said. "For treating headaches."

"What an original antidote. My mother insists on ice packs and something called Dr. Worley's Compound. I doubt that dynamite ever occurred to her. It sounds to me like a prescription that would separate the afflicted individual both from his headache and his head."

While exchanging witticisms with the Star Route mail carrier, Eleanor had grown conscious of the change in the air. The transformation of the white glare of the open road and pastureland behind them to the yawning chill of the sunless forest was like something expressed in chiaroscuro. The air temperature had dropped sharply. High overhead, the lights flickering in the treetops gave the appearance not of a general settling of morning sunshine upon the forest, but of light rays retracting everywhere to their source. It gave Eleanor gooseflesh. It reminded her of her cold damp cellar back home, when her mother sent her downstairs to get a Ball fruit jar of piccalilli or preserves. The forest put her in mind of accounts she had read of great cathedrals; she even wondered if the planners and builders of those solemn edifices, into which light was admitted so scantily, weren't perhaps driven by some hidden atavistic recollection of the great vanished forests of Europe.

As earlier, the thudding pace of the horse, and the ever-constant kaleidoscopic patterns of tree trunks and boulders shifting past, discouraged conversation. Looking about, Eleanor noticed on the wagon bed behind her a couple of blankets, a tarpaulin, a feed bag for Ben, a galvanized pail, and, most prominent—sitting beside her own canvas rucksack—Mr. Walker's big, timeworn leather mailbag. They were a mile or so into the wilderness when, from somewhere in advance of them, came echoing the distant but unmistakable sound of rushing waters, announcing the existence of a modest but leaping fast-flowing stream. It appeared to view at the next turning in the road. It rushed away to their left, to the west, as though late for an appointment.

The road, as in polite deference to its ancient counterpart, swung sharply and followed the brook upstream. At a broad clearing in the trees, Myron steered the horse off the road for a brief rest. "Ben's not what he was for uphill hauling," he said. "For that matter, he doesn't like downhill work. Ben's like a bowler or billiards man. He likes a level surface." Mr. Walker got down, and went with his pail to the brook to water the horse. Eleanor climbed off the wagon to stretch her limbs. The general sunlight shining amid the grasses and low-lying juniper was refreshing on her skin. She examined the cloudless dome of the sky, and imagined Evangeline Sewell stopping here, dismounting, and leading her magnificent ink-black mare to the brook nearby.

"That," said Mr. Walker, indicating something with his eyes, as he set the pail before the horse, "was once a house."

Eleanor realized right off what he meant. Following his glance to a spot several yards back, she recognized a declivity in the earth as the remains of a foundation. She followed him in on foot.

"There would have been pens and sheds, and a barn," he said, "but the house stood here."

In the overgrown depression, nothing remained to indicate what had once been there, except for the suggestion of a wall of fieldstones half buried in earth and grass on one side, and an actual column of chimney stones covered with moss and brambles that jutted up forlornly at the back of it.

"This was someone's farm?" Eleanor asked. "It was small, Mr. Walker," She looked about at the clearing, which amounted to three or four acres.

Mr. Walker disagreed. "Not so small. Those trees out there are also second growth. They started up," he said, "when things stopped here."

"How long ago was that?"

"Thirty or forty years. Not long after the Civil War. Lots of farms shut down because the men didn't come back, but these farms were failing, anyway. They couldn't keep up. When you can't grow or make everything you need, and you can't sell the little bit you do raise, you're not a farmer anymore."

Eleanor followed the Star Route man back to the wagon. Her heart was touched by the grassy ruins.

"Are we still within the boundaries of East Becket?" she inquired, as she put her foot up and clambered aboard the wagon.

"Nope." Mr. Walker emptied the pail, and tossed it into the wagon. "This is Cold Spring," he announced, and smiled up at her.

He knew that she fancied the designation given to these old town-ships. "You're upcountry now."

AS THEY DROVE ON, Eleanor took account of her surroundings. The cedars and firs had given way to stands of hardwood. Occasionally, through a break in the trees, a vista opened out to the north, a sudden panorama of rolling, smoky hills. Within a mile, they passed two houses. The first was an unpainted ramshackle affair, set among the trees, where a dog darted down to the road and barked menacingly at Ben. Mr. Walker reached lazily and took up his whip. The second farmstead, perched at the edge of a gully, was busier. There were henhouses connected to a stable, and a small barn connected to the house. Farther back, near the tree line, could be discerned a pigpen.

"Who lives there?" she asked.

"Woman lives there by herself. Not very friendly," he added, "But then, she ain't got much to be friendly about."

Eleanor turned in her seat. "A woman alone?" she exclaimed. "Is that possible?"

"She gets a little help from our own Mr. Conboy. He saws and cords her firewood. Does some scything. That sort of thing. She repays him with eggs, smoked ham, blueberry preserves. Her name is Jane Rollins. She and Everett understand each other. The only people who understand Everett, and who Everett understands," he said, "nobody else understands."

"You can be so cryptic," Eleanor remarked.

"Cryptic?" He looked at her.

"Speaking in code, Mr. Walker. In your own secret code. Do you ever stop and talk to Miss Rollins?"

"No reason to," he said.

"Doesn't she ever get mail?"

"Not in my lifetime."

About a mile on, from a rise in the road, Eleanor could discern the roof peak of a church or town hall, and guessed they were approaching Cold Spring proper. Along the way, several houses came into view. All looked habitable, but a clogging of bushes and tall grasses imparted an air of neglect. From one rooftop came the high-pitched, rusty squeaking of a weathervane. At the next house, a missing window had been replaced on the inside with what looked like a sheet of cardboard. At the third house, Mr. Walker steered Ben off the road. Eleanor guessed the reason.

"Mr. Hewlitt?" she said.

"The one and only," he breathed back.

In minutes, the two of them were in the kitchen with Jonathan Hewlitt.

"We were coming up this way, anyhow," Mr. Walker explained, making their purpose sound incidental, "and thought we'd stop and ask after the missing girl. This lady is Miss Eleanor Gray, our new schoolteacher."

"I'm glad you stopped, Myron." Jonathan lifted the stove lid, and inserted a log endwise. He was a graying, older man, rather loose-limbed and bony, with a ruddy complexion and noticeably alert eyes. He wore a brass-buttoned denim jacket with patched sleeves. Eleanor took to him on sight.

"Lillian okay?" Mr. Walker inquired of the other's sister-in-law, the midwife.

"Lillian's fine. She's up to the Orcutt place. Baby boy up there's got the croup." Here Jonathan turned to Eleanor, and fixed a chair for her by the stove. "So, this is Miss Gray we hear about?"

"I'm very pleased to meet you, Mr. Hewlitt! What do you suppose," she asked, "has happened to Evangeline?"

"She was supposed to be here these past couple of weeks, but she never showed. That ain't such a surprise, though. She goes her own way," Mr. Hewlitt observed, as he stepped out of the kitchen to get another chair.

Eleanor turned at once to the Star Route man. "Don't mention Aunt Beulah on the lake," she said, softly. "It's not our place to say anything."

It pleased Eleanor unaccountably to put herself in the part of Evangeline Sewell's secret collaborator. It was a kind of unexpressed bond between them.

"A couple of years ago," said Jonathan, as he returned to the kitchen carrying a chair for himself, "she spent three or four days camping by herself up at the quarry. That was the quarry that her mother jumped into."

"I have heard about that," Eleanor put in quietly.

"The two Jabish boys, who don't live here anymore, got worried, and went up to see." Jonathan turned now to Mr. Walker. "Myron," he said, "she had built herself a lean-to up there that would make Teddy Roosevelt himself proud to be alive! Did it all with an ax. As rainproof as this kitchen."

"Never heard that story," said Mr. Walker.

Eleanor was following Jonathan Hewlitt's account with unconcealed fascination.

"Was she camped at the place," Eleanor asked, "from which her mother leaped?"

Mr. Hewlitt nodded matter-of-factly. "She was coming to terms with things, I suppose."

Eleanor said nothing, but marveled at the thought of it. She tried to imagine the fourteen year old, equipped with an ax, building herself a shelter!

"She's an unusual one." Jonathan pointed toward the outdoors. "I saw her kill a blue racer out here last summer. Not twenty feet up the road."

"Blue racer?"

"That's a king snake," he explained to Eleanor. "We call them blue racers. They can grow to about six feet. This one was sunning himself on the gravel, stretched crosswise, looking like an old piece of motor belt. Suddenly, the snake came alive, and slithered off for the blackberry bushes like lightning. 'Vangeline's horse reared! Startled the daylights out of it. Almost got her thrown. So," he said, "she gets down from her saddle, gets herself a rock about the size of my fist, and goes after it in the berry bushes. I'm watching her all this time. Next thing I know, she reaches down—calm as you please—and picks it up."

"She sounds so capable."

"Very," the man said. "Her mother was that way, too—but not so much as this one."

"I never knew the mother," Mr. Walker put in. "I never came up here much, and she, far as I know, never went down there much."

"She knew men up in Hinsdale. She used to go regularly to Hinsdale." Jonathan reached for his pipe. A brief lull fell over the kitchen, broken by the metallic squeal of the rusted weathervane next door. Eleanor sat stock-still next to the stove, her hands in her lap. She had a great many questions she would like to have put, but had lately grown increasingly wary of revealing to others the ever-deepening extent of her interest in the truant Miss Sewell. Still, an instant later, a question leaped from her lips without a moment's forethought. "Was she as beautiful as Evangeline?"

"If she were alive," said Jonathan, "and they walked in that door, I think I'd be hard-pressed to tell them apart. Of course, our memory plays tricks. Yes, she was a beauty."

During this while, Myron Walker signified to Eleanor, as discreetly as he could, that they should move on. As they stepped outdoors, it occurred to her to ask Mr. Hewlitt if he had seen Everett Conboy and Justin. She explained that they had come up this way three or four days ago.

He nodded. "I was outdoors, and the boy walked up to me and asked if I could give him some kitchen matches. 'For Ev's pipe,' he said." Mr. Hewlitt smiled at the remembrance. "He's a lovely boy."

"I think so, too," said Eleanor.

"He's a very trusting boy." He turned to Myron. "I'll bet he's never had a bad thought in his head. I'll bet he wakes up every morning with that same sweet smile on his face that he fell asleep with."

"Where were they headed?" asked the Star Route man, as he gave Eleanor a hand up onto the wagon.

Mr. Hewlitt gestured with a jerk of his head toward the north. "Up above."

Eleanor laughed gaily. "Mr. Hewlitt," she cried, "you use the word *up* in just about every sentence. *Up* the road, *up* at the quarry, *up* at the Orcutts'. I," she said, "am upcountry for the first time in my life, and I thought everyone *up here*—upcountry—would be using the word *down* on a regular basis. *Down* in East Becket, *down* by the Housatonic, maybe even *down Boston way.*"

The two men reacted heartily to Eleanor's witty recitation.

"Where," she said, "is 'up above'?"

"Up by the lake, Miss Gray."

"Tell me, Mr. Hewlitt, where would you say is the uppermost place upcountry? Because I know it can't be a lake. I have heard further"—she was pulling on her gloves—"that the lake, which is situated up above everything else, doesn't even deserve a name anymore. One travels, hour after hour, up roads that are vanishing, to a lake that sits above all else, and which to worsen matters, has been deprived of its name."

"Told you she was a smart one," said Myron, taking up the reins.

Eleanor waved to Mr. Hewlitt as they returned to the road.

"We've learned that much." said Mr. Walker. "Miss Sewell's up at the lake."

"Mr. Conboy was supposed to bring something for her to the blacksmith, Calvin Tripp, in Wisdom Way. But he and the boy must have continued on north to the lake."

"If that blacksmith told Conboy where exactly she was lodged up here, he'd've continued on there himself. Everett," said Mr. Walker, "has a funny kind of worshippy way of looking at and talking about that girl."

"I have noticed!" Eleanor laughed. "He refers to Evangeline as *herself.*"

About a hundred yards from Jonathan Hewlitt's house, at a turning in the road, Eleanor and Mr. Walker came upon a grassy clearing that was once a town common. It was flanked by a run-down church on one side, and a grange hall with a swayback roof on the other. This was the church, Eleanor realized, where the reverend Howard Allen held Sunday services. This was the church where Reverend Allen had apotheosized the fourteen-year-old Evangeline. Eleanor looked upon it carefully. It was derelict.

"The air is feeling raw," said Mr. Walker, examining the sky.

"This town gives me a chill!" she said.

"See that block of granite?" He pointed. "There used to be a minuteman statue on it. There was a similar one up in Wisdom Way. The joke was . . . that the statues got down and walked away."

"I wouldn't blame them," she said, looking about. "What a lonely place to wind up."

In her secret heart, however, Eleanor thrilled to the notion that Evangeline Sewell derived from these desolate mountaintop towns, where the wind went through the sheds and shabby houses like an angry landlord, banging doors, shaking the well pump, kicking up leaves. She imagined Evangeline riding ahead of them on the gravel road, leading the way, processionally, across her desiccated domain, a countryside dotted with fallen barns and fallow fields and on, at a stately pace, to the precincts of Wisdom Way itself, her birthplace—her capital city!

"Mr. Walker," she said, "will we see the house in which Evangeline was born?"

The Star Route man turned and regarded Eleanor for a long moment. "I guess you've taken quite a shine to the young lady," he said, grinning.

Eleanor blushed at once, and looked away. "I don't even know her," she said. "I only know of her."

"I can't say where she got herself born," he said. "But I suspect it was at her grandmother's place. That's where she lives now when she's upcountry." He touched the reins to Ben's flanks. "That's what they tell me, anyhow."

Eleanor's forehead was still smarting from her friend's earlier remark. She took her rucksack from the wagon bed and opened it on her lap. She was still blushing.

"Shall we stop for sandwiches?" she inquired.

"Yes," said he, "but not here." Mr. Walker signified something on their right with a tilt of his eyes. "That's a graveyard," he said.

Indeed, Eleanor descried amid neighboring saplings and grasses the gray crowns of a scattering of headstones, a section of cast-iron pipe, and, farther on, the remains of a stone gate. As they rode past, she looked on in dismay. "No one comes to clear the clutter—the underbrush, whole trees!"

Mr. Walker had thoughts of another sort. "I don't like that sky," he said, flicking his head.

The heavens to the north were leaden, while overhead vaporous gray clouds came streaming—distinct from one another—like outriders detached from the main formation—all hurrying.

Eleanor and Mr. Walker drove on now past a one-room farmhouse with an attached cow shed. Nearby, stood a small barn whose sides appeared slatted. Alternating vertical boards were either propped open or missing. It was a tobacco shed, said Mr. Walker. A half mile on, they stopped and disembarked to stretch. Eleanor got out her thermos of tea, sandwiches and an extra cup. As she did so, she could not have guessed what the next five minutes held in store for them. On the road ahead, a man came into view leading a bull. Mr. Walker's horse reacted with alarm.

"This road is too narrow for passing!" The Star Route man had got down, and grabbed at Ben's bridle.

The horse's dread struck Eleanor as something communicable, sending cold tremors up her spine.

"Ben don't like bulls!" said Mr. Walker. He made Eleanor take hold of the bridle. Starting up the road, he shouted and waved his arms. Eleanor tried to place herself in front of the horse to obstruct his view.

Despite Mr. Walker's hollering at them, the man and bull came on. The man was leading the animal with the use of a long pole attached to its nose ring. To Eleanor's surprise, Myron came back to the wagon to get his whip.

"Don't you do that!" the man yelled. "I'm comin' by!"

By this time, Ben was shying and whinnying, and straining toward the trees. Eleanor was holding the leather straps of the bridle in her hands with all her might. Once or twice, Ben started to raise up in the shafts, and actually lifted Eleanor off her feet. The horse was quaking everywhere. Eleanor's instincts took over. "Mr. Walker!" she shouted. "Cover his head with a blanket! Cover Ben's head!"

The Star Route man scrambled past her to the wagon. For want of a better idea, he leaped to take Eleanor's advice. The right front

wheel of the wagon was by now lodged against the base of a hem-
lock, holding the horse in place, as Mr. Walker tossed the blanket.
Ben raised up once more in the shafts, neighing in terror, and lifting Eleanor off her feet as before. Mr. Walker joined her in holding
him. Eleanor turned to see, as the man and bull came past on the
other side of the dirt road. The man was a smallish, knotty individual, wearing a crusty jacket and trousers. He was struggling to
keep the bull under control. The bull's head was cranked painfully
to one side under the force of the twisted nose ring. Now and
again, the bull grunted and surged, his hooves kicking up gravel.
Eleanor had never seen a sight to match it in all her life, the spectacle of the infuriated bull, his muscles shaking, head pulled downward, eyes enraged.

Mr. Walker shouted something after the man, and the man
flung back an obscenity. Eleanor still had her arms under the blanket, clasping the bridle with both hands, and reciting Ben's name
over and over again to calm and restrain him. She and Mr. Walker
watched as the man and bull went their way laboriously down the
road, the bull giving out a roar now and again, which, at a distance,
was more like a screech.

Mr. Walker appeared rather shaken himself, but he made light
of the encounter. He patted Eleanor's shoulder with his fingertips.

"Welcome to Wisdom Way," he said.

twelve

BY **LATE MORNING,** Eleanor and Myron Walker approached the house of Calvin Tripp, the blacksmith
whom Evangeline had mentioned in her instructions for
Mr. Conboy. The house and small church facing it stood in open
country, on a hilltop field sprawling away to the north. The church

was utterly forsaken. Its windows were gone, and part of the roof at the rear was missing. The coldness of the landscape filled Eleanor with a sense of uneasiness; it assailed her confidence in the appropriateness of her journey. As she looked away to the north, she was visited by the idea that she would remember the lonely prospect of these December fields as long as she lived. Why that would have been so, she did not know. But years from now, in the fullness of her life, even on to dotage, she would remember this particular moment. She would remember herself sitting at Mr. Walker's side, the rhythmical thud of Ben's hooves, and the cold, blowing grasses.

"There are things, Mr. Walker, about myself," she spoke up, "that I do not understand. Things that I cannot even identify."

Touched by the young schoolteacher's words and tenor, the Star Route man nodded, and said nothing.

"They are like that lake," she added, "that has no name."

Eleanor waited on the wagon, while Mr. Walker climbed down from his seat and banged on the blacksmith's front door. Eleanor examined her surroundings. She could see some of the blacksmith's tools hanging on the wall of the open shed next to the house, a well pump by the side door, and a scattering of fruit trees off to one side. The house itself was as shabby and rundown as any she had seen so far this morning. Nevertheless, the roofline was straight, and the windows appeared to be intact. A rain barrel stood in place under a metal drainpipe, and an impressive quantity of firewood was piled in a neat stack alongside the shed. For the past hour or more, Eleanor had envisioned the young Evangeline Sewell lying abed in just such a house as this one belonging to the blacksmith—a crude drafty dwelling—being doubtless attended by some illiterate rural midwife. It was like a tableau from the Dark Ages—a living picture of the past. She thought of the little gifts she was bearing, and of how frivolous and ineffectual they seemed when considered amid these mean, timeless conditions.

As Myron Walker rejoined her on the wagon, Eleanor sought reassurance. "Mr. Walker," she said, carefully phrasing her words, "it was very much my idea to journey up here this morning—and very kind and thoughtful of you to have brought me—but I have a growing dread that my arrival will not be a welcome one."

Her friend was not of two minds on the point. "Oh, you will be welcome," he declared. "You are doing the very thing that many might like to have done, or should've done, but couldn't do."

"Do you think so?" she asked, as they resumed driving.

"I told Truman last night what you planned to do, and he said, 'I wish she'd've asked me to take her.'"

"I feel a lot better, hearing you say that."

"Everyone admires you. The girl will be the same. She'll see the smartness and the goodness in it."

Eleanor pointed to a juncture about fifty yards ahead, where a road started away to the left, and ran northward straight as a die across the fields. "Where does that road go?" she asked.

"If you were going to Hinsdale, you might take it. It goes to the lake, too, but it's a longer way and not used much. I've never been up it. We go this direction." He pointed a gloved finger straight ahead. "Through Wisdom Way itself."

"I thought *this*," she gestured round herself, at the church ruins and the northward sprawling fields, "was Wisdom Way."

He shook his head. "It's another mile or more on to the old town hall, and what was a village green."

"Because," Eleanor stressed, all at once, "I don't think we can go this way." She had spotted a big wooden sign nailed to a road-side tree not twenty yards ahead. She was able to read the painted lettering.

"What are you looking at?" he asked her.

"Can't you read the sign?"

"I used to have glasses," he said, "but they broke." He drew Ben to a halt.

Eleanor read it aloud: *"'The bridge is out at Wisdom Way.'"*

The Star Route man grunted. "Well, that's happened before," he said.

"Is it from flooding?"

"There's no flooding in December, miss. It's just *out!*"

"It was the blacksmith who posted the sign," Eleanor remarked. "I can see his name in the corner. Calvin Tripp."

"There's no sense chancing it," said Mr. Walker, sighing. "The bridge is about a half-mile off. We'd just have to come back to here, anyhow, and take this other road."

Eleanor and he paused in their reflections, and gazed up the northern road to a point where it tilted from view.

"This road," Mr. Walker explained, "runs about six miles to where it meets the road coming out of Hinsdale, and they go east together like a married couple to the lake." Mr. Walker eyed Eleanor to see if she appreciated his poeticism. "Calvin's about the only person who's used this road, but for going to Hinsdale, not to the lake." The Star Route man laughed. "But Calvin broke some furniture and some beer and whisky bottles in a tavern up in Hinsdale, so even he doesn't use this road anymore." He laughed into his fist again. "Calvin's a wanted man in Hinsdale."

Eleanor called to mind the spectacle of the foul, runty man leading the bull—the devilish look of the man, and the expletive he threw back. "These men are so violent."

"Not at all!" Mr. Walker crooned back. "Calvin's as gentle as a lamb."

"But if that lamb is wanted by the authorities in Hinsdale, Mr. Walker, that lamb has some qualities in him that we don't readily associate with baby sheep."

On that note, Mr. Walker turned Ben's head toward the north, and they commenced their detour. Eleanor poured her companion another cup of tea from her thermos. As she reached into the rucksack, she laid her fingers on Mr. Chickering's elegant compass. She removed it from its case and velvet pouch. She examined its needle.

"Look, Mr. Walker," she said. She handed him the compass. "Look at the arrow!"

"Well, I know we're going north," he protested gently, while gazing at the device. Eleanor's tone perplexed him.

"But the arrow, Mr. Walker, divides the road precisely in two!" We are not just going north. We are traveling *exactly* north."

"That's called true north, Miss Gray."

"I *know* that," she teased back. "But I was talking about the road, not the location of the North Pole."

Eleanor looked back at the sign that Calvin Tripp had posted, and at the road leading into Wisdom Way. The road dissolved from sight in a gray tangle of trees. The leaves were all down. The trees stood out like a stencilling. While looking back, she observed a sudden curtain of snowflakes go whisking past the naked treetops. Then, above and beyond that, a second and similar cloud of snow. She pointed it out to her companion. "The sky," she said, "is snowing over Wisdom Way."

Mr. Walker dealt it a cursory backward glance. "Weather changes fast up here," he said.

Eleanor didn't say as much, but ever since the fright she experienced over the sight of that struggling infuriated bull, she felt that certain occurrences befalling her this morning held out some portentous significations. She thought about the impassable bridge. She fell into a brown study. She was imagining how Evangeline would look in her splendid black coat. She smiled inwardly at the thought of Evangeline coming out of Wisdom Way, riding out of her upcountry redoubt, on her way to settle accounts with somebody. She could hear the thudding of the hooves on the floorboards of that same bridge. She could see Evangeline sitting solidly in her saddle, the reins clasped in the ball of her fist.

Eleanor was snapped out of her ruminations all at once, however, by a sudden explosive tattooing of wings near at hand, a frantic drumbeat that set the air vibrating all about her, and the swift upward onslaught of a brace of birds. They came spiralling up in a swooping helix. Eleanor flinched instinctively, and cast her arm before her eyes. She gave a shout of surprise.

"Those are partridges, Miss Gray!" said her companion—who had also shot a hand reflexively up to his face. The birds vanished in a second, spinning away willy-nilly among the veil of branches.

"I think I am being tested." Eleanor laughed, after regaining her composure. She ran her fingers over her forehead, and took a deep breath.

"I think we are both about to be tested," he said. With his eyes, he indicated the sky ahead. "That's snow," he said.

Eleanor followed his glance.

"I don't need spectacles for that," he added.

"Are you worried?" she asked, and looked at him.

"We've got something else to think about, too."

"What is that?"

Mr. Walker finished his cup of tea, and gave the cup an upside-down shake. "This road," he said, "forks."

As before, Eleanor followed the tilting gesture of the Star Route man's head and eyes. He leaned round and put away the cup. As Ben continued plodding solemnly under the trees, it became apparent to Eleanor that the narrow gravel road upon which they were travelling did indeed fork up ahead.

"Which way do you suppose is correct?" she asked, licking her lips, and looking about at the woods, as though the trees themselves might return a sign.

Mr. Walker spoke to himself. "I never knew there were two roads up here. I didn't think there were two places to go up here!" He reined the horse to a stop. By now, the air was blowing about with a light snow.

"It must be to the right," she said, "because Wisdom Way is east of here, and the lake is north of Wisdom Way."

The Star Route man listened to her in earnest.

"If we go to the left," she said, "we'll end up somewhere west, or northwest, of where the right fork is going. So, that wouldn't make a lot of sense."

Mr. Walker ruminated, rubbing his neck, and grunting.

"Unless one of them peters out," she said.

"A road that's being used doesn't just peter out, Miss Gray. It doesn't peter out till it gets to where it's been going."

Eleanor was sitting up straight on the wagon seat. She pulled her knit hat down to her ears. She tried mentally to picture the course of each of the two roads.

"If the right way is the wrong way," she said, after a moment's consideration, "we will probably be offered some sort of indication along the way of that fact. Something," she added, "that we cannot anticipate while sitting here."

Mr. Walker's reply to that was not as oblique as his words might have suggested. "If the right way is the wrong way," he explained, quietly, "by the time we get back to this point, we may need a sleigh."

Eleanor felt the disappointment building within her. "If you'd like to turn back," she allowed, "I am perfectly ready to do so. I'm so grateful, as it is, for all you've done. I have been such a burden to you."

For the first time, Myron Walker regarded her with a very lingering look. She returned his gaze.

"I want to go on," he said, "because I know how important it is to you. I know how much you want to find her."

Eleanor flushed with color, but continued to hold his gaze. She was touched by his solicitude, and felt that he alone in all the world understood that she was being impelled by forces that she could perhaps not comprehend. She felt a pressure of tears coming, and didn't even mind if Mr. Walker noticed. She had never felt so kindly toward anyone. "You are a prince," she said. Feeling her lips shudder, Eleanor looked away. Her companion set Ben moving, reining him to the right, and peering on ahead into the swirling flakes.

"How different it is—a road like this—from the streets of Fall River, from the cobblestoned highways going in and out of those cities. This is what a road really is. A path in the wilderness."

To pass the time, as they trundled along, Eleanor asked questions of her friend. The man with the bull, he explained, was named Isaac Jessup, a "mean cuss," who couldn't read or write, who had no friends, and whose wife left him, taking their boys with her, and departed the mountain altogether.

Eleanor desired to ask Mr. Walker about her colleague, William Bayles, but could not bring herself to raise the subject. Lately, she avoided her fellow teacher, not only in the Harrison house, but even in the privacy of her thoughts. Instead, she asked Mr. Walker about Howard Allen, the young minister from Otis. Howard, he replied, came from a fire-and-brimstone family that spent their summers praying and preaching up in the campgrounds of the burned-over country. Up New York state way.

"*'Burned-over country'?*" she interrupted.

"That's what they called it. The fire-and-brimstoners scorched everything they touched. The countryside was black with it. From Rensselaer and Troy all the way out to Chattaqua. Rochester was what they called 'the burned-over capital.'"

"But the Reverend Allen seems anything but a firebrand."

Mr. Walker had pulled down the earflaps of his peaked red-plaid cap, and was wearing mittens now. The steel-rimmed wheels banged noisily on a protruding stone now and then. As always, Eleanor's thoughts turned like the arrow of a compass to Evangeline. Mostly, though, by keeping up her talking, she was trying to busy Mr. Walker's mind, to shift attention from the growing squalliness of the weather, while attempting a show of her own indifference to it.

It was windless under the trees. The ticking sound of the snow in the bare branches overhead, and on the withered leaves blanketing the earth under the beeches and sycamores through which they were passing, reminded Eleanor of the insistent rattling of the telegraph in her father's office at the mill. She looked about herself. God's telegraphy, she thought, was not so easily deciphered. Eleanor buried her chin in her scarf. The secret thought came and went in her mind that her mission was evolving, mile by mile, into a stoical errand, and that Evangeline would know, by her coming upcountry today, coming of her own will and devising, and withstanding the elements, that she was now openly the other's proven confederate.

"Sometimes, Mr. Walker," she spoke up, "I have such unusual . . . such unbidden . . . such hard-to-place thoughts."

Myron Walker's reply was a thoroughgoing non sequitur. "I don't know where we are," he said.

He was gazing into the snowfall.

"There's a brook and a bridge up ahead," he added.

"If this is the stream running down into Wisdom Way, where

the bridge is out, it's the one that Mr. Chickering called the East Branch."

"This one's smaller 'n that."

The planks of the bridge rumbled and complained under the wheels. Eleanor could make out the remains of a low structure on the bank of the stream a few yards away. The snow both defined and distorted its shape. To Eleanor, it looked like a cartoon creature lifting its head from a hole in the ground, with snow on its shoulders, a gaping shadow for a face, and a cocked powdery white tricorn hat. She questioned her companion.

"Was probably a grist mill," he said.

After a second, Eleanor sought again to plumb the other's estimation of their circumstance. "Are you getting worried?" she asked.

"This road," he said, "can't make up its mind to go north."

While Eleanor knew it to be a greenhorn sort of thing to do, she took out Mr. Chickering's compass, and opened its lid.

"We are going due east," she affirmed. "But if we continue to do that, we will necessarily cross the road with which you're familiar, the one going straight up to the lake from Wisdom Way."

"You're right about that, miss."

"How far have we come from the fork?"

"Maybe half a mile. Maybe three quarters."

"Do I hear *sawing*?" she asked, suddenly.

Mr. Walker reined in his horse. They listened. Her suspicion was confirmed. From up forward came the systolic, back-and-forth rasp of a handsaw. Ben, sensing a possible respite, set a smart pace. Presently, a house appeared to view. It stood in a small clearing. The big trees brooding about it on all sides gave it the look of a toy house. A boy in a mackinaw coat, breeches, and high-cut boots came out of the adjoining woodshed at the sound of the approaching wagon. He was carrying a bucksaw.

"Who lives here?" Mr. Walker called to him, as they drove up. The boy gaped at them, wide-eyed, with open mouth, before answering.

"The Morgans," he said, in a changing voice.

"I should have known," said Mr. Walker. "This is about the only place up here I've never seen."

Eleanor, however, had just taken note with dismay that the road they had been following for quite some while ended here. "We have come the wrong way," she said.

Before her companion could respond to that, a woman came out the front door of the house, and eyed the two of them with suspicion. A figure of older years, she had the lean, hard-bitten look that Eleanor now associated with these upcountry dwellers.

"You must be Joanna," he said. "I'm Myron Walker. We," he said, nodding at Eleanor, "got ourselves lost."

"You come along indoors." She turned to the boy. "You lead that shuddering beast of theirs into the shed, Cy. Put a blanket over him."

"Cy's a good one," she said, as she led the two of them inside. "Weren't for him, I'd be cracked. That's my little brother's boy. He's my nephew. He's my favorite nephew, and my only nephew. With a nephew like Cyrus," she said, looking back, "you don't need two."

The interior of Joanna Morgan's house was oddly appointed but inviting, and struck Eleanor as a reflection of the eccentric, sharp-tongued woman who led them into it. The walls of the kitchen were covered with magazine illustrations and full-page advertisements from Montgomery Ward catalogs. A collection of framed photographs, some of which may have been daguerrotypes, stood atop the icebox, six or eight old-fashioned portraits of bearded, furious-faced men and their indomitable women. The big cast-iron kitchen stove, behind which lay a brown-and-white beagle fast asleep, set a sudden obstreporous popping as the logs within rearranged themselves.

In the minutes to follow, Eleanor made known the purpose of their journey.

"Who is the *father* of this miracle-to-be?" the Morgan woman cut in, mincing no words, brushing aside any pretense at being discreet.

"I don't know," Eleanor colored.

"Or don't they talk about that down there?" Settling into her rocker, Joanna gestured vaguely at the surrounding forest. "Here," she said, "we always knew. You've got to be really *swank* to create a reason not to know." She laughed over her own joke.

"Do you know her?" Eleanor asked.

"I know her from when she camped up here by the quarry. I boiled some eggs for her one morning, and gave her some bread and grapes."

Eleanor interposed at once. "We're near the quarry?" she blurted, making an exclamatory note of it.

Joanna Morgan showed the young schoolmistress a bemused expression. "Where do you think you were headed?" she said. "This was the original road to the quarry. Forty-five years ago, my father was superintendent up there. This house," she said, "was his. But a day came along, out of nowhere, when my father was paid a visit by a superior reason for him to get up in the morning. He went to war!"

Eleanor knew instantly what the woman was about to say. "I'm a stranger to this part of the state," she said, "but I am familiar with the great heroism and sacrifices made by the men from this district."

"There's a lot of bull in that," said the old woman, showing Eleanor the corner of her eyes. "They were killed!"

Eleanor blushed at having been upbraided.

"If they gave medals and ribbons for dumbness and hardheadedness, my father would have been decorated front and back. The man was forty years old!" Joanna cackled over the irony of it. "My mother begged him not to go. I remember it like yesterday. She was sitting where I'm sitting, just like this, with her hands on her knees. 'If you go, you'll never come back,' she said. '*None* of you.'" Joanna laughed at the remembrance. "And those were Americans they were after. It's one thing to shoot some Spaniards down in Cuba. You don't shoot your brother."

Eleanor thought she had never met anyone so cynical as Joanna Morgan, but could not help admiring her. Mr. Walker, she noticed, as a veteran of those campaigns, seemed visibly to be taking exception with the old woman's remarks. He looked away, his hatchet-cut profile etched against the kitchen window and the snow squalling past.

Joanna Morgan nodded conclusively. "We got the news on the first day of October, eighteen sixty-four. I was about your age," she said to Eleanor. "How old are you?"

"I am twenty."

"Exactly my age on that horrible day. Mr. Lincoln himself signed his name at the bottom of the page. The Second Company of the Third Massachusetts was wiped out. I remember my father and the others, in the days just before they all left. They were marching around with shovels on their shoulders on the town common in Wisdom Way, with some idiot on the bandstand, blowing on a bagpipe. . . ." Joanna paused in her diatribe. Her face darkened. *"Spotsylvania!"* she spat out. "I hate the name! I hope when the skies open up, and Jesus returns to resurrect the dead, I hope He starts in Spotsylvania. They were fools," she said to Eleanor, "every one of them, but we loved them all uncommonly."

Joanna Morgan put her fist to her lips, as though she might cry. "All was different forever after."

Eleanor didn't know what to say. She had never known a moment when that receding war had stood up so vivid before her. Joanna's eyes sparkled like sapphires.

"Fifty men went down to the Secession War fields, and sixteen came back. People used to say, 'What's worse, they came back on twenty-nine legs.'"

Unexpectedly, the Morgan woman lost her cynical reserve. "And what brave Yankee girls we all were!" she declared, in earnest.

Myron Walker's eyes went again and again to the window, beyond which the snowflakes created a spinning, shadowy veil. A rush of icy air preceded the advent of the boy carrying in an armload of split logs. He made straight for the wood box. He was a pink-faced boy, with protuberant ears, and a shy, evasive glance.

"He plays the ukulele!" the woman cried out, happily. "Don't you, Cy?"

He nodded embarrassedly, while opening the lid of the woodbox.

"When I beat him at pinochle enough times, he plays it for me.

He plays and sings the 'Red River' song as good as anybody you ever heard. He's got the sweetest voice." She beamed at the boy, who was standing with his back to her.

Eleanor was studying the back of his head, as he leaned over the woodbox—the nape of his neck and the look of his peaked cap over his eyes—and her heart moved at this configuration of innocence. "I am glad there are no more such great wars to inflict such suffering," she said.

"Oh, there will be," cried the old woman, in an access of her customary cynicism. "But they won't be coming up here to fill their rosters."

As Eleanor and the Star Route man prepared to leave, she couldn't help wondering how the woman and boy provided for themselves. "Does anyone else live with you?" she asked.

"I've got a daughter and a son up in Dalton. They're in business up there. They come by regularly enough—bring me my patent medicine, some foodstuffs, kerosene, tobacco. I like my tobacco. Me and the boy smoke a pipeful of shag every evening. *Don't we?*" she cried at him.

She followed Eleanor and Mr. Walker outdoors. "Mostly, I like being down here, away from the two of them up there, and they like me being down here, away from the two of them up there." She laughed drily over her own humor. "Myron," she said, "you got a lantern on that buckboard of yours?"

"In fact," he said, "it's a little low on kerosene."

"Cyrus!" she said, "Attend to Mr. Walker's lantern. I'm going indoors. I ain't twenty, like this one." She squeezed Eleanor's arm in passing, and glanced upward at the tall snow-whitened trees.

"It's been a joy meeting you, Mrs. Morgan," Eleanor responded. "I'm glad we lost our way."

"She's got a nice way of putting things," she said to Mr. Walker. She spoke from the open doorway to Eleanor. "I hope you find the Sewell girl. Tell her that Joanna misses seeing her, and hopes her baby is a girl. Wisdom Way is unkind to boys." She slammed the door behind herself.

Mr. Walker backed Ben out of the shed, while the boy replenished the fuel in the well of his lantern. Eleanor shook some silver from her little drawstring money bag in her pack, and brought it to the boy. The effect was remarkable. He stared in disbelief at the coins in the palm of his hand, and in wonderment then at Eleanor as she got aboard.

AS THEY RUMBLED their way back along the quarry road, Mr. Walker had to get down from the wagon, and lead the horse by hand through the swirl of flakes. Eleanor sat alone on the seat, with a blanket over her, acknowledging from moment to moment the bitter fact that her upcountry errand of comradely love had failed. There was no chance that they might turn north at the fork, and continue on the five miles to the lake. It was getting well into afternoon by now. It was enough to contemplate—if conditions worsened—where they would put up for the night. Returning to East Becket was out of the question. If the snow kept up, even getting back to Cold Spring might be an arduous undertaking. Eleanor chastised herself. The sight of Myron Walker, with a piping of snow decorating his cap, and forming white shoulder-tabs on his coat, as he trudged stolidly ahead, filled her with recriminatory feelings. Mr. Walker was not a young man. He had given so much of himself today.

Eleanor let herself down from the slow-moving wagon, and went quickly to his side.

"I have made such a blunder of things today. I've put you to so much needless exertion and discomfort."

Mr. Walker smiled at her cannily. "I like doing it for you. I don't get as many chances to do things like this as I probably used to. Forget what you're thinking. . . , It was a brave idea."

Eleanor clasped his free arm.

"Besides," he added, "this ain't much of a storm."

"It looks quite awful to me," she said.

"You should've been alive in 'eighty-eight," said he. "Blizzard like that blows up maybe once in five hundred years."

"They talk about it no end in Fall River."

"All the way up and down the seaboard!"

When at last they came rolling out from under a canopy of

boughs onto the road from which they had departed, where it forked, Mr. Walker deferred to his companion.

"What'll it be, Miss Gray? Shall we go north?"

"You are very gallant," she replied.

She looked off in both directions. She had a sense of their standing at the center of a dome. "I think we should let Ben decide."

"We both know what that'd be."

"I think," Eleanor concluded, "we should seek shelter."

Mr. Walker nodded. "We'll come back in the morning," he said. "If the snow makes it necessary, we'll stable Ben someplace, and return on foot. It's only a two-hour walk to the lake." He showed Eleanor a reassuring look.

AS THEY TURNED south at a walk, headed back toward Calvin Tripp's, Eleanor had a thought: "If Mr. Tripp is not at home," she said, "we could put up in that abandoned church."

"Do you know," the other echoed, melodiously, "that's not a bad idea!"

"I'll bet that Ben will be the first horse in history to march in at the door of that consecrated house."

For all her apparent light-spiritedness, however, Eleanor knew herself to have been unequal to the trials of the day. A leaden feeling dogged her footsteps. She had been of no earthly use whatsoever to the other young woman.

thirteen

ELEANOR AND MR. WALKER looked in at the deserted church. While the walls and floor were intact, all the windows were gone, and at the back of the little wooden building, snow was falling through a hole in the roof. As it was relatively dark indoors, the sight of the snow coming in at the roof, and spinning steadily downward in a shaft of light, gave the derelict church an inexplicably spectral feel. A circular apron of snow lay on the floor at the approximate spot where the pulpit would have been. Eleanor reflected in passing upon the many hundreds of people who had worshipped here over the years, going back especially to those long-ago times, as of the Civil War years, and before that, when Wisdom Way had doubtless been a lively mountain town.

Mr. Walker went across the road to Calvin Tripp's workshed, and was back presently with a sheet of tin and an armful of kindling.

Eleanor teased him. "My Promethean hero," she said, "the bringer of fire."

In her heart, she still felt guilty over having put him to such a power of trouble. While he unhitched the horse, Eleanor brought their things in from the wagon. Within minutes, he led Ben into the church. The boom and rumble of Ben's hooves on the old floorboards of the Wisdom Way church sounded like thunder rolling in from afar.

"Can't imagine where Calvin is," he remarked.

"My instincts tell me that he is up at the lake," said Eleanor. "He is a man Evangeline counts on, I'm quite sure." But Eleanor had something else on her mind. "Mr. Walker," she put in, while following him and Ben to the opposite front corner of the church, "I am concerned that I might have thrust you into a perilous situation here. I'm a city girl, I'm afraid, but I do know that a person untutored in the wild can easily underestimate the caprices of nature— of bad storms, perhaps—or just being exposed too long to the elements. Are we in danger?"

The Star Route man laughed, as he reached to unbridle the horse. Ben nuzzled his hand, as he did so.

"This is not the Yukon, Miss Gray. We'll be comfortable here overnight, and continue on north in the morning."

Mr. Walker got the horse his oats, and put a blanket over him. That done, he set the sheet of tin on the floor near the other corner, and in short order had built up a neat blaze.

"You are making us a very comfortable bivouac," she remarked, with intentional primness, while opening her rucksack. "I would like to give a name to our encampment." She signified their portion of the church, including the sight of the firelight flickering and playing upon the walls. "I would like to call it the 'Southwest Corner of Things.' That was an expression that my preacher grandfather—Eugene Lloyd Gray—coined for himself. He meant it to describe and define his own modest angle on the world." Eleanor sat down on the blanket by the fire, and folded her legs beneath her. "Of course, he wasn't modest, at all. I think he was a rampaging egoist. It was no wonder that my father bolted. My father believes in mechanics! *Beauty*—to my father—is something to be found in the predictability and the smooth running of a well-designed, well-built, well-oiled machine."

Mr. Walker smiled with pride over his young friend's verbal flights.

"I haven't heard the word *bivouac* in years," said he. "I was on bivouac! There wasn't an army in all history that could bivouac like the Army of the Potomac. Miss Gray," he said, his voice going up, "if General McClellan hadn't finally got fired, we'd *still* be on bivouac down there!"

Eleanor laughed aloud over the thought of Mr. Walker camped for decades on the banks of the Potomac.

As the fire expanded, the two of them, sitting in the corner with their backs to the walls, removed their coats. Mr. Walker was wearing an imposing pair of yellow-and-green suspenders that brought a smile to Eleanor's face.

"I think my father would be quite astonished to see me right now. He would wonder what on earth I am doing."

"You often mention your father, miss."

"Well, I love my mother equally, but somehow it's his confidence and approval that guide my thoughts and actions. I think I could not bear being a disappointment to him."

Mr. Walker had lifted his eyes to the gaping hole in the roof, where the snow came pouring down in silence. "You would not be a disappointment to him tonight."

"Do you find it odd, Mr. Walker," Eleanor inquired with some embarrassment, "that I have taken such an unusual interest in Miss Sewell?"

"I do not."

"Because I don't know what impels me to do so." Eleanor looked down at the tin cup she had taken from her pack. "She comes and goes in my mind all day long."

The Star Route man watched Eleanor with a look of unmixed affection. The fire made his face ruddy. "You've packed quite a nice picnic there."

"*My* fondest hope," she said, "is that we don't get eaten by bears."

"Our Berkshire County bears are little bears. They like to get at the grain and feed bins. They like leftovers. They'll eat anything. Right now, Miss Gray, to put your mind at rest, they're all sleeping. They'll be sleeping till the ice melts and the crocuses come out."

"Do they really hibernate?" she asked.

"The ones I know do."

Eleanor poured tea from the thermos, and set out sandwiches, chicken, and pickles. "I also have brown bread and butter," she said, "for later."

Mr. Walker reached up a drumstick. "I'll start here."

"Is it nightfall yet?" she asked, while corking the thermos.

"It's still afternoon, miss, but it's as dark out there as it is any night of the year."

"Mr. Walker!" She suddenly realized something. "Tonight *is* the darkest night of the year! This is St. Lucy's Day. It's the winter solstice. The shortest day. The feast of lights!"

"That a fact?" he sang back, indifferently, while chewing.

"How unimpressed you are! It's a very special night. Tonight's the night that blackbirds, black widows, black beetles, bat wings and all such, all get refurbished. God paints them once a year. Everybody knows that."

"Maybe in Fall River," he said, "everybody knows that. Out here, we don't know a fraction of what everybody back east knows. Or out west of here, for that matter."

"You make such interesting company," she exclaimed, happily.

His eyes came up. "It's because I keep interesting company."

"And you are much too quick for me."

"A fox," said he, "is not too quick for you."

Suddenly, Eleanor's heart jumped. "Mr. Walker!" she cried. "Someone is at the door!"

There came a report of someone stamping his feet, and cursing, when the broken front door of the church was thrust in. It gave a grinding sound. Eleanor was sitting bolt upright. However, Mr. Walker's expression remained placid as before. He paused, peering over the drumstick in his fingers, as a man stepped in. The man was tall and bearded. He looked at the two of them, and then glanced at the opposite front corner of the church, to where Ben was feeding.

"Evening, Cal," said Mr. Walker.

"I should've known it'd be you, Myron," said the other.

Eleanor had her hand flat to her bosom. "That was startling!" she said to the intruder. "Are you Mr. Tripp?"

"Yes, and I believe I know who you are."

"I'm Eleanor Gray."

"As I thought," he confirmed, in a deepish, pleasant voice, with an accompanying nod. He approached the two of them. Eleanor took note of his long, tan-colored coat—a type of coat that, oddly, she associated with horsemen, with brigands; it went back to a picture or daguerrotype that she recalled seeing of some John Brown raiders. In all, Mr. Tripp was a most impressive-looking man. He extended his hands over the fire.

"Borrowed a piece of tin from you," Myron Walker let fall, and indicated the metal sheet underneath the fire.

"You're welcome to it," came the baritone reply. Turning his attention to her, Calvin Tripp delivered Eleanor of an easy smile. She held his gaze. She guessed him to be a man in his forties, and guessed further that he was an individual to be counted on.

"Would you like something to eat?" she asked.

Mr. Walker spoke up simultaneously. "We were headed up to the lake, Cal, but I took the wrong road a ways up from here, where the road forks."

Eleanor made a joke of their folly. "We had the pleasure instead of meeting Mrs. Joanna Morgan."

But Calvin Tripp looked quite somber. He was watching Mr. Walker with a steady gaze. "I just came from the lake," he said.

The gravity in Mr. Tripp's eyes and tone of voice sent a shudder through Eleanor. A dire announcement hung in the air. She was sure of it.

"Mr. Tripp," she burst out. "What is it?"

"Evangeline," he said, "gave birth to a baby yesterday night, a little while after midnight. He died this afternoon."

Eleanor put her hands to her face, but continued staring at him through her fingers. Her heart had come to a stop.

Mr. Walker spoke up, at length. "What about the girl?" he asked, worriedly.

Mr. Tripp nodded once. He looked at them in turn. "She's okay, Myron." He fell quiet for a second. "It was a hard night and a hard day today. They had a midwife, woman named Richards, down from Hinsdale. She did fine. But that baby couldn't somehow get started. He was working at it, too. He was working hard at it every minute he was alive." Mr. Tripp passed his hand over his beard, and looked away, and looked back. "It was hard to watch—him pulling for air like that, hour after hour. I felt bad for him. It isn't supposed to be that hard for a new one to join the rest of us."

Eleanor had started to cry.

"You rode down in the snow, Cal?" said Myron.

"I walked down. I just got back. There was nothing for me to do up there. Not for Beulah, and not for the girl. The Richards woman knew her art, I'd say. She was sent down from Hinsdale, you know, by one of the Billings men."

Eleanor looked up at the mention of the Billings name. It was the second time today she had heard it uttered.

Mr. Walker apparently noticed the coincidence also. He glanced at Eleanor.

Calvin Tripp enlarged on his remark. "He heads some young women's Christian society up there that looks to assist women in trouble."

Eleanor would like to have remained silent for a while with her thoughts, but felt the need to show Mr. Tripp a hospitable manner.

She could all but feel the blacksmith's grief. She sensed that he was trying to hide it. As for herself, her thoughts were racing. A long minute elapsed. "Mr. Tripp," she put in, softly, at last, if only for the sake of saying something, "is Mr. Conboy still up at the lake?"

"No," said Calvin. "He and the boy headed home yesterday. Only reason he was up there at all was to fetch the midwife from Hinsdale." He forced a smile. "I'd've gone for her myself, but they've taken a lively dislike to me up in Hinsdale."

Mr. Walker smiled back. "I did hear about that," he said.

"They would arrest me," said the other, matter-of-factly. He stood as before, with his hands out above the fire. The firelight glimmered up and down his flowing tan waterproof coat. "They would arrest me right here, if they could. But they don't come here. They don't come up to Wisdom Way." He showed Eleanor an amused expression. "They tell ghost stories," he said, "about Wisdom Way."

Eleanor watched and listened all the while to the tall, bearded blacksmith. He struck her as being very much a man of these up-country townships. Though Mr. Walker had likened the blacksmith to a lamb, he struck Eleanor as a figure of biblical provenance.

Mr. Tripp added with amusement, "And they don't want to become a part of one of those ghost stories."

"If Everett has gone back down to East Becket," said Mr. Walker, "how is it, I wonder, we didn't see him about?"

"I haven't a notion," replied the other. "He and Justin upped and headed back yesterday."

"Then they don't know yet about the baby," Eleanor realized.

"Not unless they got special powers. Nobody knows," he added, "except you two now. How could they? It's only been about three hours."

"Jonathan Hewlitt and Lillian have been wondering for days where the girl went," said Mr. Walker. "You didn't tell them?"

"She didn't say to," said Calvin, simply as that.

The laconic, yet deferential character of the blacksmith's utterance reflected an attitude toward Evangeline identical in Eleanor's mind to that of Mr. Conboy. In all her Fall River years, and on through the time of her studies at Framingham, Eleanor had never known anyone who had transmitted to others such mysterious imperatives. Nor was Eleanor unaware that she was herself similarly magnetized. She, too, was drawn in. She, too, did Evangeline Sewell's bidding, kept her counsel, and thrilled in her secret heart to have been thus acknowledged.

Eleanor surprised herself by articulating aloud a peculiar thought of the moment. "I wonder where we were," she said, sadly, to Mr. Walker, "when the baby passed on." Eleanor felt choked still. "I suspect we were at the place where the road forked, where we went the wrong way. That's when the baby died," she said. Eleanor could not control her emotions.

"Nothing wrong with crying," Mr. Tripp sympathized. "Wisdom Way's got a corner on crying." He turned to the Star Route man. "Evangeline's going to bury her baby down in East Beckett."

"What a remarkable thing." Mr. Walker appeared uncharacteristically incredulous.

"She told me herself this afternoon. 'That's where he came from,' she said, 'that's where he's going back.'"

Eleanor would like to have recited to them the granite avowal Evangeline made in her secret letter to Reverend Allen, the one Eleanor had steamed open.

"The two of you should come across the way with me, and spend the night in the house," said Calvin.

Eleanor could read Mr. Walker's thoughts. "We'll be fine to stay here," she said. "A church is a good place to be."

Calvin Tripp looked up at the snow falling into the cone of light at the back of the church.

"We've got enough blankets here to sleep a regiment," said Mr. Walker.

"We're quite fine," Eleanor repeated, looking up at him. "But it was kind of you to invite us, sir."

"I just need to get an armful of wood," Mr. Walker added. "Been putting it off."

"You should finish eating first," Eleanor was quick to advise, unconscious of her schoolteacherly inflection. Both men laughed.

"I'll do what you say, Miss Gray."

"You should digest your food," said Eleanor, in earnest.

"Was it you sent the coat?" Calvin asked Eleanor out of the blue.
Eleanor was taken off guard. "Coat?"

"Was it you sent the lady a coat?"

"Yes, it was!" Eleanor brightened. "I'm so happy to hear, Mr.
Tripp, she got it!"

Calvin turned away toward the door, with a pleasant bemused
smile. "That's some coat," he said, departing.

For a long while, Eleanor and Mr. Walker sat by their fire, sipping tea and talking like friends met of a snowy night.

"Four months ago," said Eleanor, "I could not have dreamed of
the adventures to come. I could never have dreamed of a night like
tonight."

She looked about herself. Darkness by now had fallen. The
church grew dimensionless, the rafters and roof all but dissolving.
Mr. Walker lighted his pipe, and put away his tobacco pouch. He
blew up a plume of aromatic pipesmoke.

"You look like an Indian maiden," he said, "wrapped up in that
blanket of yours."

"And you a sachem, sir."

There were many things that Eleanor might wish to have said,
or to have questioned Mr. Walker about, but inwardly her spirits
were flagging. As long as she lived, she felt, the memory of this day
and night would be one of enduring perplexity. For she knew now
that her love of Evangeline was something that transcended the ordinary, and eluded her own simpler understandings. With the firelight warm upon her face, Eleanor, feigning drowsiness, closed her
eyes to think. Her pilgrimage today, hopeless from the start, was,
she realized, less like a sojourn into the upcountry world of these
barren townships than it was into a domain even more forbidding,
an inner country, pathless and unexplored, a place of noiseless
storms, riotous undergrowth, metaphysical brambles underfoot at
every step. This was her own private upcountry "settlement."

Swaying before the fire, she seemed to be looking down on herself from a height—as from the rafters swimming in the darkness

above—or from afar—beyond the gaping nightlit windows—looking in on herself—as upon a stranger.

Later in the evening, as Mr. Walker snored softly under a heap of blankets, and the snow had ceased falling into the church, Eleanor rose in her blanket and went to the door. She stepped outside. The snow had stopped and the sky was bright and clear from one end to the other. The Milky Way shimmered like jewels. Across the way, Calvin Tripp's house stood in black profile against the snow-whitened trees beyond. She pulled her blanket wrappings about herself and stood stock-still, alive to the night, the immediate and the far, from the snow-bearded trees to all the universe, in its vast systematic glory, spread across the sky. She stood a long while in the doorway of the Wisdom Way church. From somewhere, a fox barked. Eleanor listened. She could feel the tears starting. She had, for the first time, distinct intimations of lonelinesses to come.

AT FIRST LIGHT, Mr. Walker harnessed Ben, and they started back. As they trundled west out of Wisdom Way, past the overgrown graveyard, and the turning in the road where yesterday they had encountered the bull, Eleanor was not inclined to look back. Her instincts told her that she would not come this way again.

Yesterday's storm left little more than three or four inches of snow. The morning sun shining on it set the road and nearby fields aglare. Had the snow come squalling an hour or two later yesterday, she and her friend would have continued on successfully to the lake—only to have arrived there at the most unfortunate time imaginable, shortly after that hour when the infant expired. Either way, her journey north was a failure and a mistake. Still, she wished to think that Evangeline would hear in time of how she had striven to come to her in the time of her troubles, and of the hardships she had met, and of the sorrow she had felt.

"I've often noticed," Eleanor spoke up at length, while examining her surroundings, "how different a landscape or countryside looks when one is traveling the selfsame road in the reverse direction."

"Well, they tell you, Miss Gray, when walking in deep woods," he said, "to look back behind you now and again, for that reason. So you'll know what it looks like when you're going the other way." He looked at her. "So you won't get lost."

Eleanor didn't respond at once. She felt inexplicably fragile this morning. She felt inwardly rattled. "Have you ever been lost, Mr. Walker?"

"In some ways or other, I suppose."

By midmorning, they had turned south through Cold Spring, and gone on past the Hewlitt place and the houses nearby. Within an hour, they had re-entered the forest, the profound world of massed hemlocks and cedars that had worked such an impression yesterday on Eleanor's senses. The sky overhead narrowed to a blue band, looking like a prodigious pail handle.

"Do you believe, Mr. Walker, that Evangeline will truly transport her baby to East Becket to be buried?"

"Well, if Calvin says that she said it, she said it. And if she said it, it will happen. That's what they're like. I'll say that in their favor. They never speak to no purpose."

The boughs of the hemlocks along the roadside were layered lightly with snow. The faintest breeze sent down a shower of snow dust. Ben's tail swept slowly to and fro, like a metronome clocking his hoofbeats, while the steel wheels of the wagon, going over frost heaves and stones jutting up in the roadbed, made occasional clashing sounds.

"As Miss Harrison said of them," Eleanor remarked, after a pause, "they do seem a hard people. I think that Evangeline Sewell is hard. But I don't admire her any the less for it. It brings her through things that would shatter another so young. The tragedy of her mother. A life lived in want. Her child dead in a day. Yes, I agree, Mr. Walker. She'll bring the baby down."

Eleanor was affected for a few minutes by the thrust of her own remarks regarding Evangeline's misfortunes, and her bravery, and the steeliness of her character. Secretly, she liked thinking of the Sewell girl as hard, unwavering, clear of purpose. Once or twice during the course of their wagon ride home, Eleanor found herself beset by graphic mental pictures of the other actually giving birth, enduring the agony of delivery. Each time, she cast it from her mind.

The last hundred yards of the road leading to the edge of the trees, to where the sky opened out over East Becket, recalled for Eleanor the look of the wilderness "door" into which she had passed yesterday, and back through which she would now debouch. From the cool, shadowy interior of the forest, the gap in the massed trees up ahead was indeed a perceptible slot. Eleanor remarked on it.

"I feel we are approaching a doorway, Mr. Walker—as between one set of things and another set of things. The dark and the hidden behind us, the evident up ahead. Forest and fields." Eleanor was staring out at the gulf of sunlight. "As my Latin teacher, Mr. O'Donnell, liked to say, 'And *that*, Miss Gray, is the he and she of it.'"

The Star Route man offered a related thought. "I get different feelings here when going different ways. Right about here," he specified.

"So does Ben, evidently." Eleanor smiled on noticing how Mr. Walker's horse had picked up the pace.

A moment later, the wagon rolled out into the sunlight. A fine layer of snow lay over the rocky pastureland like a linen tablecloth cast carelessly down. A blazing blue sky gave down torrents of light. Eleanor shielded her eyes.

"Thus," she said, with a poetic sigh, "do the Magi return to their valley fires, their journey a forfeit, their gifts untouched."

fourteen

AFTER **ELEANOR** had brought her things upstairs to her room, she returned outdoors. Alonzo Klaw had set up his easel on the porch by the back door, and was painting a winter landscape. Up the roadway to the east, Myron Walker was still in view.

"You should include the Star Route man and his horse and wagon in your watercolor."

"I was just admiring that! But it's too late, I'm afraid, for me to relocate the road in my picture. If I placed him upon it, it would skew everything else." Mr. Klaw gazed inquiringly all this while at Eleanor.

"The news is not very happy," she said, at last. "Mr. Walker and I never did reach our destination. There were blinding squalls. But Mr. Calvin Tripp told us what happened. Evangeline gave birth to a boy two days ago. He died yesterday afternoon. He never really took hold. He just couldn't hold on to the world. Mr. Tripp said that the baby strove every second and every minute to make it, but failed."

The look of intensity in Alonzo Klaw's face, as he absorbed Eleanor's meaning, matched her own.

"If you would tell Miss Harrison and the others," she added, "it would spare me having to do so. . . . Some things are almost harder to say than to hear."

He nodded his assent. "Where did you spend the night?" he asked.

"In an abandoned church in Wisdom Way. Mr. Walker was

very resourceful in putting us up. Under other conditions, it would have comprised a charming adventure."

"I understand."

"I know that you do, Mr. Klaw."

"The girl," he said, hesitantly, "is all right?"

"There's every reason to think that she's quite hale—more than just up and about. Altogether herself."

For a split second, Eleanor was tempted to apprise Mr. Klaw of Evangeline's intention to bring her dead infant down to East Becket for burial, but thought better of it. It would serve no foreseeable purpose. Besides, Eleanor treasured the unspoken confederacy she shared with the young woman from upcountry, even though she suspected Evangeline Sewell was not of a sentimental disposition.

"Mr. Tripp," she said, "remarked on the extravagance and beauty of the coat you sent her. He said that it was 'some coat'! Have you ever met Mr. Tripp?"

"Yes, I have," said Alonzo, as he reached and shook two or three paint brushes in a can of water. "There was an agricultural fair down in Otis. He was doing some forging."

"He is a very impressive man. With his great, long waterproof coat and furious beard!"

"I remarked him," said the painter.

"He has a look of history on foot," said Eleanor. "It was he who was to have fetched the midwife from Hinsdale, but he had committed some brash act or other up there, and thus made himself a figure of considerable interest to the authorities who maintain the peace."

Alonzo and Eleanor both laughed over her manner of characterizing Calvin Tripp's civic status.

"So," Eleanor explained, "Evangeline summoned Mr. Conboy, and sent him to get the midwife. That was several days ago, of course."

"Everett is back," said Alonzo. "But he has said nothing to anyone."

"He doesn't know anything," said Eleanor. "That is to say, he may know of the birth, but not of the baby's passing. He returned, I was told, two or three days ago."

"Strangest thing," Alonzo interrupted her. "Conboy is over at the Billings house. He 'opened' the Billings house."

Eleanor's eyes widened in perplexity. "I don't understand."

"Neither does Marjorie Treadwell, who told Alice about it. She saw the two of them up there—the man and the boy. She can hear woodchopping. There's smoke from the chimney. There's lantern light in the windows at night."

Alonzo Klaw was referring to the imposing red-brick house standing on the wooded hill adjacent to the ruins of the jute mill. Eleanor's thoughts were racing. Last night, Calvin Tripp stated that it was one of the Billingses up in Hinsdale that had arranged the midwife for Evangeline. Clearly, Evangeline had dispatched Mr. Conboy to Hinsdale with that understanding in mind.

"I think Evangeline is coming back to East Becket," said Eleanor. "I think she is coming back to that house. You, Mr. Klaw, having spent so many hours drawing her, probably know her as well as anyone. Has she ever spoken of the Billings family?"

"Never," said he. "But Alice says that Everett Conboy served in the war with one of them. They own a lot of property, you know."

"Yes, I have heard."

"She says that Everett's one-room shanty and the acre under it that he occupies were probably given to him by that man, as tribute for something he had done. He's lived in that little house about fifteen years. It didn't seem a coincidence to her, Alice said, that Everett took ownership of the place on the last day in May of that year. It was Decoration Day."

"Where did he live before that?"

"I'm a stranger here, like you. But it's obvious he has lived in these parts all his adult years, keeping to himself, scratching out a life." Alonzo smiled. "Where I come from, we would call Everett Conboy something more than a hermit and eccentric. The man is a bona fide Yankee crank."

"I have a suspicion that Mr. Conboy hails from upcountry!" Eleanor laughed. "He has all the earmarks."

While speaking, she examined Alonzo Klaw's work-in-progress. He had caught to perfection the blue sheen of the snow, the small copse of haggard trees in the distance, the immaculate sky. She looked out at the living landscape, from which by now Mr. Walker and his horse and wagon had vanished from sight.

LATER THAT DAY, in the hour before supper, Alice spoke briefly in private to Eleanor. "I am so sorry," she said, "that your trip north involved such hardship and such an unpleasant discovery."

"It was all to no purpose," said Eleanor. "I needn't have gone." She was visiting Alice in the kitchen, helping to get out the dinnerware. "Still," she added, "I am not sorry I went, even though we lost our way and were essentially balked at every turn." Eleanor took up a stack of plates, while falling into a sudden thoughtful mood, repeating to herself, "I will never be sorry for that."

While tying on her apron, Alice remarked on Eleanor's colleague. "William headed home this morning," she said. "He comes from a big family. They make a great fuss over Christmas. I've heard that they're all ingenious!" Alice stooped and took a galvanized pail from the cabinet under the sink. "One of William's brothers patented an invention for some type of contraption used on motorcars. Don't ask me what it is!"

Eleanor felt a tremor go up her spine at the mention of his name. For the life of her, she could not fathom the man's behavior. She could only wonder at what must have been transpiring in his mind during all these weeks—most especially, these last few days, when it was all but general knowledge that the birth was imminent.

Alice started for the back door with her kitchen pail, but Eleanor insisted on fetching the water for her.

Outdoors, a gloomy, late-afternoon chill invaded her clothing and set the roots of her hair tingling. She set the pail on the boards beneath the spout and rubbed her hands together briskly. She was shivering. As she reached and began pumping, the cold iron handle of the well pump stuck to the palm of her hand, as though it were reacting with resentment. She used both hands to work the pump. The wintry sky stretching south toward Blandford and East

Otis reminded her unaccountably of the sickly gray-white hues of the fishermen's catches back home, of the cod and halibut and such, in the fish stalls.

For a minute or more, her thoughts circled round the figure of her colleague. Try as she might, she could not imagine that the young Mr. Bayles was anything but responsible for what had happened—and for what was perhaps yet to happen.

THAT EVENING, after returning upstairs, Eleanor heard Mr. Chickering speaking out boisterously. He had not come to supper tonight. At the table, Miss Harrison had remarked playfully upon his absence. "Charles," she said, "went ahunting today!"

"This has been the longest winter day I have ever endured," he announced, aiming his remark at Eleanor coming toward him in the hall.

"On the contrary, Mr. Chickering," she said. "It is the next-to-shortest winter day."

"Shotgun in hand, I followed the trail of a wounded buck from one desolate ridge to the next, from one watercourse to another! Only Orion," he exclaimed, "could appreciate the futility of it. Believe me, I was more overmatched than ever was that Nimrod of the stars."

"I'm not sure about that," Eleanor said. "Orion carries only a club."

"Yes, but he has a dog, Miss Gray. He has a good-luck belt! And while he may not overtake his elusive stag, he never falls back. He never loses ground!"

Eleanor had grown very fond of Mr. Chickering. Tonight, in his woodsman high-cut boots, butternut hunting jacket, and the big-brimmed hat he sent scaling onto his dresser, he was every inch one of those men of the new century who had drawn from their former president, Mr. Teddy Roosevelt, something of his boisterous vitality. Mr. Chickering leaned his shotgun against the wall and began removing the scarlet shotgun shells from his coat, standing them in a squad on his desk. "I went out with eleven shells, and returned home with an equal number."

"Then how in heaven's name did you manage to wound your buck?"

"I didn't!" he thundered, turning to her. "I never even saw him."

"Then how do you know it was a deer, at all? How do you know it was a buck? How do you know he was wounded?"

"By the *snow,* Miss Gray. By the snow." Mr. Chickering lighted a second lamp, a big-globed Victorian affair, which, he claimed, was given him years back by the wife of the commandant at West Point. "Someone shot the creature up around the Boston and Albany train tracks, and apparently gave up pursuit. I, the greater fool, took it up. Not only took it up. Made it into a sacred quest. My father, who deplored all of it—hunting, fishing, trapping, and every other such primitive pastime—would have laughed himself into conniptions. Oh, how that man ridiculed me!" He laughed at the memory of it.

"If he did," said Eleanor, stepping into the room, "and I doubt very much that he did, it surely had a most salubrious effect on you."

Mr. Chickering peeled off his hunting jacket. "The conditions for tracking were perfect. Three or four inches of snow powdering the ground. Not enough to hinder the hunter on foot, but more than enough to leave an indelible record of the quarry in flight. Bloodstains big as silver dollars," he said, making a circle of his thumb and forefinger. "After the first two or three hours, though, the trail of blood grew faint, and vanished. I should have known by then. That was up by the old Brindamour logging camp. It was obvious, too, that his stride was opening out. Why," he added, "he's up past Lake Champlain by now. He's headed for the Arctic Circle. And having a good laugh at my expense."

"Do your failures always bring out such lively spirits, Mr. Chickering?" she inquired.

"Whatever the issue of my pathetic undertakings, a day in the woodlands is its own reward."

"I wish I could say as much for my own undertakings."

"I should have asked." Mr. Chickering's face altered instantly. "I have been so full of myself these past few minutes."

"Mr. Walker and I were forced to turn back, but learned from the blacksmith up in Wisdom Way that Miss Sewell gave birth two days ago, to a baby boy. He died yesterday. . . . He never made it, the blacksmith said."

Mr. Chickering stood motionless by his desk, a portrait in embarrassment.

"I am so sorry," he said, at last.

"There was nothing to be done for her. She had proper care. It was just as well that Mr. Walker and I failed to reach her. Had the bridge not been out at Wisdom Way, I think we would have arrived at her aunt's house at about the hour of the infant's death." Eleanor reflected briefly on that possibility. "She would have hated us forever."

Mr. Chickering's voice dropped to a whisper. "It was ever so decent of you to have gone."

Eleanor repeated herself. "There was nothing to be done."

"What did you think of the country up there?" he asked, in an apparent effort to change topics.

"I found it to be as you all said it to be. It's a bleak place. There is a dimension to it that I do not understand. I sensed a corrosive cynicism, which, I think, invests everything, Mr. Chickering. I think it affects the trees!"

"Interesting that you should say that. It is, in fact, the most acidic soil I've ever tested. There is a magnificent American elm standing at the center of Wisdom Way that turns yellow with autumn in July."

"I guess, then," she said, "if the earth is bitter, the people who live on her have every right to be bitter, too."

As Eleanor spoke, she had an abiding desire to confide in Mr. Chickering about her feelings for the other. It was a part of being human, she thought, to make a thing real by making it public, that a true secret is anathema to the social principle. She kept her tongue, however. "You are so late getting back," she said.

"I stopped at the general store for some notions and some lozenges, and I was enticed into downing a cannikin or two of Bob Treadwell's precious applejack."

"I thought your cheeks looked unusually rosy!" Eleanor piped.

With that, she stepped in, and handed Mr. Chickering his canvas rucksack.

"Did you make use of any of these items?" he asked.

"When we felt sure that we were lost, the compass confirmed it. It didn't point the way we should go. It merely indicated that the way we had gone was the wrong way to have gone. And, of course, we already knew we had gone the wrong way."

Mr. Chickering laughed over Eleanor's cleverness. "Should you ever become lost in our Eastern woodlands, Miss Gray, you have only to follow Mr. Thoreau's unerring advice. 'Walk downhill till you come to water, and walk downstream into the clear.'"

Eleanor replied with irony. "I think that I, more than most, should commit that simple formula to memory."

She was tempted to ask Charles Chickering if the Treadwells had said anything about Mr. Conboy having commenced work around the Billings house. But she saw no advantage in it. After returning to her room, Eleanor dwelt on the fact that she and Mr. Walker alone were conscious of an unfolding of events that was certain to create a scandalous stir. She wondered if her guarding of this knowledge was a violation in any way of her civic duties. Not that it would alter her behavior. She would never broadcast Evangeline's intentions, even if it imperilled her job. Smiling to herself, while taking Alonzo Klaw's pencil portrait of Evangeline from her closet, Eleanor likened herself to the heroine of a melodrama, languishing among aliens, but in secret receipt now of the impending descent of the unstoppable hero.

In fact, she would like very much to have been able to tell someone about the unprecedented feelings that came and went in her breast these days. She had always known herself to be a person of optimism and cheerful spirits, but she had never known emotions quite like these.

While musing thus, Eleanor sat, kneading her knees with the heels of her hands, staring into space.

THE FOLLOWING MORNING, not long after breakfast, she set out on foot for the Billings house, determined to discover from Mr.

Conboy and Justin what was happening. She made up her mind, too, that she would not be easily put off by Mr. Conboy's gruff ways. The news that she bore of the death of the baby conferred some special authority on her, as did the fact that it was she, Eleanor, who had actually given Mr. Conboy Evangeline's instructions that evening at the schoolhouse, and who had brought him Alonzo's coat to take with him. Nevertheless, Eleanor felt certain in advance that he would be more than reluctant to divulge anything of consequence to her.

The sky to the west this morning was roiling with gray tones, as though stirred up with a paddle. As she made her way past the pastures toward the bridge, she could hear the cattle lowing in a nearby barn. She was walking briskly. From the bridge, she could make out long delicate panes of ice that had formed along the edges of the stream below, and hemispherical shells of ice shimmering atop the stones and boulders exposed in the stream bed. On reaching the town common, she recalled the afternoon that Evangeline came plodding under the elms on her black horse. As often, Eleanor wondered how one so young could command such attention and respect from others. She wondered also how much of her own deep interest in the other might not have derived from that, from the responses of others to her. By the time she reached the cart road that led down to the ruins of the mill, she could hear the sound of hammering.

Evidently, it came from the wooded knoll opposite. Because of the trees on all sides, she noticed how the echo of the hammer seemed to come from all directions, or from no direction. It resounded this way and that in the branches overhead. After just a few more steps, she caught a glimpse of the rear of the red-brick house, and started up the hill toward it. Much of yesterday's snow powder had blown away, or been blown into declivities. She spotted the boy first.

He, Justin, was standing big as life atop an elegant-looking carriage. He was standing by the driver's seat, with one foot up on the dashboard. Seconds later, Mr. Conboy came into view. He came out the double doorway of the stable, carrying a strip of lumber in one hand, a hammer in the other.

"Look!" said the boy. He pointed out Eleanor, who was making her way toward them through the trees. As she got closer, she noticed a narrow gap in the floorboard of the carriage, which, clearly, they were repairing. More outstanding, though, was the look and condition of the small carriage itself. It was the sort of carriage that one saw on Sunday mornings in the wealthier neighborhoods back home. It was of a dark green lustre, with two brass lamps, and a raised black hood that sheltered the upholstered seat situated behind the driver. Eleanor smiled at the thought of how the reverend Howard Allen, with his fancy cabriolet, might have admired this one. Waving, Eleanor dealt Mr. Conboy an elegant verbal salute.

"Good morning to you, sir," she called to him. "I heard the report of your hammer on the wind, and knew beyond any doubt that you were performing good works."

He, the man before her, was less effusive. He just stared at her. Eleanor did a quick appraisal of the back of the house. While it certainly did not look lived in, there was nothing derelict or neglected about it. It was just empty. A latticework bower by the back door leaned to one side, though, and the rose vines that covered it were long dead, not quiescent with winter. The windows of the house glittered vacantly. A brick well situated by the carriage barn had been boarded up.

Before engaging Mr. Conboy, Eleanor gave herself quick counsel on two points. For one, she must respect the man's feelings for the young woman up north, and respect the fact that the mortal news about the baby might genuinely distress him. Second, however, she was convinced she would learn more about what was happening, and more about Miss Sewell's intentions, if she portrayed herself as possessing greater knowledge than she did. For all she knew, Mr. Conboy, when being told what had occurred up at the lake, would have reason to think that Eleanor's coming to him this morning would have definite bearing upon whatever he was doing. He could not help seeing her as Evangeline's emissary. As she walked up to the two of them, Eleanor endeavored to suppress the cheery manner she had just shown them.

She started right in. "I was up at Wisdom Way yesterday, Mr. Conboy, and I have some unfortunate news to pass on to you."

Mr. Conboy stopped in his tracks, his face an inexpressive blank. Justin Judd, standing atop the carriage, must have sensed his friend's alarm, however, as his eyes went back and forth repeatedly from Eleanor to the man. Eleanor stated the matter with formality.

"Two days ago," she said, "your friend Evangeline lost her baby boy forever." Eleanor felt her own heart contracting as she uttered the words. "He couldn't make it," she said.

She looked up at Justin, standing above them; he appeared not fully to understand. Mr. Conboy had meanwhile not moved a muscle. He stood by the wheel of the carriage, with his mouth open, his arms slack at his sides, looking quite transfixed. Unable to withstand the suspense of it, he put the obvious question to Eleanor, employing the gravest of tones. "What about herself?" he asked, drily.

Eleanor nodded. "She's altogether vigorous."

Mr. Conboy's relief was transparent. He ran his hand flat across his forehead. He looked up then at the golden-haired Justin, and at Eleanor again.

In her next remark, Eleanor struck a conspiratorial note contrived to win the man's trust. As Everett Conboy was about the most taciturn man she had ever met, she knew the point of her statement to be redundant. "I think we should say nothing to anyone, sir, about Evangeline's determination to return." With that, Eleanor glanced round at the house. She reflected in passing upon how exactly she might learn more about the purpose of Mr. Conboy's activities, and, of even greater interest, about the authority underlying them.

"Surely nothing should be said," Eleanor continued, further showing herself to be intimate with Evangeline's circumstance and plans, "of her resolve to return with the child. Because that is what she is resolved to do. She intends to bury the babe here. In East Becket. She said, 'That's where he came from, and that's where he's going back.'"

Mr. Conboy was still showing his relief that the bad news Eleanor brought pertained to the infant only. "You hear that, Jus?" he called to the boy over his shoulder. "She's up and about!"

Intuiting Mr. Conboy's happiness, Justin smiled radiantly. "I heard."

Here Eleanor paid Mr. Conboy a compliment that would further exhibit her knowledge of what was going on. "I learned," she said, brightly, "that it was you who made the trip up to Hinsdale—that Mrs. Richards, the midwife, was a good one—and that one of the Billingses, a man from your old regimental days, was most helpful."

For the first time in their short acquaintance, Everett Conboy showed an emotion. He turned ruddy with pleasure. "You learned all that?" he said, darkening.

"Yes," Eleanor added. "The blacksmith told me. He told me that if he had gone to Hinsdale, rather than you . . . that . . . well . . . he'd be in jail up there." Eleanor laughed outright.

Suddenly enlivened, Justin Judd contributed an observation of his own concerning Calvin Tripp, the blacksmith. "He broke bottles up there!" he cried.

On inspiration, Eleanor put a question to Mr. Conboy that would satisfy her curiosity. She spoke to him now with the quiet authority of one who had the right to know the answer, and who, in aiding Evangeline, might need to know the answer. The question required guessing. Till now, there was no substantial reason to conclude that Mr. Conboy's "opening" of the Billings house had any bearing on the young woman up north. But Eleanor could feel it in the electricity between herself and the man standing before her. There wasn't a grain of doubt in her mind. Evangeline was coming here.

"Since it's the case," she began, "that Miss Sewell may be coming back *earlier* than planned . . ."—Eleanor paused. She scrupulously avoided looking at the house. She held Mr. Conboy's gaze. "Will your preparations be finished on time?"

Mr. Conboy shot a telltale look at the house. "There ain't that much to do, Miss Gray."

Emboldened by his polite employment of her name, Eleanor persisted cannily. "I'm sure, Mr. Conboy, that Mr. Billings was specific about what was to be done, but I would guess that Evangeline had her own instructions for you."

Mr. Conboy gave Eleanor a quizzical look that persisted for seconds. He looked away at the trees, and looked back. "I don't know what you're talking about," he said.

Eleanor shifted ground instantly, attributing to the blacksmith something that Alice had told her about Mr. Conboy's acquaintanceship with one of the Billingses. "Calvin Tripp," she said, "implied that Mr. Billings might have assisted you."

Mr. Conboy continued to stare hard and perplexedly at Eleanor. This time, he was even slower in responding. The rising tone of his voice matched his bewilderment. "It all comes from herself!" he declared.

"Now, Mr. Conboy," she came back at him pleasantly, but thinking fast, "we all know that Evangeline needs to have got the authority to open the house in order *to* open the house."

"That's more than I need to know," he pointed out. "I only need to know to open the house. I do what she tells me to do."

Eleanor was staring deep into the man's eyes. Till now, she had been alive to Everett Conboy's singleminded devotion to the young woman. Here, for the first time, she saw a light burning in his pupils that seemed unaffected by what the eye itself was looking at. The mere thought of Everett Conboy's obsessive dedication to the girl set Eleanor's senses tingling. She would have said more, but Mr. Conboy turned away from her. He handed the narrow floor slat up to the yellow-haired boy, and prepared to climb up onto the carriage. Eleanor was left standing by herself.

"Mr. Conboy," she said, in an effort at humor, "I think that Evangeline Sewell has become like a local Joan of Arc. She has an observable following."

Without turning to her, Mr. Conboy—speaking not in humor, but from a near-perfect ignorance of history and foreign tongues—dismissed Eleanor with a final, gruff remark. "Joan of Arc was a Frenchman!" he said.

Eleanor nodded to that, pivoted on her heel, and started away, calling a pleasant farewell. "Good morning, Mr. Conboy. Good morning, Justin."

fifteen

ABOUT AN HOUR before noon of that same day, Eleanor laid eyes upon a most remarkable sight. She and Mr. Chickering had just come outdoors. They were on their way to the woodlot situated behind the town hall to find and bring home a proper Christmas tree for Alice's parlor. While Mr. Chickering excused himself and stepped round back to the toolshed, Eleanor waited under the elm tree by the road. For the past hour or so, she had marveled at the thought that Evangeline might have ordered Mr. Conboy to his task of opening the Billings house with nothing more substantial—or lawful—behind it than a willful spirit. It set Eleanor's nerves jingling, not because she feared the consequences of Evangeline's arbitrary decisions, but because she secretly admired the recklessness of it!

Eleanor was staring into the distance, lost in thought, when a carriage materialized from within the darkness of the covered bridge. She saw first the bobbing of the horse's head, but in nearly the same moment, above that, the crown of golden hair of the driver himself. She recognized him at once. It was the boy, Justin. He was standing up at full height at the dashboard, legs apart, reins in hand. As the carriage emerged into the wintry daylight, its brass fixtures and lustrous green woodwork seemed oddly out of place; it were as though the gleaming vehicle and its youthful driver had been abstracted from one landscape, or category of composition, and set trespassing on another.

"Will wonders never cease?" Mr. Chickering exclaimed,

speaking up from behind her. Reaching, he put on his little gold-framed spectacles.

The horse and carriage grew steadily in magnification, coming on between the open meadows approaching the crossroads, the boy standing proudly at the reins.

It was obvious to Eleanor that the carriage was empty. She could see the pale daylight shining in on the leather upholstery of the seat behind Justin. Not wishing to express anything of what she knew about the carriage, Eleanor let fall a pointless remark.

"They form quite a picture!"

"I recognize that horse," said Mr. Chickering. "I've hired him myself from Truman Rogers. He's a beauty. Look at the way he shakes his head."

"I am surprised," said Eleanor, maintaining her ignorance, "that anyone would entrust such a handsome contraption to a boy like Justin!"

"Oh, you are wrong," Mr. Chickering objected instantly. "The boy is a wonderful driver. A year ago this past summer, he drove sulky for Todd Trumbull in the trotting races out at the Great Barrington agricultural fair. He is very talented." Abruptly, Mr. Chickering interrupted himself. "Where the dickens do you suppose he's going?"

As he had reached the crossroads, Justin readjusted his footing and stance, and could be seen steering the horse round smoothly to his left onto the northern road. Eleanor was visibly enthralled by the colorful spectacle unfolding before her. "He looks like a charioteer from ancient times!" she brought out. While she could not divulge her secret understandings, it appeared certain that Justin was headed for the lake. He was headed upcountry to get Evangeline. As Evangeline would have had no way of getting word to Everett Conboy, Eleanor could only guess that he was following an earlier plan, that she had intended to come back by Christmas, with her newborn. And that Mr. Conboy—despite the baby's death—was obeying her to the letter.

"It's clear now what Conboy's been up to at the Billings place," Mr. Chickering concluded, putting his own construction on events.

"He's likely been hired to fix that carriage, and send it up to one of the Billingses in Hinsdale."

Eleanor said nothing to that.

Mr. Chickering took down his glasses. "Well, the boy won't get close to reaching Hinsdale before nightfall. He'll have to put up along the way."

It tickled Eleanor to picture Justin rolling on in the darkness of night, standing stiff-legged at the driver's seat, with the brass lanterns behind him to left and right casting their narrow separate beams past the horse's head onto the road unfurling in the forest.

As Eleanor and Mr. Chickering started out on foot toward the bridge, she glanced away repeatedly toward the luminous carriage withdrawing to the north. When the cast of the sunlight was just right, she could make out from afar the slot in the long black palisade of cedar trees where the road to Wisdom Way entered the wilderness.

For the balance of the afternoon, Eleanor was visited by a medley of feelings. One moment, she would suddenly fill up with nervous apprehension at the thought of Evangeline's imminent return, and of her own secret knowledge of the fact—and of the even more notorious secret, that she was bringing her baby with her. At other times, however, she grew unexpectedly buoyant, and would have to stop what she was doing, and take a long breath to restore her equilibrium. She guessed that this was how persons felt when the return of a dear one could be measured, at last, in hours and minutes.

In the pine woods behind the town hall, Mr. Chickering asked Eleanor to select the tree of choice for Miss Harrison's parlor. She picked out a Scotch pine and watched with some amazement as her companion, swinging a long, glittering scythelike tool that he called a brush hook, felled the little tree with one blow. The severed tree literally leaped into the air.

"How accomplished you are," she exclaimed.

"A brush hook is a wondrous device," said the other, beaming. "My father taught me how to do that."

"I'll pull it home for us," she said.

"Not a chance," said he, grasping the pine by its lower branches, and starting away with it. As they walked toward home, traversing the common and heading down to the bridge, Eleanor wished there were some way she could broach the subject of her upcountry journey. She wished she could tell Mr. Chickering about the travails of her trip. Try as she might, she could not find the words. Also, she felt in her heart—though probably mistakenly—that others were by now looking upon her with a rising bewilderment, at the way she had exercised herself over the troubles of a sixteen-year-old truant unknown to her.

That afternoon, Eleanor went across the road to the schoolhouse to fetch home one of her books. But she knew on entering the front door that what she really wanted was to sit at her desk and write down her thoughts. Before beginning, she stuffed the stove with paper and kindling, set it aflame, then carefully inserted a log. For probably the first time, she acknowledged that the greater part of her fascination for the young woman derived somehow uninterruptedly from her imagination. She had never once spoken to the girl. In fact, she had seen her only rarely—and even then in mere glimpses. The notes written back to her were the products of a blunt, unschooled, really quite presumptuous spirit.

She cleared the top of her desk, set out a sheet of writing paper, and took up her pen. She would write some words to Miss Sewell, although she knew at the start that she would never transmit the letter to the other. Eleanor liked to think on paper. She lived in words. "Dear Evangeline," she wrote. "I would never have guessed at summer's end, four months ago, that I had embarked on a journey that, in the weeks to come, would introduce me to hallways and rooms inside the house of my heart that I had never known were there. I think it is because I am a stranger here, dining at a strange table and sleeping in a strange bed, far from home and all things familiar, that these secret chambers—these spaces—have become known to me."

Pausing, Eleanor put her fingers to her forehead and closed and opened her eyes. She was moved and troubled by the thrust of her own words. From where she sat, she could look out the back windows of the schoolroom all the way to the line of the forest. Her thoughts went again to the sight of the handsome green carriage coming out of the shadows of the bridge this morning, with the golden-haired boy standing straight upon it, clutching the reins. It was dreamlike. Like a jaunting car being sent out to collect the fabled maiden.

She loosened her cardigan sweater, and looked about herself. She had the odd sensation that she was following the track of her own thoughts unspooling on the paper before her. As though one part of her were leading another part, step by step, word by word, toward some hidden revelation.

"I do not understand," she wrote, "the meanings of my own discoveries. It has been for me like discovering a riddle that was not there before, but whose solution is nonetheless at once required."

Eleanor paused to dip her pen. Her heart was rising inside her.

"Only thereafter, during the passing of autumn, as I learned more about you, did I come to possess a full appreciation of your qualities—of your look and bearing—your magic. Now," she went on, "I am sitting in the schoolhouse, awaiting your return tomorrow with great anticipation. While I worry about what might befall you here, or what bold, impulsive acts you might yourself commit, I find myself all but giddy at the prospect.

"Last of all, I grieve for you, and for the indescribable loss you have sustained. I have prayed many times for the safe arrival in that kinder Other World of your beloved infant, who, I have been told, fought so hard to stay here with you in this one."

Eleanor got up and walked about the room. It was cold in the corners, and cold by the windows, and the floor grumbled icily underfoot. She stood, gazing away to the north, when she was visited by a most unusual notion. During the fall, William Bayles had taken his class on an all-day bird-watching expedition. They had made use of a pair of field glasses, she recalled. Eleanor had an impulse to get her hands on them. Without hesitation, she let herself into the other classroom. Following a brief search of the oak cabinet at the back of the room, she located them behind a stack of maps and paper supplies. Returning to her own room with the big field glasses in hand, she was reminded of the day she had steamed open Evangeline's letter to Howard Allen! It was so uncharacteristic of her. At the window, she raised the binoculars to her eyes and began slowly adjusting the lens. The results were remarkable. The doorlike opening of the road into the far-off wall of conifers materialized with astonishing clarity. Eleanor performed some mental calculations. Justin would reach the lake before nightfall. At dawn tomorrow, the day before Christmas, Evangeline Sewell would take her place in the carriage, with the coffined baby, and the fated journey would begin. By noontime, or a little while thereafter, she would appear to view, coming out of that opening in the wilderness. Eleanor lowered the field glasses, then raised them to her eyes once more. Tomorrow, she thought, she would come here to the classroom and hold vigil for the first appearance of the elegant carriage and its upcountry passenger.

FOLLOWING AN EARLY SUPPER, Alice Harrison and her guests set about the trimming of the Christmas tree. They were joined in the front parlor by several neighbors, as well as two or three members of Alice's choir. Even Mr. Walker showed up for the occasion.

"Wherever you find Eleanor," Miss Harrison teased the Star Route man, as she asked for his coat, "Myron Walker is bound to appear."

"It's well known," Ivy Trumbull confirmed, playfully, "that Myron is more than smitten with our young teacher."

"I don't hide the fact," he replied, beaming. Mr. Walker looked unusually flushed, as perhaps from alcohol, as he stood under the archway in the front hall. The atmosphere was festive. With lamps burning in all the downstairs rooms, and fires going in both of the fireplaces and in the big black parlor stove, Alice's house was unusually bright and cheerful. From time to time, Alonzo Klaw put a roller in the piano, and pedalled out a Tin Pan Alley tune. Mr. Chickering was stringing popcorn.

"When called on to perform a task requiring even the most rudimentary manual skills," he said, holding up his needle and thread in one hand, and a kernel of popped corn in the other, "one can appreciate the artisans of old. The Cellinis," he said. "The Ghiberties."

"Well, the artisans of old," Eleanor spoke up, as though defending Mr. Chickering against his own depreciations, "knew next to nothing of what you know about water tables!"

"The engineers out of Rome who raised the aqueducts of Spain, Miss Gray, knew more about water tables and the shifting of waters from one place to another than I shall know in a hundred years."

"Or need to know," Alonzo put in.

"Or need to know," Mr. Chickering agreed, pleasantly.

"I understand," Ivy Trumbull addressed Eleanor, "that you and Myron ran into a storm up north."

"Yes...," Eleanor answered her cautiously, hesitating. "But Mr. Walker was equal to the depredations of nature every inch of the way, every hour and minute."

"My goodness!" exclaimed one of the choir ladies, admiring Eleanor's reply, and turning to her companion. "How brilliant the girl is! We're all such clodhoppers out here."

Ivy Trumbull maintained Eleanor's eye. "The news was very unhappy, wasn't it?"

Eleanor could not read Ivy Trumbull's thoughts or intentions. "It could not have been unhappier."

Evidently, others in the room had overheard the oblique allusion to Evangeline Sewell and the news of the death of her baby, as the room fell quiet. Eleanor had a sudden dread that Mrs. Trumbull, who was a forceful lady, might suddenly put questions to her that she could not evade, and that would leave her revealed as a meddler, or worse. She excused herself.

"Mr. Walker," she said, stepping away, "we have hot cider. Would you help me bring it from the kitchen?"

Myron followed her through the central hall.

"I have something to report to you," she breathed out, upon entering the kitchen. "I am quite sure that Evangeline is coming tomorrow to East Becket. Justin Judd went north earlier today with a carriage." She was speaking at close range. "I saw him go."

Eleanor's words riveted Mr. Walker's attention.

"Todd Trumbull," he said, "is intending to go over to the Billings place in the morning. He wants to talk to Conboy. He wants to know what he's doing there."

"Why would he choose to do that?"

"Because he's justice of the peace here, is why."

Eleanor reacted with alarm. "This is dreadful," she said. "It's obvious that Evangeline is headed for that house. I spoke to Mr. Conboy this morning. He's following her orders! Mr. Walker," she exclaimed. "I think it was Evangeline who ordered him to open the house. Not someone else. I think she was intending to come back to East Becket tomorrow, the day before Christmas, with her living baby, and she sent him here on Wednesday to prepare things."

Even as she spoke, Eleanor marveled over the temerity of it, the defiance. She pictured the action in her mind of Evangeline's summoning Everett and the boy to her side, and dispatching the two of them to do her bidding. She would show them her mettle. She would bring her Christmas baby into their midst.

"Everett Conboy knew nothing, of course, of the baby's death. That was why I went to him this morning," Eleanor explained. "He was working on the Billings's carriage, getting it ready—a wonderfully handsome vehicle, if ever there was one. The news was clearly upsetting to him—behind that inexpressive face—but had no effect, I'm sure, on his carrying out her commission. I feel certain of it, Mr. Walker. She commanded him to send her that carriage today. He's obsessed with her. But we must warn him. The *justice of the peace?*" Eleanor asked.

"Truman told me he hired Conboy a horse."

"Was there . . . an exchange of money?" she asked. "I don't imagine Mr. Conboy has had a dime in his hands in years."

"He doesn't like or trust money. That's a fact. He promised Truman 'some fair work in return.' Those were his words. Because it's Christmastime, Truman hired him his 'prancer.' His personal favorite."

"It's important that Mr. Conboy be warned! What will happen if Evangeline arrives, with the baby, and no one is there? It could be even more tragic."

A commotion at the front door of the house, followed by a rising uproar of greetings, and a sudden wave of cold air that curled into the kitchen, announced the arrival of the East Becket Atheneum's evening guest speaker. Eleanor stepped sidewise to look up the hall. The man in question was a divine. He had a name that caught Eleanor's attention. She had heard her father speak of him, characterizing him as a "platitudinous villain" who liked discussing pastoral communes in public, but who in private railed violently against the "hordes of Canucks" that were destroying eastern Massachusetts. The man's name was Hezekiah Hicks. He was a deep-voiced, well-dressed, blustery-looking man, with sidewhiskers and furry eyebrows, who claimed to be the boyhood bosom friend of Oliver Wendell Holmes, Jr., as well as an expert in New England wildflowers and a phrenologist. Eleanor's father lumped Hezekiah Hicks together with his own father, as a pair of fast-talking, but not-so-deep-thinking preachers who thrived on the lecture circuit. "Trained bears," he called them. Eleanor smiled to recall her father's remark about Mr. Hicks's wildflower searches: "Hezekiah Hicks can't ascend to the pulpit or the rostrum without trailing some arbutus behind him."

Alice could be seen leading Mr. Hicks up the front stairs to his lodgings for the night, while the others trooped into the crowded parlor. In short order, everyone would march across the road to the grange hall, where they would be joined by many other townsmen. Notwithstanding the flurry of activity, Eleanor was not diverted from her determination to warn Mr. Conboy. However, Mr. Walker was not helpful.

"Everett and I don't speak," he said, with finality.

Eleanor gave a nervous shudder. "Will you take me there later tonight?" she implored him. "I don't want to feel that I was in possession of a certain knowledge, of which I *am* in possession, and see a consequent disaster take place before my eyes. . . . I have forebodings, Mr. Walker."

"We'll leave the grange hall early. I'll think of a reason. I'll run you over there," he said, "and wait for you."

"You are so understanding. You spoil me left and right."

At that same moment, Eleanor wheeled around at the sound of a familiar voice, and was startled to discover Calvin Tripp, the Wisdom Way blacksmith, advancing in the hall. He entered the doorway of the kitchen.

"Mr. Walker!" she piped up, brightly. "Look who is here!"

"I thought it was you!" the blacksmith exclaimed.

On the occasion of their original meeting, Calvin Tripp had made a lasting impression on her. He struck her as being one of those solid, strong-minded types who are capable of making history. Quite naturally, she saw him also as the embodiment of that upcountry domain that had fostered the likes of Evangeline Sewell. As previously, he was wearing his long, tan-colored waterproof coat. His beard glistened in the light.

"You are the last person I would have expected tonight!" Eleanor's happiness was transparent. She was collecting glass cups onto a tray. "You have come tonight to listen to Mr. Hicks?"

"That I have," said the other. "He and my mother, and my mother's brother, were raised as orphans in the same house. About fifty or so years ago. They said that Hicks and my uncle, as teenaged boys, got to arguing about John Calvin—which is where I got *my* name—and that neither one of 'em would stop, and never did stop, and haven't either of them, stopped talking since."

Eleanor was instantly charmed. "But you seem yourself a man of few words, Mr. Tripp," she said, over her shoulder.

"My uncle used it up. Talking was like money, my mother said. One person in the family could spend it all. My mother sometimes didn't talk for a week."

While delighted with his words, Eleanor was wondering all the while if Mr. Tripp was somehow alive to what Evangeline was planning. What if his arrival was something more than a coincidence? While she knew the thought to be insupportably romantic, Calvin Tripp seemed to her the sort of advance element, the lonely outrider, that will appear out of nowhere on the eve of great developments. If so—if he were here to look after and safeguard his young "countryman"—which was less than likely—he would be a formidable player.

Mr. Walker bore the punch bowl of hot cider into the front parlor, Eleanor trailing a step or two behind him with her tray. The liveliness of the room sent her spirits leaping once more, unexpectedly, as had been happening all day. Through the front windows, she could see the lighted grange hall. Visitors were arriving. Near at hand, Alonzo Klaw was helping the aged Mrs. Sampson to attach little tin candleholders to the boughs of the tree.

"Mr. Klaw," Eleanor teased him, "does your faith permit you to share in the joys of Christmas tree trimming?"

"My faith, as you call it, does not prohibit me from doing anything that is both festive and silly. Whether," he added, "you be Polynesians or Hottentots. If you suddenly started chopping coconuts in two with firemen's axes, I would fetch me a fireman's ax faster than you could say, 'Praise the Yuletide!'"

"Whatever his professions may be," put in Charles Chickering, "Alonzo's a Universalist Unitarian at heart. One of those for whom all things and views are accepted as valid, and all things and views simultaneously rejected."

"I had heard," chirped Eleanor, who loved always witty bantering, "that Mr. Ralph Waldo Emerson was too extreme in that direction *even for* the Universalist Unitarians. But if what you say is true, I think they could have found a seat for him in their parish house. They could have seated him, while at the same time *not* seated him."

"Correct," said Alonzo, "as he would not have been there."

"He would not have been there if he wished to be there, and been there if he wished not to be." Mr. Chickering's eyeglasses flashed in the lamplight.

"This dialectical broth has grown too spicy for me," said Eleanor. Turning, she saw Miss Harrison descending the front stairs. Her guest, Mr. Hicks, descended behind her, talking without letup. Eleanor's gaze moved about the room, and settled on Calvin Tripp. She enjoyed looking at him. He was far too young to be called patriarchal, and too full-blooded and mature to be thought of as a swain. He was, in that way, she supposed, quite perfect as a speci-men male. He was talking soon thereafter to Hezekiah Hicks. That is to say, he listened while the other rattled on and on with ob-vious relish, doubtless upon some abstruse subject. Alone for a sec-ond with her thoughts, Eleanor indulged herself with a fanciful picture of Evangeline Sewell making an appearance in the room. She imagined how she must look—or might look—in glimmering holiday satins—with her snowflake complexion and the long pane of wheaten hair—and that look of strength about her. Evangeline was an inch or two shorter than Eleanor, but made up for it in her posture and the look of solidity. In the portraits that Mr. Klaw had done of her, Evangeline's hands were closed lightly, as in fists. By chance, during this interlude, Calvin Tripp caught Eleanor staring at him, and grinned at her from across the room.

When the tall clock beside her began to chime seven, the laugh-ter and rising conversation all about her was such that she could scarcely hear it. Its soft tolling seemed to be coming to her alone, as in bearing her a secret, from very far away.

IN THE GRANGE HALL, Mr. Hicks regaled the assembly with story after story of his boyhood, while reading out "snippets" from his weekly newspaper column. He grew increasingly charmed by his own voice as his recitation continued. He grew redder in the face.

Eleanor whispered an amusing remark to Alonzo Klaw. "The dictionary meaning of the word 'voluble,'" she said, "is not elastic enough from this night forward."

Mr. Klaw proved equal to Eleanor's witticism. "I," he said, in a subdued voice, "have had to rearrange my entire outlook and phi-losophy of life five or six times in the past forty minutes."

Eleanor suppressed her delight over Mr. Klaw's rejoinder by placing her fingers to her lips and pretending to have found amuse-ment at some invisible spectacle elsewhere in the room. Alice Har-rison and others were putting out sandwiches and cake and bever-ages on a long table at the rear of the hall. Mr. Walker appeared then beside Alice. He spoke to her, then beckoned to Eleanor. She followed him to the coat room.

"I said that you were worried about young Justin Judd, that you thought he didn't look well."

"But, Mr. Walker, Justin is upcountry! He's not in East Becket."

"Well, I can't think of everything," said Mr. Walker.

Eleanor laughed. Going outdoors, she took Mr. Walker's arm. The yard beside the grange hall was crowded with wagons and carriages. The blanketed horses stamped their feet. Overhead, the moon was wafer-white behind slips of clouds as Mr. Walker steered onto the road.

"I'll bet Ben is happy to get started."

"I don't know about that," Mr. Walker offered back. "Ben's a sociable horse, who likes being with other horses." He looked over at Eleanor. "He likes their company."

After passing under the covered bridge, and rolling up the gravel incline and on past the church and town hall, Eleanor became alive to the pervading brittleness of the wintry night. She could imagine things snapping in two. She thought about animals deep in their burrows tonight. According to Alice, the first big snow was late coming this year. Alice had spoken about it as though it were a train or streetcar late for arrival.

"I'll walk you up close to the house," said Mr. Walker, minutes later, as they approached the mill ruins. The Billings place lay hidden in darkness on the opposing hill. Eleanor comprehended his meanings. "I am not frightened of Mr. Conboy," she said.

"He is not a bad man," said Mr. Walker, "but he is an unpredictable man." He fell silent momentarily. "I'll be in shouting distance."

"I feel like we're conspirators."

For a full minute or so, Eleanor's thoughts turned to Evangeline, and to the deep satisfaction that she felt whenever she conceived of herself as the other's confederate. And it was not as though the dilemma that entangled them were something inconsequential. To the contrary, it was a drama from life at its fullest. She reflected on a future time, long after the resolution of these difficulties, when she and Evangeline would look back upon these days — upon this hard passage — with great sympathy and understanding. Eleanor could even picture it, a casual scene. She could envision the two of them sitting at a fire, herself on a straight-back chair, her hands in her lap, clasping a book perhaps—and Evangeline, a few years older than now, looking very at one with herself, sitting back in a big wing chair, with her legs crossed. It titillated Eleanor to picture the other young woman holding a glass tumbler in hand, with a measure of whiskey in it! She smiled to herself. She had a suspicion that an upcountry girl was no stranger to hard liquor, and Eleanor was more than sure that she could be accepting of a little intemperance in her friend, insofar, she thought, as we all have our failings.

"Mr. Walker," she spoke out. "I have become an incorrigible romantic. My friends at school wouldn't know me."

Within minutes, after tethering Ben, the two of them were making their way on foot up the wooded hill toward the house. As they approached, the pale echo of a lantern or oil lamp could be discerned in one of the windows.

"Have you ever been in the house?" she asked.

"No," said the other, "nor have I ever been this close to it before."

"I am going to peek in that window." Eleanor touched Mr. Walker's arm as a sign that he should go no further, and continued soundlessly on her own. Secretly, she was grateful that her dear friend had accompanied her tonight, as it somehow emboldened her to confront Mr. Conboy. She stepped directly to the window. Everett Conboy was sitting at a table in the middle of the room. The room looked to be a spacious pantry. Shelves reaching to the ceiling were laden with kitchen implements, rows of tin canisters, cheese boxes, magazines, and various indefinable articles. A pine cabinet stood beside a low wooden vegetable bin. At either end of the room, she noticed, was a swinging door, giving Eleanor to realize that the room was a butler's pantry, a chamber that communicated between the kitchen and dining room. On the table in front of Mr. Conboy stood a copper oilcan and wrench. He was holding in his hands what appeared to be a bicycle sprocket and chain. Lest he suddenly look up and spot her, Eleanor departed quickly along the side of the house. Mr. Walker stood among the trees nearby, watching, as she stepped up and knocked loudly on the back door.

Mr. Conboy responded in short order, yanking the door open with visible impatience. He was obviously a fearless man. The ray of his lantern lighted Eleanor's face, while obscuring his own.

"It's important, Mr. Conboy, that I speak with you."

He stood glaring at her. "About what?" he said.

Eleanor experienced a rare flash of anger. "I insist you ask me indoors!" she pronounced. "You have no idea what I am about to say, nor do you dare not *listen* to what I am about to say."

For a second, as he lowered the lantern, Mr. Conboy appeared noticeably chastened. He stepped back, and Eleanor entered the house.

"I have come here at great inconvenience to myself," she went on. "There is an Atheneum meeting in the grange hall, and I was compelled to sneak away in order to come here. I don't know why you are so brusque with me. Our interests are similar." It pleased Eleanor to add, "We are both resolved to help Evangeline. There is no denying it, Mr. Conboy. We are both serving her interests."

Everett Conboy set the lantern down on an enormous black cooking stove, its nickel fittings glittering in the light. Slowly, the room about them assumed form. They were standing in the kitchen.

"I," she emphasized, "am helping her in my way, just as you, I know, are doing your best."

Eleanor knew that she had the man's attention now, and was conscious of her "schoolteacherly" manner and tone of voice. Equally impressive to her was the realization that she could speak to him about Evangeline—could actually *show* her devotion and concern—as to no one else on earth. There was something exhilarating in that. She enlarged on her point.

"Two days ago, I tried getting through a blizzard to reach her, up in Wisdom Way. This morning, I made my way to you with the bad news of what had happened. Mr. Conboy," Eleanor insisted, "it's time you trusted me."

As before, Mr. Conboy stared at her. He had a face that Eleanor thought of as saturnine. He struck her as a glum, distrustful man.

"Why didn't you tell me this morning that you were sending Justin upcountry in that carriage?"

"You didn't ask," he said.

Eleanor showed him her consternation. "What a remarkable thing to say!" she cried. "How could I possibly have asked about something that could not have been predicted on any basis, by any human being alive? Others who saw the boy departing assumed that he was headed for Hinsdale, to deliver the repaired carriage to some member of the Billings family. I, however, knew that to be very unlikely, Mr. Conboy." Eleanor stared back. She waited patiently for his reply. She knew he could not risk challenging her will at this moment, as she had not told him yet her reason for coming to him tonight.

"You guessed right," he muttered, after an interval, in a baritone growl.

Eleanor's pulse quickened. "Yes, I did guess right! And I guessed further that you were following earlier instructions."

"I do what I can, when I can," he grumbled back.

As the lantern light spread through the kitchen door into the hallway, Eleanor perceived chairs, a low table, and what looked like a long oriental runner on the floor.

"Mr. Conboy!" she remarked. "Is this house furnished?"

Slow to respond as always, Everett nodded. "Some parts of it," he said.

In the next moment, while taking in her shadowy surroundings, Eleanor was visited by a sudden tremulous sensation. She couldn't suppress the following question. Her voice turned hollow. "Am I *trespassing?*" she asked.

Mr. Conboy glanced away with an expression of unconcealed cynicism.

"Am I breaking the law by being here?" Eleanor added, in the same tone.

"You asked to come in," he said.

"What a magnificent evasion!" she cried. She didn't know whether to laugh or to worry about her status before the law. Her mind went reflexively to other moments of questionable behavior, such as some of the intricate little lies that she had let fall, or the half-truths, or the silences that amounted to prevarications—not to say the steaming open of Evangeline's letter to Howard Allen on that autumn afternoon (which seemed an age ago), or, most recent of all, her taking home William Bayles's field glasses from the science cabinet in his classroom. For the first time, Eleanor sensed that her involvement in Evangeline Sewell's plight could become a public fact, something quite blameworthy, even though she was not sure what variety of social transgressions she, as schoolmistress, had actually perpetrated. She only knew that if Evangeline Sewell created a violent mess of things, in taking out her revenge upon the citizenry of East Becket at large, or upon some young man in particular, she, Eleanor Gray, in the wake of it all, would be left standing at the very centerpoint of the damage. The townsfolk would be scandalized. She would be openly vilified. What is more, the culpability attaching to her would be an exact exponent of the possible severity of Evangeline's actions. By this odd devolution, she was at the mercy of events yet to come, the character and extent of which would be determined by Evangeline herself—a person now known by Eleanor to be hard at the core, strong-minded, impetuous.

Grown nervous, Eleanor got to the point.

"I heard it said tonight that Mr. Trumbull is going to 'look in' on you tomorrow morning."

Everett Conboy grunted. "The man is a galoot."

"He is also justice of the peace," Eleanor observed.

"He won't come around me."

"That's reassuring to hear," Eleanor came back at him, "if it were true, but there is a strong chance that he will indeed look in on you."

"You didn't hear him say that!" Mr. Conboy's eyes flashed with menace.

"How are you so certain of yourself?"

"He doesn't come around me," Mr. Conboy repeated. "We go a long way back, him and me. I go where I please, and he stays out of my way every step I take."

Eleanor studied the expression of dark resolve in Mr. Conboy's face.

"He don't worry me."

"That's obvious, Mr. Conboy. But what happens if Miss Sewell arrives here tomorrow, as I have every reason to think she is going to do—with her dead infant!—and comes into this house—*moves* into it—as I know in my bones she is going to do—and violates the law—and is perhaps even apprehended—and might conceivably be prosecuted? It's too awful to think about. She's suffered enough unpleasantness already."

Mr. Conboy took a different view of things. "You are forgetting something."

"Indeed, what am I forgetting?"

"You're forgetting about herself," he declared. His dark eyes penetrated Eleanor's gaze for a long moment. "She told me to repair the carriage, send the carriage, and wait. I repaired the carriage, I *sent* the carriage, and—"

"Yes, I know," Eleanor interrupted, "and now you're *waiting*."

"Her word's enough for me," he threw out, "and if you're what you say you are to her, it ought to be enough for you."

"I wish I had your faith."

Abruptly, Mr. Conboy complimented Eleanor with an unexpected observation. "You had enough faith and enough love to go into a blizzard for her!"

Startled, Eleanor reacted with a surge of pleasure. "Mr. Conboy! What a lovely thing to say." She was visibly moved. "Of course, you are right. Now, that you've said it, I see it, and am sure you're right. I was forgetting about . . ."—Eleanor hesitated—"about herself. She, after all, is the principal player. I shall have more faith, you'll see."

In the gloom of the kitchen, Eleanor blushed to the roots of her hair over what she was about to say. The words came out softly, with conviction. "I do, of course, love her."

Everett Conboy looked away with a smirk. "Then act it!" he said, and took up his lantern.

AFTER RETURNING from the Billings place, and after the Star Route man had gone home, Eleanor and the others joined together in completing the tree trimming. Hezekiah Hicks was still across the way in the grange hall, holding forth. While Mr. Hicks would naturally be headed home in the morning—tomorrow being the day before Christmas—Alice had invited Calvin Tripp to stay over as a guest in her house for the next two or three days.

"I have plenty of room," she said, "and you'll add so much to the good feelings in the house during these special days." Alice turned to Eleanor. "Wouldn't you agree," she asked, playfully, "that Calvin will be a welcome addition?"

Eleanor smiled at Mr. Tripp, who stood facing her, his hands in his pockets, his back to the fire.

"He will be a very *handsome* addition," Eleanor replied, flirtatiously.

From behind the tree, Charles Chickering exclaimed, "My love of Eleanor Gray goes now unrequited."

"And mine," put in Alonzo. "She's found herself an upcountry love, I'm afraid."

Alice Harrison agreed with Eleanor. "Calvin does cut a figure."

To everyone's surprise, the elderly Annie Sampson, who was sipping her cider, put in her own observation on Calvin's looks. "*He ought to be painted!*" she suddenly cried.

Mr. Tripp gave a shout of laughter. "Last time I got painted, the law put up posters of me. To me," he said, "getting painted is getting stone-blind drunk."

"If you ask me," Eleanor joined in, laughing. "I think that our upcountry neighbors have a noticeable liking for distilled spirits. I met a lady in Wisdom Way, named Joanna Morgan, who made no secret of it."

"Joanna's cough syrup is eighty proof," Calvin said. "She could hold her own with Diamond Jim Brady."

During this while, Eleanor was wondering if Mr. Tripp was aware of Evangeline's intentions, and was eager to speak to him alone. From outdoors, the sudden screech of Hezekiah Hick's laughter on the winter air heralded his arrival in the house.

"The man is quite a talker," Calvin allowed.

"Oh, he is more than that," Eleanor amended. "He is loquacious to the point of mental derangement. I've noticed, too, that if the person to whom he is speaking *speaks,* the volume of his own broadcasting goes instantly to another register."

Minutes later, Eleanor apologized to Calvin for her remarks. They were standing in the kitchen. "I know he is a relative, or close, lifelong intimate of yours. I hope I was not being disrespectful." She spoke in low tones.

Calvin smiled. "Carry on," he said.

"I wanted to ask you if you saw the boy, Justin Judd, today?"

"I did," said the other. "He was driving quite a fancy affair. Went right by my place. Didn't stop, didn't even look over."

Eleanor decided all at once to trust Calvin, and to appraise him of her dilemma. "Obviously," she said, "he was headed for the lake. Have you told anyone what Miss Sewell is proposing to do? Because I have not."

Mr. Tripp regarded her at length. As before, she noticed the inky shimmeriness of his beard, and his steady gaze. She wondered how he would reply to that.

He made a face. "We don't do that," he said.

Eleanor's eyes widened. *"'We'?"* she said.

"What's Evangeline Sewell's business is Evangeline Sewell's business. But I don't mind your asking."

Eleanor nodded, but felt he had avoided her question. "You see, Mr. Tripp, only I know that something quite extraordinary may come to pass—something unacceptable to all—and one part of me insists that I reveal this information to the people I live among, while the other part of me instructs the opposite." Eleanor sought to frame her point of view in more passionate terms. "Evangeline and I are only remotely connected. I have written her, and she has written me. But I think I know her well, and I think she knows me well. And I have taken her side of things—even though. . . ," Eleanor hesitated, "her ideas of justice and moral rectitude may differ wildly from my own. I have to take her on faith. And I think I have done that." Eleanor felt her feelings surge. "I wouldn't betray her for the world."

"Well, she will never trick or deceive you," he attested.

"I believe that utterly."

He teased her then. "We don't do that," he repeated, and smiled at her. "We are not inventive enough. We're not deep thinkers."

Eleanor glanced toward the central hall to confirm their momentary privacy. "I would like to tell you in confidence that Everett Conboy and Justin have opened the Billings house on instructions from Miss Sewell, and are obviously waiting for her to arrive with the infant. It was I who had to tell Mr. Conboy what happened to the baby. He didn't know. Behind the cold facade, he was clearly distressed. I have a fear, Mr. Tripp, that he and the boy are trespassing, and that Evangeline is about to do the same. She strikes me as altogether brash, bullheaded, reckless—as very 'up-country,' that is—and would probably welcome a fight of some sort. She feels wronged, Mr. Tripp. And she has been wronged."

"I don't see it as your worry, Miss Gray."

Realizing that she had grown excessively emotional, Eleanor sought to collect herself. "Is there a possibility," she asked, "that Evangeline may have the approval of one of the Billings family?"

Calvin was staring at Eleanor, with a wondering light in his eye. "If she does," he replied, presently, "she didn't say so."

On inspiration, Eleanor changed the subject. "Mr. Tripp, I happen to know where Miss Harrison keeps a bottle of brandy. I'm going to get you some." Eleanor was back from the pantry in a second with a squat, square-faced bottle in hand. "It will be our secret," she said, and poured a measure of the colorful liquor into his glass.

Mr. Tripp showed her the glass in the way of toasting her. "To a lady full of secrets—whom I'm glad to know." He drained his glass.

IN THE FRONT ROOM, Mr. Hicks was excited to learn that Eleanor was the granddaughter of Eugene Lloyd Gray, the author and itinerant preacher. "Is your own father a man of the cloth?" he asked.

"He is an engineer," she replied, politely. "He works at the Held McDermott cotton mills in Fall River."

Hezekiah Hicks stood in the middle of the room, looking very flushed from the briskness of the air outdoors, as well as from his own hearty spirits.

"I never met your father," he boomed back at her, "but his father would have been an exemplum on earth impossible to match."

Eleanor experienced an instant flash of resentment. "If you have never met my father," she said, "you are the poorer for it, sir—for *his* father was but a shadow in the fields next to *my* father."

Eleanor was standing perfectly straight, fidgeting with the satin ribbon at her throat. She disliked what he had just said.

The Christmas tree was by this time fully decorated, and Charles Chickering was lighting the tiny candles that set all the glass trimmings aglow.

"*Our* exemplum," Mr. Chickering remarked, amiably, to Hezekiah Hicks, "is the daughter and granddaughter of those two men."

Alice Harrison had a suggestion of her own. "Calvin," she declared, "would you like a glass of brandy?"

"I would not say no."

"What an original idea!" said Eleanor, in a return of good spirits. She showed Mr. Tripp an affectionate expression.

"And you, Alonzo? And you, Charles? Anyone?" said Alice.

"I'll drink from your cupboard," said Alonzo, "if only to mark the pagan holiday. The winter solstice!" he cried.

"As will I!" Eleanor joined in. "To the feast of lights everywhere."

UPSTAIRS, LATER, with the heated soapstone in place under the blankets and quilted counterpane, Eleanor slid into bed. She got comfortable. She had her journal in hand.

She began:

December 23, 1910. While I have been very jittery all day—and it has been a very *long* day—experiencing sudden anxious jolts—still there is no one alive who should be deprived forever of an experience like mine. I am sure it is a very special time for me, one that may never be duplicated. Tonight, by some inexplicable transposition, I feel that it is I who require rescue—that I am the maiden in distress!—and that my hero is coming. I cannot deny any longer that my love of Evangeline Sewell is not just a form of "schoolteacherly" compassion.

Eleanor paused in her writing, as tears of confusion had begun gathering in her eyes. She set her pencil carefully to one side and put her hands to her face. Lest someone suddenly knock at her door and discover the state of her feelings, Eleanor reached and extinguished the oil lamp.

sixteen

F ELEANOR longed for a romantic picture of the returning Evangeline, she was not to be disappointed. It came to pass, as though supplied by the Fates themselves. She had guessed the carriage ride from the lake would take about four hours, and that Justin and Miss Sewell would appear to view, therefore, some time before noon. Earlier that morning, Eleanor had walked out past the common to Marjorie Treadwell's general store to purchase some little gifts to put under the Christmas tree, and had remarked on the cold purity of the day. It were as though the air itself were holding its breath. Her heels rang to the frozen ground underfoot.

On leaving the general store, she glanced off in the direction of the Billings place, and recalled in that same moment how the reverend Howard Allen would likely be passing this way at noontime on his way up to Cold Spring, for tomorrow's Christmas services. She wondered if he and Evangeline might not encounter one another, therefore, on that upcountry road—and what he, the clever young minister, would make of that development. Of Evangeline and her dead infant—about which he could have known nothing yet—headed south into East Becket! The words of Evangeline's first letter filtered through her mind. "Then I will come back," she wrote. "Then we will see who is strong and who is weak."

By ten o'clock, or a few minutes on, Eleanor had returned to her room with her parcels. She put William Bayles's field glasses in her satchel, with two or three textbooks, and started downstairs, going down the back way. Calvin Tripp was sitting at the kitchen table, drinking coffee and eating pie, when Eleanor appeared. He was talking to Alice Harrison about horses. "I had a sorrel once," he was saying, "that voted for president!"

"Mr. Tripp!" Eleanor exclaimed gaily, stopping in place. "One never knows what you're going to say next."

Alice laughed along with them.

"It's true as it gets," he said, and held up his hand in oath. "Her name was Trudy Belle. She was an enrolled Republican up in Middlefield."

"Did she walk to the polls alone, or in harness?" asked Eleanor, while admiring the way Calvin Tripp sat at the table, solidly, with his feet splayed, his elbows out.

Mr. Tripp laughed. "She mailed her vote. It was for McKinley, I think."

"She told you so?"

"She couldn't talk, Miss Gray. She was a horse." As he spoke these words, he raised a piece of blueberry pie to his lips on his dinner knife.

Eleanor reacted with astonishment at this mannerism, but said nothing. Her mother had told her once that all Northerners were Yankees to people in the South, and that Yankees were New Englanders to people in the North, but to New Englanders, Yankees, she said, were people who ate blueberry pie for breakfast—on a knife. It gave Eleanor a squeamish feeling.

ARRIVING IN THE SCHOOLHOUSE across the way, Eleanor stood on a chair and set the wall clock going, timing it to Alice's kitchen clock. It was a quarter to eleven. That done, she pitched in and made herself a fire in the stove. The back windows of the schoolroom looked out onto the northern pasture, all the way to the black line of the cedars in the distance. By now, as the hour of Evangeline's return actually drew near, Eleanor found it hard to credit that the carriage would in fact materialize. Standing at the window, she lifted Mr. Bayles's binoculars to her eyes, adjusted the lenses, and focussed on the narrow opening in the trees where the upcountry road erupted to view.

As often lately, the surreptitious nature of her actions set her nerves on edge. Her fingers shook. She had become like a spy in the midst of the people who paid her wage and entrusted their children to her. Other times, though, it made her giddy. She thought of the notes she had exchanged with Evangeline, of the coat she had sent her, of the night spent snowbound in the abandoned church, not to say her latest clandestine errands to the irascible Mr. Conboy.

She stood at the window, with the field glasses lowered in her hands, her eyes glazed with a dreamy, preoccupied light. In the twenty-year record of her days on earth, today seemed the most momentous so far. Returning to her desk, Eleanor removed her coat, sat, and opened a book. The idea of sitting vigil for Evangeline appealed to her. And if the other did not return today, to carry out her "ideas," she would return tomorrow. Or, if not then, on the following tomorrow. There was something mortally predictive about Miss Sewell. That she was coming back was like something ordained in the schedules of the constellations.

Eleanor had not very long to wait. She later imagined that she had anticipated the other's appearance prior to any sensible contact. She couldn't remember having got up from her chair, and gone hurriedly to the window. She saw nothing in the field glasses. The line of sunlight at the foot of the mile-off trees was unbroken by any detail. Then, like an apparition, the vehicle gathered form in the shadows. Eleanor, her heart beating, was squinting, and grasping the glasses tightly in her fingers.

After a second, the green glittering carriage burst into sight, coming out of that doorway in the trees, into the light. Eleanor could hear her own breathing. The gold-haired boy, she noticed, was sitting. With the magnification, she could almost make out his features, his expression. And Evangeline was there. The sun coming from Eleanor's right illuminated part of the passenger seated under the hood behind the boy—the shoulder and arm of her black coat, the side of her neck, a long, broad strand of her cornsilk hair. They were coming at a trot. Evangeline's black mare, she noticed, was tethered to the back of the carriage, trotting along in tandem. Eleanor stood stock-still at the window. She had never witnessed a spectacle anywhere near so gripping to the eye and the imagination as the vision formed on the lenses of her binoculars. The formality of it! The beauty of the carriage, the gold-haired driver, the brisk pace!

She could see Justin's face clearly now, although he had turned his head, as in listening to something his passenger was telling him. Then he stood up from his seat. Clearly, he had just been enjoined to do so.

Eleanor shivered at the thought that Evangeline, sitting back in the shadows, had ordered him to his feet. Adjusting the lenses fractionally to compensate for the distance narrowing between them, she focussed the field glasses upon the boy. The deadpan look on Justin Judd's face would have dignified an accomplished charioteer. One would never have guessed from the look of him that the boy-driver was in any manner impaired. He stood wide-legged at the dashboard, proud, with head erect. The horse was indeed, as Mr. Chickering pointed out, something of a prancer. As for the mare, following at the back of the carriage, she wove rhythmically from side to side, sometimes swinging out of view altogether. Repeatedly, Eleanor tried to make out Evangeline. By the time the carriage had covered half the distance from the wall of the forest to the crossroads nearby, the shadows inside the carriage had begun to dissipate. Evangeline was sitting in the middle of her seat. Her posture was perfect. Her hands and face were separating themselves now from the dimness of the interior, like a developing photograph attaining clarity in solution. Short of breath, Eleanor brought down the binoculars.

The thought of the infant, the dead boy, riding with her suddenly dismayed Eleanor, and compelled her to realize the banality of her own passions and daily life. If, she imagined, she lived in the world a hundred times, she would never find herself at the center of such troublous events. Hers would always be the part of on-looker. It was sobering to recognize as much.

Now, she could hear the carriage—could hear it coming—the muffled echo of steel wheels and the icy report of the horses' hooves. She raised her binoculars. This time, Evangeline showed up clearly in magnification. She sat unmoving beneath the shiny, lacquered hood of the carriage. She seemed not even to be blinking. Eleanor remarked under her breath, "How beautiful."

The carriage was not more than two hundred yards away, when a horse and wagon slid unexpectedly into view in the periphery of her sight. It was Mr. Walker. He was coming toward the intersection of the roads, toward the schoolhouse. To see her reaction, Eleanor focussed at once on Evangeline's face. She could see—practically *hear*—her ordering something of the boy. Justin turned his head, then turned back. But Eleanor *saw* the command! She had yelled something. It was not difficult to deduce its intent, for the boy looked straight ahead of him, his face a mask of glass. "Drive on!" she had said. Or, "Don't speak!" Or, "Don't stop!" A quick imperative! Something not to be argued, or even thought about—just as the brilliant green carriage swung into its arc at the crossroads and they rolled on rapidly past Mr. Walker. In the next instant, Evangeline and the carriage shot from view.

Instantly, without a moment's thought, Eleanor let herself into Mr. Bayles's classroom next-door, the windows of which faced west, and trained the glasses anew on the retreating vehicle, headed for the covered bridge. The tall black mare trotted behind. Eleanor gave out a moan at the sight of a small box sitting at the back of the carriage, directly behind Evangeline. Mr. Walker, in the meanwhile, was drawing near. Before going outdoors to call to him, Eleanor trained the field glasses a final time upon Evangeline Sewell. The wintry sunlight pouring in at the back of the carriage ignited clearly the yoke of her black coat and the long colorless tail of hair.

Eleanor put the field glasses in her crocheted bag and went out to meet her friend.

"Mr. Walker," she exclaimed, in suppressed tones. "She's done it. She's come back."

The Star Route man stepped down from his wagon onto the frosty grass. Eleanor's eyes followed the distant carriage. As it rolled on into the shadows of the covered bridge, the goldenrod glow of the young driver's hair winked out like a flame.

"She didn't come alone," said Mr. Walker, significantly.

"I saw!" said Eleanor, turning at his words. Clearly, the small wooden box riding aboard the carriage had transfixed their attention. "What a cross for her to bear. Not just for now, or today, but in all of time future. I would like so much to do something for her, Mr. Walker. And yet, I feel constrained—all but sworn, really—to stay back and say nothing." On impulse, Eleanor indulged her feelings of ardor. "We have, I think," she said, "an unspoken understanding, Evangeline and I."

Mr. Walker surprised her with his next remark. He nodded in the direction of the departed carriage. "She'll be talking to that young minister from Otis about now."

"Howard Allen?" Eleanor exclaimed. "He's here?"

"He's up at the Treadwell's. I just saw him. He was buying some holly berries and silver pine cones to decorate his fancy go-cart."

Before Mr. Walker had completed his last utterance, the bell in the far-off church tower commenced tolling. The crisp air resonated with it. It was noon. "I should have remembered," Eleanor said. "He always gets here by twelve o'clock the day before his services up in Cold Spring. He told me so. If they do speak, Mr. Walker—if she does stop for him—he is going to be more than startled by what he discovers."

ELEANOR KEPT TO HERSELF that afternoon. As much as she tried to busy herself with chores, such as wrapping her little gifts in Christmas foil, the presence of Evangeline Sewell, barely a half mile away, magnetized her thoughts. She was certain that the rumors were flying by now. How could it be otherwise? It would not have been possible for Evangeline to carriage her way to the brick house on the knoll without having been seen. Twice, Miss Harrison's telephone rang, and Eleanor listened as best she could from the stair head. As there were so few telephones here, she felt sure it was Ivy Trumbull calling. Eleanor strained to hear, but failed to isolate even one significant phrase. One thing was all but certain, though: It was unlikely that anyone in East Becket could even have guessed about the box Evangeline had brought with her, and its pathetic cargo. She and Mr. Walker knew about it, and Mr. Tripp might readily have guessed at it.

From time to time, Eleanor experienced a sudden shortness of breath. She felt restive and unnerved. It was not just the luridness of what was happening—nor the uncomfortable knowledge of her own secret understanding of what was happening—that set her so on edge. It was the bare fact that Evangeline was here. Her presence in the town was like a lodestone that put an electromagnetic charge on the air. She could picture Evangeline at this moment striding through the rooms of the Billings place—giving instructions to Mr. Conboy—dispatching Justin on errands—doubtless anticipating her actions to come.

Eleanor stood a long while in her window, looking down at the kitchen doorway where she had first set eyes on Evangeline.

As the afternoon wore on, the sky turned from slate blue to a gun-metal gray. By four o'clock, the eastward yawning shadows of the trees and the roofline of the house were drawing in the dusk. Going downstairs with her coat, Eleanor encountered Alice in the hallway below.

"I suppose you have heard the news," Alice declared, with embarrassment.

"Yes," Eleanor anticipated her. "I was in the schoolhouse, and saw her arriving."

Alice winced with discomfort. She appeared shame-faced for the sake of the young woman. She was toying with a collection of several keys dangling on a black ribbon about her neck, while appearing at a loss for words. "Why would anyone do such a thing?" she remarked, at last. "It isn't just outlandish, for her to come to town on the day before Christmas. It's mysterious. It is also unbelievably thankless. Evangeline Sewell has been practically a ward of our town since the day she started school. We have boarded and sheltered her at our own expense for nearly ten years."

Thinking rapidly, hoping to avoid open questioning, Eleanor sought to inject an innocuous reply. Her sense of being deceptive brought a blush of color to her cheeks. "Maybe she wishes to shock people."

Alice disagreed with that notion. "No. I think she is not like that. She is quite indifferent to the opinions of others."

In a change of subject, Eleanor remarked on the fragrant smell of the cooking coming from the kitchen. Alice smiled appreciatively. "Annie is keeping me company," she said. "She helped with the dressing, and insists on preparing the cranberry relish." Alice's expression grew nostalgic. "Today was always my favorite day of the year."

"Mine, also," said Eleanor. "I think it is both the merriest and the most hopeful of all days. I'm going now to the Treadwells' store, but would be pleased to help when I get back."

"Oh, we are well along! Everything is splendid this year, you'll see."

At the door, Eleanor raised her heavy knitted scarf over her head like a shawl, closed and buttoned her coat, and pulled on her big green woolen gloves. Twilight was coming fast. By the time she reached the bridge, it was nearly impossible to make out the boulders or the splashing icy waters below. In the distance, the town common was filling up with darkness. The stately elms that presided upon it stood like Brobdingnagian giants, up to their waists in rising black waters. It was to be a moonless night.

As she strode on briskly past the church toward the general store, Eleanor could not help gazing off in the direction of the distant knoll, even though the Billings house could not be seen from this angle and distance. Eleanor wished that she could just continue on, and climb the wooded hill, and knock on the door. She wished for a day to come when such an innocuous thing to do would be as commonplace as saying hello. Tonight, the red brick colonial standing among the hardwoods was more like a fortress, or citadel, in which the magnetic upcountry girl had installed herself, than a local historic house. At every step, feelings of intimacy toward her secret ally coursed through her breast. How nearby she was! Of one thing she was certain: A day was fast coming when she and Evangeline Sewell would meet up. It would be a very special occasion, she was sure of that. What such an hour might mean to Evangeline, she could only guess; but she hoped against hope that it would be an hour long remembered by her, also.

At the Treadwells', Eleanor spotted instantly Reverend Allen's two-wheeled cabriolet. It was parked outdoors at the back of the house, tilted forward onto its shafts. It stood underneath a tar-papered lean-to type shelter attached to the stable. A lighted window at the rear of the house illuminated it. The fact that Howard Allen had not continued north to Cold Spring today—as he must surely have planned to do on setting out this morning—could mean only one thing. That he had been intercepted, and—incredibly!—had elected to skip tomorrow's church services. Before Eleanor could reflect on the point, she heard footsteps approaching along the side of the house. It was the young clergyman himself.

"Reverend Allen!" she said, in greeting, and removed her hand from the door latch of the general store. "It's me," she said. "Eleanor."

"You frightened me!" he tossed out, airily.

"Frightened you?" she countered, pleasantly. "It's you who are skulking round in the shadows."

"I am not skulking, Miss Gray. I am doing the work of the world." He held up a burlap sack. "Oats!" he said.

"Where is your horse?" she asked, and stepped away from the Treadwells' door. She kept her voice down.

"They are not for my horse. They are for another horse, and *another* horse."

Eleanor nodded. "I see."

At close range, the minister seemed more surprised upon encountering her than his cheerful exclamations might have signified.

"I know what horses you are talking about," she added.

The minister, however, did not stop walking. He came brushing past her. His behavior struck her as rude. She called after him, employing his given name. "Howard!" she said. "What about your parish up north? What will they do tomorrow morning?"

He replied over his shoulder, as he headed out to the road. "I have another parish." He was vanishing by then in the darkness, stepping round a great shadowy lilac tree at the foot of the pathway.

She called again. "Is it a *parish of one?*"

The young man was gone. His rudeness left Eleanor smarting. For perhaps the first time in her life, she felt distinct stirrings of jealousy. There was no way he could have heard about the fate of the baby, but he could have known that Evangeline planned on returning to East Becket today in any event. After all, he went up-country every week. For all Eleanor knew, he might have visited her up there. Eleanor had to acknowledge that Howard Allen might have been a good deal closer in Evangeline's heart than she could hope to be. It gave her a bitter taste. She did not like having invidious feelings toward another human being, but could not help envying the young clergyman's proximity to the other. If Eleanor had proprietary feelings about Evangeline, she felt she had earned them. She had held high the lamp of good faith all this autumn. She pictured the two of them indoors together, with a fire going in one of the big marble fireplaces, and Howard falling all over himself to ingratiate himself to her—yes, and she susceptible to his glib tongue! For he was very clever.

Even more to the point, if he had made up his mind to cancel his holy duties tomorrow in Cold Spring, mightn't Evangeline Sewell respond with a depth of pride over his skewed priorities—at having undermined his sacred calling—at having appropriated his highest motives to her own gratifications? Because there was no denying that had happened. He was fetching oats for her horse!

Eleanor had been walking along slowly all this while, in troubled spirits, but not toward home. She was pacing the other way, in the direction of the knoll. The emotions roiling inside her were not, she knew, those of a disappointed friend. These feelings were weightier than that. They absorbed her thoughts. Nonetheless, she had to admit, it was not all unremittingly bad. There was a pleasurable reverse side to it. She had never felt so quickened by life. There was even a dark pleasure to be taken in the idea of how she would enjoy showing deference to the youthful upcountry girl. The teacher as pupil, the pupil as teacher. That, she knew, would gratify Evangeline's nature.

Eleanor was startled from her dreamy reflections by a metallic clinking sound that shot through the darkness, followed after a second by a narrow beam of light swinging in a sudden arc through the trees on the knoll ahead. Someone was coming down the hillside. The ray of light came from the narrowed lens of a lantern, that was obvious. She discerned the sound of their footsteps in the frozen leaves, then spotted their two silhouettes. Mr. Conboy's long, loping stride instantly identified him, as he made his way forward with dispatch. Justin, coming hurriedly in his wake, was carrying a shovel over his shoulder. The long handle of the shovel reached above the two night-lit figures like the sprit sail of a fast-moving skiff. They passed within ten yards of her. Eleanor stood still, breathless with surprise. She was standing in the open, in plain sight, perfectly still, as the man and boy marched quickly by, following the dancing pencil of light. She watched them step out onto the roadway, the light of the lantern swinging to and fro like a pendulum.

There was such audacity in it. For the intent was clear. Mr. Conboy and his fast-stepping, gold-haired companion were on their way to dig a grave in the frozen earth. As Evangeline had "opened" the house, likely with no permission, she was now going to open the most consecrated earth in all the township, the graveyard of the church. That she had ordered the eccentric pair to their task would surely strike the townspeople of East Becket as the most profane act of all. Eleanor, for her part, saw matters differently. She saw Evangeline, for better or worse, as a young lady of considerably ingenuity, not to say bravery. Who else—especially of her young years—would have the courage to stand up to all?

Headed back toward the general store and common, Eleanor kept to the shadows at roadside. Ahead of her on the road, the light was extinguished, but she saw the two of them heading in at the churchyard gate. She heard the icy report of the iron latch of the gate. The graveyard stood on the hill behind the church. She caught one glimpse of Everett and the boy headed up the graveyard road. They materialized in silhouette on a distant rise amid trees and dark headstones, then subsided from sight, with only the oarlike shovel wavering against the night sky. Then, it, too, vanished.

MISS HARRISON'S CHRISTMAS EVE TABLE was laden to capacity with food and beverages, including an array of pretty serving dishes that she only set forth at holiday time. The heart of the table was decorated with candles and a delicate porcelain vase containing a dark plume of evergreen sprigs. Charles Chickering did the honors with the carving knife, then removed the gleaming turkey to the sideboard. All were present, save William Bayles, of course, who had gone home. Alonzo Klaw wished to toast Alice.

"Oh, let me do that, please," said Eleanor, thrusting back her chair, and rising to her feet. She took up her glass of apple cider. "I have never proposed a toast, but I've never had such good reason to do so as tonight. With your permission," she said.

"By all means!" Alonzo waved his hand deferringly.

"I could not have dreamed in the closing days of last summer," said Eleanor, "back in the time before my leaving Fall River, what a wonderful world *I*—while being no Samuel de Champlain or Brigham Young—was about to discover." She turned to Alice Harrison. "I have not rehearsed any words, or given even a moment's thought to making you a speech, Alice, but I believe you are everything a lady should be, or could ever be raised up to be. You are modest, generous, loving, and forbearing of the flaws and frailties of others."

Mr. Chickering applauded softly. "Bravo."

Eleanor rested her left hand affectionately on Annie Sampson's shoulder, as she continued toasting Alice. "I hope I am not being impolite to anyone, or too regionalist, in saying that I think you are the living emblem of our matchless New England history. You make me so proud." Eleanor's eyes filled with tears. While she realized that her feelings of the moment were mixed with the perplexing emotional entanglement she felt for Evangeline, her admiration for Alice was indisputable. The words came easily. "I have spent quite a lot of time and thought considering what a modern woman should be all about. There is certainly a new age coming for us. You can feel it in all the cities of America. If I had to choose a road to the future, a road leading to the future American woman, whomever she may be, and whatever qualities she may possess and portray, or a road leading to *you*—I would be beside myself—in a perfect quandary—to form such a decision—despite," she said, "all of my heartfelt protestations over the injustices that women have endured." Eleanor turned to the three men at table. "I hope I am not offending you."

"Some things require saying," Alonzo allowed.

"Mostly," said Mr. Chickering, as in agreement, but with a little reserve in his tone, "many of these popular movements are appropriate to the new era."

Eleanor had turned, and was smiling now at Calvin Tripp, as she anticipated a characteristically original response. (As before, she liked the way he was looking up at her.)

"I make tools," he said. "I shoe horses. I hammer things that can't hammer back. My opinion, ladies, isn't worth five cents. The world out there," he gestured, "changes without my changing it, or trying to change it, or trying to stop it from changing."

Miss Harrison was beaming all the while over the attention being shown her. She laughed pleasantly. "Calvin can get around a question better than any man or woman in the Berkshire hills!"

Mr. Tripp, while turning his eyes to his plate, concluded his thoughts. "If things were up to me, I'd keep things as they are."

Eleanor nodded in satisfaction, then raised her glass once more. Her eyes shone wetly. "To Miss Alice Harrison, the heart and soul of this secret valley, this green and pastoral town, this blessed house."

Eleanor put Mrs. Sampson's brimming wineglass of cider in her hand, and all raised then their glasses in toast.

"I could listen to Miss Gray orate for hours and days," Alonzo rhapsodized, as Eleanor returned to her chair.

Alice squeezed Eleanor's hand. "You are the most brilliant person I have ever met. I think the new century is safe, and our great and fair nation safe—with a generation such as yours—with persons like you—to guide it."

Mr. Tripp let fall a playful, provocative line. "Fall River makes good women."

"So long as they keep axes out of their hands," Charles Chickering joked back.

All had commenced dining by now. Eleanor helped Mrs. Sampson add a serving of butternut squash to her plate, and buttered her bread for her.

"You would be a wonderful subject to paint," Alonzo remarked abruptly.

"No," said Eleanor, "I have no qualities worth preserving on paper or canvas."

Alonzo disagreed, while holding a forkful of bread dressing aloft. "You are quite beautiful," he said. "You are beautiful to look at. You stand beautifully, and walk beautifully, you have a beautiful nature, and you speak with inspiration. Alice got it right." He looked to the other men. "The new century is safe."

Eleanor's feelings let go. Just like that, she set down her bread, and put her hands over her face. Her emotions were uncontrolled. Mrs. Sampson saw what was happening, and put her arms around her. Eleanor leaned her head instinctively onto the elderly lady's shoulder. "I am making a spectacle of myself."

"She's homesick," said Calvin.

Eleanor nodded, but without taking down her hands. "Yes, I suppose so."

"I have a new subject matter to introduce," said Mr. Chickering, in an effort to restore equable spirits. "Has anyone seen the sky tonight?"

"I have," said Eleanor, straightening. "It's moonless."

"Moonless," said Charles, "but not a cloud moving across it from here to New York State. The man with the white beard and reindeer has clear sailing tonight—all the way."

DURING THE BALANCE of the supper hour, no one at Alice's table so much as mentioned the name Evangeline Sewell. While the omission was conspicuous, Eleanor was not surprised. It was often the custom at festive times that certain unpleasant subjects be tacitly proscribed. Eleanor wondered how they would all have reacted if they were aware of the inflammatory dimension of the thing. Of the coffined baby, or the already accomplished fact of Mr. Conboy's digging a grave out there. The knowledge left Eleanor feeling queasy inside. It made her all but complicit somehow; and so far as she could tell, Mr. Tripp was not informing anyone of what he knew, or of what he might at least have guessed at. It occurred to Eleanor for the first time that these several figures were all of them outsiders—Evangeline, Howard Allen, Mr. Tripp, Mr. Conboy, Justin, and, of course, herself. Together, through the person of Evangeline, or led by Evangeline, they seemed on the threshold of defiling something. What was worse, of them all, Eleanor alone was resident here. Her East Becket host admired and trusted her. While she dined at her table, she kept secret counsel. She gathered information. She sent notes. She saw herself in her mind's eye standing in the schoolhouse window today, with her field glasses trained upon her returning hero, the cold and resentful one, coming back to settle differences. It made her into a spy of sorts, and might later bring down on her the wrath of those who had kindly taken her in and trusted her. Hers was an invidious part. She sought a name for it, and it came to mind. It was the whited sepulcher.

Upstairs, she had a moment alone with Calvin Tripp. She had gone up to collect the little gifts she had wrapped for the Christmas tree, and met him in the hallway. He was carrying an ironstone pitcher.

"I have an unusual question," she said. "As you know, I have chosen to keep secret certain intelligences that have come my way—or, frankly, that I have sought to obtain. I needn't tell you what they are, as you already know what they are."

Eleanor was aware of a dark tangle of lights in Mr. Tripp's eyes, as if he might even have been pleased by her dilemma. But she could not be sure.

"Am I doing right," she said, very quietly, "in being as reluctant to speak of it as you are?"

Mr. Tripp's response did not surprise her. He was often terse to the point of being enigmatic. He stood flat-footed before her, smiling intimately. "Who'd know better than you?"

Eleanor nodded matter-of-factly. "I think she hasn't many people on her side, Mr. Tripp. She's been alone up north all this while. She has some moral right in her position. Even," she added, "if what she intends doing may be ill-advised."

"Who can know?" he said.

Eleanor tried then a different tack. "Am I helping her, would you say, by keeping quiet?"

"It can't hurt her," he said.

Again, Eleanor saw the dark smiling lights swimming in his eyes. In her next breath, though, she astonished herself.

"Am I wrong to show her my loyalty and my love? I mean," she amended, quickly, "am I wrong to place her above others?"

The glow of the Palladian window at the end of the hall spread a milky panel of light along the floor. The voices of those in the downstairs parlor arose through the stairwell. Calvin touched a finger to his beard, as though mulling a reply. Eleanor would have said more, but heard a flurry of activity at the front door below. She recognized the voice of the visitor at once.

"It's Mr. Walker!" Eleanor excused herself at once, and started downstairs.

The Star Route man, looking up at her, was outfitted in his most eccentric costume: a full-length rabbit-skin fur coat, a voluminous affair, which reached down to the tips of his boots, and a big matching rabbit fur hat.

Eleanor was immediately charmed. "Alice! Come quickly to the front door!" she cried. "You won't believe your eyes. It's Mr. Walker—back from the Klondike!" On impulse, Eleanor went to him, and kissed the Star Route man's cold cheek. "You always surprise me. You are a true original, sir."

Mr. Chickering appeared in the arched doorway of the front parlor. "However he may look, Miss Gray," he pronounced in a big voice, "he's your gentleman caller!"

"And altogether welcome!" Eleanor echoed.

Alice, coming along the central hall from the kitchen, called forward to the three of them. "When Myron turns out in his furs," she remarked, happily, "you may be sure that winter has begun."

"It's a fact," said he. "The icehouse pond out by the old Mayberry place froze up solid last night. You could walk an elephant across it this morning."

Eleanor's spirits were sailing. "Mr. Walker is indeed my beau," she said, turning at the waist to face them all. "My confidant and my beau."

"Half the time," he observed, "I don't know what she's saying, but I like the way she says it." Mr. Walker was beaming at her. His affection for Eleanor was transparent.

Charles Chickering injected an amusing thought. "Well, you did spend a night together."

"That's true, isn't it?" she remarked back.

"Yes," said the Star Route man, "though there was a horse in the room."

Miss Harrison contributed an unlikely observation, which started all laughing. "I don't think Ben will compromise you, Myron."

"Would you like some hot cider and cinnamon?" Eleanor asked.

"I've just stopped for a few seconds," he added, "to warm my feet, and to give you all my best wishes for Christmas."

Minutes later, Eleanor followed Mr. Walker outdoors. As he removed the blanket from Ben, and climbed up onto his seat, she told him about Mr. Conboy and Justin. "It was just after twilight. They had a lantern and shovel, and entered the churchyard."

Eleanor watched as Mr. Walker pulled on his mittens and took up the reins. He gave no sign of replying to the news, but stared at her a long moment, as though trying to interpret the passion in her eyes. The night wind moved her hair. She spoke to her friend in confessional tones.

"Mr. Walker," she confided, softly, "she is in my thoughts all day. She interrupts whatever I am doing."

seventeen

IN CHURCH the following morning, she made up her mind to pay Evangeline a visit. After all, it was Christmas Day. Eleanor was schoolmistress here. She had a moral right to project herself into situations where other persons might be loath to go. A few months ago, Evangeline Sewell was sitting at her desk in the East Becket schoolhouse, a pupil like any other. By law, she was still a child. Eleanor could walk up to the door of the brick colonial, therefore, and ask after her, or, in the event Evangeline came to the door, expect to be admitted.

In the meanwhile, the little white-haired minister had been at the pulpit nearly thirty minutes, rambling on with considerable charm about the journey of the Wise Men, and of how he, Reverend Winslow, had once ridden a camel about four hundred yards from the Euphrates to his hotel, and was appreciative thereafter of any similar undertaking that might measure, say, four hundred miles. Occasional eruptions of laughter reminded Eleanor that she was not listening.

She was fooling herself, she went on thinking, if she imagined that she could be as bold and purposeful as all that, when the time actually came. In truth, she feared Evangeline. That was one of the unexpected consequences of her own behavior this fall; that she had built up and aggrandized the other to an unintended extent; she had sent her propitiatory notes; she had journeyed up-country like a pilgrim seeking the blessings of a minor deity. Eleanor suspected that the other probably deprecated her by now. She thought back with embarrassment to the excitement that she felt each time she discovered one of the other's primitive notes lying in her mail slot. Crude notes containing blunt instructions to be carried out. She had pandered to Miss Sewell's vanity. She had raised her up. They both knew it, too. If the other were to accost her suddenly—out of the blue—she, Eleanor, would probably be tongue-tied. Still, by this hour of the morning, she was resolved to bring the matter of her preoccupation to a head, even if it meant losing her voice when the time came, or, conceivably, being shut out.

The church choir had a guest vocalist this morning. It was a very plain-looking adolescent girl named Hazel Jones, from the town of Cummington, who instantly proved herself a soaring soprano. Everyone in the church turned to look when the stupendous voice came out of her. To the hymn "Abide with Me," the girl imparted a thrill that Eleanor Gray—despite her more cosmopolitan origins—had not experienced before. The customary coughing and shuffling of feet gave off, as many parishioners swiveled in their seats. The girl, standing in front of Alice Harrison and the other choir members, was remarkably short in stature, almost stunted-looking. She had dark pigtails and a freckled face. She delivered her solo with such intensity, her eyes fixed on an imaginary point in space, that she might have been possessed. Her voice grew so thin and penetrating as it climbed the scale toward its musical destination that all present held their breath in anticipation. After a moment, the climbing, dwindling voice vanished into nothingness. Eleanor was left with her spine tingling, and a distinct sensation of having been lifted up bodily from the floor.

Later, she could not recall the exact moment when someone in the church had looked outdoors and spotted the approach of the dark green carriage, coming along the road past the Treadwells' house, but Eleanor associated it in her mind with the heavenly flight of Miss Jones's miraculous voice, which, in the very moment of its disappearance, had summoned to existence the picture of the carriage on the road. The sight of it took her breath away.

The young Reverend Howard Allen was leading the way. He paced along in front of the gleaming carriage, looking altogether ceremonious. He carried his book. Behind him, Evangeline's majestic mare was in the shafts, and Justin was standing up at the dashboard, the reins in his hands. The sun lighted up his hair. This time, there was no doubting Evangeline's presence inside the glittering conveyance; the low slant of the wintry sun lit up her figure perfectly. She sat in the middle of her cushioned seat, the black leather hood of the carriage providing a dramatic frame to her head and the entire silhouette. Someone—clearly it would have been Mr. Everett Conboy—was walking in the wake of the slowly advancing carriage.

Like everyone around her, Eleanor found herself gazing in stupefaction out the side windows of the church. She seemed nearly as astonished as they. She should have known. She should have seen it coming. That Evangeline would seize on one of the most reverential hours of the year to come at them.

Presently, no one in the crowded church was left in doubt about what was happening, as the boy, Justin Judd, drew the big mare slowly around to his right, following behind Reverend Allen, and came rolling over the frozen path toward the iron gate of the churchyard. The church service had stopped altogether. No one, though, spoke out. Eleanor was seated in the heart of the church, flanked by Calvin Tripp and Charles Chickering, surrounded by townspeople on all sides. Across the way, Truman Rogers and his wife and son got to their feet, the better to see what was happening outdoors. Then others stood, including Eleanor and her two companions. Mr. Chickering's muttered observation to Eleanor—"It's got to be the baby!"—was doubtless what everyone else had inferred. Someone in the choir rapped a stick, as to waken the congregation to the theme and purpose of their being here this morning. No one paid attention.

"This is beyond anything," said someone.

The carriage was not twenty yards from the church windows.

When Howard Allen reached the iron gate, Mr. Conboy came forward to unlatch it. His long, purposeful stride was familiar to all, as he stepped past the green-spoked wheels of the carriage. It was at this moment, as the carriage slowed and swiveled round in front of the gate, that the baby's casket came into view. It sat by itself on the back of the carriage. It was not the squarish black box that Eleanor and Mr. Walker had seen yesterday, however. This was made of plain pine boards. It had a fresh, clean look. Obviously, Everett Conboy had made it last night. The actual sight of it threatened Eleanor's equilibrium. Somehow, she had never acknowledged the existence of the baby quite so impressively as when looking out on it now. She stood dreamlike, holding her prayerbook to her lips. At what point Eleanor lost her inner restraints, or what impression in particular it was that started her moving, she did not know. But she seized her coat from the pew behind her and excused herself, pushing her way past Mr. Chickering and the person next to him, and had taken several steps along the central aisle of the church, before she realized what she was doing. As she threaded her way forward, and headed for the door, the parishioners stared at her in disbelief. Their faces in passing shone like wavering moons.

Eleanor got outdoors just as Mr. Conboy was swinging wide the black iron gate. The boy touched the reins to the flanks of the mare. Howard Allen, wearing a long silvery silk scarf over his black topcoat, led the way into the churchyard. Everett Conboy stood to one side, as the gleaming carriage moved formally past him, its wheels echoing icily. Looking his usual dour self, Mr. Conboy fell in behind the back wheels and took up the funereal pace. Not an arm's length away rode the small pine box. There was a steel gleam of wood screws. Eleanor's attention went at once to the figure of Evangeline, sitting upright on her seat not six feet in front of her.

In seconds, Eleanor fell in behind Mr. Conboy, who had not so much as glanced at her so far. Justin stood rigidly, steering the horse and carriage up the nearest cart path toward the pines at the crest of the hill. Now and again, through the sunlit triangle of the boy's forked legs, Eleanor caught a glimpse of Reverend Allen leading the way on foot, his scarf trembling in the morning air. As the carriage rattled its way up the frosty incline, the steel-rimmed wheels banging out a discordant rhythm, Mr. Conboy rested his hand on the little coffin. As for herself, Eleanor knew that she had crossed an invisible barrier. A sense of oppression weighed on her.

Evangeline never once turned around in her seat, or even so much as averted her head. The steady mechanical progression of the carriage climbing the frozen hill in the graveyard struck Eleanor as something inexorable, like a machine part advancing in spasmodic jounces across a living tapestry of pine trees and time-blackened headstones.

At the crest of the low hill, at that approximate point where Eleanor had seen Everett and the boy vanish last night—with Justin's shovel wavering over the twilit horizon like an oar—the carriage path turned to the right. The young minister was out of view momentarily, as Justin worked the mare with the reins. The carriage was pivoting, and Eleanor found herself staring at Evangeline Sewell in profile. For just a second or two, the pale chinalike face— the seashell cheekbone, the blond eyebrows and lids—stood out in relief in the gray morning air.

Miss Sewell must have sensed someone there, because after turning away, she spun round instinctively and looked back. Eleanor, gaping at her, found herself the subject of an arresting scrutiny. The dark blue gaze seemed to reach out and grip her, in the way a jacklight might paralyze a deer. The effect was startling. Until today, Eleanor had imagined that her first meeting or confrontation with Evangeline Sewell might prove very disabusing of her expectations, that the other young woman would reveal herself as a simple country girl, ordinary in the extreme, one upon whom Eleanor had elaborated dimensions from her own romantic imagination. She knew better now.

Looking directly through the interior of the carriage, past the seated Evangeline and Justin standing in front of her, and off to the left of the plodding black mare, Eleanor spotted the gravesite. Against the frosty background, the pile of earth next to the open grave put her in mind of a dark prehistoric beast lying among the

headstones. Beside her, Mr. Conboy strode slowly but determin-
edly, his gloved hand resting on the pine box. Whenever Eleanor
contemplated the infant, she expelled the thought. She tried not to
visualize the ice-cold baby in its casket.

During the many minutes of the carriage ride up the incline
from the churchyard gate, no one had spoken. It were as though
Evangeline alone were empowered to do that. When she did speak,
her voice resonated in the icy air. "Stop here!" she said.

Justin pulled up obediently on the reins, and the reverend Allen,
halting a few feet short of the grave, took a step or two back toward
Evangeline and the carriage. Mr. Conboy stood rigidly at the back
of the carriage, like a sentinel at his post. Eleanor's eyes were glued
to Evangeline's back, when she stood up from her seat. Mr. Conboy
brushed past Eleanor, and went directly to the running board. Eleanor naturally followed, a step or two behind. She stopped by the
rear wheel hub. She could feel the hesitancy being shown by the
three males toward the young woman. She was not wearing gloves.
As in Alonzo's portraits, Evangeline's hands looked rather fleshy,
and were partially balled, as into fists. As she descended a step onto
the running board, and then to the ground, she looked at no one.

Mr. Conboy summoned Justin to the back of the carriage. To
Eleanor's surprise, Justin was given the pine box to carry. At close
range, staring at the boy's face, and at the expression in his eyes of
great seriousness, Eleanor's heart rose up inside her. The sight of
the boy carrying the little coffin in both arms threatened to undo
her senses. The boy carrying the boy, she thought. Justin Judd must
have been instructed what to do, because he marched on past Evangeline, the casket in his arms, and fell in behind the minister. Mr.
Conboy signified to Eleanor that she was to follow Miss Sewell. He
came last.

As a site for the baby's burial, Mr. Conboy had chosen a space
lying just over the eastern side of the crest. At some distance stood
a scraggly white pine, a tree whose odd, twisted shape testified to
the ravages of a century of hilltop winds. Five or six slender grave-
stones, all unquestionably old, shared a nearby plot. Time and
again, Eleanor forced the baby out of her thoughts. She wondered

instead how Mr. Conboy had managed to break through a half foot of frozen topsoil without a pick. It must have taken him hours, she thought. She reflected also on how the congregation up in Cold Spring must have discovered by now that their pastor, always punctual to a fault, would not be conducting their Christmas services this morning. She could picture the assembled farmfolk facing the empty pulpit. But as Eleanor drew close on foot now to Evangeline, she could no longer deflect her thoughts. There was great dignity, she was compelled to notice, in Evangeline Sewell's pace and posture, the squareness of her shoulders, the erectness of her head, the solid, clocklike rhythm of her legs.

On reaching the grave, Howard Allen paused, and indicated politely where Justin was to set the pine coffin. Evangeline halted. Standing behind her, Eleanor marveled at her own circumstance. During all the long autumn, she could never have dreamed that her anticipated encounter with Miss Sewell would take such an outlandish form as this morning's bleak undertaking, or that she would need to have transgressed moral or social barriers to be here. She stood behind Evangeline like an acolyte.

Justin Judd placed the tiny coffin on the near side of the grave, straightened now, and stepped back. The minister had moved round to the other side of the grave, facing the four of them, and signified with his eyes that Evangeline should approach the grave. Only he was in a position then to discover that a sixth party was joining them. Eleanor had heard the crunch of icy footsteps behind her, and turned to see. It was Calvin Tripp. He was wearing his long waterproof coat and flat-brimmed hat. Everett and Justin turned to look. Eleanor was quick to notice, however, that Evangeline did not so much as move a muscle. She stood four or five feet in front of Eleanor and the others, and a similar distance from the pine casket. As Calvin Tripp halted beside Eleanor, they exchanged a look. They watched then, to their surprise, as Evangeline stepped forward, removed her black knitted shawl, spread it over the small box at the side of the grave, then moved backward a step or two. Instinctively, Eleanor squeezed the sleeve of Mr. Tripp's coat.

The revered Allen paused significantly before commencing. He regarded Evangeline for a long moment.

"When all others are gathering today," he began, "to commemorate and to celebrate the birth—many years ago—of God's own son and missionary, we come to this hill this morning to observe the departing from us, and the laying to rest, of a boy of no possible fame or attainments." Reverend Allen raised to view a sheet of paper, his prepared words, before continuing. Eleanor found his words remarkably affecting, more than she would have anticipated.

"It is not possible," the young minister continued, his eyes going from the paper in his hand to Evangeline facing him, "for a soul to pay a briefer visit to this vale than this small being whom we have come here to bury. He lived one day, and he lived one night, and we are here to mark that sacred interlude, and to thank our Creator for revealing him to us, for that one night and that one day. Not, if you will, to make us better. Not for any such apparent reason. There is no moral lesson here. There is too much mystery in it. We can only say, he arose from mystery, and has returned to mystery. That's all we know. The crowing of the cock and the song of the whippoorwill at dusk are one and the same."

With that, Reverend Allen bowed his head. Eleanor was sensibly touched by the young man's eloquence. Beside her, Calvin held his hat in his fingertips. He was staring at the crude pine box with the shawl upon it. She was trying in earnest to find the words that she might express to Evangeline at the end of the service. It pained Eleanor to realize that she wanted their acquaintanceship to become an open thing today, to take life now, and that that ambition was separate from any concern she might have felt for Evangeline in her actual grief. It was a contemptible motive.

Howard Allen was reading aloud from his prayer book. As before, Evangeline was standing with her back to Eleanor and the others, motionless as a post. Then, to Eleanor's surprise, the minister closed his book, and looked over at Mr. Conboy. An instant later, Everett and Justin stepped forward past Evangeline to the grave. The boy gave Mr. Conboy his hand, then jumped down into the grave, and disappeared. The grave was deeper than the boy was tall. Only his hands showed when he reached up to take the pine box from Mr. Conboy. Before passing the shawl-covered coffin to the boy, however, Mr. Conboy turned to Evangeline, as for permission. The picture of the gangling, eccentric Mr. Conboy, holding the box at his waist, and looking round at the young woman in her long black coat, engraved itself on Eleanor's mind. A brief interlude elapsed. Eleanor and Mr. Tripp were staring at the crown of Evangeline's head when she gave a very distinct nod, and Mr. Conboy turned back to the grave. Justin's bare, ungloved hands appeared to view, looking disconnected from all the world outside the grave. The pine coffin vanished from sight. After a moment, Mr. Conboy, leaning, reached a long arm and pulled the boy up. Justin glanced about nervously at everyone, to see if he had done properly.

There followed a most unexpected development. Mr. Conboy had just fetched his long-handled shovel from behind the mound of earth at the head of the grave, and the minister asked that all recite the Lord's Prayer, when Evangeline spoke up out of the blue. Her voice was clear as the crisp December air.

"I said I would bring him back," she declared, "and I have brought him back!" She spoke the words in a ringing voice.

The remaining minutes of the burial rite were all but lost to Eleanor as a consequence of Evangeline's startling pronouncement. The Lord's Prayer was recited. Reverend Allen sifted down a handful of earth, and read then from his book. Mr. Conboy went meanwhile to Evangeline to see if she wished to toss down the ceremonial first shovelful of soil. She shook her head, but stepped forward to the lip of the grave, and looked down. All five parties stood silent and still. Evangeline addressed the baby in his coffin.

"I am giving you a name," she said, "for your trip. You are Elijah."

Eleanor felt gooseflesh running up her arms.

Evangeline turned sidelong then to Howard Allen. Her alabaster face in profile riveted Eleanor's gaze.

"The burial is over," Evangeline informed him. She turned then to Everett Conboy, and signified with a quick declension of her chin that he was to bury the coffin. That done, Evangeline started for the carriage. Justin came hurrying behind her. She came directly past Eleanor and Calvin Tripp, her gaze fixed on the carriage parked behind them, her eyes shining moistly.

The sight up close of the upcountry girl pacing past left Eleanor weakened and visibly moved. She was gripping Calvin Tripp's coatsleeve. "She isn't like anyone."

Mr. Tripp nodded, but said nothing. He was fumbling with his hat.

Everyone but Mr. Conboy started away from the gravesite. Justin went quickly to the mare, got hold of her by the bridle, and began backing her up and turning her about. Evangeline climbed aboard with great agility. From behind them, the sound of Mr. Conboy's shovelling assumed a steady systolic beat. Howard Allen stepped alongside the carriage and handed his prayerbook up to Evangeline, evidently bestowing it on her. He went on ahead of the mare, then, as Justin Judd climbed aboard. Eleanor and Mr. Tripp followed behind the carriage. As they reached the low crest of the hill, the spire and then the church below came into view. Eleanor looked back once to the grave, to where the angular figure of Mr. Conboy shovelling, working industriously, swung back and forth. Time and again, Eleanor had to take deep breaths to restore her calm.

As Justin started the horse and carriage down the icy cart path, Eleanor could see through the carriage to where the churchgoers were coming outdoors, headed for their wagons and carriages. Several, however, had stopped, and were looking up the hill. The pale eastern light flooding down from the churchyard illuminated their upturned faces. Eleanor was conscious of the difficulties. She was sure that Evangeline had ordered Mr. Conboy to open up a grave at any place on the hill that he thought fit. What's more, the illegality of the gravesite enhanced the likelihood that she had acted similarly in opening the Billings house—not to mention in appropriating to her own use the brightly lacquered carriage. And here was she, Eleanor Gray, the new schoolmistress, witness to the unlawful funeral on the hill, and pacing along dutifully in Miss Sewell's funeral train.

The double perspective, of the adults clustering below in their Sunday best and of the headstrong upcountry girl, seated not five feet in front of her, left Eleanor feeling skittish. It was one thing to have journeyed up to Wisdom Way with Mr. Walker, but a very different matter to have given her moral approval to actions that others would surely regard as egregious, even sinful. She thanked her stars that Calvin Tripp had joined her on the hill. His presence might provide some small ratification of her own participation. Eleanor said as much.

"I am so glad, Mr. Tripp, that you decided also to pay your respects this morning—however unusual the circumstances."

"I came up here," he said, "to accompany you."

Eleanor inquired, anxiously, over the rattle of the wheels. "You would not have come otherwise?"

"I don't know about 'otherwises,'" he replied, in a laconic manner that reminded her of the Star Route man.

"But she is one of yours," Eleanor added, even more softly.

Evidently, Mr. Tripp had no more to say on the question.

Eleanor's next remark was more an exhalation of worry than a statement. She spoke softly to herself. "I don't know what to do," she said.

Mr. Tripp then offered a sentiment that gave Eleanor some reassurance. He was speaking of the baby. "He was entitled to decency," he said. "No one asked him to come here."

Eleanor nodded gratefully at that, regarding Calvin from the side of her eye. "I am glad you feel that way," she put in.

"A baby doesn't have to earn decency," he said. "Certainly not his very first day."

Eleanor wiped at her eyes. She hadn't really given too much thought to the baby, and realized now that he was all alone back there, with the man shoveling, and in an hour would be forever alone.

Eleanor naturally found herself caught between opposing forces. She worried about the East Becket townspeople, always so lovely to her, and what they would make of her actions, while at the same time picturing Evangeline standing over the wintry grave, giving the boy a name. But the resolution was an accomplished fact. She had given her loyalty to Evangeline Sewell, and never felt as sure about it as she did this morning, in her actual presence. That she was powerfully infatuated only seemed to strengthen and confirm her in the rightness of her actions. Nothing that felt so good, she thought, could be anything other than good.

At the bottom of the frosty grade, it would be necessary for Justin, turning the mare toward the iron gate, to drive directly past a significant number of parishioners. Most of the congregants were departing the church grounds, calling salutations to one another, and starting away, but others could not keep their curiosity in check. Some whispered, and looked away. Others gaped. It occurred to Eleanor that most of the townspeople of East Becket regarded reverend Allen not only as presiding minister at this morning's outlandish burial rite, but also—in the minds of many—as being the actual father of the infant! Which could only add to the general outrage. Clearly, Reverend Allen was jeopardizing his future, although Eleanor felt sure that his upcountry congregation would not censure or vilify him for what he had done. Being a bitter people, they might even extoll him for it.

From her place at the back of the carriage, Eleanor could not see the minister's face, but his pace and physical bearing bespoke calm.

As for the individuals milling about up ahead, beside the church and under a nearby oak, without exception they were staring now at Evangeline. If Eleanor had one other concern right now, it was the remembrance of the way Evangeline had blurted out, with ironlike insistence, that she had "brought him back!" From that, one might have worried that her feelings of wrath eclipsed her grief. For the sake of the boy on the hill, Eleanor hoped in earnest that was untrue. She was meanwhile looking round in the vain hope of spotting Mr. Walker.

Moments later, Howard Allen went on ahead, unfastened the iron gate, and swung it wide. As the gleaming carriage bounced and clattered its way through, Eleanor witnessed at point-blank range the expressions of dismay on the faces of a dozen men and women. Some of her own pupils stared at her in perplexity. An unpleasant, clammy sensation invaded the skin at the nape of her neck. Then, unexpectedly, Evangeline turned full around in her seat. She looked lengthily at Calvin Tripp, and then at Eleanor, and nodded, in the way of thanking them.

Eleanor wanted ever so much to say something, to make some expression of sorrow or sympathy, but the moment was gone. Evangeline called something forward to Howard Allen. He left the gate open, and stepped up onto the running board—as Justin, without any apparent urging, picked up the pace. Eleanor and Mr. Tripp watched as the horse and carriage rolled out onto the sunlit road, its wheels grinding noisily in the gravel, and started away toward the Billings house. The green-lacquered body of the carriage, with its shiny black hood and matching brass lamps, gave off an eerie incandescent glow in the morning light.

18

NTERING THE PARLOR, Eleanor could hear Alice Harrison moving about in a nearby room, and felt a sudden pang of anxiety at the thought of encountering her. For Miss Harrison's disapproval of Eleanor's actions would trouble her more than anyone else's. For the first time in all these months, she felt herself a stranger in the house. The furnishings in the parlor took on an alien cast. There were photographs atop the upright piano that she thought she had not seen before. The big green jardiniere on the floor by the hallway door looked like a decapitated head. Even the presence of the Christmas tree put her ill at ease, an observable reminder of her status as guest here.

Eleanor retreated upstairs to the privacy of her room. Just the act of closing the door behind herself gave her some comfort. Now and again, the windows of her room rattled noisily, as it had grown remarkably windy outdoors. In the hour to come, she contemplated taking the little gifts she had got Evangeline and Justin, and marching out the front door, and straight up the road past the common to the Billings house. But she knew in her heart that that would be improper, and that she would not have the courage. It was the baby's funeral day. She had no place going anywhere near that house today. She wondered if the reverend Allen was with Miss Sewell at this hour. Wishing that he were not, she guessed that he probably was.

She took out the big pencil portrait of Evangeline that Alonzo had given her. It reminded her impressively of that moment at the churchyard gate when Evangeline swiveled round and showed Eleanor that brooding, hypnotic look. Eleanor marveled at the astonishing likeness that Alonzo had captured on paper.

Her attention was drawn to the outdoors, to where the wind came sailing around the house, shaking the doors and windows importunately, demanding admittance. The day was getting blustery.

At one point, Eleanor heard Calvin Tripp and Mr. Chickering talking in the hall. There was laughter, then the sound of one of them going down the back stairs, and then a knock at her door. It was Mr. Chickering, looking noticeably flushed and robust.

"I have permitted myself two glasses of Christmas port, and would like nothing better than your agreeing to join me for another."

"My last visit to your chamber, sir," Eleanor replied, with feelings of relief, "was entirely profitable. You outfitted me for the wilderness."

"Yes," he said, "and if Myron Walker is to be believed, you comported yourself with great inventiveness and fortitude up there. Enough to make any frontierswoman of our great Wild West red with envy."

"It is *green* with envy, Mr. Chickering."

"He stands corrected!" said Mr. Chickering of himself.

Eleanor followed him down the hallway. She hadn't seen him since he stood beside her at church this morning, and wondered if she might not sound him on the reactions of others to her compulsive departure, not to say her active participation in what many of them would have considered a grotesque funeral cortege. Even now, she could not remember with clarity the specific moment when she had seized her coat and pushed her way out of the church.

Charles left his door ajar, as he admitted her. She was struck anew by the handsomeness of the man's room, with its gleaming dark-wood furnishings, the glass-shaded lamps, and tasteful framed prints. The two side windows of Mr. Chickering's room opened onto an expansive vista. The afternoon, she noticed, was remarkably alive. Fast-scudding clouds occupied half the sky, like a blue-black armada sailing up from the south.

"What an ominous look to things," she remarked, and thought instinctively about the baby, Elijah, buried under six feet of soil, with his first big rain coming, and what a sad thing it was to reflect upon the closing down of the darkness of his very first day alone.

Eleanor strove to hold in her feelings. Within minutes, she and Mr. Chickering were discussing the obvious.

"I'm afraid," Eleanor was saying, "that I made a spectacle of myself this morning, and have probably raised some hackles. I feel very sorry about that. And," she added, "I worry about it."

Mr. Chickering temporized. "Well. . . ," he paused to open the glass door of his little china cabinet, "it wasn't so much your joining them, as it was the simple shock of what was transpiring out there." Mr. Chickering laughed. "I," he said, "am not so easily offended."

"You are an outsider," Eleanor reminded him. "Like myself."

"Too true," he replied.

"Was everyone put out?"

"Oh, yes," he crowed back, automatically. Turning, he set down two tumblers. "But that was the idea behind it, wouldn't you say? If it weren't for the mortal character of the thing, not to say its likely consequences, I'd say it was bully! Nothing was left out. Christmas Day! The infant! The-death-in-the-birth! The return of the prodigal daughter!"

"The Judas?" Eleanor put in, alluding to herself.

"No, that is the other end of the year. This is the child in swaddling clothes."

"It is the child in his shroud," Eleanor corrected him, and instantly regretted having said it.

"Well, if they wanted mystery," Mr. Chickering rattled on, not fazed by Eleanor's interjection, "it was all there."

As he leaned to pour port into Eleanor's glass, she noticed the high color in his cheeks, and a slight telltale glaze over his eyes. In the moments to come, her thoughts went again and again to Evangeline. She pictured her pacing about the downstairs room of the brick house. The crystalline porcelain face appeared and reappeared in her mind's eye. Not for a second was Eleanor mindless of the fact that there was nothing high-minded about her actions today. It was not the plight of the infant that compelled her to do what she had done. To suggest such a thing, as she was surely doing, was a hypocrisy.

"What did you mean," she said, all at once, "about the 'likely consequences'?"

Mr. Chickering gave Eleanor her glass. "Your guess is as good as mine on that score. Miss Sewell violated the East Becket burial ground."

"By putting a baby there?" Eleanor replied, looking up.

He nodded quickly, concedingly. "I am only hypothesizing."

"It is just a piece of ground."

"It's hallowed ground," he allowed. "It is also private property. Someone doubtless owns it. Where is the grave?" he asked, as he corked the bottle.

"Just over the top edge of the hill."

"Looking east," he said, glancing up.

"Yes," said Eleanor, with feeling. "Looking toward morning."

Mr. Chickering considered for a moment what he was about to say. "Some of the selectmen are meeting tonight to talk about it."

Eleanor reacted instantly, setting down her glass. "Mr. Chickering!" she exclaimed. "Where did you hear such a thing?"

Charles Chickering's manner had convinced Eleanor that he had consumed a sufficient quantity of alcohol this afternoon to have blunted his judgment.

"I'm sure nothing will come of it," he replied, evasively. "They haven't the spunk"

"To do what?" Eleanor demanded to know, in a sepulchral voice. She had straightened in her chair.

"One or two of them want to disinter the coffin, I heard someone say."

"*Disinter?*" Eleanor was flabbergasted. Her cheeks colored. "What a horribly sinful thing that would be to do!"

"It's been done a million times in a million places." He gestured philosophically, as at the world at large.

"The baby's grave is not one of a million places, Mr. Chickering. It's *his* place." Eleanor couldn't hold in her tears. "I helped bring him there!"

"I'm sorry," he replied, chastened by Eleanor's tone.

"It is a perfect place for him to rest," she insisted. "He had no say in it. He went where they brought him. It was prepared for him. In all the world, in all the vast acreage of the world, he should be allowed to sleep there."

"I'm very sorry," Mr. Chickering repeated, looking at Eleanor with a tender expression. "Every year, on the night following Christmas, the selectmen meet in the grange hall, to review the year gone by, and look at the year to come. This year, they have moved it up a day, evidently."

Eleanor was staring at the window. The air outdoors had darkened. The first raindrops struck the windowpane like a handful of peas.

Her first impulse was the more reasonable one, namely, to go to Miss Harrison right away, downstairs, and use all her persuasive skills to forestall any such hideous notion as of the town's disinterring the infant. But in nearly the selfsame moment, she chose the less reasonable course. Without thinking as much, she had wanted a reason all day long to go to the other; it had been gnawing at her thoughts for nearly three hours. By coincidence, Mr. Chickering was simultaneously articulating the obvious solution.

"If you," he was saying, "put your case to the board of selectmen—Alice being one of these elected officers, as you know—you would be a very formidable advocate."

"I feel sure," Eleanor countered, "that they would not listen to me, at all. I think I have become anathema to them."

"They are very fond of you."

Mr. Chickering watched in perplexity, as Eleanor stood up to leave. She indicated her glass. "If you will save this for me," she said, "and if you'll forgive me for going, I'll return for it this evening. You are always so kind to me, and so wise."

He followed Eleanor to her room, visibly puzzled by her peremptory departure. Eleanor's pulse was racing. To worsen matters, she had left her big pencil portrait of Evangeline standing on the needlepoint chair by the fireplace. Had she not thrown her door wide, Charles would not have seen it. Eleanor reddened. It was clearly on show. It was like a tangible display of her obsession. In the gray afternoon light, Miss Sewell's face lighted up as though haloed. It shone like an icon.

"I hope you're not thinking of going outdoors," he said, as Eleanor reached and pulled on a cable-knit sweater. Stepping past him, she took her raincoat from the closet. Her forehead prickled with embarrassment, but she couldn't stop herself.

"I think the rain is not so bad," she said.

Mr. Chickering pointed to Eleanor's window. "The wind is coming from the north," he said. "The clouds are coming up from the south."

"I don't know what that means, or what it portends," said Eleanor, with an uneasy smile, "but I am sure you are able to tell me."

"Being from the coast, you should know," he said, "It looks like a nor'easter coming in."

"When it comes to the elements, Mr. Chickering, I don't know a hawk from a handsaw." Eleanor closed up her raincoat. "But if I'm going to breast a storm for someone, I'm pleased to think that it's a storm with which I should be familiar."

"I'll go with you," he said, following her out the door.

But Eleanor was not of two minds on that point. "No," she said.

"I'll go alone, please." She was making for the back stairway. Her rain a and umbrella were kept on a coat peg by the woodbox in the kitchen.

Mr. Chickering was plainly distressed at having told her what he did. "I should not have said that—about disinterment!" he protested. "I'm sure no one would go that far."

Eleanor glanced back at him, as she started down the steps of the box staircase. "I believe they may. What's more, they would have every right to do so. There will even be those who say that they are obliged to do so—in the name of some sacred consideration or other—some self-serving principle over which my own grandfather must have waxed eloquent more than once."

Eleanor arrived in the kitchen just in time to see Alice going out of sight up the central hall near the mail desk. She had evidently heard Eleanor coming down the steps, and despaired of what to say. Eleanor took down her umbrella and yellow oilskin rain hat, and headed for the back door. In truth, the rainfall was light, but the wind was like a voice, like someone angry, turning over things, looking for something lost or misplaced. Her umbrella would be of no use to her.

While she knew her reasoning for going out in the rain to be facile, even false, the prospect of actually going to Evangeline's door, bearing her important news, drove her on. It could only commend her to the other. When she got out to the road at the front of the house, her umbrella blew inside out.

Overhead, at treetop level, the wind blew a sheet of brown corrugated cardboard from nowhere, like a kite, and kept after it for a hundred yards. Mr. Chickering was right about the wind. It was not coming from the direction of the advancing storm. It was coming from the north. It was coming from the direction of upcountry. Eleanor cast aside her umbrella. Just as she reached the crossroads, the rain came squalling. She could actually see it coming in a wall along the riverbank trees and pouring across the nearby pasture. It seemed to be looking for her. That quickly, it swirled over and about her in a blowing sheet, soaking her to the skin.

Sometimes the gusting wind stopped her in her tracks, and thrust her roughly backward, or to one side, like a chess piece suddenly shifted from one square to another. Under any other circumstances, Eleanor would have turned for home. The memory of the snow blowing tumultuously at the fork up on Wisdom Way—not three days ago—and of her electing to turn back—pushed her on. Besides, the distance to the covered bridge up ahead was not greater than the distance already covered from Alice's.

The wind and rain were stinging her face like frozen confetti. Up ahead, the trees flanking the bridge were being buffeted, sometimes turning round and round like screws. Eleanor heard the hail before she saw or felt it. Hailstones were hitting the roof of the bridge with an angry clatter. Not five seconds later, she lost her footing and went down.

She fell sidelong, full-length on the road, with a startled gasp. The roadway was a shower of hailstones. They came down like marbles, bounding and leaping. The sound rolling past was shockingly loud. It was like gunfire. Eleanor scrambled to regain her footing, ran a step or two, and fell again. "Dear Mother," she was saying, as she got up a second time, and made for the bridge. As long as she kept her face down, the hail of ice-stones was harmless enough, peppering her shoulders and rain hat. But the road underfoot was treacherous, a carpet of ice. Two or three times, while hurrying the last few yards to gain the shelter of the bridge, her footing was threatened. She slipped and slid. The dark interior of the covered bridge loomed before her with unworldly appeal. She had no thought but to gain sanctuary under that roof.

On the apron to the bridge, not three feet from shelter, Eleanor's feet shot out from under her. She scrambled to grab hold of the vertical chestnut stanchion at the side of the bridge, and twisted out of control. A second later, she went down sideways over the embankment itself. She fell through the air several feet, and landed on her side. Her hip and thigh took the full impact of her fall.

In near shock, Eleanor started up the embankment on all fours. One of her gloves was missing; her yellow oilskin rain hat, which had flown off her head, lay in plain view on the bank of the stream below. The absurd spectacle of the yellow hat unhinged her senses. It seemed a picture of her inner condition, of something gone flagrantly wrong. With difficulty, Eleanor clambered her way back up the icy slope onto the bridge. As she stood up and made her way forward, her right leg pained her at every step. Notwithstanding the fright of what had happened, and the blow she had taken, she felt desperately foolish.

The roof of the bridge was perfectly rainproof, and the floor planks dry. Eleanor sat down in the middle of the bridge, impassive for the moment, and listened to the rattle of the hailstones on the roof and showering down in the trees nearby. She was staring up the road in the direction of the common, when a living picture materialized of someone sitting on a wagon under the side portico of the town hall. She recognized the wagon and driver by the orange paint on the side and on the wheel spokes. It was Truman Rogers. A second horse was tethered to the wagon. Eleanor's brain was working slowly, as she concluded that he must have gone up to the Billings place to retrieve his colt from Mr. Conboy, and on returning had taken shelter under the portico.

As soon as the hailstorm passed, and she could hear again the groaning and swinging about of the trees, and the incessant splatter of the rain, she saw Mr. Rogers coming forward in the storm, which convinced her that he had seen what happened to her. Otherwise, he would have stayed in place till the weather abated. Clearly, he was alarmed for her. His approach—the horse was coming at a trot in the rain—reminded Eleanor that here she had been loved. That they had loved her, and taken her into their hearts, as one of their own, and she had traduced them.

Mr. Rogers got down hurriedly from his wagon not a moment after arriving on the covered bridge. His coat and trousers were soaked black from the rain. He wore a worried expression.

"Miss Gray!" he exclaimed, his mouth dropping open, his tongue lolling. "What happened?" He stared at her with great concern.

For one reason or another, Eleanor remained sitting a little while on the floor of the bridge. The horses stamped and shook themselves. Mr. Rogers was shivering. Eleanor was looking up at him, and was slow to reply. She smoothed her wet hair with the flat of her hand. "I fell, sir," she said.

FOR THE NEXT QUARTER HOUR, she sat next to Mr. Rogers on the wagon, waiting for the rain to subside. She was drenched from head to foot. On climbing onto the wagon, Mr. Rogers had to help her up. Her right leg was impaired.

"Did you collect your horse from Mr. Conboy?" she asked, at length, in an effort at casualness.

"Yes, I did," he said. "Everett is reliable, but he's got his hands full right now." He looked at Eleanor significantly.

Eleanor felt that Truman was probably probing to see how much she knew about the strange goings-on. He had been at church this morning, and surely saw her go hurrying outdoors. She determined to speak plainly.

"Between his chores and his grave-digging," she remarked, "he is very occupied, I agree. He is obviously very devoted to Miss Sewell. He would go to the ends of the earth for her."

"They were always close," Mr. Rogers said.

"I didn't know that."

"He was devoted to the mother in the same way."

"Truly?" Eleanor was genuinely amazed. "He was close friends with Evangeline's mother?"

"They weren't what you'd call friends, any more than *they two* are friends," he said of Mr. Conboy and Evangeline. "He worked for her at anything she might need, and at anything he thought she might need, and at anything he thought she might ever need. There's a side to Everett that's a particular puzzle. But you have to respect it. It ain't selfish!" he cried. "Whatever it is, it ain't that."

Truman Rogers had parked the horses and wagon by the rails on the side of the bridge to avoid the rain gusting in from across the way. Looking down, Eleanor could see the little river swelling by the minute. The black coursing waters had risen to within inches of where her hat lay. The yellow hat with its disklike brim looked like a surveyor's marker.

Eleanor persisted in her plain speaking, anticipating that an open manner might produce unexpected news. "I am afraid," she said, "that my joining that sad procession into the churchyard this morning has probably raised questions about me. I am sorry for that."

Mr. Rogers nodded, but said nothing for a considerable interval. He had taken out a shiny silver tobacco pouch, and was checking the dryness of the tobacco. "There's two sides to everything," he observed, at last, in an ambiguous tone.

"I have a worry," Eleanor went on, while trying to disengage the wet collar of her coat from her bare neck, "that the townspeople may decide to exhume the baby."

"Do what?"

"Dig him up," she said

Mr. Rogers stopped fiddling with his tobacco pouch. His expression changed. "That would be a rough business," he replied.

"I think so, too."

"I don't mean it that way," he said, turning to her. "I ain't talking about the coffin. I'm talking about him."

"Mr. Conboy," Eleanor confirmed, tentatively.

"That young woman may be in the right," sang Mr. Rogers, "or she may be in the wrong—but it don't matter either way to him, because he don't think like you or me." Again, he nodded decisively. "It'd be a rough business."

Eleanor waited a moment. "Because of what he'd do," she guessed.

"No telling what he'd do. Eight or nine years back, he dug her mother's grave, and that man, if you ask me, has no intention of digging her grave. Nobody else probably feels so strong about him as I do, but *I* think, if she told him to, he'd put his Remington twelve gage to any man, woman, or child who took a shovel to that grave."

"I can see now," Eleanor let out, "how Evangeline can be as brazen as she is, with a force like that protecting her from others."

"Naw," said Mr. Rogers, rejecting that. "She'd be just as brazen as she is. Maybe it's even her being the bold one she is that makes him what he is." Reflecting a second, he added to his thought. "She's rough."

Eleanor felt an emotional surge at the mention of her. Her eyes went to the sight of the yellow oilskin hat on the rocks below. Any second now, the turgid waters would carry it away.

"Is it because of Mr. Conboy that no one has sought to expel her from the Billings house?"

"Not that simple," he answered, in a melodious voice that suggested he had given some thought to the idea. Eleanor awaited his reply. "You see," he said, "if she's a *right* to be there, and you go there to take her out of there, *she's* a right to shoot you dead." Truman Rogers savored his words. He looked across the bridge downstream to where the rain continued dancing and flashing.

"For trespassing," Eleanor put in.

"That's the word," said he.

"But not if you have police powers, Mr. Rogers."

"If you're an official," he continued, "and you go there to take her out of there, then she or he would have no right to shoot you dead. But chances are, you ask me, one of 'em would shoot you dead anyway. . . . Devil take the hindmost," he added.

"Since it wasn't necessary for Miss Sewell to use that house in coming down here to bury her baby, maybe she does have that right." Eleanor straightened in her seat.

"Oh, I would doubt that," said Mr. Rogers, as he started in to pack his pipe. He showed Eleanor the corner of his eye. "I'd say she's just on the loose."

"'The loose,' sir?"

Truman chuckled under his breath. "The fox in the henhouse."

"Mr. Rogers," Eleanor interrupted herself. "You must have just seen her!"

"I didn't see much of her. She was in the front room, someplace. Everett went from the kitchen to ask her if it was all right for him to give me back my horse." Truman smiled to himself over the absurdity of it. "She asked him something back, and he came into the doorway again, and said why'd I want it? . . .'Only 'cause it's mine.' I said. 'No other reason.' That's when I saw her. She was coming down the long hall to the kitchen. At the door, Everett practically jumped out of his skin to get out of her way. But seeing her like that—today, of all days—I wanted to say something, and I did. I said, 'I'm sorry about your misfortune.' She sort of nodded, and turned to Everett, and said 'Send J.J. to get Truman his horse.'"

"And that was it," Eleanor deduced.

"Turned away, and went back up the hall!" he said.

"What was she wearing?" Eleanor asked, trying to picture the scene.

"There was clothes lying about in the kitchen, and a good hot fire in the stove. She was wearing pants and a big sweater. There was a steamer trunk open on a table, full of clothes, like old-fashioned shoes and ladies' hats and things. Must have come down from the attic. From the old jute mill days."

When Eleanor next looked down at the frothing, swollen waters below, her oilskin hat was gone. She turned reflexively toward the opposite side of the bridge just in time to see her yellow hat speeding downstream, darting and spinning. Truman Rogers was meanwhile examining the weather speculatively. He had located a dry match, lighted it with his thumbnail, and set it to his pipe.

He took several quick puffs, then turned to Eleanor, as in the way of an afterthought. "Where were you going in this storm?" he asked.

Eleanor considered her reply, and answered him truthfully.

"I was going to Evangeline," she said.

19

Y THE TIME Eleanor got back upstairs to her room, climbing Alice's front stairs with some difficulty, it was manifest she had sustained some ugly bruises. But as she changed out of her wet things, pulling on a flannel petticoat and long woolen skirt, she scrupulously avoided the mirror, and didn't once look down to examine her thigh. It was enough to have humiliated herself in Miss Harrison's eyes, not to say those of Charles Chickering, without her having to look upon the very signature of her shame. Instead, she lay down on her bed, fully dressed, and pulled the calico counterpane over herself. She would have welcomed sleep, but her thoughts circled back again and again to the incident at the bridge, the violent winds and slashing hail, and the picture that Truman Rogers had drawn of Evangeline Sewell standing in the kitchen door—in her pants and sweater—ordering Justin to fetch Truman his horse.

It was during this interlude that Eleanor made up her mind, for the second or third time, to be loyal to the other, no matter what the future held. Also, it was not lost upon her that others might wrongly believe that Evangeline, having bearded the town, and buried her infant, would depart now for the north. Eleanor knew better. It gratified her to realize that she alone knew about the other's promise to return. "Then we will see who is strong and who is weak," she had written. That vow was set down long before the child had died. Had the baby, Elijah, lived, Evangeline was coming back, anyhow. Everett's behavior, in opening the house, further attested to it, for when doing it, he had not known of the boy's passing.

As suppertime approached, Eleanor dreaded going downstairs to take her place at the dining table. She was all but certain that Alice had seen her getting down from Truman Rogers's wagon, limping and rain-soaked, because just as she had stepped down onto the ground and turned toward the house, she had seen someone closing the curtain of the front parlor window. Alice, it was obvious, was ashamed of her. Eleanor had a half mind to take her supper to her room, but that sort of evasion would intensify matters. Better to meet things head on.

At the table, Eleanor endeavored to be engaging, and, if possible, cast a humorous light upon her disastrous outing.

"Mr. Chickering," she said, as he stood to light the two tall Christmas candles, "as an expert on watercourses and rainfall, you are delinquent in your calling for not having been at the river today."

"Nor'easters are beyond my education," he said. "I am not a seaboard man."

Alonzo Klaw tried also to keep up a civil tone at table. "Rumor has it . . ."—he turned to Eleanor, while unfolding his napkin— "that you have no fears of these famous Atlantic storms."

"I wanted to see," said Eleanor, with studied brightness, "how fast the waters of our little river could rise, when put to the test. I swear," she said, "it became a living creature right before my eyes. And ever so indignant! It took on every unpleasant characteristic known to humankind. At one point, it stole my yellow hat, and ran away with it."

While speaking, Eleanor glanced surreptitiously at Alice Harrison. But Alice kept her eyes down all this while.

"Tibetan priests wear yellow hats," said Mr. Chickering. "Maybe there was a lamaist priest in the vicinity."

"If so," said Eleanor, turning aside to help Mrs. Sampson, "he is richer tonight by a lemon-yellow oilskin rain hat."

Calvin Tripp, who had been the first guest to arrive at the table, and was not embarrassed to say that he was unusually hungry, looked round in turn at those speaking, but said little. A taciturn man, he liked listening.

Within minutes, though, a silence fell over the table, interrupted only by polite requests for this side dish or that, the passing of bread, a word of thanks. Eleanor ate with difficulty. She was sure by now that most others at table were in possession of a knowledge being denied her. Some bleak resolve was in the offing. One had only to look at Alice to know that the townspeople of East Becket were deeply offended.

No word was spoken about the sacrilege committed in the churchyard that morning, nor any reference whatever made to Evangeline. No one spoke of Eleanor's purpose in breasting the storm, or said a word, for that matter, about her physical condition. While she felt herself a distinct failure in the eyes of her townsmen, the worry and sympathy she felt for the beautiful upcountry girl mounted by the minute.

After supper, Eleanor managed to accost Calvin Tripp. Of all those present, he, she felt, might appreciate her extreme views. She didn't mince words with him.

"Mr. Tripp," she said, "I am in desperate need of your help." She admitted him to her room, and closed the door.

"It's become obvious to everyone, doubtless even to yourself, that I have taken Miss Sewell's side in the midst of these bewildering circumstances. I have done so without any real knowledge of her feelings or intentions. I am taking her on faith alone. In doing so, I have brought down on myself the displeasure of just about everyone."

"Seems to me," said Calvin, "that the thing'll die down soon enough."

Eleanor disagreed. "It is going to get even more intense. Miss Sewell is a very determined young woman. She is strong and capable. I am, Mr. Tripp, very admiring of her."

He gazed steadily at Eleanor. "You were headed over there in the storm?"

"Yes."

"To warn her?"

Eleanor hesitated, as she knew in her heart that her motive was nothing more selfless than to show the other her trustworthiness and devotion. Eleanor's glance went instinctively to the pencil portrait—to the riveted eyes and alabaster cheekbone.

"Yes," she said, at length.

By coincidence, she heard the report of the back door downstairs, and from the window saw Alice going around the side of the house.

"Several of the selectmen are gathering tonight in the grange hall," she explained "There is talk of their ordering the disinterring of the baby. I think they feel that this holy day has been openly desecrated, and intend to rectify matters. I am sure they have the right to do that. I learned of their intentions today, and wanted to notify Evangeline of that possibility. Not that she could stop them doing so!" Eleanor allowed. "But advance word to her *would* prepare her for the shock to come. It would give her time to think about it— and to consider her response." Eleanor stood with her hands folded together at her waist. "I want to ask you a question, Mr. Tripp."

"What is it?" he leaned to her, almost conspiratorially.

"It's about Evangeline." Eleanor winced over her own words. "Is she violent?"

Calvin Tripp's smile revealed a humorous ambiguousness, as though the question were not altogether preposterous.

"I don't mean," said Eleanor, "might she perpetrate some violent action. But she has a man with her who would obey any instruction of hers, of any type, however lawless it might be. He has already proven that. Does she have the violence within her to loose him upon others?"

Calvin continued smiling to himself, while nodding conjecturally. Eleanor construed his expression as assent.

"Truman Rogers told me," she went on, "that Mr. Conboy was once all but slavishly devoted to Evangeline's mother. You, being from upcountry, Mr. Tripp, would know the answer to that."

"There's truth in it. His mind fixes on something, and stays fixed. Don't misunderstand. He's no lunatic. It's just the way he's built. Also, the mother liked knowing that he was nearby. And he kept his distance from her. But like the daughter, she knew he'd go to any lengths for her."

"It was he who buried her, wasn't it?"

"Yes," said Calvin. "He did the work."

"Were you there?"

"Naturally," he replied.

"And Evangeline, of course, was there."

"It was her mother!" Mr. Tripp exclaimed.

That's what I mean," said Eleanor. She paused. "In a few minutes," she said, "the selectmen will be meeting and deciding what to do. You and I know each other only a few days, Mr. Tripp, but I have great trust in you, and wonder if you would do me a kindness."

"I think so," he replied.

"I want to send written word to Evangeline. I would go there myself—tonight!—right now!—but I have concealed the extent of the injury I sustained this afternoon. I fell down the frozen embankment by the bridge. I'm afraid even to look at my leg."

Mr. Tripp's face changed. "I'm so sorry to hear that. You're one of those persons that I can't imagine such a thing happening to. You *fell*?" he said.

"On the hailstones," she said. "I fell headlong. . . . If I started out tonight, I would not get halfway there, but I want desperately to communicate with her. If Mr. Walker were anywhere around and about, I would have him take me. He is very understanding of me." Eleanor's need to express her deeper feelings prompted her words. "I think he is the only person who understands the strange compulsion that has gripped me, and that governs my . . . well, not just my actions, but nearly all my waking thoughts. Where my understanding stops, his," she said, "goes on." Eleanor smiled. "That, I suppose, is why they call him the Star Route man. It's also why he tried so hard to get me through that storm up in Wisdom Way, and on north to the lake. . . . I think he saw that as *my* Star Route."

Eleanor permitted herself a moment of self-pity. The emotions rose inside her. Just the thought of the rain-soaked clothing that she had taken off this afternoon in this room—or the way Mr. Rogers had looked at her as she sat on the floorboards of the bridge. . . .

Mr. Tripp watched Eleanor crying with a pained look.

"You want me to go to her," he affirmed.

Eleanor nodded, and turned away in shame at having lost control of herself. She went to her desk, and took out her writing tablet. While Calvin went for his coat, Eleanor began her note. Notwithstanding her emotional shakiness, she elected to employ a brisk, businesslike style.

In writing to Evangeline, it pleased Eleanor to assume the manner of the efficient subordinate addressing her superior. She wrote the note out rapidly, in a fluid, legible hand.

December 25, 1910

Dear Evangeline,

I am sending Mr. Calvin Tripp to deliver you news of an urgent character. The East Becket selectmen are meeting tonight—at this very hour—to consider the possibility of removing your infant from his resting place in the churchyard, and, conceivably, even perhaps to discuss legal steps that might be taken against you. I have discovered this information at some peril to myself and to my post at the school. I tried coming to you earlier, but was caught in the wind and hail, and injured myself badly. Despite these regrettable developments, I hope to continue as your most loyal friend, and am prepared to follow any further instructions that you send me. Mr. Tripp is, as you know, our most reliable ally.

Please tell me what next to do.

Yours, in devotion,
Eleanor

As Mr. Tripp took the envelope in hand, and closed up his coat against the cold, Eleanor asked his indulgence. "If you please," she said, "it's very important to me that Miss Sewell appreciate the efforts I have made in trying to help. Tell her, Mr. Tripp, that my heart is with her—and that I wish very much to do more . . ." Eleanor paused in her impassioned request. "Tell her that the townspeople whom I serve are turning against me, but that she, Evangeline, is my first loyalty."

"You followed her into the cemetery this morning, Miss Gray. That ought to be enough."

"Tell her what I said," Eleanor insisted, softly. She could feel the pathos behind her words, but wanted nonetheless that Mr. Tripp honor her wishes.

She followed him down the back stairs. Twice, her leg seized up. She had sustained, at the least, a severely pulled muscle. Each downward step sent an electrical jolt the length of her leg. After Mr. Tripp set off outdoors—the crunching sound of his boots resonating on the frosty earth outside the kitchen windows—Eleanor got out the tea kettle. She could hear Charles Chickering and Alonzo Klaw in the front parlor, apparently busy at a game of chess. While heating water for tea, she looked about in the icebox and pantry for the jar of honey. Her temperature, she now realized, was climbing.

Sitting at the table with her tea and a slice of brown bread, she tried to formulate how best she might represent her actions to Miss Harrison and others, in order to mitigate matters. She thought of the disappointment she would bring to her parents if she were dismissed—especially as all of those persons who ever knew her were keenly aware of her lifelong ambition to be a teacher. She was first in her class at Framingham Normal, and had earlier won statewide recognition for her high school writing achievements in Fall River. But the prospect of dismissal, or of her even perhaps resigning her post, was replaced in mind by thoughts of Evangeline, and a corresponding sense of the unpredictability—of the bizarreness—of the events that had overtaken her here. For the first time, Eleanor allowed certain forbidden thoughts to come forward onto the lighted stage of her mind, and linger there. These were thoughts that had a little history now, that had taken form only lately, emerging stealthily from the shadows of her consciousness, which until now she had reflexively expelled. They were like certain specimens in nature that only appear at twilight or dawn. Tonight, she would let them persist a little while. Tonight, she would look at them.

She was studying idly the pattern of the kitchen-table oilcloth, unconscious of her surroundings, while acknowledging the romantic character of the feelings she felt for her friend. That, after all, was one of the more insidious, persisting ideas that had sought a purchase on her thoughts. That her love of Evangeline was a love full-fledged, not the response of an iron-filing coursing toward a magnet. The idea that she wanted to possess and be possessed by her. There was nothing grotesque in that. There was nothing to be ashamed of there.

She was sitting perfectly motionless at the table, hands in her lap, leaning over her tea. She had known solitudes in times past — as when, for example, she had detected first a sign of slowing in her father, or the first gray stands in her mother's hair, and the unsettling knowledge of a day to come when they would be taken, and exist in her thoughts only. It was one of the more poignant fates, she had always thought, of the only child. It was something she had characterized in her diary, as a high-schooler, as the "bereavement of bereavements," and "as inevitable as tomorrow."

This particular solitude, which settled over her tonight in Alice's kitchen, was different from that, probably not so frightening to the diarist of a few years back, but the sense of her aloneness was acute and painful. She had had the thought lately that one's passage through life was accompanied perhaps by a reciprocating growth of that inner solitude. But whether it was true or not, knowledge of the thing was no comfort at times like this. There were simpler truths. Eleanor brought to mind the most elemental of them all. She would like to have been lying in Evangeline's arms. She would like to have known the soft sensation of the other's lips upon her fingers, her cheekbone, her throat. What, after all, was the guessing at or knowledge of things metaphysical *next to that?* Especially when it seemed tonight that this separateness from the world bypassing was doubtless general for her, and might mean a life without any expression of the richest form of love that God confers. It didn't seem fair.

Voices echoing from the outdoors announced the arrival of Alice and others. If the selectmen were coming into the house, Eleanor would meet them here. Something in her nature required it. She would withdraw no farther; not just for reasons of love or loyalty to Evangeline, but to what was irreducible in herself. Here were her palisades. She took up her teacup, to discover it was cold. She set it on her saucer, and straightened in her chair. She could hear the water bubbling still in the kettle, and thought back to that September afternoon when she unsealed Evangeline's letter, and set in train the long sequence of events that led her straight to this point tonight.

AS ELEANOR SUSPECTED, Miss Harrison and her colleagues did wish to speak to her about "Miss Sewell" and the events transpiring about them during this holiday season. The Trumbulls were present, along with a man named Willis Beauchamp, whom Eleanor had never seen before. He was a small man, with a dark, leathery complexion and craggy features. Eleanor liked him on sight. He struck her as cordial and probably fair-minded.

"Your reputation," he said, smiling, "is spreading even to the neighboring towns, such as to my town."

"You are not a townsman here?" Eleanor returned, interrogatively.

"I am," he said. "Technically, I live in East Becket, but I live much closer to Otis, and my practice is in Otis, and my daughters live in Otis —"

"Are you a lawyer?" Eleanor interrupted, wondering at once if Alice and the Trumbulls were not perhaps reaching out for legal advice.

Alice set out teacups for her guests.

"I am a physician," he said, and made an effort at a joke. "You can probably tell as much by the fashionable cut of my clothing." He gestured at his coarse woolen shirt and at his suspenders, which were as big as any braces Eleanor had ever seen.

"I think," Eleanor responded with ease, "that the country doctors of New England *are* the most stylish physicians anywhere!"

"I'm a member of the board of selectmen here," he explained. "They elect me, and I serve. It's a six-mile ride to get me here, but I serve! To my family and neighbors, my periodic trips to East Becket are judged to be part of a secret life I lead!"

Alice Harrison was looking meanwhile uncomfortable, as she brought tea and a platter of warmed-over biscuits to the table. She was embarrassed for Eleanor.

Ivy Trumbull brought up the matter at hand without preamble. "The funeral that took place this morning," she said, "came as a blow to a good many people."

"I understand that to be true," said Eleanor.

"It seemed a vicious thing to do," Ivy added.

Mr. Trumbull, whom Eleanor recognized readily from Sunday morning church services, improved on his wife's remarks. "It was calculated," he said, "as vicious."

Eleanor regarded the two of them. She remarked again Ivy Trumbull's impressive prettiness, her deep indigo eyes and rosy face. While immense in size, she gave off a sense of great vitality.

Eleanor spoke to the heart of the matter. "I'm afraid that my going out and joining her this morning gave the appearance to some that I had contributed the weight of my post to my own personal or private approval of Miss Sewell's unexpected actions."

"Did you know she was going to do that?" asked the doctor.

Eleanor, in replying, used the doctor's own word. *"Technically,"* she said, "no."

"You do write back and forth," said Mrs. Trumbull.

Eleanor's eyes went at once to Alice, as only she and Mr. Walker could have known anything about the exchange of messages. Alice turned away to the stove.

Dr. Beauchamp cut in. "On what basis, Miss Gray," he inquired, in a perplexed allusion to her earlier words, "does your approval of Miss Sewell's actions rest?"

Eleanor turned back his question. "In the part of my mind or heart where I form the private conclusions that govern my behavior, I sit alone, Dr. Beauchamp. A silent Buddha. It is only my actions, I believe, that may be impugned or brought to public judgment."

Miss Harrison contributed at last a quiet observation. "We are all very admiring of you, Eleanor." After a moment, she added. "We don't think you did wrong."

"On the contrary," said Eleanor, over her shoulder. "There is not one person on the town's side of things who would not censure me for it."

Dr. Beauchamp persisted in his own line of thought. "I do admit," he said, "that your reasons for aiding the young woman—who, you'll agree, can be disagreeable and rebellious—"

"I agree to no such thing," Eleanor cut in. Her feelings for Evangeline were rising within her. Her love of the other was etched in her face.

"You are extraordinarily fond of her," Ivy Trumbull observed, while loosening a delicate lavender scarf at her throat. "Aren't you a stranger to her?"

At any point in the conversation, Eleanor knew that she could suddenly invoke the baby, revert to the pathos of the child on the hill, and put all three of her interlocutors in an awkward position. But as she knew them *not* to be morally at fault—and had decided on her own to defend this small corner within herself—this mysterious corner—she waived the opportunity. In a thousand future situations, she would employ skillful, pragmatic arguments, she was sure. But not here and now. Here she would be true to herself, by being true to Evangeline.

"If I am a stranger to Evangeline," she replied, "as I may very well be, she is nonetheless no stranger to me."

Eleanor was sure by now that the subject of disinterring the baby would not be mentioned, but was equally certain that that decision had been reached tonight.

Alice apprised Eleanor of something she did not know. "Ivy," she explained, "has been trying to telephone Aaron Billings up in Hinsdale, but Mr. Billings is away for Christmas."

"He's in Glens Falls," said Ivy.

"Do you have any idea, Miss Gray, of the basis on which Miss Sewell is occupying the Billings house?"

"I have no idea," Eleanor admitted.

You see, if the matter ended here," said the doctor, thoughtfully, as he spooned sugar into his tea, "we could correct the . . . ," He searched for the proper word.

"Malfeasances?" said Eleanor.

"Yes, we could get by all that. Feeling tonight was . . . ," he added, referring to the meeting at the grange hall, "that she is apt to do anything next, and has a man behind her who is as indifferent to consequences as she herself."

Eleanor said nothing to that. She imagined Calvin Tripp to be arriving about this time at the Billings house. She could picture him striding under the trees, and going up to the back door. The secretness of her emissary bearing her message to Evangeline gave Eleanor a dark satisfaction. She savored, even, the duplicitousness of her sitting at the kitchen table, responding to these exploratory questions, at that very moment when Evangeline would be unfolding the handwritten letter and perusing her words of warning. She likened this shared secret—especially as it was anything but frivolous—to the sort of high intimacies that have bound lovers together since the beginning of time.

"I am going up to bed, Alice," she suddenly announced. Eleanor could feel herself getting weaker.

"You look quite flushed, Eleanor."

"I am running a fever." As she rose to leave the table, she moved very carefully, so as to hide somewhat her injury. At the door to the box staircase, she paused. She decided, after all, to express that point of view that she knew was morally improper, but doubtless served Evangeline's purposes. She addressed all four of them.

"When you go up onto the hill," she said, "and dig down, and take the box in hand, tell him that there was a solemn vote taken to disturb him." Eleanor turned, and reached for the door latch. "His name is Elijah."

ELEANOR FELT BITTER with herself at having struck a recriminatory chord, especially toward Alice Harrison, whom she knew to be the salt of the earth. To worsen matters, Eleanor was feeling increasingly sickish. She added kindling and a beech log to the waning blaze in the fireplace, and sat down beside it. The afternoon storm had drawn away to the northeast hours ago, but the winds blowing in its wake were strong and vociferous, like the rearguard of a marauding force, shouting and shaking the house, and vowing one day to return.

After sitting, Eleanor reflected idly on her past life. She thought about the many Christmases past, during all the time of her growing-up years, from the very mistiest of memories, as of a three-year-old playing on the kitchen floor with a big, colorfully painted top—and how she had always been the living raison d'être of her mother and her father. She knew, in the meanwhile, what she most wanted to do at this moment, but felt a nagging reluctance to carry it out. At last, she rose, opened her closet door, and prepared to examine her leg in the tall door-mirror. Reaching, she pulled her long woolen skirt and flannel petticoat carefully up her leg, revealing first her calf and knee, and then, going higher still, slowly uncovering her thigh. The result of her fall exceeded her worst expectations. She could scarcely credit her eyes. From a point inches above her knee reaching all the way up to her hip, appeared the most livid discoloration—a swath of blue-black flesh that widened and grew uglier all the way up to her hip.

Eleanor quailed at the grotesqueness of the thing. She had never seen anything so nasty. The firelight rippled up and down the length of it, setting off iridescent flashes. If thunder itself had a color, she thought, it had painted her leg with it. She dropped her skirts. She shut the closet door. While a mounting fever left her dizzy, she determined to hold vigil until Calvin returned. The sight of her leg had shaken her for the moment, though, and occupied her thoughts. At one point, reflecting on it, she attributed the damage she had sustained to the uncoiling upon her of a moral universe; at other times, as the badge and emblem of her fervor and sacrifice.

She was nodding and dozing in her chair, when she heard the report from below of the outside kitchen door. It was still the middle of the evening, not nine o'clock yet. She was certain that Calvin Tripp had returned, but worried lest he join the others in the parlor. She could hear the melodic plinking of the player piano, and could picture Mr. Chickering sitting on the bench, pedalling away at it boyishly. The question as to whether or not Mr. Tripp would think it important to apprise her at once of his errand was resolved by a soft knock at her door.

"Thank goodness," she said, upon admitting him.

"You don't look well," he observed, at once.

"I'm feverish," Eleanor said. "I'll be all right. Did you see her? Did you see Miss Sewell?"

"I did," said he, stepping into the room.

"She must have been pleased to welcome a . . . 'countryman.'"

Mr. Tripp smiled over that. "We are all countrymen," he replied, in a deepish baritone, and removed his wide-brimmed hat.

"If you don't mind, sir, I am going to close the door behind you," she said.

"Suit your fancy."

He and Eleanor faced one another by the fire. "Do you have any news?" she asked.

"They don't seem particularly worried. I asked her right off about the burial plot, and whose it was, and she waved her head at Everett to answer my question, and he said, 'It belongs to a tree.'"

"A tree," Eleanor repeated, mystified.

"When he said that," Mr. Tripp continued, enlarging on his remark, "Evangeline and the boy laughed."

"I am not keeping abreast of you, Mr. Tripp." Eleanor was feeling wobbly on her feet, and reached and set her fingertips to the mantel for balance. She had pulled on a bathrobe over her skirt and sweater to reduce the chills.

"Everett said that the biggest chestnut tree in history once stood there. He knew, he said, because it was he who chopped it up back in 'eighty-eight, the year it came down. 'Chopped it up,' he said, 'and carted it away.'"

Calvin wiped his lips with the back of his fist. The firelight glimmered in his beard, and sent tiny splinters of light in and out of his eyes.

"That's hardly justification for her appropriating the ground to her own purposes," Eleanor interposed, softly.

"We were in one of the front rooms," he continued.

"Describe it, please, Mr. Tripp," Eleanor urged, in a suspenseful tone.

"It was a big room, with four big windows, empty bookshelves going all the way up to the ceiling, and a lot of old furniture, some of it covered up. They had two kerosene lanterns burning out in the kitchen, I noticed when I came in, but just a pair of big candles going in this front room, along with the fire. She said something strange. She was looking right at me, too. 'God took His tree back to make way for Elijah,' she said."

Eleanor was visibly moved. "What an extraordinary thing to say!"

When Eleanor closed her eyes, the room spun slowly around her in a circle.

"I asked Everett straight out who'd given him the right to do it—"

"I know what you're going to say," Eleanor interrupted.

"Then you say it," said Mr. Tripp.

"He said, 'Herself!'"

Calvin Tripp laughed aloud, while unbuttoning his long coat. "I didn't even need to go there!" he said. "You've got 'em figured backward and forward. . . . How'd you know that?" he asked.

"I knew it came from Evangeline, because it all comes from Evangeline, and it is all a secret, Mr. Tripp, and no one can see beyond the surface of things—of the things that are simply happening. There's no seeing through to the core of things, nor with reading her mind. I think Truman Rogers got it right. 'She's on the loose,' he said."

Eleanor would like to have pictured the scene at the Billings house. She envisioned Evangeline sitting back importantly on a leather couch, or pacing this way and that. "What were Mr. Conboy and Justin doing while you were there?"

"The boy was working on her riding saddle. He had Evangeline's saddle propped up on the back of a big easy chair, and was saddle-soaping it for her. Then Everett brought her a tin cup of hot coffee, and she waved the cup at her saddle, and told Everett to take over. 'Show J.J. how to do that,' she said."

Eleanor nodded, impressively, as before. "She tells them what to do, then?" she ventured.

"There's no doubt about that," Calvin replied. "But then, the Sewells, going all the way back, are like that."

Eleanor thrilled in secret to Mr. Tripp's allusion to Evangeline's nature.

"Mr. Tripp," she said, "how did she appear? It's been such a short time since her 'laying in.'"

"Oh, she's fit!" he exclaimed, broadly. "That didn't surprise me none."

"It wouldn't have surprised me either!" Eleanor attested. It pleased her to affect an intimate understanding of the other, as though the blacksmith and she possessed that good fortune in common. "I think she is very strong," she said. "Very bold and resourceful." Eleanor dropped her voice in embarrassment, as she added a more extreme tribute. "She can be hard when she needs to be." Eleanor colored, and looked away, adding, "I have never been sorry that I allied myself with her."

Eleanor was finding it awkward to ask what she most wanted to know. "Did you give her my note?" she inquired, finally. "Did you talk about me?"

Eleanor could not mask her ardent feelings. Her fingertips trembled, as she touched her lips, then smoothed back her hair.

"Yes," he allowed, "she looked at your letter."

"Did she read it?"

Calvin shrugged, and made a face. "I suppose she read it!" he said. "She opened it. She looked it over. I don't think anything in it worried her, if that's what you're wondering. I did, though, tell her what you said for me to say."

"And what was that?" Eleanor asked, hopefully.

Mr. Tripp smiled, and recited his answer like a school lesson. "I said, 'Miss Gray's heart is with you. She is doing everything for you she can think of. She'll do anything else you want.'"

"You actually said that?" Eleanor whispered back.

"You told me to say it, and I said it."

"*And?*" Eleanor pressed, after an interval, studying his face all the while with great scrutiny.

"That's all," he replied. "I said it."

"And she?"

"She," Mr. Tripp pointed out, "doesn't say much."

"I understand." She liked thinking of Evangeline Sewell as being reticent to the point of curtness, just as she respected her steeliness. Eleanor saw herself as being different from that, as being more talkative and engaging, and liked to think that these were agreeable reciprocities that persons such as Evangeline and she might come to enjoy in one another.

Eleanor had an unexpected insight. It flashed upon her, as she lowered herself onto her chair by the fire. "It's all so unusual," she declared. "It's the most remarkable thing. That *I,* the stranger of strangers here, know far more about this secret drama, and have learned more about it, as it has unfolded, from point to point, than anyone else!"

Calvin Tripp was amused. He lowered his voice to match hers. "That's why you're whispering," he said.

"What's more," she said, "as has been the case all along, the more I learn, the less I am able to express the truth of it. Till it is become very like *my* secret. That her world, secretive and illicit, is my own lawless place." Eleanor smiled at the thought. "That I am my own unfolding secret."

Eleanor's recondite remarks left Mr. Tripp in the dark as to her meanings. He made signs of leaving, spinning his hat in his hands. "You seem pretty certain, then, that she's defying the law."

Eleanor considered it. She sought to frame an elusive thought. "I don't believe she wants the sanctions and protection of the law. In a manner of speaking, she is the law. Tell me," she added on impulse, "where is the young minister? Where is Reverend Allen?"

"I didn't see hide nor hair of him. Probably at the Treadwells'."

Eleanor agreed. "Yes," she said. "I saw his carriage there yesterday at twilight. I think he may not want to link himself to something unlawful—such as their having entered that house!"

Mr. Tripp shook his head. "I see it different," he said. "He's wherever she told him to be."

"And doing whatever she told him to do," Eleanor confirmed, automatically.

"That's how I see it."

"Maybe Miss Sewell is sparing him any sort of guilt by association. Something that could do harm to his future."

"Makes sense."

"Which only argues further," said Eleanor, reasoning her way, "that she and her two accomplices are, in fact, trespassing!"

"I've no way of knowing that," said the other.

"One thing is clear. Whether or not he has hired himself a room for tonight at the Treadwell's, he shirked his church duties up in Cold Spring this morning to stay close to her. He is very much under her sway, I think. Like her own private minister!"

"This'll interest you, Miss Gray." Mr. Tripp interjected, smiling at the thought of it. "She was wearing something tonight that I'm tempted to guess wasn't hers."

"Really?" Eleanor was instantly animated. She had intimations of something revelatory in the offing.

"A pair of boots," he went on. "She was wearing those same twill pants of hers, but you could see the shiny boots showing under the cuffs." He laughed. "Like a gentleman's riding boots. She must have found them upstairs."

Eleanor saw the humor in it. "Found them, and pulled them on!" she said.

Mr. Tripp's voice rose musically. "It's the Sewell way!" he intoned. "I was thinking, while walking back, that maybe she's come back to return to school."

Eleanor was not of two minds on that point. "I have good reason to know, Mr. Tripp, that that'd be the last thing she has in mind."

"You never know," he countered. "She asked if Mr. Bayles was back yet from home. He's her teacher, ain't he?"

Eleanor's pulse slowed to a cold drumming. She was gaping up at him wide-eyed from her chair, while gripping her knees with both hands. "She said that?"

"As I was leaving," he answered.

"How did you reply, Mr. Tripp?" she added, in hollow tones.

"I told her what I know. He's coming in by stage from Lenox tomorrow. I heard Chickering tell it to that artist fellow. Said that Bayles'd be coming back the day after Christmas, and was bringing some radio telephone parts. Those are the words he used."

"Radio telephony," Eleanor corrected, quietly.

"Yes. He said that Bayles was making himself a 'set.' I can't guess what a 'set' is, but it's something he's making."

In her distraction, Eleanor spoke her wonderment aloud. *"She is waiting for him."*

"That's what I was thinking," Mr. Tripp rejoined. "That's what I just said."

Eleanor focussed and refocussed her eyes on him. "It isn't like that," she breathed out. "It isn't like that at all." She pressed him further. "How did she say it, Mr. Tripp? Tell me, please. What was her manner?"

"It's when I was going out. She was standing back in the middle of the room, with her two hands flat in her front pants pockets. Everett was seeing me out to the kitchen and back door. 'Calvin,' she said, when I got to the hall door. She signalled me to come back into the room."

Unconscious that he was impersonating the young woman, Mr. Tripp slid his hands downward into his own pants pockets, and put his shoulders back.

Eleanor studied him expectantly. "What exactly did she say?"

"Just that. She didn't move an inch. She just called it to me. 'My teacher get back yet?' she said. 'William get back yet?' So, I told her what I told you I said."

"Tomorrow."

"Yes," said the blacksmith.

As Eleanor rose now, to see Mr. Tripp out at her own hall door, he noticed for the first time her condition.

"You're limping bad," he said. He showed Eleanor a pained look.

"It's what comes of falling," she bantered back. "It's what comes of overstepping."

213

20

EXT MORNING, Eleanor took her breakfast alone, bringing her tea, toast, and oatmeal up to her room. She was running a temperature, and was disheartened to notice that the soreness and stiffness in her right leg had worsened. Yesterday had been the longest, most trying day she had ever known. Her recollection of the Christmas morning church service was as of something recalled from the ages; the sight of Justin driving Evangeline up to the churchyard gate in her glossy green carriage likewise seemed forever ago. She thought about the hailstorm, her oilskin hat speeding downstream, the baby buried on the hill. Her mind skipped from one worrisome thought to another. She recognized the obsessive character of her thinking, but to identify a devil was a very different thing from expelling a devil.

Later, she heard voices coming from the front of the house, then someone calling upstairs to her by name. It was Mr. Chickering. "Someone to see you!" he sang out, in a pleasant melodious voice.

At first, she guessed it might have been the Star Route man—to judge by Mr. Chickering's happy accents, given the way everyone kidded her about Mr. Walker being her gentleman caller. But her spirits jumped wildly at the sudden rare notion that her visitor might be none other than Evangeline herself! It was not all that improbable, as the Sewell girl had shown herself as having no compunctions about doing such things. It would be just like her to march straight into Miss Harrison's house. To beard the lion in its den. An image of the upcountry girl flashed into Eleanor's thoughts; she could picture her standing in the hallway below, her hands thrust down flat inside the pockets of her twill pants, the beautiful posture, the ice-eyed bearing. Eleanor went at once to the front staircase, and started down. On reaching the landing, she was startled to discover the boy, Justin Judd, standing at the foot of the stairs. He was holding Alonzo Klaw's magnificent black coat in his arms. The big coat was folded neatly. Justin held it ceremoniously, as one might hold out a ritual offering. Eleanor was immediately dismayed, and could not hide her shocked feelings. They were returning the coat to her.

"What a dreadful thing to do!" she cried, as she came down the steps.

The boy was smiling up at her. He stood at attention, his features glowing. Sprigs of bright blond hair stuck out at the sides of his cap. He addressed her cheerfully. "She don't need it," he said. "'Vangeline *got* clothes!"

Eleanor was clasping the newel post at the foot of the stairs. She was clearly beside herself. "I can't imagine anyone doing such a thing!" she exclaimed in anguish. "Why would anyone do this to me? I went to such lengths to obtain it for her—and to send it to her at the lake."

Eleanor's reaction caused Mr. Chickering, who appeared embarrassed by her outburst, to withdraw from the hall into the front parlor.

The boy had meanwhile changed expression. The confusion grew in his face. He held the coat out farther, as though perhaps she had not understood why he was there.

Eleanor was close to being indignant. "You take that coat back!" she said.

The boy made as though to respond.

"You will do as I tell you," Eleanor cut him short. "Didn't she know that it was a gift? That I strove to get her something for the winter that was just right for her? What was she thinking?"

All at once, Eleanor made up her mind to return the coat with an accompanying note. "You come upstairs with me," she said.

Justin followed her obediently up the front steps, the folded coat lying flat in the cradle of his arms. Eleanor fought back the tears.

She could feel the beat of her heart. She was sure that Alice Harrison had heard every word that had just transpired, and could only deduce further the extent of her involvement in the arcane activities of the past two days, but she was beyond turning back.

She commenced her note, setting the words down with passion, her temples heating up.

Dear Evangeline:

You have disappointed me terribly this morning by returning to me this splendid greatcoat, which I was so honored to find for you, and so honored to send to you — indeed, as a gift from me, and as a reminder of the great affection in which I hold you. I thought it represented a proof of my ability and my eagerness to serve you. You have made me very unhappy.

Eleanor paused, as by the wildest chance, she heard a man's laughter coming from the stairwell at the head of the corridor, and recognized it at once as that of William Bayles. The timing defied all probability. He had just arrived in from Lenox. To make certain, Eleanor got up from her desk and went to the hallway. He and Charles Chickering were talking by the mail desk.

The boy, Justin, stood all the while immobile in the middle of the room, mouth open, a look of bewilderment distorting his face, still holding Evangeline's coat.

Eleanor resumed her note. The word came readily to hand.

I have given you also the gift of trust. Besides hurting myself physically, I have jeopardized my post and place here in the community by putting myself at your side, by believing in you, in your goodness and importance. I shall now give you further earnest of that faith — by reporting to you here that the person whose return to Miss Harrison's house you are awaiting arrived home not five minutes ago. He is here.

When I contemplate your intentions, or what might happen to you in consequence, my blood runs cold. I need ever so much to see you. I have a morbid premonition that you will suddenly vanish. If you can,

please come to me. While I ask nothing in return for my actions, I have
the right to expect your recognition of those things I have done, and am
doing, on your behalf. It should be obvious by now that my devotion to
you is total. I would walk through fire for you.

Your loving friend,
Eleanor

To be sure that no one would intercept the boy, Eleanor saw him
out. First, though, she remembered the little Christmas parcel of
honeycakes and peanut brittle that she had wrapped for him in silver foil. She slipped it into the side pocket of his plaid jacket. "It's
something sweet," she said. With that, she led him downstairs to
the front door. Outside, in the icy air, she instructed him on his errand home.

"You mustn't forget to give Evangeline my letter. It's important."

The pale lights, moiling and swirling in the boy's eyes, touched
her heart. He had fallen to staring at her.

"You're very beautiful, Justin," she said.

The boy lingered a moment, his eyes brightening and dimming,
then he turned about, and dashed out to the road.

Going back indoors, Eleanor had suddenly to clasp the door-
jamb to maintain her balance. A sharp pain darted up her right
thigh at every flex of the leg. By now, though, following her dispatching of Justin with the coat and her letter, she had already
made up her mind to enlist the help of Myron Walker, her closest
friend in all East Becket. She would prevail upon him to drive her
to the Billings house this afternoon. She was sure he would indulge
her. He was always acceding to her desires. While the thought of
imposing herself on Evangeline—of actually going to the door—
left Eleanor feeling shaken inside, the reverse prospect of their not
meeting up at all—as, for example, were Evangeline suddenly
compelled to depart the town, and of her never perhaps seeing
her—was far more appalling. Sometimes it is imperative, she
thought, to improve upon a fleeting opportunity.

Because her own windows at the rear of the house gave her no view of the road, Eleanor took a book and a blanket, went down-stairs, and stationed herself on the big sofa by the front parlor win-dows. About an hour after noon, Calvin Tripp started out for home. Eleanor could hear him in the kitchen thanking Alice for her great kindness to him. He stopped to bid Eleanor farewell.

Eleanor sounded fatalistic. "An inner voice tells me that I will never see you again, Mr. Tripp."

Calvin Tripp expressed some doubt. "The world is not so wide," he said.

Eleanor was looking up at him with admiration from her place on the sofa. She always liked the way he stood, his head back, his feet splayed.

"I have never known anyone," she said, "who more surely occu-pies the space on earth that he *is* occupying than you, sir." She smiled.

"You'll come upcountry again one day."

Eleanor didn't know whether to nod or shake her head. "I only dream that that may be true." She was sitting with her legs tucked beneath her, her book on her lap.

He tilted his head toward the outdoors. "It looks like snow," he said.

"I would wager anything," she said, "that it's snowing hard up in Wisdom Way. I have never known a place like it, even though I never really quite got to it. It is certainly the one most memorable place I have ever been, or, at least, *hoped* to get to. I think," she added, " you are the walking embodiment of Wisdom Way. They say that it's on the way to being unpeopled—that it is something turning to nothing—but as long as you are there—or Evangeline Sewell is there—I think it is a magical place on earth." Her eyes shone wetly.

Calvin Tripp seemed on some level to understand her meanings.

"I am sorry you have to walk all that way." Eleanor teased him. "I will remember you," she said, "as the blacksmith who had no horse." She extended her hand to him. "Good-bye, Mr. Tripp."

A minute later, she watched as he strode vigorously across the front lawn toward the elms at roadside, his tan waterproof coat shaking in the wind, the flat-brimmed leather hat riding atop his head like a cup and saucer. Then he was gone from sight.

Twice in the next hour, William Bayles walked by the hallway door. She avoided looking at him. She felt certain that he knew all about the events of the past few days, regarding Evangeline Sewell's occupation of the house on the knoll, and of her having buried the child in the East Becket churchyard yesterday. He had probably even been told by now of her own accountable actions— of how she, Eleanor, his colleague and subordinate at the school, had been in cahoots all this fall season with Miss Sewell. As always, Eleanor made no pretense of understanding him. She judged him to be one of those persons who shut their eyes to unpleasant prospects on the assumption that even the most insidious matters will unravel harmlessly if left alone. She imagined his mind taken up instead with the occult technologies involved in the creation of his radio set—with his talk of currents and frequencies, of coils and condensers!

As she gazed out onto the wintry afternoon, she took a dark pleasure in conjuring an image of Evangeline standing in front of the fireplace in the Billings house, or maybe sprawling back boy-ishly on a big leather couch, with Eleanor's letter in hand, reading with the sharpest interest Eleanor's secret report to her that William had just returned. She wondered if her behavior was sin-ful. The fact that no one in the house interrupted her vigil im-pressed Eleanor as a sure sign that all were embarrassed for her now. They saw her as someone whom they had sorrily misjudged. The comely, well-bred "normal school" teacher imported from Fall River had shown herself an unpredictable quantity, a figure governed by inexplicable impulses and a secretive nature.

When the tall cherrywood clock by the side wall struck four, the chiming slowed with each tone. The clock was winding down. El-eanor wondered in passing if a person's descent into folly, or iniq-uity, might not be signified to them at some critical point, disclosed from without—as by Nemesis, the elastic response of that which is orderly and correct in the universe to that which is grown false, wanton, out of place. A tremor under the floor, perhaps. A clock that slows to a stop. She listened carefully. Indeed, the parlor clock had stopped. A light wind rattled the windows, like the tapping of a watchman announcing the onset of night. Gathering up her lap blanket and book, Eleanor arose and made her way back upstairs.

Not a minute later, as she closed her door, there arose a commotion from the front hall below. There was a sudden clashing sound, of the front door thrown wide, followed by running footsteps on the stairs. It was the boy. Eleanor recognized his voice at once.

"Mr. Bayles!" he was yelling "Come quick! Everett says for you to come quick! You got raccoons in the schoolhouse!"

Eleanor's heart was in her throat. She could hear Justin pounding on the schoolteacher's door, then William Bayles's voice, then Justin again. Mr. Conboy had sent Justin to fetch Mr. Bayles in a hurry. That much was clear. Raccoons, the boy repeated, were wrecking things in the schoolhouse. Justin sounded genuinely alarmed. Eleanor was certain he had been put up to it; that Mr. Conboy had instilled a great sense of urgency in the boy.

Eleanor was standing by her door, her hands to her face, listening breathlessly to the drumming sound of the teacher and the boy going noisily down the front staircase. She was certain something violent was impending. The mere idea of it rooted her to the floor. She was, after all, inextricably wound up in it. By alerting Evangeline to Mr. Bayles's presence in the house, she might even be said to have set certain events in motion.

By the time Eleanor went out her door and made her way forward to the low Palladian window at the front end of the hall, Justin and the schoolteacher were out of sight. They were doubtless just entering the school. She could make out beyond the elms by the road only the edge of the schoolhouse window. It was weakly illumined by lantern light. Eleanor was crouched uncomfortably on her knees by the decorative, floor-level window. As her eyes grew accustomed to the twilit yard below and to the road beyond, her gaze returned more than once to the stand of lilac trees situated far to the left, in the direction of the crossroads. Gradually, a silhouette materialized in the shadowy mass of the lilacs. She pressed her face to the cold window pane, the better to see. The form moved now and again. It gained definition. It was the head and neck of Evangeline's mare! Eleanor was sure of it, though she could see but a small portion of the overall figure. She was sure that Evangeline was sitting there astride her horse, and had watched just a moment ago as William Bayles and the boy hurried across the road to the school.

Eleanor's thoughts were racing. She tried thinking of a superior vantage point from which she could see across the road. Within seconds, she was going down the back staircase, headed for the out-doors. At the foot of the darkened staircase, in her frenzy, she nearly lost her balance. Once outside, she made her way quickly to-ward the toolshed attached to the corner of the house. The air was frigid. There was a brittleness in the atmosphere that made her eyes sting and set her knees quaking. The instant she came round the toolshed, however, she knew her timing to have been exact. Evangeline was coming along the road on horseback, advancing unhurriedly, at a walk.

Eleanor put a hand to the corner of the house to steady herself. The sight of the other in her flowing black coat, her hair glowing like phosphorous, was unforgettable. The frozen surface of the gravel road glittered iridescently, like black glass, under the light tapping of the horse's hooves, as the horse and rider closed the dis-tance between the dark mass of lilac trees on the left and the dull glow of the schoolhouse window. There was something hypnotic, machinelike, in the motion. Evangeline Sewell was leaning for-ward a trifle, her right arm draped at her side, the reins clasped high in her left fist. Her body rose and fell rhythmically to the gait of the mare. The icy tapping of the horse's hooves accentuated the sense of something malevolent unfolding.

Evangeline was still in view on the roadway when Eleanor's at-tention was diverted to something else, a noise coming at her from behind, a sudden metallic click. The door out which she had come was still ajar. The kitchen window, closer at hand, cast a panel of light onto the ground nearby. Eleanor detected a movement in the light. It was Alice herself, standing in the window. She was looking down at Eleanor with alarm.

Without a moment's reflection, Eleanor crossed the yard and re-entered the house. She was shivering from head to foot, her senses in riot, as she started up the back staircase.

FOR A LONG half hour or so, she sat by the fire in her darkened room, filled with worry. She tried over and over again to divine what exactly was going on. Whatever it was, Alice would surely associate her with it. For the life of her, Eleanor couldn't rid her mind of the look of shock in Alice's eyes on discovering her skulking about outdoors, at the back corner of the house. Eleanor's reflections were abruptly interrupted by the sound of someone making his way up the back stairs. Every instinct told her that it was William Bayles—that it must be he—and she prayed that it *was* he—as she had been considering the direst possibilities. Eleanor went stealthily to her door and listened. Indeed, the soft report of a door closing a little way up the hall all but confirmed her speculation.

It was nearly supper hour. Eleanor felt that she would not have the courage to face anybody tonight. It was to her good fortune that Mr. Walker stopped by. She heard his voice below, and opened her door a crack. He had been told about her fall, he was saying to someone. Then she heard him coming upstairs. She opened the door to him with unconcealed relief. "I'm so happy to see you," she exclaimed.

The Star Route man stood in the doorway. His rabbit coat and hat showed a light dusting of snow. While taking off his fur mittens, he signified her room with a tilt of his eyes. "You're living in the dark?" he said.

"More than ever," Eleanor replied reflexively, unable to forgo the pun. She lighted the hurricane lamp, and moved her desk chair to the fire for Mr. Walker to occupy. She draped his enormous coat over her bedstead, then seated herself opposite him. Aware of the agitation of her pulse and breathing, she set her hand to her breast and took a long deep breath. Her nervousness was apparent in her voice.

"I have never known days like these," she said. "Something of an extraordinary nature is going on, and I am at the heart of it, and I don't know what it is." She looked away to the window, then looked back. "Mr. Walker," she added, in a suppressed tone, "when you drove up just now, was there a light burning in the schoolhouse?"

Mr. Walker shook his head. He was evidently trying to accustom himself to Eleanor's anxious state. He watched her worriedly. "You don't look yourself," he said.

"You're sure it was in darkness," she persisted.

He nodded. "I'd've noticed."

Eleanor felt herself a prisoner of her own knowledge. She couldn't reveal to anyone, not even to Mr. Walker, her confidant and closest friend, all that she knew. She did, though, describe to him how the boy, Justin, had come running into the house, hollering for the young Mr. Bayles to come quickly, that Everett Conboy wanted him at once. She cited the ostensible reason for his alarm.

"*Raccoons?*" said Mr. Walker.

"I'm sure it was a ploy," she said. "I'm sure it was something else."

More than ever, Eleanor longed to tell Mr. Walker everything she knew, but could not even bring herself to describe the sight—the vision, really—of Evangeline Sewell riding quietly up the glassy road to the schoolhouse.

"I wish you had come earlier," she said. "I wanted so much for you to drive me to the Billings house, Mr. Walker!"

"Forgive my saying it, miss. You're not fit to go anyplace. Look at you," he said, with concern. Mr. Walker's great affection for the schoolteacher shone in his eyes.

"I do have the chills," she agreed. "I am not myself tonight."

"Truman told me about your accident at the bridge."

Eleanor's lips were shaking. From time to time, her right leg trembled spasmodically. She pressed her hand on her knee to stop it. "I am afraid," she confessed, "that I am quite a mess."

A long interval passed between them. Eleanor was unable to look up.

"You are as good a friend as I ever had," she added, at last. "Because these have been hard days for me, Mr. Walker." Eleanor's eyes came up to meet his. "And without your understanding—or even if your understanding is *not* an understanding, but just an expression of trust radiant with sympathy—without that, I think my ignorance of who I am, and what I am going through, would disassemble me."

Mr. Walker had no rejoinder, but was visibly touched by Eleanor's condition and by her words. He stared at her in silence.

A puff of wind sent a flurry of snowflakes against the windowpane. Eleanor smiled on noticing it. "Nature punctuates," she said.

twenty-one

TWICE DURING THE NIGHT, Eleanor arose, and went to the window. Visibility was negligible. The night grew windless. She looked out upon the snow falling with almost perfect verticality. The flakes crowded down past the window with a sense of urgency, a silent multitudinous army.

The second time she got up, she revived the fire and took her chair to the window. She wanted to watch the snow. Something of the awesomeness and indifference of the night rendered her own drama more bearable, as it seemed small and peculiar by contrast. Before sitting, she indulged a childish impulse. She stood Evangeline's portrait on the pine lowboy by the window, then opened the closet door to a point where the portrait was reflected in the tall closet mirror. The effect was uncanny. The drawing itself, dimly illuminated, was as hauntingly beautiful as always. But the reflection of it in the distant mirror was an impression of another order altogether. It was barely perceptible in the depths of the looking glass, like a postage stamp afloat in a solution, or a vision of someone standing perfectly still at the end of a darkened corridor.

She leaned her head against the icy window glass, watching the endless stream of flakes spinning slowly down. She thought of the valley all round filling up with snow. Tomorrow, she determined, she would bring matters to a head. For her to falter now would be to nullify all of her hopes and actions of these past weeks. Tomorrow, by one means or another, she would go to Evangeline, whatever the cost to her pride, and proclaim her feelings. She would make the seriousness of her purpose crystal clear. Such an honest protestation, she was sure, could work no harm, for no human being on earth had the moral latitude to ridicule or make small of a confession like that. She knew that Evangeline would not.

In the morning, Eleanor could scarcely recall having left her chair by the window the night before and gone to bed. She was awake at dawn, and went downstairs to make herself a breakfast. The snow outside the kitchen window was deeper, she judged, than any snow she had ever seen during her years on the coast. It had stopped snowing. She could see nearly a mile to the east. The rolling fields resembled an Arctic landscape. The sky was gray and featureless. While preparing biscuits and stewed blueberries, and taking her place at the kitchen table, she was pleased to realize that her fright last night over what had happened, or might have happened, in the schoolhouse was much dissipated in the morning light.

A muffled banging sound coming from the road was followed by the appearance a second later of a snowplow and oxen. While at that distance, Eleanor could not identify the teamster, she guessed it to be Truman Rogers. When she went upstairs, she was not surprised to encounter Alonzo Klaw emerging from his room. He was dressed for zero weather. His winter costume was topped off by a five-foot-long royal-blue scarf and a matching knit watch cap.

"My goodness," Eleanor exclaimed, "you are bringing East Becket fashion to its knees, Mr. Klaw!"

He stood beaming before her in the hall. "Myron Walker appointed me as the official recording artist of the modern snow clearance techniques employed in this valley."

Eleanor laughed. She was feeling surprisingly buoyant following her early morning ruminations.

"This year," the artist went on, "I have added picture-taking to my repertoire." He showed her the box camera he was carrying.

"I'm sure Mr. Walker will vote you a citation. Not just for your artistry, which we all already admire, but for your native resourcefulness."

"Try as I will," said Alonzo, "I can never keep pace with your wit. You are always fifty feet out front of me, darting back and forth, vanishing from sight. It's your Boston upbringing."

"I am not from Boston, sir. If I were, I'd be a good deal more clever than I am. As it is, even New Bedford puts a strain on me."

"You see?" he bantered back. "You are doing it again."

"I think that Mr. Walker, for all his good sense, had no idea how his snow clearing techniques would be memorialized this morning. Museums," Eleanor piped, "will cherish and protect for a thousand years the results of what he has commissioned you to do."

"I am about to record you," said Alonzo, "if you'll come downstairs to the front door."

Eleanor was game for it. She was enjoying a minute's respite from her preoccupations. As she stepped past Mr. Bayles's door, headed for the stair top, she envisioned the schoolteacher secluded in his room, more than severely chastened, probably afraid to come out.

"How is your leg?" asked Alonzo Klaw, looking back over his shoulder, as he started down the staircase ahead of Eleanor. "I heard that your fall was uglier than we thought."

"We have all fallen, Mr. Klaw. Do you know your *New England Primer? 'In Adams's fall,'*" she recited, "*'we sinned all.'*"

"I *am* familiar with it!" he said. "I think it is the dreariest little book the world was ever asked to look at. The Puritans' idea of cartoons!"

"That is quite *Nasty,* Mr. Klaw," Eleanor responded with a pun.

"Do you see what I mean?" He stopped on the stairs. "You take ten steps to my one."

Once outdoors, Mr. Klaw readied his camera. The snow lay deep on all sides, like a white sea that had come to a stop.

"Stand by the door," he said, indicating where she was to pose. "I am about to enter history."

"No, no," said Eleanor. "I would rather do it the other way." She was clasping the elbows of her sweater, shivering the length of her body.

"There aren't two ways to do it, Miss Gray. One person poses, and one points the camera."

"I mean," she said, "I'll stand out there, and you stand at the door."

The snow was shallowest by the front door, the lea side of the house in last night's storm.

Eleanor stood with her back to the road and valley.

"Isn't it peculiar," she said, "that everything that will be in the picture is what I do not see, and that everything I do see will not be."

"Yes," he remarked, wryly. "They call it photography."

"Do you suppose," said Eleanor, rubbing her hands, "that the future will capture on film all that is not to be seen, and leave out all that is to be seen? Because if that is the case, this new century is off to a tottering start. We'll all be toting mirrors, or walking backward much of the time, hoping to see what we were not intended to see, but most needed to see."

"Stop talking, please," he said, peering into the viewer.

"It is how I have felt for some while now," she said. "That I am confronted with the wrong side of things, while not seeing any part of what I most wish to see. Let alone, touch," she added.

She fell silent. In the next moment, while standing motionless, staring into the lens of Mr. Klaw's camera, something poignant rose up inside her. She imagined that all of the days she had spent here would be reduced to a lonely photographic image. A blurry picture of a young woman standing against a bleak background of snow-covered farmlands and distant vaporous hills. The individual in the picture—genial looking, with pleasant features and dark hair—would be known to no one. Eleanor felt the power of the moment. She reflected on the hill towns upcountry, where houses foundered into the earth, streams regained their primeval anonymity, and how those subsiding settlements were a better prognosticator of things to come than the bursting silos of this fecund valley.

"What are you thinking about?" Alonzo asked, as he cranked the camera for a second picture.

"Oddly, I was thinking about Wisdom Way, and what an appalling amount of snow must have fallen up there last night, and of how I will likely never go there again. It may not even be there. It's an irony that my favorite town in all the world is well on its way to becoming the opposite of a town. To what it was before it was a town."

Alonzo raised the camera a second time. "Wildernesses return," he agreed.

Eleanor smiled into the lens. "I will always remember you said that."

ELEANOR DRESSED SPECIALLY for the day. She got out her dark ruby-red dress of merino wool, the one she saved for important occasions. While dressing, she stole a second look in the mirror at her bruised thigh. The blue-black discoloration down the side of her leg was gruesome. She pulled on a flannel petticoat, and promised herself that she would avoid looking at it for days to come. It was unsightly.

The prospect in front of her of going now to Evangeline set Eleanor's nerves on edge, but not without its having an exhilarating side. Her blood was up. If she felt a stab of anxiety over it, as she did at regular intervals, she saw the foolishness in that. It wasn't as if the other had any reason on earth to be put out by Eleanor's decision to go to her. For it would have been as plain to Evangeline as it was to Eleanor herself that she had been Evangeline's true and sole confidante in all the valley all these many weeks. That was made clear in their letters, as well as in the fact that Eleanor, in each case, had fulfilled the other's blunt demands. Nor could either of them deny that theirs had been a secret bond, an all but conspiratorial understanding. Her case was even stronger than that, as it was she, Eleanor—the only one of the more than two hundred East Becket worshippers—who had hurried outdoors to join the funeral cortege on Christmas morning, and imperiled—most likely ruined— her respected place in town by doing so.

Of all her involvement, though, her latest show of loyalty was the most difficult for her to countenance herself; that was the note she sent yesterday telling the other of William Bayles's return. Eleanor couldn't think of it without experiencing a cold, sinking sensation. In her mind's eye arose the picture of Evangeline emerging on horseback from the shadowy lilacs, in her flowing coat, her hair aglow, advancing quietly to the sinister tapping of the horse's hooves on the icy roadway. It set her nerves on edge. More than once this morning, she thought about rapping on William's door, knowing that just the sight of him, standing before her, physically sound, would dispel this particular anxiety.

Two or three times during the course of the morning, a light snow began to fall. Each time, it amounted to nothing, but the sky remained low and overcast. By ten o'clock, the time had come for her to make good on her word. She was sure if she went outdoors onto the road that she could hitch a ride with one of the men involved in the snow plowing, or with any passing wagon or carriage. The roads looked quite clear. While the idea of seizing the nettle, and actually going to the other, of confronting her, placing herself in a position where she might in fact be humiliated—while all that was worrisome—she felt also a surge of excitement that only a twenty year old caught up in such a passion might know. The excitement was palpable. It made her giddy. All of her hours and days in the Harrison house pointed to the present time.

As it happened, the events of this iron-gray December morning did not so much originate with Eleanor as with others. Charles Chickering had gone outdoors to shovel a path from the front door to the road, and was coming back inside for a cup of hot cocoa. Eleanor heard him calling to someone, then he came in, clapping his gloved hands and stamping his feet. Eleanor went immediately to see who it was, and discovered Mr. Conboy and Justin approaching on foot from the direction of the crossroads. They were headed past the house. Mr. Conboy had what appeared to be a knapsack or bedroll on his back. He was carrying his shotgun. They were going home! Eleanor went downstairs as hurriedly as she could, and out the front door. Mr. Conboy was striding along in his long-legged, determined gait, but the boy had turned, and was wading in through the deep snow, and then coming up the shoveled path toward Eleanor. The man in the road paused to wait for the boy. Eleanor was filled with misgivings.

"Where is Evangeline?" she demanded. "What did she say?"

Justin stopped in front of her. He was sniffling from a head cold. "She says she got nothing to say!"

"That is unacceptable!" Eleanor cried, instantly. "I want to know what is happening. I insist you tell me."

The eyes of the boy reflected his confusion. He was not able to grasp what was being asked of him.

"You gave her my note?" Eleanor pressed him. "Did you?"

The boy nodded, then answered as before. "'Vangeline says she's got nothing to say."

Notwithstanding her concern for the boy's incapacities, Eleanor had a powerful impulse to reach out and shake him by the shoulders! Her voice was thin with alarm. "I have every right to know what is happening. I insist you tell me, Justin! What happened last night? What happened in the schoolhouse?"

Justin fell back a step. He stared openmouthed at her, his face blank as a dinner plate. A moiling of lights rose and fell in his eyes. He was visibly distressed. Suddenly, he blurted his reply. "She *horsewhipped* him!" he cried.

With that, the boy turned on his heel and fled in the snow, leaving Eleanor gaping at him in astonishment from the front door. She could scarcely credit what she had just heard, and yet knew it at once to be true. William Bayles had not emerged from his room all morning, and had not spoken to anyone. He was doubtless laid up. Not just injured, she guessed, but shamed and badly shaken. The sight of Mr. Conboy and Justin going side by side up the road gave Eleanor to realize all at once that Evangeline had dismissed them—that she had brought matters here to a close. She had, in short, sent them home!

Eleanor could not later recall by what stages she had got herself upstairs, or whether she had encountered anyone along the way, but she had thrown open her closet door, and was pulling on her winter coat, hat, and mittens. All at once, she had the dismaying realization that Evangeline was about to leave the valley. Considering what the other had done, there could be no doubt now on that point. No one could countenance what she did last night. The vicious retributive justice that she had inflicted on Mr. Bayles in the schoolhouse would place Miss Sewell forever beyond the pale. As Eleanor started from the room, her insides were shaking. She had lost control. She was not equal to the events that were sweeping her before them, and saw now the folly in all her assumptions of these past weeks. She had assumed all along that she and Evangeline were being borne forward, as by fate, toward some point of convergence. She had honestly believed that.

It pained Eleanor to see Alice standing in wait of her at the foot of the stairs, her temples pink with embarrassment. Eleanor descended the steps, determined to go to the Billings house one way or another, on foot if necessary, whatever the cost to her leg, or whatever others might think of it.

Alice attempted gently to intercede, to dissuade Eleanor from going out. "We're all aware, Eleanor, that you have shown Evangeline a great heart—"

"Please don't say anymore," Eleanor cut her short.

"She's stubborn, she's ungrateful—"

Eleanor stepped around Alice. "I think she is worth a great deal!" she said.

Outside, the iciness of the morning air attacked Eleanor's face and eyes. As earlier, a light snow was flying. Now and again, too, when the air gusted, the fallen snow lifted up in a sudden powdery screen, like something alive. Eleanor had barely closed the door behind her when she experienced the most extraordinary sensation. For at the very second of her turning, there was Evangeline—at the crossroads, not a hundred yards away—turning the head of her mare to the north, homeward. Through a sudden snow flurry blowing sidewise past the elms, the shadowy image of the horse and rider looked like an apparition, like something apocalyptic.

Eleanor was instantly aware what was happening, and started down the partly shoveled path toward the road. Her heart was jumping. Where the shoveling came to an end—with the handle of Mr. Chickering's shovel jutting up forlornly—she waded into the deep snow. The hem of her long skirt billowed about her, the snow invading her boots. There was not one moment when she had paused to consider her actions, or given a thought to those persons who were surely watching her from the window. By the time she had clambered over the snowbank and onto the plowed rod, the distance between herself and Evangeline had widened. The great mare was proceeding at a walk, but now and again would pick up the gait, trotting a few steps, her hindquarters shifting sideways.

Eleanor called to Evangeline once, but knew that her voice was lost in the leaden air. By the time she got to the crossroads, the figure of the black-coated rider and her mount had receded perceptibly. Evangeline's hair shone with a talismanic glow. Eleanor was keenly aware of the ridiculousness of her attempt to overtake the other on foot. She imagined in passing what an absurd spectacle it would have made to someone peering down from the sky, at the two tiny figures moving microscopically over the white landscape, one behind the other, the first oblivious of the second, and the interval between them expanding with geometric precision.

Far ahead on the road, however, a team of oxen emerged to view, seeming, really, to materialize out of the white tableland itself. They were coming up from a declivity in the road. They were snowplowing. The northern road, leading to Cold Spring and Wisdom Way, was the least used road, and therefore the last to be cleared. Eleanor could not identify the teamster at that distance, especially as he was moving away from her, but soon enough she recognized him by his coat and fur hat. It was Mr. Walker. He was about halfway between Evangeline and the far-off slot in the trees, where the road entered the wilderness. The long palisade of cedars stretching to left and right was covered in snow, the pointed treetops like a hundred white spears.

Eleanor knew now that Evangeline would be made aware of her presence. When she reached Mr. Walker on her mare, he would turn around at the sound of her approach, and, in turning, see Eleanor. She would have stepped along more rapidly had she been able, but was genuinely impeded, and knew anyhow that she was going to meet up with Evangeline. She was certain of it. Presently, up ahead, she could see where Mr. Walker had indeed halted his team, and was looking back at the rider. The two individuals, and the horse and team of oxen, formed a dark, complex configuration against the snow. Then, after a minute's time, it was evident that the Star Route man had in fact spotted Eleanor.

The snow rose up and blew in a swirl across the road. When it had settled, Evangeline could be seen sitting sidewise on her mount, looking back at Eleanor. There was naturally no hearing them at that distance. But there was no need to hear what they were saying. She knew what they were saying. Mr. Walker was telling her how she, Eleanor, had done everything conceivable to help. Mr. Walker was praising her to Evangeline. Nothing was surer under the sun.

By something of an illusory nature over the distance, something blurry and dimensionless, Eleanor perceived that Evangeline had in fact detached herself from Mr. Walker, and had already advanced some little distance toward her. She was coming back along the road at that same unhurried pace as before. Eleanor continued on. Her thoughts were everywhere. She recalled out of the blue the afternoon in September when Evangeline came by on horseback, the glacial face, the percussive rhythm of the hooves, the sight of Mr. Conboy treading behind her—and how that moment had been without any precedent in her life, and yet, was precedent itself for so much that followed.

The cold packed snow underfoot clung to the soles of her boots. The steady gait of the approaching horse seemed not so much a fluid movement in time as a chain of articulated segments. The blond globe of Evangeline's head reiterated the clocklike motion, bobbing at every step, as she drew closer.

In the final moments before Evangeline got to her, Eleanor resolved to express herself as well and bravely as she could. After all, expressing herself with some clarity was the one thing that had distinguished and sustained her so far in her young life, and which— doubtless—would redeem her more than once in the long years to come. Anyhow, it was all she had this morning.

Eleanor stopped walking, and waited the last few seconds for

Evangeline to reach her. She was sure that Miss Sewell was a young woman of very few words. Eleanor could only hope that if speech were ever to come easily to her that it would do so now. She shivered from nervousness, her head and neck quaking. Evangeline halted, was staring down at her with an open but curious expression. As always, the paleness of her complexion and hair was startling, and made even more emphatic by the blackness of her mount and greatcoat.

Thankfully, for Eleanor, the words came with ease.

"I should not have followed you on the road just now," she said, "but I wished to speak to you before you went away."

Evangeline listened with apparent interest. She lurched gently as the horse beneath her fidgeted and twitched. Eleanor could feel on the air the body heat of the great animal. At the moment, however, she was more than conscious that this was the first time she had ever communed with the other face-to-face, and she, Evangeline Sewell, was as prepossessing in person as Eleanor might ever have guessed her to be.

"This has been a long and difficult season for me," Eleanor went on, "but I will not ever duplicate it." Eleanor could feel her eyes heating. "Ever since my first seeing you, and ever since our first written notes, you have been first in my heart. I have never placed anyone before you."

Eleanor uttered these words with difficulty, but was relieved to realize that what she most wished to say—even perhaps dreamed of saying—was coming from her with great naturalness.

Evangeline spoke for the first time. "You've been good to me," she said.

"If so," said Eleanor, "it is not because I am a good person. Everything I have done has served my self-interest. Everything I have done was done to promote me in your eyes."

An hour earlier, Eleanor would have guessed that such a protestation as that would have embarrassed the other. It didn't. Evangeline nodded. She was pulling off her gloves. She raised her bare hands to her lips, and blew into her fists. Eleanor was studying her in the meanwhile, from the slight fleshiness of her face and throat,

and the perfection of her temples and cheekbones, to the solidness
with which she sat on the mare. The sides of her coat draped down
over her thighs and knees. She was wearing the riding boots that
Calvin Tripp had mentioned. They peeped out from beneath the
legs of her twill pants.

"When you get upcountry," Eleanor asked, "what will you do?
Will you stay—or go?"

Evangeline turned her eyes to her, but said nothing.

"You know, of course," Eleanor said, more brightly, "that I tried
reaching you up there. Mr. Walker drove me. There was a big
snowfall. We spent the night in the church."

"Yes," Evangeline remarked, in a tone that impressed Eleanor.
"I heard about the hailstorm, too."

Eleanor sought a light rejoinder that would permit her to say
what she greatly desired to say. She was smiling up at Evangeline.

"Every time I tried to show my love for you, nature stepped in
the way." She gestured prettily at the sprawling snowfields. "This
storm is only the latest manifestation of that. I think—I think it is
not just nature," she added. "I think it is God who got in the way."
Eleanor smiled again. "Probably a family curse. Something in the
blood."

"They said you hurt yourself."

"Oh, there is truth in that," Eleanor came back, melodiously. "It
was I who hurt myself. It was not someone else who did it to me."

The sun was not out this morning, but there was a glow nonetheless behind Evangeline's head and back. Eleanor raised her
hand flat above her eyes. "I fell down the embankment at the
bridge. I was trying to reach you. I wanted to warn you about the
selectmen, and what I thought they intended to do." Eleanor debated whether or not to mention the buried infant. "About Elijah,"
she added, at last.

Evangeline was staring down at her still. She was studying Eleanor. It was apparent she was going to say something. After a moment, she urged the horse somehow fractionally into a sidelong position. She disengaged her foot then from the stirrup, and leaned
decisively with her hand extended. "I'll ride you back," she said.

Eleanor stood before her like a fencepost, but was wonderfully charmed. It was the last thing she had expected.

"I have never been on a horse."

"It's as easy as being off a horse," said Evangeline. She fluttered her fingers impatiently.

Eleanor took hold of her hand. While the act of reaching her foot up to the stirrup imparted the most painful sensation to her bruised thigh so far, it only lasted a second, as Evangeline drew her up behind herself with unexpected strength and speed. Eleanor fairly soared upward. She wavered to and fro precariously, and took hold of Evangeline instantly with both arms. Then she extracted her foot from the stirrup. Evangeline kicked her own foot back into place, and gave a sudden forward jolt of her body that set her mare in motion.

"I hope you'll go slowly," Eleanor entreated. "Otherwise, I'll end up on my forehead."

Evangeline said nothing to that. While riding behind her, Eleanor was aware of the other's posture. She could all but feel the stiffness of Evangeline's spine, and the lift of her head. Most impressive, though, was her closeness. Evangeline's hair was not inches away from her face. Her coat smelled of the woods at close range, as of leaves, earth, fire smoke. Certain that a second opportunity would never come about, Eleanor determined to give utterance to her most precious secret thoughts. Her chin grazed the collar of Evangeline's coat. The mare settled into a mechanical plodding. Up ahead could be seen a faint banner of smoke rising from each of Alice's two chimneys. The house looked like a steamer traversing a white ocean.

"If this were a fairy tale," Eleanor put in, quietly, "we would be going the other way. You would be carrying me off to your wilderness." She held Evangeline around the waist. "Your wilderness redoubt," she added. "I had hoped last week to see your house, where you were born and raised."

"It shakes in the wind, and leaks in the rain," said the other, tersely. She turned her face sidelong to Eleanor.

"Your eyes," Eleanor offered, "are cobalt blue. I think these little towns, upcountry and down, have found their most perfect expression ever in you."

"I am not beautiful," said Evangeline, matter of factly.

Eleanor disagreed. "You are as beautiful as Nature ever gets," she said. Her cheek brushed Evangeline's hair. Her senses were swimming. "Everything is going every which way inside me. During all these weeks, I had looked forward to our coming together—to our being bound closely in great friendship. I was so sure of it. It was all a pipe dream. I can barely believe this morning that you are leaving."

The jouncing of the horse gave their bodies a single rhythmical pulse beat. "Would you do me one kindness?" Eleanor asked the other. "At the crossroads, would you turn right, and ride us as far as the covered bridge—and then back again?"

Evangeline, characteristically, did not reply, but began beveling the black mare to her right over the snowy surface of the road, headed toward the bridge.

Eleanor rested her cheek on the other's shoulder. "In a world that never stops," she said, "in a universe without ending, some such small things should go on for a while."

Shortly, Evangeline had turned her mount onto the road to the bridge. The plowed snow lay in a high furrow on either side of the road ahead. As before, a light snow was falling.

Eleanor offered an amusing remark. "Mr. Tripp," she said, "told me about your new boots."

Evangeline said nothing. But when it was apparent that Eleanor was not going to enlarge on the point, Evangeline did. "They were somebody else's," she said, "and now they're mine." She looked around. It was the first time Eleanor had seen her smile. She was quite sure by now, on the strength of that insignificant response, that Miss Sewell *had* in fact commandeered the Billings house—had ordered Everett and the boy into the place, appropriated the carriage to her own use, strode into the place herself, probably rummaged about upstairs, came upon some fancy riding boots that fit, and pulled them on! The thought of it excited her admiration. But she declined asking about the Billings house, as some things are better left in mystery.

Eleanor wished to speak the other's name. She repeated her earlier question. "When you get up home," she said, "will you be staying, Evangeline, or going?"

"Nobody stays in Wisdom Way," said the other, after a pause.

Eleanor's heart was flooded all the while with warm feelings. "There will never be a time," she said, "when I will have forgotten you. The days of this autumn and winter will stand out for me always as the most beauteous of all."

Eleanor thought of saying something heartfelt about the infant Evangeline had lost, but thought better of it. She reflected, too, on William Bayles sequestered in his room this morning, and the harsh justice of the horsewhipping that Evangeline had inflicted upon him, but said nothing of that, either. For a long moment, she contented herself with reaching her arms around the other, and leaning against her. She pictured the busy streets back home. She pictured the elementary school she had attended—and her father's house—and her book-crowded bedroom—and knew that this East Becket world of lush farmlands and of the barren upcountry townships might soon hold no more reality for her than something mythical, something more ancient than history. Eleanor here admitted to the obvious. "It is clear to me now," she confessed, quietly, "that I, too, am going away. That I shall be going home now to Fall River."

Evangeline remained silent. They had reached the covered bridge. The clashing sound of the waters striking the rocks in the riverbed below seemed noisier than usual. Evangeline had brought the mare to a halt, and turned her about. "They will never get another teacher like you," she said.

"They will do far better. I have disgraced them all. I am the outsider they must naturally shun. I bear them no grudge. I am in their debt. Truth is," Eleanor continued, dreamily, her head on Evangeline's shoulder, "I am in debt to everyone. I have been given everything that a person could want, everything necessary to a full and bountiful life. It's just the irony of a lifetime that the one thing

I have that is most precious is an abstraction, a supposition, something wished for."

Evangeline had started them back toward the Harrison house. Eleanor looked up at the road unfurling before them and the snow-covered fields to the east. At the crossroads, she glanced away to the north, to the distant sight of Mr. Walker and his oxen and plow, dark specks on the snowscape. "How will you manage to get home, Evangeline, if the roads upcountry are not plowed?"

"The snow isn't deep under the trees," said the other. "Anyhow," she added, "I have all day." For the first time, Evangeline turned full around in the saddle and regarded Eleanor at point-blank range. Eleanor stared into her eyes, her heart moved by the intimate moment.

By this time, Mr. Chickering had finished shoveling the path from the front door out to the road, and was returning to the house. Eleanor guessed he was embarrassed at the sight of the two of them. Evangeline walked the horse up the pathway. The fact that William Bayles was inside the house meant nothing whatever to her. That was obvious.

"I'll help you down," said Evangeline.

"I'm not a child," said Eleanor.

Evangeline dismounted, nevertheless, and took Eleanor's hand as Eleanor reached her foot into the stirrup. A moment later, Eleanor was standing on the snowy path. Evangeline stepped past her, and swung back up onto the mare.

"Before you go, I want to give you something," Eleanor said. "I will only be a minute."

She went indoors quickly, and up the stairs to her room. Among a small collection of books standing on the mantel was a slim blue volume. Eleanor inscribed the book to Evangeline, and went back downstairs with it. She was breathless. Evangeline sat patiently on her mare, as Eleanor came back outdoors.

"When my father was a young man of my age, of twenty," she said, "he had a famous father who lectured and preached and wrote books. But he was a dismal father. My father wrote a little book of his own, in his twentieth year, and produced it himself. It is called

Wanting Someone. There are only three or four copies in existence. This is one of them." Eleanor stood, looking up at the other. "It will have no meaning to you, or value to you. I give it to you, Evangeline, for one reason only, because it is so precious to me."

Eleanor reached the book up to her. The other took it in hand respectfully, examined it, turned it over and back in her hands, and slid it into her coat pocket.

"These are my only words of farewell," said Eleanor. Reaching, she touched Evangeline's hand. "I will always remember you. I will always miss you."

Evangeline Sewell, as ever, said nothing. She nodded understandingly, and turned her horse to go. She started down the path to the road, and did not pause or look back.

Eleanor watched her go.

22

THE FOLLOWING MORNING, Mr. Walker was to make his buggy ride to Westfield for the mail. Eleanor would be with him. She pulled her leather Boston bag and small trunk from the closet, and began carefully to pack her books, clothing, and personal things. In that same hour, she wrote her letter of resignation to the board of selectmen. She made no apologies and offered no explanations. There was no need of it. She ended the note, saying, simply, "I regret I was not equal to the opportunity."

As she might have guessed, even anticipated, the day of her departure was glorious to look at. The sunlight came down in torrents. The snowfields appeared endless. The tall leafless elms, standing by the road, swaying in unison, looked buoyant, like a pair of travelers waiting for the next coach.

While Eleanor said her good-byes indoors, Mr. Walker carried her baggage down the pathway to the road. He was visibly downcast. Eleanor, who was usually talkative and forthcoming, realized she had nothing to say to anyone. Alonzo Klaw accompanied her outdoors. He gave her a tiny oil painting, no bigger than a postcard, of a green and gold summer landscape. On the back, he had titled it, *East Becket Harvest Time 1910.*

"Everyone is so kind to me," she said. "None more than you."

"Except for your beau, Myron Walker," said Mr. Klaw.

"Except for my beau," Eleanor agreed, with a smile.

Alonzo was slow to frame his good-bye. He rubbed at his mustache. He was touched by the moment. "It's been enriching knowing you," he said, finally, with feeling.

Eleanor studied the painter momentarily, then offered her hand. "Good-bye, sir."

She walked down the path to the road, to Mr. Walker's wagon, where the horse was stamping impatiently. "Everyone is eager to get to other places," Eleanor remarked, as she put her foot on the iron cleat, and raised herself up onto the driver's seat. "Even," she said, "if it means departing Eden itself."

As the Star Route man touched Ben with the reins, and started him along, Eleanor wished to express a special regret. "More than anything," she said, "I feel that I have done something unfair to Miss Harrison. I took the side of one whose ways, whose actions, Alice could never condone. She has stayed upstairs this morning to avoid my departure. She feels bad for me. I am a disappointment and perplexity to her. Others, I suspect, feel the same."

Mr. Walker nodded comprehendingly, but excepted himself. "I don't," he said.

"I know that is so, sir."

Within minutes, they were heading out into open country. In a half hour, East Becket and its beautiful valley farmlands would vanish into memory, just as Evangeline herself had now passed. Eleanor would make no mention this morning of William Bayles, but was sure that everyone knew by now what had happened to him. Mr. Chickering had brought his breakfast up to his room this morning.

Eleanor pulled a heavy wool blanket over her shoulders, and wound it about herself. Ben was clopping along smartly, evidently enjoying the beauty of the day unfolded. While rolling east, past the Trumbulls' farmhouse and barns, Eleanor wanted to look back, to catch a last glimpse of that slot in the cedar trees far to the north, where the road leading upcountry entered the wilderness. She fought the impulse. But as they rode on, she wanted once more to talk about Evangeline Sewell.

"What do you suppose, Mr. Walker, will happen to Evangeline? Will she be happy? Will she ever come back?"

"Hard to imagine her coming back," he replied.

"Yesterday afternoon," Eleanor remarked, "all afternoon, while she was going home upcountry, I sat in my room and pictured it. I pictured her riding onward under the trees, past Mr. Hewlitt's house, and the abandoned graveyard, and the fallen church that we visited, until she came to the sign about the bridge, and I could see her no more." She turned to the Star Route man. "I didn't know the depths of my feelings before coming here. I didn't know that such feelings were possible. I have loved her all these many weeks, each day more than the last, each hour more than the last, up to this very minute."

All at once, Eleanor lost control. She turned her head away, and put her hand to her face. She raised the blanket to her eyes. The Star Route man said nothing.

"I won't do that again, Mr. Walker. It will not ever happen again, not in all the times to come." She kept her head averted, her gaze fixed on the snowfields to her right.

"Where is my learning now?" she said. "I am like nothing."

"No," Mr. Walker objected to that. He turned to her. "You are everything that anyone might hope for—in any human being or creature that ever got itself born here. I think," he said, thoughtfully, fumbling with the reins, "that we individuals are worth exactly what we lose. What we are capable of losing."

Eleanor nodded appreciatively.

"Not more, and not less," he said.

"I'll remember," she said.

A silence ensued, with the rhythm of Ben's hoofbeats articulating the interval. They were climbing. Looking round, Eleanor noticed how the town of East Becket grew both smaller and larger. The houses dwindled in size, while the valley opened out for miles to a magnificent panorama. She remarked on it. "Isn't it peculiar, Mr. Walker, that things get smaller," she said, "that other things might get bigger?"

Now and then, a gust of wind blew up a veil of snow. Eleanor's bags, on the bed of the wagon behind her seat, were dusted in it.

At last, impulsively, she turned around the other way, and looked far off to the north, to the palisade of evergreens, toward that specific point—not clearly visible any longer—where the road entered the forest. Much as she strained her eyes, she could not discern it.

She attempted a light tone. "Or how things vanish, Mr. Walker, that others might appear."

Only after they had reached level ground, and the valley behind them fell from view altogether, did they resume speaking. And for the balance of the journey, they spoke just once of Evangeline, and of Eleanor's love of her. The Star Route man had the last word on the subject. "I think," he said, "we love the person that God appoints us to love."

Eleanor adjusted her blanket, against the long, cold ride ahead. She saw the wisdom in Mr. Walker's words.

READING GROUP GUIDE

QUESTIONS FOR DISCUSSION

1. The author begins the novel with the arrival of Eleanor in East Becket and her sense that she is somehow traveling back in time. How does this shape your expectations of the story about to unfold? What further contrast is provided by the knowledge that even Eleanor's "modern" life in Fall River would appear old-fashioned to the contemporary reader?

2. Eleanor looks forward to her life in East Becket as an "adventure among the familiar." What does such a phrase suggest about her character? About her expectations? To what extent are these expectations fulfilled or unfulfilled?

3. Almost immediately upon her arrival Eleanor finds herself behaving in a manner she considers uncharacteristic—eavesdropping on a conversation. What does this incident suggest about the course that the story will take? At what other points in the novel does she find herself behaving in uncharacteristic ways?

4. How do the residents of East Becket regard the natives of the "up-country" villages? When Alice Harrison says they are "a hard people," how does this shape your understanding of both groups and the relations between the two?

5. Myron Walker later remarks of the upcountry residents, "I'll say that in their favor. They never speak to no purpose." What does this suggest about the similarities and differences in values and outlook between the two groups? In what ways does Eleanor register or fail to register the differences?

6. The residents of East Becket, and especially her fellow boarders, frequently comment on Eleanor's manner of speaking. In what ways

does this signal both her distinction within and her isolation from the community?

7. Though she is introduced early in the story, and subsequently becomes central to Eleanor's thoughts, Evangeline Sewell appears only rarely. How do you respond to the author's decision to keep her "off-stage" for so much of the novel? How does it shape your understanding of her?

8. Howard Allen says that Evangeline is "one of those figures whom people like either to romanticize or demonize." Is this observation borne out by the behavior of the other characters in the novel?

9. The phrase from Evangeline's letter—"Then we will see who is strong and who is weak"—takes on a foreboding significance for Eleanor. To what extent do questions of "strong" and "weak" become important in the novel?

10. How does the nature of Eleanor's obsession develop and change over the course of the novel? What is her own response to her obsession? How is it viewed by the others in the community?

My introduction to historic New England came to me by way of my mother—who, interestingly, was born in the Canadian-French tenement district in the mill town of Holyoke, Massachusetts. She spoke no English as a little girl. But by the "vagaries" of life, she was sent away as a nine year old to live with strangers in the town of Tolland in the Berkshire hills. That was in 1910. My mother's parents split up that  year, and her mother feared that her father was going to try to steal her away. Many years later, when my mother was 80, I asked her about her having been spirited away to the hills like that. "It was the worst year ever," she said. I felt bad hearing her say that. After all those years, it was her most enduring remembrance: that 1910 was the year long ago when her parents split up, and she was sent away.

The irony of it all was that my mother's years in the Berkshires—from 1910 to 1916—were idyllic! The lady in whose house she went to live was the principal lady in town. Her name was Alice Harrison. Miss Harrison lived in a big colonial house at the very crossroads in town. She was a member of the board of selectmen, headed the Grange, ran the town post office in her house, and boarded the two schoolteachers. In fairly short order, however, my mother became a virtual ward of the town—as her own mother (working at a paper mill in Holyoke) proved unable to pay for her room and board. But Miss Harrison, who had no spouse or children, came to love my mother dearly—the little girl whom she took into her life for free. Thus was my mother on her way to becoming a bona fide Yankee!

The overall setting of the book, of *The Romance of Eleanor Gray*—as well as the depiction of the manners of that era—not to say of the thrifty, hardworking, fair-minded Yankee farmers themselves who populated that world!—came directly to me from my mother's vivid recollections of the days of her girlhood. My mother had a definite flair for storytelling. She could really paint a picture, so to speak.

But the characters in the novel are all inventions. I retained the name Alice Harrison, and the name of one of the boarders in the Harrison house—namely, Alonzo Klaw, a Jewish fine arts painter from Park Avenue, who came to the hills periodically for respiratory reasons. But I only know their names. My mother does not appear whatsoever in the pages of this book, nor does anyone remotely similar. This is the story of Eleanor Gray.

This is your eighth novel. In what ways was the experience of writing this book similar to or different from the experience of writing your others? From your perspective as the author, what connections, if any, do you see between this book and your others?

I am told that my novels differ noticeably from one another, as in spirit, or maybe even genre, and I agree there's some truth in that. One of the eight books, entitled Lulu Incognito, *has a distinct gothic feel to it, as it portrays the destruction of a sensitive young girl at the hands of a "vengeful society lady." Another book,* Ride a Cockhorse, *is unquestionably comic. It is the story of an attractive middle-aged lady—a banker, no less—going on a manic high, seizing power from anyone who crosses her path. Nevertheless, these two books—very different on the surface—do have something in common. Each rests on an erotic foundation. Just about all of my books have an erotic thread—with the exception of* The Bitterest Age, *the story of a heroic German schoolgirl, set in World War Two. There was no room for eroticism there!*

Would you say that *The Romance of Eleanor Gray* is therefore erotic?

Not at all. But it has its moments! The sixteen-year-old Evangeline Sewell, who is the object of Eleanor's affection and of her fantasies and gathering desires, is very much a figure who holds an authoritative sway over others. A blind following, one might say. One incident comes to mind right off. One of the lesser characters in the book, Mr. Charles Chickering, a former Army officer, describes to Eleanor how Miss Sewell recently rode horseback eight miles up a country road to a nearby town, followed on foot every mile of the way by the redoubtable Everett Conboy, a dark-tempered, violence-prone man in his sixties, who is thoroughly—fanatically—devoted to the young lady. He does not walk at her side. He follows behind! That moment, to me, is singularly erotic. Not in a gothic, sinister way, not in a comic way, but realistically so.

Like many of your recent novels, this book features a female protagonist. What intrigues you about or attracts you to female protagonists? Is it a deliberate choice on your part to make female characters central to your books, or does it just happen? If it is a choice, why do you make it?

Well, I would have to question the question. Because I think it is true that the greatest novels in the Western tradition are about women, written by men. The Scarlet Letter, Tess of the D'Ubervilles, Vanity Fair, Anna Karenina, Wings of the Dove, Daisy Miller, Madame Bovary. *The list goes on and on. In my own case, though, I do like to see the story unfolding through a woman's eyes. To see a woman at the heart of it. Hey, women are morally superior to men! Who could deny it? I say that not jokingly.*

How did you come to write this particular novel? What about the story or the characters appealed to you? Which came first? Did the basic situation come to you fully formed, or did you develop it over time?

The Romance of Eleanor Gray *began as a ghost story. In the opening pages, I tried to begin a story about a young "upcountry" girl who had been gotten pregnant by her school teacher, and who had withdrawn to her village up in the hills. By page five, I knew it was impossible to tell. My protagonist was gone, and I was left to tell the tale from the villain's point of view — which is an aesthetic enormity — that is, is out of the question. Then Eleanor appeared! And all was changed. I went back to page one and started anew.*

Most of your novels, including this one, are set in New England. What is important or significant for you about the region? How important is the sense of place for you when writing a novel? How important is it to you as a reader?

I always write about New England because it's where I come from, because it's the region of the world that I love best, and I honestly believe that our New England history and culture are unmatched in moral brilliance throughout all time. To illustrate that in a word or two, when you have a cultural setting of such morality and high-mindedness that it could produce, as it did, the finest lyric poet who ever lived anywhere, or in any age, as in Emily Dickinson, you challenge that assertion at your risk! And Miss Dickinson of Amherst is but one example in a pantheon.

What is the significance of the "upcountry" villages?

I don't know where the "upcountry" towns came from in my imagination, but the conception is a favorite of mine in this book. These are towns that lie beyond the dark wall of trees to the north. They are cut off. They are impoverished towns. Life is hard in them, and the people still living in them are themselves hard and bitter. That is Evangeline's world. And she is "hard." Taken in all, these desiccated towns provide a dark, subconscious backdrop to the innocence and good health of the sunlit, bountiful valley below.

What prompted you to set the story in this particular time and place: western Massachusetts in 1910? Is the setting important to the story you wanted to tell?

As I've said elsewhere, my mother went to live in the Berkshire hills as a little girl. She was Canadian-French, born in a Massachusetts mill town, and then more or less abandoned to live out there as a virtual ward of the town. That was in 1910. From her stories, and vivid recollections of her long years living in Yankee country, I have always been able to re-create her life in my imagination. She lived in the town of Tolland. I changed the name of the town to East Becket. And, yes, for the purposes of this story, I wanted to place it in a rather pastoral setting—in just such a modern but pre-Freudian time, as that would deepen the mystery of it all for Eleanor, of her infatuation with another young lady—as she struggles to understand what is going on inside her heart.

What attracted you to Eleanor Gray as a character? How would you compare her to the women from some of your other novels? How did she develop as a character as your worked on the novel?

I love Eleanor Gray. She is so sensitive, so thoughtful of others, so politic, and ever so quick in her thoughts and responses. And my view of her is not so different, I hope, from the responses to her of all the characters on stage, so to speak. And that is the essence of the story. That she is that endearing, lofty-minded young lady whom they know her to be—but whose drives and actions, whose compulsions and necessary secrecy, must inevitably put her at odds with all of the townspeople. She is drawn into a battle she cannot win.

What were the important considerations in opening the story?

It's quite appropriate that Eleanor be a stranger in the world that she is about to enter, just as she is a virtual stranger to herself in the drama about to unfold. I began with her arriving by horse and wagon in the town of East Becket—an idyllic town in the Berkshire hills—about to take up her first teaching post, feeling understandably unsure of herself. If she feels that she is traveling backward in time, as to a paradisal agrarian past, that too seems correct. She is entering Eden. There she will be tested.

I wanted Eleanor's drama to begin at once, almost within the hour of her moving into Miss Harrison's house. She overhears an exchange of voices on the stairs outside her door. She eavesdrops. As Eleanor does so, her story begins. From that moment forward, her behavior becomes increasingly secretive and clandestine. Step by step, she is drawn into the world and predicament of the beautiful young Evangeline.

What were the challenges in presenting Evangeline?

By keeping Evangeline "offstage," it is easier from a storytelling point of view to render her ever more fascinating. We hear interesting stories about her. She sends one-sentence notes to Eleanor. We see her at a distance—as a solitary figure on horseback. Therefore, she becomes—at least, I hope she does—everything mysterious that we want her to be. All that is necessary from the author's point of view is that when we do *see her up close—as in the graveyard scene on Christmas morning—the author has to deliver! Such a scene is critical. For without Evangeline's mystery, and her ability to dominate such a scene, the tale would suffer. Incidentally, in that particular graveyard scene, it is the solemn, step-by-step ceremony of the funeral itself that (once again) keeps everyone at a distance from her, further precluding any mundane contamination. In that way, it is hoped that Evangeline will retain her "heroic" stature.*

What is the significance of the phrase from Evangeline's letter—"Then we will see who is strong and who is weak"?

I like the fact that Evangeline says something as threatening and sinister as she does early on—a remark that Eleanor discovers upon steaming open a note. Evangeline says she'll be back, "Then we will see who is strong and who is weak." If this rather scary admonition works an effect on Eleanor's impression of Evangeline—that is, as of the other's hardiness and resolve—it only further enhances Eleanor's respect and growing obsession. The girl upcountry is not a wallflower type! Not a figure to be crossed. She will not be just another female victim of a man's faithlessness and immorality. Evangeline's words—portentous of something violent in the offing—help to fuel and sustain the ensuing action.

How has your writing practice changed over the course of your career? How do you go about developing a novel?

A novel usually begins for me with an image. So, I start writing about it— describing it. It is, of course, always dilemmatic. There's something wrong in the picture. As for the scene or setting, it's already there. It is the background of the image, so to speak. And it's invariably a place I have known—somewhere at some time. My characters, though, are not drawn on persons I have ever known. They just take up residence in that familiar scene. Then they take me for a ride!

How has the literary and publishing landscape changed over the course of your career? Any developments that have particularly excited or depressed you?

The publishing world has changed rather dramatically over these past forty years. My first agent was Henry Volkening, probably the finest agent in the world. He was like a father to me. Well, he is a vanished breed. The publishing world is a worsening mess—which many small presses like University Press of New England are endeavoring successfully to resuscitate. However, I remember one day when I was in college, and was criticizing the current state of the arts, a fellow student of mine promptly cut me short. "The arts," he said, "will take very nice care of themselves, thank you!"